A MOTHER'S SECRET

BY
SCARLET WILSON

MILLS &
BOON

Published in Great Britain 2014
by Mills & Boon, an imprint of Harlequin (UK) Limited,
Eton House, 18-24 Paradise Road, Richmond, Surrey, TW9 1SR

© 2014 Scarlet Wilson

ISBN: 978 0 263 90764 3

Harlequin (UK) Limited's policy is to use papers that are natural,
renewable and recyclable products and made from wood grown in
sustainable forests. The logging and manufacturing processes conform
to the legal environmental regulations of the country of origin.

Printed and bound in Spain
by Blackprint CPI, Barcelona

Dear Reader

As I started writing this book about a surrogate mother who keeps her baby I automatically called it my 'bad surrogate' story. Poor Gemma. The last way she should be described is as a *bad* surrogate.

Needless to say my heroine with a difference has a very genuine and valid reason for keeping her baby. But she's been labelled that way by the press after a prolonged court case and she comes to the Scottish island of Arran for a fresh start for her and her daughter.

Arran is a beautiful island just off the west coast of Scotland. The places described on the island are factual, as is Crocodile Rock on Millport, the Isle of Cumbrae, but the people, of course, are entirely fictional.

My hero Logan has lived on the island most of his life and has a real connection with and love for the people there. But like in any small community as soon as he's seen with the new lady doctor rumours start to fly.

Logan turns out to be Gemma's knight in shining armour—only his white horses are on the sea rather than on dry land!

I love to hear from readers. Feel free to contact me via my website: www.scarlet-wilson.com

Happy reading!

Love

Scarlet

**These books are also available in eBook format
from www.millsandboon.co.uk**

**Praise for
Scarlet Wilson:**

'HER CHRISTMAS EVE DIAMOND is a fun and interesting
read. If you like a sweet romance with just a touch of the holiday
season you'll like this one.'
—*harlequinjunkie.com*

'WEST WING TO MATERNITY WING! is a tender, poignant
and highly affecting romance that is sure to bring a tear to your
eye. With her gift for creating wonderful characters, her ability
to handle delicately and compassionately sensitive issues and her
talent for writing believable, emotional and spellbinding romance,
the talented Scarlet Wilson continues to prove to be a force to be
reckoned with in the world of contemporary romantic fiction!'
—*cataromance.com*

Dedication

This book is dedicated to my long-suffering work colleagues
and partners in crime Kathleen Winter and Sharon Hardie.
Is it Friday yet?

It's also dedicated to my lovely, shiny new editor Laurie Johnson.
I'm sure I'll wear you down at some point!

CHAPTER ONE

'Look, Mummy, that's our island!'

Isla was bouncing up and down and pointing through the ship's railings. Gemma put her bags at her feet and rested her elbows on the railings. 'Yes,' she said quietly, 'it is.'

The ship gave another shudder as it moved away from Ardrossan Harbour and out into the Firth of Clyde. Arran looked so close she could almost reach out and touch it. But, then, it had looked that way the whole time they had driven along the Ayrshire coast.

Her stomach gave a little flip—and it wasn't from the choppy waters. Her hand settled on Isla's shoulder next to her little red curls—the only permanent reminder of her father. This would be better. This would be safer for them both.

A chance for a new start. A chance for some down time.

A chance to meet some new friends who knew nothing about her past and wouldn't stand in judgement of her. Glasgow and the surrounding area had been just too small. Everywhere she'd gone someone had known Patrick or Lesley. They'd gone to medical school together, or been on a course with one of them, or knew a neighbour. The list was endless.

As were the whispers. *The bad surrogate.* The woman who'd made the papers when she'd 'stolen' another couple's baby. Not strictly true. But true enough that it had caused her a world of pain, a court case and five years of sleepless nights.

But now it was finally over. Now she could finally move on.

Now, in accordance with the law, Isla was officially hers.

She stared out across the water. Arran. Twenty miles long and ten miles across. A population of ten thousand that swelled to twenty thousand over the summer holidays.

It was perfect. Even down to the cottage she'd purchased over the internet for her and Isla to stay in. Two days' work as a paediatrician all year long and one day's work as a GP over the busy summer months. That, along with an occasional emergency shift in the island hospital, would be more than enough.

Some of her friends thought she was crazy, moving to a place she'd only ever visited on summer holidays as a child and making a new life there. Taking up a new job with some extra part-time hours when she hadn't even sorted out her childcare for Isla yet.

That did make her stomach give a little flip. But she'd had long conversations with the head of the GP practice and he'd assured her he had a few people in mind he could vouch for to help with Isla's care.

Time with Isla was precious. She was starting school in August. And although properties on the island could be expensive, the sale of her flat in Glasgow had given her a healthy profit. She didn't need a big income. She wasn't looking to be a millionaire. She just needed enough to keep her and Isla comfortable.

'Mummy, can we look at our new house again?'

The brisk sea wind was whipping their hair around their faces. The sun was shining brightly but the wind was cutting straight through the thin material of her summer dress. Maybe she'd been a little over-optimistic when she'd dressed that morning. It was always the same in Scotland, the first glimmer of sunshine and the entire nation pulled out their summer clothes in case it was the only chance they got to wear them. Gemma held out her hand. 'Let's go inside and get something to drink. We can look at the pictures again then.'

They settled in with tea, orange juice and two crumpets with jam. Isla pulled the crumpled piece of paper from Gemma's bag for the hundredth time. She flicked over the pages, her little finger stroking down the paper over the pictures. 'My room's going to be yellow, isn't it, Mummy? It will be *so-o-o* beautiful.'

She had that little wistful tone in her voice, with the slightly dreamy edge to it. Isla hadn't wanted to move at first. She was only five but the thought of starting school without her nursery friends had caused her lots of sleepless nights. It had almost been a relief when she'd started to romanticise about their new house and her new bedroom—all set on a Scottish island.

The extra expense of buying her a whole new range of bedroom furniture, along with letting her pick her own curtains and bedding, had been worth every penny.

Gemma had arranged with a local contractor to paint the inside of her house before they arrived. The removals van had left a few hours before them and caught the earlier ferry. Hopefully, by the time she got there most things would have been unpacked and the new carpet she'd bought for the living room would be in place.

She was trying not to concentrate on the fact that the contractor hadn't answered her emails or phone calls for the last few days. She'd had more than enough to think about. He was probably busy—busy in her new house, making it ready for their arrival. At least, she hoped he was.

The ferry journey was smooth enough. Thankfully Isla hardly seemed to notice the occasional wave swell and Gemma finally started to relax.

Isla had started to draw a picture with her crayons. 'Look, Mummy, here we are on our new island.'

Gemma took a sip of her tea. 'Who is that?' she asked, pointing to a third figure in the drawing.

'That's your new boyfriend.'

Her tea splattered all over the table and halfway down her chin. 'What?' She grabbed napkins and mopped furiously.

Isla gave her the glance of a worldly eighty-year-old instead of an innocent five-year-old child. 'We might be able to find you a boyfriend on the island, Mummy. We couldn't in Glasgow.'

There was so much innocence in her words. Isla had never, ever mentioned Gemma's lack of a boyfriend before. It had never been an issue. Never come up. But she'd obviously given it some thought. 'Tammy's mummy at nursery got a new boyfriend. He bought Tammy a laptop and took her to the transport museum.'

Ah. She was starting to understand. Understand in little-girl terms.

'I think they might all be taken. Arran's quite a small

island. And Mummy really doesn't have time for a boy-friend. She's starting a new job and we need to visit your new school.' She ruffled Isla's red curls. 'Anyway, you're much too young for a laptop.'

Isla shook her head, her little face instantly serious. 'I think I might need one when I go to school. I don't want to be the only person without one, Mummy.'

Her blue eyes were completely sincere. If it had been anyone else in the world Gemma would think she was being played. But she already knew that her five-year-old had concerns about making friends and fitting in at a new school. Sometimes she felt Isla was too old for her years.

Gemma had tried her best. But the flat in central Glasgow hadn't exactly been the most sociable area for kids. Isla really only had her friends to play with at nurs-ery, and then again on the odd occasion she'd been in-vited to a party. Juggling full-time work, childcare and single parenthood wasn't easy.

And that had been part of the problem. Part of the rea-son she'd wanted to get away to a different style of life for her and her daughter. Being a full-time paediatrician in a busy city was frantic. Particularly when a sick kid came in minutes before you were due to finish. Thank goodness for an understanding childminder. But even she'd had her limits and had eventually told Gemma she was struggling.

She gave Isla a smile. 'I've seen photos of your new school. They've got some lovely computers there. I'm sure the teachers will let you work on them.'

Her phone buzzed in her pocket once, then went silent again. Weren't they still in the middle of the Firth of Clyde? Apparently not. She turned her head. They looked only moments from the island. She pulled her phone from her pocket. It was an unknown number and her signal had vanished. This was supposed to be the best network for the island but it looked as though the coverage wasn't as good as she'd been promised.

Looked like she still had a lot to learn about Arran.

A loud passenger announcement made her curiosity around the phone call instantly vanish.

'All passengers, please return to your vehicles prior to arrival in Brodick.'

'That's us, Mummy!'

Gemma smiled and took a last gulp of her tea. Isla's hand automatically fitted inside her own and she gave it a little squeeze as they joined the queue to file down to the car deck.

Her little red car was packed to the rafters. There was barely room for her and Isla to scramble back inside and get their seat belts in place. The removal van was similarly packed and the costs of moving to an island had proved much more prohibitive than moving somewhere inland. As a result most of their clothes were squashed into the car around them, along with a large amount of Isla's toys.

She tried to remember the directions that she'd been given as the cars slowly trundled off the ferry. It wasn't too far between Brodick and Lamlash—the capital of the island and the place where they would be staying—and the journey was over in ten minutes.

It didn't take long to find the house and her heart gave a little flutter when she saw it. Their new home.

Gemma spotted the removals van immediately. There were also a number of men, dressed in their uniforms of black T-shirts and matching trousers. They'd been ruthlessly efficient back in Glasgow, their removal expertise putting her to shame. Trouble was—right now, none of them were moving.

She pulled the car up outside the cottage and couldn't help the smile that appeared on her face and Isla squealed in excitement. 'Is this it, Mummy?'

Gemma nodded and helped Isla from the car. The cottage was everything she'd hoped for—two bedrooms, a study and a small conservatory on the back. That, combined with a view over the Firth of Clyde, was more perfect than she could have imagined.

There were even little shutters at the windows. From the look of them they were only decorative and could do with a lick of paint. But they added to the character and she loved them immediately.

Before she could stop her, Isla had raced through the open front door.

Gemma gave her hair a shake, pleased to be out of the stuffy car on such a clammy day. One of the removals men approached her straight away. Her stomach was already jittery with nerves. 'Something wrong, Frank?'

He nodded. 'I think so.' He pointed to the front door. There, sitting next to the steps, was a row of large paint tins. Gemma walked over for a closer look—pale yellow for Isla's room, mocha for her own bedroom, magnolia for the hall and living room. There was a tightly wrapped parcel at the end of the row. She peeled back some of the wrapping to reveal the purple wallpaper she'd picked for the feature wall in her living room.

Her brow furrowed. 'What's all this doing here? I'd an arrangement with a local contractor to have painted and decorated for us before we got here.'

Frank shrugged. 'He's obviously bought the materials and intended to do it. Something must have happened.'

Gemma let out a sigh and walked into her cottage. There it was. That instant feeling.

It made her catch her breath.

People said that you made up your mind in the first thirty seconds when you viewed a house. And even though the deal was done Gemma knew immediately she'd made the right decision. She walked around. Some of her furniture and most of her boxes had already been put in some of the rooms.

She ran her finger along the wall. The place looked a little tired. If it had been decorated it would have been perfect. But she could live with it in its current state. If need be, she could do the painting herself.

Frank tapped her shoulder. 'There's another little issue.' He pointed back outside.

Gemma followed him to find her brand-new purple sofa sitting in the driveway. 'What's wrong?'

He pointed to the doorway. 'It's too small. We can't get it in.'

She spun around. 'You're joking, right?'

He shook his head. 'Did you ask for the dimensions of the door before you bought it?'

She could feel the colour flare into her cheeks. Of course she hadn't. She'd fallen in love with the colour immediately, and once she'd sat in it in the showroom her mind had been made up. Dimensions hadn't even entered her brain. Not once. 'Could we take the door off?'

He shook his head. 'We've already tried that. It's just too big.'

Just like she thought. Ruthlessly efficient. She'd half a mind to invite these removal contractors to work with her in one of the big hospitals in Glasgow to see what changes they would make. They would probably have the whole rambling hospital running seamlessly in a matter of days.

One of the other men approached. 'I've checked the back window—the one that's broken and boarded up. If we take out the window frame we might get it in there.'

'I've got a broken window?' She was trying not to let her chin dangle open. This was just getting better and better.

'You didn't know?'

She shook her head, her long strides taking her back into the house and following the pointing fingers to the window at the back of her living room. There were a few remnants of broken glass caught in the window frame, but someone had done a good job clearing up the floor and ensuring it was spotless. The carpet in this room had been slightly worn and damaged in the pictures she'd seen so she'd given instructions for it to be lifted. Her new carpet was currently rolled up inside the removal van, waiting to be fitted—another aspect of the efficient company.

She touched the edge of the window. 'I knew nothing about this. I guess I'll need to phone the estate agent.' She sighed. 'If taking the frame out is the only way to get the sofa in then just go ahead.'

Two other men appeared with the underlay and carpet, ready to fit it. One of them gave her a smile. 'I take it you just want us to go ahead, lift the old carpet and get the new one laid?'

She gave a little nod. She'd have to worry about paint stains later. The removals company had covered just about every angle. It was just a pity the decorator hadn't fulfilled his duties.

Her phone rang sharply and she pulled it out of her pocket.

'Dr Halliday? Are you here yet?' It was a deep voice and one she didn't recognise.

'That depends. What "here" do you mean? And who are you?'

'Sorry. It's Logan Scott. One of the GPs you'll be working with. I needed to see if you could cover a shift.'

She let out a laugh. 'Cover a shift? I've just got here. And my house isn't painted. A window's broken, I haven't unpacked a thing and I would have no one to look after my daughter. So, Dr Scott, I don't think I'll be covering any shifts any time soon.' She winced at the snarky tone in her voice. She was taking her frustrations out on a perfect stranger—and, worse still, a new workmate.

'You have a daughter? I didn't know that.'

She felt herself bristle. What did that mean? And what business of his was it that she had a daughter? But he continued, 'You're at the cottage? I'll be there in two minutes.'

Before she could say another thing he'd hung up. She shook her head and walked back inside, just in time to see the wooden board being taken off the window and the window frame being slid out of place.

The underlay was already down on the floor and was being anchored in place. These removal guys really didn't waste any time. Then again, she could bet none of them wanted to risk missing the last ferry home and being stranded for the night. She'd been warned in advance that the Arran ferry could be cancelled at the first gust of wind.

She walked along to Isla's room. Her bed was nestled in the corner with the new bedding and curtains sitting on top of it. Isla was on the floor with one of her boxes upended and toys spread across the floor. She was already in a world all of her own.

Gemma's eyes ran over the room and she gave a groan.

No curtain poles. She hadn't even given it a thought. She'd just assumed there would be some still in place. Another thing to add to the list.

Isla's oak wardrobe and chest of drawers had been put in place—in the exact spots where Gemma would have positioned them herself. Most of Isla's clothes were in the car—still on their hangers—it would only take a few minutes to pick them up and start to get Isla's room ready.

She walked outside and opened her car door. The wind was starting to whip her dress around her legs and she grabbed it as she leaned inside to grab a handful of Isla's clothes. The last hanger slid from her hands on to the floor between the front seats and the back. She leaned further, her feet leaving the ground as she stretched as far as she could, just as the biggest gust of wind caught her dress and billowed it upwards.

'Well, there's a sight I don't see every day.'

'What?' Panic filled her chest as her cheeks flared with heat. Her left hand thrust out behind her and caught the wayward fabric of her dress, pulling it back firmly over her underwear as she scrambled back out the car, pulling Isla's clothes with her. Several of the items landed on the ground at her feet. So much for keeping everything on their hangers to save time.

She pushed her hair out of her face. She couldn't really see properly. The cheeky stranger was standing with his back to the bright sun, which was glaring directly at her.

'Look, Mummy!' shouted Isla. 'There's one! I told you we'd find you a boyfriend on Arran!'

Her eyes adjusted. Oh, no. Just what she needed. A tall, almost dark and very handsome stranger with a smattering of stubble across his face. Her biggest vice.

Ground, open up and swallow me now. Complete and utter mortification.

What else could go wrong?

Logan didn't know who to be more amused with. The little girl for just embarrassing her mum to death, or the rogue dress and sea winds, which had just given him a glimpse of some lovely pink satin underwear.

He held out his hand. He'd love to stay here all day, but he really needed to get things sorted. 'Logan Scott. It's a pleasure to meet you.' There it was. The light floral scent that he'd thought was floating in the air was actually coming from her. Hmm. He could get used to that.

Her cheeks were scarlet. Her long curly brown hair with lighter tips was flapping around her face like mad, caught in the brisk sea winds, and her dress was once again joining in the fun. He hadn't expected her to look quite so young. Then again, he hadn't expected her to have a child either. Maybe he should have paid a little more attention when his colleagues had said they had recruited someone for the summer.

The dress was really playing havoc with her. Now the pink and white material was plastered back across her body, revealing every curve, every slope and the outline of her underwire bra. Having glimpsed one half of her underwear he tried not to wonder if it was a matching set.

It was obvious she was trying to collect her thoughts. She held out her slim hand towards his outstretched one and grasped it firmly—as if she was trying to prove a point. 'Are you always so forward with your colleagues, Dr Scott?'

He shrugged his shoulders. 'Only if they look like you. Welcome to Arran, Dr Halliday.'

The little girl waved her hand. 'Come and see my new room, it's beautiful.'

Gemma tucked her hair behind her ears and thrust the pile of clothes she had in her hands towards him. Her embarrassment was still apparent, but it was clear she intended to get past it. 'You might as well make yourself useful. These are Isla's. Just hang them up in her cupboard.'

For a second he was stunned. Then a smile crept across his face. It wasn't any more presumptuous than he'd just been. Maybe he'd just met his female equivalent?

He followed the little red-haired girl into the house and fumbled with her clothes. Most of the hangers had tangled together and some of the dresses landed in a heap at his feet as he tried to slot them in the wooden wardrobe.

'Careful with this one. It's my favourite.'

She held up a pale blue dress with some obvious netting underneath. A little-girl princess-style dress. The kind of thing his sister would love.

He took the dress and carefully put it on a hanger. 'There we go. Do you want to hang it up yourself?'

She shook her head, her curls bouncing around her. 'No. Mum says that's your job.' Like mother, like daughter.

'How old are you, Isla? It is Isla, isn't it?'

She smiled. One of her front teeth was missing. 'I'm five. I'll be going to the big school after the summer.'

He nodded. 'There's a lovely primary school just around the corner. I'll show you it later if you like.' He pointed to her tooth. 'Did the tooth fairy come?'

She rolled her eyes and planted her hands on her hips.

'No, silly. The tooth fairy only comes if a tooth falls out by itself.'

He straightened his back. 'Why, what happened to yours?'

She sighed. She'd gone back to her dolls and had obviously lost interest in him now. 'I got it knocked out when I was playing football.'

He blinked. So the little curly-haired redhead who liked princess dresses was actually a tomboy?

Gemma appeared at the door with another pile of clothes, which she started automatically hanging in the wardrobe. 'I can see Isla's entertaining you with her terrifying tales.'

Logan gave a slow nod. 'Football?'

Gemma nodded. 'Football. Is there a team she can join?'

'At five?'

'Yes. She was in a mixed team back in Glasgow. They played in a mini-league.'

Logan leaned against the wall and folded his arms. 'I think the primary school has a football team, but I'm sure it's the primary six and sevens. We can ask at the surgery, someone is bound to know.'

Gemma finished hanging her clothes and turned around. 'I'm not really sure what you're doing here, Logan. I certainly won't be ready to start work for a while. Look around. My contractor hasn't appeared and one of the windows is broken.' She ran her hand through her tangled hair. 'And I have no idea where to start with that one. The estate agent isn't even answering her phone.'

Logan glanced at his watch. 'That's because it's a Thursday and it's two o'clock. Nancy Connelly will be getting her hair done.'

Gemma's chin almost bounced off the floor. What did she expect? Logan had spent most of his life on this island and could tell her the ins, outs and daily habits of just about everyone.

She started shaking her head. 'Well, that's not much use to me, is it? I would have thought she would have the courtesy to call me and let me know that my property had been damaged. I'm going to have to find out who can do replacement windows around here, and then I'm obviously going to have to find an alternative contractor since the one I've paid hasn't done his job.'

It sounded like the start of a rant. No, maybe that was unfair. She'd just arrived on a strange island with her little girl and probably wanted to get settled in straight away. At least she'd planned ahead. Her cottage was supposed to be ready just to walk into, and the reality was she wasn't supposed to start at the GP surgery for another few weeks. He was going to have to appeal to her better nature—and just hope that she had one.

He put up his hands. 'Whoa. I'm sorry. I should have got to the point but you're a bit like a whirlwind around here. Harry Burns was your contractor. The reason the work hasn't been started is because Harry had an MI last week—just after he'd delivered your paint to start decorating. The reason the window is broken is because he was up on a ladder, cleaning out your guttering, when he fell off.'

Gemma put her hand up to her mouth. 'He had a heart attack here? At my house? And why on earth was he cleaning my guttering?'

Logan shrugged. 'Because that's just Harry. He saw it needed doing, and thought he would help out. He was lucky. He usually works by himself, but his fourteen-year-old grandson was with him that day. He called us and we were lucky enough to get him to the hospital in time.'

Gemma took a deep breath. 'Do you have facilities for things like that? I thought most of the emergency stuff had to go to the mainland?'

Logan picked his words carefully. He didn't want to vent his frustration on their new doctor. It often took newcomers a while to adjust to what could and couldn't be done on a small island. 'We can treat MIs with rtPA—the same as they would get in a coronary care unit. What we can't do is an immediate angioplasty to find the problem. So we treat the clot, ensure they're stable then transfer them to the mainland for further treatment.' He looked at his watch. 'Your new window should be on the two o'clock ferry. We ordered it last week and they said they would supply and fit it today.'

There it was. A little colour appearing in her cheeks. She blushed easily—obviously embarrassed about her earlier almost-rant of frustration.

'Oh, I see. Thank you.'

Logan knew he should probably stop there. But he couldn't. He cared about the people on this island. 'Do you have to have the work done straight away? Can you wait a while? Harry is already upset about the window. If he hadn't had a heart attack I can guarantee the job would have been done perfectly for your arrival.'

Gemma looked around her. Isla seemed oblivious to the décor. The walls were marked here and there, with the odd little dent in the plasterwork—all things that Harry had been paid to fix. Did it really matter if she had to wait a few weeks for the house to be painted, and for her feature wall to be papered in the living room? Who else was going to see the house but her and Isla?

In an ideal world, her room would have been painted before she laid the new carpet, but she wasn't prepared to wait. Which was just as well as the men were almost finished. They were poised outside, waiting to try and fit her sofa through the window.

She placed her hands on her hips as she took a few steps down the corridor. The place really wasn't too bad. It just needed freshening up. 'I suppose it's not the end of the world to wait a few weeks. I guess Harry will need around six weeks to make a full recovery. But I don't want him to be pressured into working before he's ready. Maybe it would be less pressure on him if he knew someone else had done the job?'

He understood her reasoning. It was rational. It was also considerate. But this woman had obviously never met Harry Burns.

He shook his head; he couldn't help a smile appearing on his face. 'Actually, if I tell Harry someone else is doing it, his blood pressure will probably go through the roof and he'll have another heart attack.'

She smiled. A genuine smile that reached right up into her warm brown eyes. 'Well, I guess that would never do, then, would it?'

He shook his head. She was mellowing. She seemed a little calmer. But then again, she'd just moved house—one of the most stressful things to do. That, along with the fact she was about to start a new job, meant her own blood pressure was probably through the roof. He was leaving out the most obvious fact. The one that it seemed highly likely she was a single parent.

There was no sign of any man. And all the clothes

packed into the back of the little red car were obviously
hers and her daughter's.

His curiosity was definitely piqued. But he couldn't
show it—not for a second. On an island like Arran they'd
have him huckled up the aisle in the blink of an eye and
all his mother's cronies would have their knitting needles
out and asking about babies.

'About work…' he started. That was better. That was
the reason he was here.

'What about it?' she said absentmindedly, as she
opened a drawer and started emptying a bag of little-
girl underwear into it. 'I think I'm supposed to meet
Sam Allan next Tuesday. He's the head of the practice,
isn't he?'

'Normally, he is.' Logan chose his words carefully
and let the statement sink in.

Her eyes widened and she turned around. 'Oh, no,
what are you about to tell me?' He could tell from the
tone of her voice that she knew exactly where this conversation was headed.

'About Sam…'

'What about Sam, Dr Scott?' She folded her arms
across her chest.

He almost laughed out loud at the expression on her
face. Did she have any idea how identical her daughter
was to her? Even though the hair and eye colour was obviously different, their expressions and mannerisms were
like mirror images of each other.

'I think you should start calling me Logan. We'll be
working together enough.'

He could see her take a deep breath. He liked this
woman. And as soon as he had a minute he was going
to go back to the surgery and read her résumé. He could

only hope that her paediatric skills would be transferable to their GP practice.

'Sam Allan managed to fall down Goat Fell earlier today. It's about the hundredth time in his life, but this time he's been a little unlucky.'

Her eyes narrowed. Goat Fell was the highest peak on the island. 'How unlucky?'

'Unlucky enough to break his leg.' He couldn't keep the sound of regret from his voice. Sam Allan was one of his greatest friends. 'Sam's problem is he's nearly seventy but thinks he's still around the age of seventeen.'

Her words were careful, measured. 'Then, Logan, I guess it will be you I'll be meeting next Tuesday instead.'

Logan scratched his chin. Stubble. He still hadn't had time to shave. That must be around two days now. He must look a sight. Time for the bombshell.

'Actually, I was kind of hoping you could start now.'

CHAPTER TWO

'You are joking, right?'

He shook his head and lifted his hands. 'Nothing like the present time to get started.'

She looked at him as if he was crazy. 'Look around you, Logan. Do I look like I'm ready to do any kind of GP surgery right now?' She pointed at the cottage. 'I haven't unpacked a thing. My removals men are still here. I've got a broken window. And I haven't even started to look for childcare for Isla.' Her hand lifted up to her face. 'Oh, no.'

'What?'

'Sam Allan was going to put me in touch with some people who might have been able to help with Isla. He's not going to be able to do that now.'

Logan felt a little twist in his gut. He could picture in his head exactly who Sam might have had in mind. And he wished he'd talked to him about it first.

Logan's mum was as desperate to be a grandparent as his sister was desperate to be a mother. He didn't have a single doubt that Sam would have volunteered her as a surrogate granny for Isla.

And, after having met Isla, he knew instantly they would be a perfect match. His mother would love the little girl who had an old head on her shoulders. And

Isla would love the fact that she could have his mother's undivided attention.

So, why did it make him squirm a little?

His mother had been lonely these last few years. The unexpected death of his father ten years ago had been a bombshell for them all. One moment playing golf on a summer's day, next moment an aortic aneurysm had killed him instantly. Logan had just completed his first year as a junior doctor and taken up a post in a medical unit in Glasgow. Guilt had plagued him.

If only he'd come home the week before, the way he'd been supposed to. Maybe he would have noticed some minor symptoms that could have alerted him to his father's condition. The looks on the faces of his mother and sister as they'd met him from the boat would stay with him for ever. He hadn't been there when his family had needed him most.

He'd always put his dad on a pedestal, and even to this day he still missed him. He'd been a fantastic father. Smart, encouraging, with a big heart and an even bigger sense of humour. Filling his shoes as the island GP had been a daunting task. Even now, some of the older patients referred to him as 'young Dr Scott'.

His mother had probably always imagined she would have a house full of grandchildren at this point. Something to fill her days, keep her busy and keep her young.

But things just hadn't worked out that way for Claire, or for him.

He'd been an 'almost'. He'd seriously dated a woman with a gorgeous little boy for six months a few years back. All his fears about doing as good a job as his dad and having enough hours in the day had almost been pushed aside. Until Zoe had decided island life wasn't for her and she was leaving. Saying goodbye to little Ben had ripped his heart out. And he'd never dated a woman with children since.

Too difficult. Too many risks.

At least with introducing Isla it would take the pressure off him for a while. And it might even take the pressure off his sister Claire. Seven failed IVF attempts had just about finished her, and now the strain of the adoption process wasn't helping.

It should be a perfect solution all round. Only it just didn't feel that way.

He took a deep, reluctant breath. 'Don't panic. I think I might know who Sam was going to recommend.'

'Who? Is it someone reliable? Someone safe? I can't just leave my daughter with a perfect stranger. And I'm not sure how quickly I'd want to do it anyway. I was only supposed to be working one day in the surgery. We should have some time to settle in together. Have some time to meet the person and make sure I think they are suitable. Will I get references for childcare?'

She was rattling on. It seemed to be her thing. Whenever she got anxious, she just started to talk incessantly.

He put up his hand and tried to stop the smile appearing on his face. 'Oh, you're safe. I think I can give her a reference—it's my mother.'

She stopped. 'Your mother?'

He nodded.

'Oh.' First time he'd seen Gemma stunned into silence.

'Well, I guess that will be okay, then. Providing, of course, she's happy to do it—and Isla likes her, of course.'

'Of course.'

'Isla likes who?'

Isla had appeared next to them.

Logan knelt down. 'My mum. She's going to be your new surrogate granny. If you like her, that is. It means your mum will be able to work in the surgery for a while.'

It was the strangest thing. The little girl opened her mouth to say something and, from the corner of his eye, he could see Gemma shake her head. 'We'll talk about it later. Go inside, Isla.'

Logan straightened up and stretched his back with a loud clicking sound. What was going on?

'Eurgh!'

He raised his eyebrows. 'Orthopaedics not your thing?' He gave his back a shake. 'What can I say? Years of abuse from sailing.'

'You sail?'

'Just about everyone on Arran sails. That's the thing about staying on an island.'

She looked out over the water. 'I suppose. Listen, about starting right away. I only agreed to do one day a week. I don't know how much help I'll actually be to you.'

He nodded. 'I know. When are you supposed to start your paediatric hours?'

'The week after next. I'd timed it so we would have a little time to settle in and sort out childcare and things.'

He could hear the tone in her voice. The gentle implication that she really didn't want to do this. She wanted time to settle herself and her daughter. But he was desperate. The surgery was currently bursting at the seams. And would be for the next few weeks—there was no way a replacement GP could be found on an island like Arran.

He scratched his chin. 'We might be able to rearrange things. The health board are used to there being issues on Arran—and looking at flexible options. How would you feel about deferring your start date for the paediatric work? Sam will be off for at least six weeks. It would give us a little more leeway.'

She gave a little laugh. 'I get the impression you're not really listening to me, Logan. Don't you know how to take no for an answer?'

He tried not to laugh out loud. 'Only in personal circumstances. Never in professional.'

She gave a little sigh and held up her hand. 'If, and only if, I like your mother and Isla likes her, I'll agree to help you out. But not today, *definitely* not today.'

'Tomorrow afternoon? That surgery is a stinker.'

He was chancing his luck, but it was the only way to survive in these parts.

'You make it sound so appealing.'

'Oh, go on. You know you want to.'

'What about the health board stuff?'

He waved his hand. 'I'll sort that. You'll cover until Sam comes back?'

She nodded. 'Four weeks only. Three days a week. I need to start my paediatric hours soon or they'll forget why they employed me.' It was almost as if she were drawing a line in the sand.

'And a few on-calls for the hospital?'

A soft pink teddy bounced off his head. 'Only if there's absolutely nobody—and I mean *nobody*—else that can do it. I'd need to wake up Isla and bring her in the car.'

'Understood.' He held out his hand towards his latest lifesaver.

'Welcome to Arran, Dr Halliday.'

Gemma opened her eyes. Curtain poles were going to be an issue. It was only five-thirty and sunshine was streaming through her bedroom window. She made a mental note. First thing, see if anywhere on the island sells curtain poles.

She rolled over in her bed and tried to stifle a groan. Second thing. Don't let perfect strangers steamroller you into starting work early.

She should be having a leisurely day with Isla, sipping tea and sorting out some boxes. Instead, she'd be introducing her daughter to a potential babysitter and getting a guided tour of the local Angel Grace Hospital and GP surgery. She must be mad.

'Mummy, are we getting up now?'

She smiled. Isla seemed to have an internal radar and knew whenever her mother's eyes flickered open. Gemma pulled back the cover and swung her legs out of bed. 'Tea and toast?'

'Tea and toast,' Isla said, in her most grown-up voice.

Three hours later they were standing in front of a cottage with pretty flowered curtains. The blue front door opened and an older woman with an apron tied around her waist stuck her head outside. 'You must be Isla,' she said immediately. 'I've been waiting for you. I was just about to start some baking. Would you like to help me?'

There was the quick nod of a little head and Gemma was summarily dismissed. Moments later Isla was standing on a wooden chair at the kitchen sink, washing her hands, a little girl's pink apron tied around her waist.

Gemma hesitated at the kitchen door. 'Mary, thank you for this. Are you sure you don't mind? Would you like me to stay to give you a chance to get to know each other a bit better?'

She'd had a chance to have a long conversation on the phone with Mary Scott last night. Logan had been right.

His mother seemed delighted to look after Isla and had asked Gemma about her interests so she could plan ahead.

A floury hand was waved. 'We'll be fine. Go on and get to work.'

Gemma grabbed a piece of paper to write down her mobile number. 'Here's my number. Call me about anything—anything at all.'

'We'll be fine, Mummy. Go and meet Logan. I liked him.' Gemma felt her face flush, and could see the not-so-hidden smile on Mary's face. She dreaded to think what was going on in her head. Isla had lifted a glass jar of sultanas and was ready to pour them into Mary's mixing bowl.

Children were so much more relaxed. So much more at ease than adults. Her stomach had been in a permanent knot since last night at the thought of starting work early and having to meet the rest of her new colleagues. Isla didn't seem to have any such worries.

Gemma picked up her car keys again. 'Okay, then.' She dropped a kiss on Isla's head. 'See you later, pumpkin. Be good for Mary and I'll pick you up in a few hours.'

The surgery was only a five-minute drive away and the hospital five more minutes along the road. If she needed to get there in a hurry, she could.

The practice was buzzing as she entered. Patients were already sitting in the waiting room, with a number queuing at the reception desk. Gemma hesitated and then joined the queue, waiting her turn until she reached the front.

The receptionist, with long brown hair in a ponytail and a badge that read 'Julie', gave her a friendly smile. 'Are you a holidaymaker? Need an emergency appointment?'

'No, I'm Gemma. Gemma Halliday, the new doctor. I'm supposed to be meeting Logan Scott here today.'

The smile faltered for the briefest second as Gemma felt the young receptionist's eyes quickly run up and down her body. Should she have dressed more formally? Her pale pink shirt and grey skirt had suited at her last job. Maybe things were a little more formal in Arran?

The girl leaned backwards in her chair. 'Logan!' Her shout was like a foghorn. 'Our new doctor's arrived. Get out here.'

'He'll just be sec,' she said, as she picked up a pile of patient notes and disappeared through a door behind her.

Gemma turned slowly. She could feel every set of eyes in the room studying her. All potential patients. Giving her the once-over. She took a deep breath and smiled nervously. 'Hi, there.' Her normally steady voice came out as a surprising squeak. This would never do.

She jumped as a hand settled in the small of her back. 'Hi, Gemma.' Logan's voice was low, husky. Not what she expected in the middle of busy waiting room. She shifted a little. 'I take it my mother and Isla are getting along famously?'

She nodded. 'How did you guess?'

His hand pressed into her back, guiding her away from the watchful eyes in the waiting room and towards one of the consulting rooms. 'My mother could hardly contain her excitement. She spent most of last night deciding what the two of them could bake together.'

Gemma smiled. 'Yip, they were both on their way to being covered in flour when I left.' She wrinkled her brow. 'Doesn't your mother have any grandchildren of her own.'

Something flitted across his eyes. 'Not yet.'

What kind of answer was that? She instantly felt uncomfortable for asking the question. She watched as Logan poured coffee into two cups and handed one to her. He must have a wife or a partner and be trying for a family. Her eyes fell to his hand. No ring. But, then, these days that meant nothing. Lots of men didn't wear rings.

His hand gestured towards the chair opposite his as he took a seat. He gave a professional kind of smile. It seemed it was all business with him here. That cheeky demeanour she'd witnessed the day before didn't seem to feature.

'You can see we're already starting to get busy. This is just the start of the season. Arran's population doubles in the summer months.'

She nodded. 'I had heard that.' She took a sip of her coffee. 'Did you clear it with the health board about me working here for the next month?'

He gave her a smile as he gritted his teeth apologetically. 'Six weeks, actually. They agreed you can start your paediatric hours when the school session starts again.'

Her brain started to whirr. This was a new colleague. But he obviously didn't know her at all. People making assumptions about her made her temper flare. He could have consulted her first.

She took a sip of her coffee and looked at him carefully. Logan Scott was probably used to being a force to be reckoned with. On a small island like this, he probably pretty much got his own way. It was clear to Gemma that at some point they would lock horns.

'It would have been nice to be consulted, Logan,' she said simply. He had already moved his attention elsewhere and was pulling up screens on his computer for her to look at.

'What? Oh…right, sorry.'

He didn't look sorry. He didn't look sorry at all. The moment the words had come from his lips they had just vanished into the ether.

She pulled her chair around next to his to look at the information he was pulling up on the computer screen. 'That's fine. Just don't do it again.' Her voice was firm this time. Much more definite.

And this time he did pay attention. His bright blue eyes met her brown ones, with more than a little surprise in them.

The smile had disappeared from his face, replaced by a straight line. 'If you say so,' he murmured.

It only took an hour or so to familiarise Gemma with the practice systems and introduce her to the two other GPs who worked at the surgery. She seemed to pick things up quickly, only asking a few pertinent questions then going round and introducing herself to the rest of the staff.

The working-hours negotiations were a little more fraught. He'd hoped she'd be a bit more flexible. She needed to cover three days within the practice, but it would have worked out better if she could have worked some mornings and afternoons and actually done her hours over five days.

But Gemma Halliday was an immovable force. She was adamant that three full days was all she could do. No extra surgeries at all. Her time was to be spent with Isla.

They walked over to the Angel Grace Hospital. It was a nice day and the brisk walk did them both good.

'I'm hoping you're happy to see everyone who comes into the practice.'

'Why wouldn't I be? Isn't that what GPs do?' He should have asked her if she had a jacket. The breeze was rippling her pale pink shirt against her breasts, and the unbuttoned collar was flapping in the wind. Boy, she could be prickly.

'I just thought you might request to see only the kids.'

She shrugged and shook her head. 'Not at all. Happy to see anyone. If the other partners want me to see more than my share of kids, that's fine too. Obviously, they're my specialty. But that doesn't mean I won't see other patients.'

'Good. That's good.'

'How much antenatal care do you have?'

He shook his head. 'Minimal. We have around twenty-five to thirty-five births a year on the island. Our midwife, Edith, generally does all the antenatal care. It's only if someone is a complicated case that we become involved.'

'Do the mothers deliver here?'

'Most deliver on the mainland. Last year we had six home births. All planned with military precision by Edith. A few more requested them, but Edith and the obstetric consultant deemed them too risky. When we have plans for a home birth, both midwives on the island have to be on call. It can get a little complicated.'

They reached the door of the hospital and Logan held it open for her. 'So what happens in an emergency situation—for anyone, not just maternity cases—and we need to transport someone quickly?'

He led her down one of the corridors of the hospital. 'That's when we call in the emergency helicopter from the naval base at Prestwick. Surgical emergencies, unstable head injuries and maternity emergencies would get transported that way. Ayrshire General Hospital is only about ten minutes away once the helicopter gets in the air.'

He opened another door. 'We do have a theatre that can be used in emergencies, but it's a bit basic. This is mostly used for minor procedures.'

She looked around the single theatre. She'd already noticed that the hospital was an older building, probably left over from the war. 'Do you have a lot of emergencies that require the helicopter?' Even the thought of the helicopter made her nervous.

'We had ten last year. They are search-and-rescue helicopters. There are three of them and they normally get scrambled every day. They cover a huge area—twelve times the size of Wales—and we only call them out if absolutely necessary. We've transported stable patients on the main island ferry before, or we occasionally run a private boat if the ferries schedules are unsuitable, and transport patients to the mainland where we have an ambulance waiting.'

They walked further along the corridor. 'Oh, and there's also the hyperbaric chamber over on the Isle of Cumbrae—Millport. It's one of only four in Scotland and used for anyone with decompression sickness.'

'You deal with that around here?' She shook her head. She hadn't even considered anything like that. And she didn't know the first thing about decompression sickness.

He nodded slowly. 'It would surprise you, but we have a lot of diving in and around the island, and along the Scottish coast. But don't worry, there's an on-call hyper-

baric consultant at Aberdeen Hospital. He's the expert
in all these things.'

They continued along the corridor and Gemma tried
not to let the panic on her face show. She really hadn't
realised the realm of expertise that would be required to
work in an island community. At this rate she was going
to have to go back into student mode and start studying
again. They'd reached the single ward in the hospital.
Logan pointed through the glass.

'Sixteen beds, with patients that we normally reassess on a daily basis. It's kind of like a mix between a
medical ward and an elderly care ward. Lots of chest
conditions and confusion due to low oxygen saturation.
We have good permanent nursing staff that are more
than capable of dealing with any emergency. They re-
site drips, give IV antibiotics and other meds, order
X-rays and can intubate during an arrest.' He pointed
down the corridor.

'There are also a few side rooms if required and an
A and E department that is chaotic during the summer.'

Gemma's eyes widened a little. 'How is that staffed?'
His stomach curled a little. This woman could practically
see things coming from a million miles away.

'It has its own doctor, a couple of nurse practitioners
and some regular nursing staff.' He pointed to a rota on
the wall. 'If the A and E doctor isn't busy, he would deal
with any issue with the ward patients. If not, we get called
out.' He could tell from the expression on her face that she
was worried. 'Don't worry, it doesn't happen too often.'

She nodded slowly. 'I knew there would be occasional
callouts because I was covering one day a week for the
GP practice. I guess I'll just need to bring Isla with me.'

Darn it. He hadn't considered her little girl when

he'd persuaded her to work three days a week in the GP practice for the next six weeks. Her job as a paediatric consultant two days a week wouldn't have included any on-call services. He'd only been thinking of the needs of the practice, not the needs of a single parent and her five-year-old daughter. With one step he'd just trebled her chances of being called out.

He smacked his hand on his forehead. 'I'm sorry, Gemma. I hadn't even considered Isla. We'll need to have a look at the rota.'

She shrugged her shoulders. 'There's not much you can do. It's only for the next six weeks. I guess I'll just have to cope.'

But the guilt was gnawing away at him. He hadn't been entirely truthful as he'd given her the tour. Isla just hadn't entered into his radar at all.

This was the problem with being a single guy with no other responsibilities. Work was his only real consideration in life. Once he had that covered, he didn't think about much else. 'Yeah, well, about that...'

'What?' Her eyes had widened, giving him an even better view of just what a warm brown they were. She was much smaller than him, maybe around five feet two or three? The kind of small woman that men like him usually wanted to protect. It was instinctual.

But he had the strangest feeling that Gemma Halliday was the kind of woman that didn't want to be protected. She was more likely to kick you in the groin than cower in a corner.

'How about I show you where the canteen is in here?' He tried to guide her along the corridor. From the look of her small frame, the chances were slim that he could fob her off with coffee and cake but it was worth a try.

* * *

Gemma was suspicious. She could practically see Logan
Scott shuffling his feet like some nervous teenager waiting to tell you that they'd smashed the car or broken a
window. He'd been quite straightforward up until this
point, so she had a pretty good idea she wouldn't like
what he had to say.

She let him guide her down the corridor towards the
canteen. Coffee sounded good right about now. The hospital set-up looked fine. It was old, but it was clean and
functional. The patients in the ward looked well cared
for. The staff around here seemed efficient.

It was obvious she wouldn't find the latest state-of-the-
art technology here but, then again, why would she need
it? They had X-ray facilities and an ultrasound scanner.
An emergency theatre that she hoped she would never
see the inside of, and a way to transport the sickest patients off the island.

Logan pushed open the door in front of them and held
it open. It took around two seconds for her senses to be
assaulted by the smell of prime-time baking. 'Wow. What
do they make in here?'

He pointed at the counter. 'Della makes cakes every
day. And you can make requests if you find a favourite
and want it on a particular day.'

She couldn't help but smile. 'And what's your request?'

His answer was instant. 'The carrot cake…or the
cheese scones…or the strawberry tarts—they're giant.
Not like the ones you would buy elsewhere.'

They'd reached the counter. It was clear that anyone
who set foot in here wouldn't want to leave. Piles of
freshly baked scones and crumpets, some tray bakes and
a whole array of cakes. Gemma didn't hesitate, she leaned

over and picked up a fruit scone. It was still warm. She could practically taste it already.

'What kind of coffee?' Logan was poised at the coffee machine. Gemma pointed at the china mugs he was holding.

'What, no plastic cups?'

He shook his head in mock disgust. 'On Arran? Not a chance. Everything is served in china over here.'

'I'll have a latte, thanks.'

She waited until he'd filled the two cups and they settled at a table, looking out across the hospital gardens, which were trimmed, neat with lots of colourful flower beds.

Gemma started cutting open her scone and spreading butter and jam. 'What? Never seen a woman eat before, Logan? Stop gawping.'

He smiled as he started on his carrot cake. 'You don't look like the kind of girl that eats cakes.'

There it was again. His directness. Sneaking in when you least expected it. 'Because I'm small?'

He sipped his cappuccino and wrinkled his nose. It was obvious he was trying to wind her up a little. Playing with her. Obviously hoping to soften her up for what was to come. 'You're not small, Gemma. You're vertically challenged.'

She raised her eyebrows. 'Really?'

'Yip.' He leaned back in his chair. 'That's my professional opinion.' His long legs stretched out under the table, brushing next to her own. What was that? That little tremor of something she'd just felt? It had been so long since she'd had time to even have a man on her radar that she didn't even know how these things worked these days.

His shirt was pale blue, almost like a thin denim, with

a few wrinkles around the elbows and open at the collar, revealing some light curling hairs.

She was trying to place who he looked like. But the tiny blond tips of his hair were throwing her. That was it. He needed a captain's uniform. He looked like that new young guy they'd drafted in for the latest *Star Trek* movie. If his hair was only the *tiniest* shade darker he could be a clone.

She took a bite of the scone. Just as she'd suspected. Delicious. She leaned back in her chair. 'I think I'm just about to put on two stone.'

He smiled. 'The food here is good. If you have any special requests or dietary issues, just let them know.'

She raised her eyebrow. 'Dietary issues? Trying to tell me something, Logan?'

He shook his head swiftly. 'I wouldn't dare.'

Her eyes narrowed slightly. 'Okay, then, out with it. You've obviously kept the bombshell for last. Hit me with it.'

His eyes drifted away from her and he fixated on something outside. 'Yeah…about that.'

'About what?' Her voice was firm. How bad could this be?

He shifted in his seat. 'You know how I told you that if A and E is quiet the doctor will cover the ward patients too?'

She nodded. 'Yes.' She was feeling very wary of him now.

'Well, it kind of works both ways.'

She felt the hairs standing up at the back of her neck. 'What do you mean?'

He stared at her. With those big blue eyes that could be very distracting if you let them.

'I mean that if the A and E doc gets snowed under, then they usually call us out for some assistance.' He was visibly cringing as he said the words. Obviously waiting for the fallout.

She ran her tongue along her dry lips. He was worried. And a tiny part of that amused her.

She'd only agreed to help out for six weeks. She would only have a few on-calls. How bad could this be? Maybe she should make him sweat a little. After all, he had been quite presumptuous so far.

She picked up her scone and regarded him carefully. 'Think carefully before you answer the next question, Logan. I can tell you right now that if you spoil my scone, this could all end in tears.' She took a little bite. Was he holding his breath? 'Exactly how many times does the A and E doc call you out?'

Logan shifted again. 'Well, in the winter, hardly ever. Maybe once every six weeks.'

She knew exactly where this was going. 'And in the summer?'

He gave a little frown and a shrug of his shoulders. 'Probably...most nights?'

'What?' Her voice had just gone up about three octaves. He had to be joking. 'Every night?'

His head was giving little nods. No wonder he'd worried about telling her. 'More or less.'

She put her scone back down on her plate, her appetite instantly forgotten. This was going to be far more complicated than she could possibly have expected.

Logan held up his hands. 'Look, Gemma. I'm sorry. I hadn't really taken Isla into the equation. I'm so used to being on my own I didn't even consider the impact it would have on her. I mean, you are a single parent, aren't you? You don't have another half that's going to appear in the next few weeks?'

There it was again. His presumptions. And was she mistaken or did he sound vaguely happy—as well as apologetic—about the situation?

And why did she care? This guy, with his rolled-up sleeves revealing his tanned arms, was giving her constant distractions.

Like that one. Since when did she notice a man's tanned arms? Or the blond tips in his hair? Or the fact he might resemble a movie star?

She'd been so focused for the last five years. Every single bit of her pent-up energy had been invested in Isla. In the fight to keep her, and all the hard work that went along with being a single parent, working full-time.

She hadn't even had time to look in the mirror, let alone look around her and notice any men.

Maybe this was just a reaction to Isla's out-of-the-blue drawing with the feature boyfriend.

Her stomach gave the strangest flutter. Or maybe this was just a reaction to the big blue eyes, surrounded by little weathered lines, currently staring at her across the table.

She took a deep breath. Were his thoughts really presumptions? He'd helped her unpack. He must have noticed the distinct lack of manly goods about the place.

She nodded her head. She was used to this. She was used to the single-parent question. She'd been fielding it for the last five years. 'Yes, I'm a single parent, Logan. I hadn't really expected to be called out at night on a frequent basis. That could cause me a number of problems.'

She was trying not to notice the fact he'd just told her he only had himself to think about.

She was trying to ignore the tiny flutter she'd felt when he'd revealed the possibility he might be unattached. She was trying not to notice the little flicker in her stomach that Logan wasn't married with a whole family of his own. What on earth was wrong with her?

He lifted his hands. 'Look, I'm sorry. But I'm desperate. I really need someone at the surgery right now. How about I cover some of your on-calls?'

She bit her lip. 'That's hardly fair, is it?' She couldn't figure out the wave of strange sensations crowding around her brain. Then something scrambled its way to the front and a smile danced across her face. 'Don't you have someone to go home to?'

There. She'd said it.

The quickest way to sort out the weird range of thoughts she was having. He may not wear a wedding ring but he was sure to have another half tucked away somewhere on the island.

Another woman. Simple. The easiest way to dismiss this man.

He smiled and leaned across the table towards her, the hairs on his tanned arm coming into contact with her pale, bare arm. She really needed to get a little sun.

'You mean, apart from my mother?' He was teasing her. She could tell by the sexy glint in his eye that he knew exactly why she'd asked the question.

She let out a laugh. 'Oh, come on. Someone your age doesn't stay with their mother. You certainly weren't there when we arrived this morning.'

There was something in the air between them. Everything about this was wrong. He was a colleague. This was a small island.

She was here for a fresh start and some down time.

So why was her heart pitter-pattering against her chest?

It seemed that Arran was about to get very interesting.

CHAPTER THREE

LOGAN RAN HIS fingers through his hair. They'd finally reached a compromise.

He was going to cover as much of the on-call as possible, even though Gemma had been determined to do her share. She was feisty.

And so was her daughter.

He'd nipped back home after lunchtime and found his mother being ordered around by Isla. Granted, it was in a very polite manner—but the little girl clearly took after her mother.

But what had struck him most of all was the expression of joy on his mother's face. She clearly loved the interactions with the little girl. His father had died ten years ago. Logan had settled back on the island once he'd completed his GP training and bought a house just along the road. His sister Claire had been battling infertility for seven years. And his mother had been patiently knitting and stashing tiny little cardigans in a cupboard in the back bedroom for just as long.

It was a nightmare. The one thing he'd never given much thought to during his medical career. Fertility.

Sure, he understood the science of it. And, of course, he always had empathy for his patients.

But to see the true, devastating effects of unexpected infertility and how it impacted on a family had been brought home to him in the past few years. The highs of being accepted for treatment and at the start of each attempt. The lows and desperation as each failure lessened the likelihood of future success. The slow, progressive withdrawal of his sister, along with the cracks that had subsequently appeared in her marriage.

At times, Logan had no idea how his brother-in-law managed to keep things on an even keel. Claire could be so volatile now. The slightest thing could set her off. The beautiful, healthy, lively young woman had turned into a skeletal, unconfident wreck.

And it affected every one of them.

And now he'd just given his mother a taste of being a grandmother.

It wasn't as if his mum hadn't stepped in before. She'd loved little Ben as much as he had and had watched him occasionally as he and Zoe had dated. But the connection with Isla was definitely stronger. Why, he wasn't sure. But watching them together and hearing the way they spoke to each other made him laugh. It was like a pair of feisty older women, rather than a little girl and his mother. They were definitely kindred spirits.

Was he being unfair? Because his mother currently looked as if she were loving every minute of this. Isla too. And there was no question about the fact that Gemma needed trustworthy childcare.

But what would Claire think if she found out her mother was acting as a surrogate gran? Would it hurt her even more? Because he really couldn't bear that.

The phone rang on his desk. He picked it up swiftly. 'Yes?'

'Logan, we've had too many calls for emergency

appointments this morning. We're going to burst at the seams.'

He frowned. 'Have you scheduled Dr Halliday to see any of the emergency patients?'

'Well, no. You told us not to. She's supposed to be doing the house calls this week to try and find her way around the island.'

'Let's leave that for next week.' He couldn't afford the time needed for Gemma to navigate her way around the outlying farms and crofts that he could find in his sleep. 'Schedule her for some of the emergency GP surgeries this week, there's just no way we can do without her.'

He couldn't help shaking his head. Sam Allan might be in his seventies, but he was one of the most efficient doctors Logan had ever worked with. His were big shoes to fill and Gemma, with her lack of experience in a GP practice, would be struggling to keep up.

He was about to hang up but changed his mind. 'Julie? Just a thought. Dr Halliday has said she's happy to see any patients, but try and give her most of the kids, will you? She's a paediatric expert and will probably be more confident with them.'

Julie murmured in agreement and he put his phone down. He wanted to be supportive to his new colleague. It made sense to develop a good relationship with the new paediatrician on the island. After all, it would be his patients he would be referring to her.

He could think of a few kids straight away who could do with some paediatric expertise. It wasn't always easy for people on Arran to get to the mainland to see the paediatricians based at the nearest big hospital. The weather, the ferries, roadworks and even unsuitable hospital appointment times had caused numerous missed appointments. Having someone based on the island would be a real bonus for them, and would also ensure some continuity of care for their patients.

He glanced at his computer screen, checking his first patient. Rudy Sinclair. A prime candidate for a paediatrician. Maybe he should invite Gemma in and get her professional opinion?

His hand hesitated over the phone. Would she think he was testing her abilities? Because that was the last thing on his mind. He was almost relieved to think that someone else could offer a useful opinion on this little boy. He buzzed through to the nearby room. 'Gemma? I'm about to see a little boy who has frequent visits to the surgery. I would be interested if you could sit in and give me a professional opinion.'

She appeared at his door a few seconds later. 'What's it worth?' she chirped back without hesitation. There was a cheeky grin on her face.

He started a little in his seat. He hadn't expected that. There was more to Gemma Halliday than met the eye. He folded his arms across his chest. 'Dr Halliday, I hope you're not trying to hold me hostage over a child's health?'

She shook her head. 'Nope. I'm just trying to wangle out of you one of the strawberry tarts I spotted earlier.'

He laughed. 'A strawberry tart? That's your price?'

She nodded. 'Absolutely.' Then held out her hand towards him. 'Deal?' Her eyebrows were raised.

He reached over, his large hand encapsulating her small one. He tried not to let the expression on his face change as a little zing shot up his arm.

He was Logan Scott. He didn't do *zings*. What on earth was wrong with him? 'Deal,' he said as he shook her hand firmly. 'Now, let me go and get our patient.'

* * *

Rudy Sinclair had an impertinent look on his face as he strode into the surgery; his mother, juggling multiple bags, looked completely harassed. Gemma looked up from the computer. Logan hadn't been kidding. Rudy had been to the surgery on multiple occasions.

She ran her eyes over the list. Bumps and bruises, chest infections, ear infections, the odd rash—nothing out of the ordinary for the average child. Except Rudy was here much more than the average child.

Logan made the introductions quickly. 'Mrs Sinclair, this is Dr Halliday. She's the new GP in the practice and also specialises in paediatrics. I hope you don't mind her sitting in today. She's learning all the new systems.'

'What?' The woman looked a little distracted as she juggled her bags and sat down in the chair opposite. Her eyes scanned over to Rudy, who seemed to be dismantling a coloured puzzle that was sitting on Logan's desk. 'Yes, that's fine with me.'

That was interesting. Logan had implied she was there to learn the ropes, rather than there for her expertise. Was he worried the mother would object to a specialist referral?

Logan settled into his chair. 'So, Rudy, what seems to be the problem?'

Gemma liked that. She liked that he asked Rudy what was wrong, rather than the mother.

Rudy dropped the puzzle on the table and lifted his leg. 'I've got a sore foot.'

'I see. Well, why don't you take your shoe off so I can take a look?'

Rudy pouted. 'Don't want to.'

Gemma pressed her lips together to hide the smile that

could appear. She was already getting the impression that Rudy was used to getting his own way.

Logan sat forward in his chair. 'How did you hurt your foot, Rudy? Were you jumping, kicking, playing football?'

Rudy had moved over to the window and started playing with the blinds, tugging at the cord. 'Leave that, Rudy.' His mother's voice was quiet, ineffectual. As if she knew she should be saying the words but that she really didn't want to.

Logan reached over and took Rudy's hand. 'Come over here, young man, and let me see this sore foot.'

Rudy's face immediately fell into a frown. 'No.' He folded his arms across his chest.

Gemma turned to the mother. 'Has Rudy been limping?'

She shook her head.

'Did you notice any red marks or lumps on his foot earlier?' Logan was obviously trying to ascertain a little more of the history, but Gemma had an instinct for these things. And it probably wasn't going to end well.

Mrs Sinclair shook her head again. 'No. He just said it was sore.' She held up her hands in frustration. It was obvious she wasn't the person in charge in her household.

Gemma resisted the temptation to say anything. This wasn't a conversation for a seven-minute GP consultation. She settled back into the leather-backed chair and watched Logan's interactions with the little boy.

Logan was firm, without being intimidating. He knelt down on the floor, trying to talk to Rudy at his own level. His six-foot-plus frame must seem scary to a child, but he was trying his best to coax Rudy out of his shoe and sock. In the meantime, Rudy was leading them all in a merry dance. And it was more than obvious he only danced to his own tune.

Gemma watched quietly. Mrs Sinclair had dark circles around her eyes. She looked tired. She looked frazzled. But it was more than that.

She didn't seem to have any energy, or any real concern about her son. She was simply there because Rudy had told her he needed to see the doctor. Could she be depressed?

After another unsuccessful five minutes, taking them well over their consultation time and with no appearance of the injured foot, Logan gave her a look. 'Dr Halliday, do you have any suggestions?'

She looked over at Rudy again. Once more he was ignoring his mother's instructions and his hand was holding a pen, poised to write on the wooden desk. Gemma reached over and took the pen firmly from his grasp. She smiled sweetly. 'I don't think so. Rudy seems to be weight bearing on his ankle without any problems, and he doesn't appear to be limping.' She looked over at Mrs Sinclair. 'I'd just suggest you come back if you have any concerns.'

Mrs Sinclair nodded and stood up, gathering her numerous bags, and made her way to the door. It took her a few moments to realise Rudy wasn't following her, and another five minutes to coax him from the room. By the time he left he was bartering with her. 'I'm only coming if you buy me a chocolate crispie from the bakers.'

Logan shut the door firmly behind them, sagging back into his chair and heaving a sigh of relief.

He was a good GP. Even though there hadn't been anything obviously wrong with the little boy he'd tried to engage him and talk to him at his level. He'd asked all the right questions of both the mum and the boy and taken his time. He hadn't been glancing at the clock, anxious to move on to the next patient.

She could sense his frustration. But it hadn't been obvious to either Rudy or his mother, and that's what was important.

He ran his fingers through his hair, instantly upsetting the styled look and making it more windswept and tousled. She liked it better that way.

'So, what do you think?' He spun around in his chair until he faced her, leaning forward, his elbows on his knees, giving her a slightest glimpse of his dark curled hair at the base of his throat.

This was it. This was where she had her reputation decided. Was the isle of Arran ready for her expertise? How would they take to an outsider commenting on families who might have lived here for years? How would Logan take to her commenting on families he might have grown up around?

Time to take a deep breath and hope she wasn't digging her own grave.

'In all honesty? I think he's a brat.'

Logan's eyes widened and he sat back in his chair. She braced herself for his onslaught. For the *how dare shes?* and *what does she knows?*

But they didn't come. Instead, he seemed to settle himself a little more in the chair, his head tilted a little to the side—as if he were prepared to listen. 'Go on.'

She moved forward a little. 'How well do you know Mrs Sinclair?'

He lifted his hand. 'We'll discuss that in a minute. Tell me first what you think about Rudy.'

Was this a test? Was he going to let her rattle on and

then shoot everything she'd just said down in flames? She took a deep, steadying breath. This was her area of expertise. This was her professional opinion. This wasn't personal.

'I think Rudy is a little boy with no boundaries. I think Rudy rules the roost. Apart from the usual childhood ailments, there's nothing in Rudy's history that would give me real cause for concern. I don't think there's any sign of abuse. I don't think there's any sign of neglect. But I also don't think there's any apparent parenting going on in that house. She says the words. But she doesn't mean them. I think Rudy does whatever he wants and he doesn't take kindly to being told no.' She paused and leaned forward a little. 'Has he started school yet? Because I predict the schoolteacher will find him a nightmare.'

Logan nodded slowly. 'A few of the other partners have raised issues about the amount of visits. But there's never anything to really worry about. I gather the school has raised behaviour issues with Mrs Sinclair. And there was some mention about testing and ADHD.'

Gemma shook her head firmly and leaned forward. 'Rudy doesn't have any of the classic signs. If I thought for a minute there was a professional diagnosis to be made I'd refer him for all the tests myself. No. This is a parenting issue.' She raised her eyebrows at him. 'Are we allowed to talk about Mrs Sinclair yet?'

He paused for a second. And it took a few moments to realise that she'd put herself in a similar position to that he'd been in earlier. One where he could see right down past the open button of her shirt. She sat up abruptly and pulled her shirt down, her cheeks naturally flushing.

A smile crossed his face, but he didn't meet her eyes.

It was almost as if he wasn't acknowledging that fact he'd just been caught staring.

He turned to the computer and pulled up the next file. 'Natalie Sinclair is thirty-five. Rudy is her only child. She's married, no immediate health problems.'

'How well does the health visitor know her?'

His brow furrowed. 'Mags? I'm not sure.'

Gemma chose her words carefully. 'Do you think there's any chance that she's depressed?'

He spun his chair around again. 'To be honest? I'm not sure. She looked tired today, and a little disengaged. But is it depression? Or just the fact she can't deal with her son?' He gave a little sigh and leaned back again. 'Give me a straightforward appendicitis any day.'

She touched his shoulder. The heat of his body was evident through his cotton shirt. 'I haven't met Mags yet. Do you think you could arrange for me to speak to her?'

'What do you want to do?' He wheeled his chair back from the screen, making room for her to pull hers up.

'I want to get a better picture about Mrs Sinclair and how things are at home.' She gave a nervous laugh. 'Telling a parent they're not making a great job of parenting their child and setting boundaries never goes well—believe me. I'd prefer a straightforward appendicitis too.'

Their eyes met. And for her it was instant relief.

He hadn't jumped down her throat and tried to defend the mother. It was the professional acknowledgement that she needed. It felt good.

For the first time in a long time she didn't catch a man's eye and immediately want to look away. Logan's eyes were a nice shade of blue. Much brighter than the dark sea that surrounded the island.

He was looking at her with interest and, if she wasn't wrong, with more than a little appreciation.

Would that change when he found out her own personal history? Would he start to make judgements about her, and her situation, then?

Her heart sank a little. Back to square one. That's where she'd be then, with all her new colleagues discussing her personal business. Just exactly what she didn't want.

He let out a little laugh. 'I'll arrange for Mags to come and speak to you. And here was me thinking that our brand-new paediatrician would ridicule me and tell me I'd missed some unknown, vital syndrome. You've no idea how relieved I am to hear you say you think it's something much more fundamental—much more basic.'

She gave a shrug of the shoulders. 'Sometimes it's easier for an outsider to say the words that the rest of you have been thinking.'

She lifted her chin to meet his gaze. There was silence. His blue eyes were fixed on hers. They were only a few feet apart. Close enough that she could see the tiny laughter lines around his eyes, along with skin that was slightly weather-beaten by the glimpses of Scottish sun and Ayrshire winds.

It was unnerving. And she didn't like it.

She didn't like the way her stomach was doing flip-flops. She didn't like the way that even when he annoyed her he could still make her smile.

She wasn't used to this. It had been so long since she'd ever felt anything like this, she almost couldn't recognise the signs.

It didn't help that she knew next to nothing about him. For all she knew, he could be the island Lothario with half a dozen women to his name. And he was a colleague. It could only be a recipe for disaster.

She tilted her head to the side. Some of his words had triggered something in her brain. 'What would we do with appendicitis, anyway?'

He pointed skyward. 'That would be another one for the emergency helicopter and a quick transportation to the Ayrshire General Hospital.' He gave a fake shudder, 'In our worst case scenario, if the helicopter couldn't land we'd have to muddle through with our emergency theatre.'

Gemma shuddered too. Only hers wasn't so fake. 'Why wouldn't the helicopter be able to land?'

He lifted his hand. 'Lots of reasons. They could already be on a callout to somewhere miles away. Occasionally the helicopters are grounded due to engine problems. But the main issues around here are because of the weather. There can be some fierce storms around Arran, and even fiercer winds. The pilots are the bravest men I've ever met, but if it's not safe to land—they won't.'

She gave a little smile. 'In that case, bags I the anaesthetist role. You can do the surgery.'

His eyebrows rose. 'Bags? Wow. I haven't heard that expression in years—since I was about six and in the school playground.'

'You have now.' She winked. 'Maybe I'm just showing my youth, and you're really an old crock.' It was too easy. It was too easy to flirt naturally with him.

His face broke into a smile. 'All this for the price of a strawberry tart. You're a cheap date, Dr Halliday.'

She stood up and straightened her skirt. 'Actually, that will have to be *two* strawberry tarts, Logan. I'm part of a unique partnership and I can't have one without my girl.'

She walked towards the door, aware that his eyes were on her behind. She had to get it out there. No matter how subtle the words.

Every now and then he flirted with her. And while flirting was always harmless, she was part of a pair. She didn't want him to think for a second she could entertain him without giving thought to her daughter.

It was better to just have it out there, right from the start.

Her hand reached for the door. He hadn't said anything. Maybe it was for the best.

'Gemma?'

She spun around, just a little too quickly for her own liking. 'Yes?'

'The strawberry tarts. I'll bring them around tonight.' He turned back to his computer and started typing.

She sucked in a breath and tried to stop her feet from running down the corridor. What on earth was she doing?

CHAPTER FOUR

LOGAN PULLED UP outside the house and ran his fingers through his hair. He'd hardly had any sleep last night and had just jumped in the shower and dressed without even taking a look in the mirror. Hardly impressive. Ouch. His finger scratched the stubble on his chin. He hadn't even thought to shave.

Gemma pulled open the door and strolled over towards the car. Funnily enough, she looked as though she'd had the best sleep in the world. Her hair was loose and shiny, her red dress skimming her curves. There was nothing unprofessional about her appearance—every part of her that should be covered was covered, with only the tiniest glimpse of some tanned legs and red sandals. But that hadn't stopped an instant temperature rise in the car.

He tried to hide his smile. Gemma Halliday certainly wasn't sore on the eyes.

He rolled down his window. 'Ready for the island tour?' They'd arranged this last night—before he'd been kept up most of the night. It only seemed fair that he showed her around a bit more. Then at least Gemma could do some of the outlying surgeries or some of the more rural home visits.

She held up the big lump of grey plastic in her hands.

'Just as soon as we get the car seat in. Isla's looking forward to it.'

He opened his door. 'Isla's coming with us?' Darn it. He hadn't even considered the little girl.

Gemma nodded. 'Your mum had something on this morning, and since we're only going around the island in the car—and not seeing any patients—I assumed it wouldn't be a big deal.'

She leant passed him, pulling his seat forward and expertly situating Isla's car seat in the back of the car. He hadn't missed the 'argue-with-me-if-you-dare' slant to her words.

She folded her arms across her chest and leaned against the car. He shook his head. 'Sorry, Gemma, single man occupational hazard. I should have invited her along. I'd love to have Isla come with us.'

She smiled. A smile that reached right up into her deep brown eyes. 'I thought you might say that.' She looked over at the house. Isla was now arranging her colourful toy ponies on the front step. 'Two, Isla, you can only bring two,' she shouted, as she walked back to the front door.

There was a tiny mother-daughter altercation on the step, with a little tugging and pulling between the brightly coloured ponies before a few were left behind the locked door.

Isla stomped over to the car, brandishing her prizes. 'This is Whirlwind and this is Lightning.' She held up first a green and then a pink pony. She rolled her eyes. 'I wanted to bring Stargazer so you could meet him too, but Mummy made me leave him behind.' Without further ado she jumped into the back of the car and fastened her own seat belt, giving her mother a stern look.

Logan gave Gemma a wink as she climbed into the passenger seat. 'How about I introduce you to some real live Shetland ponies at one of the farms today, Isla?' He gave her a smile. 'They might not be pink or green, but they're just about your size and I'm sure you'll be allowed to touch them.'

'Will I? Really?'

He climbed in and started the engine. 'Really.' He turned to face Gemma, who was looking at him with a clear glimmer of amusement on her face. 'I take it that's all right with you?'

She half laughed. 'I was wondering how long it would take her to wind you around her little finger.' She leaned forward, her hair brushing against his arm. 'I'll let you into a secret, Isla Halliday has it down to a fine art.'

He laughed. 'Where do you think she learned it from?'

Gemma pressed the button to put the window down and let some of the sea air rush through the car. 'I have no idea what you're implying, Dr Scott,' she teased, as a whole wave of her light perfume drifted over towards him.

She leaned back in the car seat. 'I know I agreed to work longer hours, but this is the last few weeks of the summer holidays.' She cast a glance backwards to where Isla was carrying on a conversation between her two ponies. 'And I just can't bear the thought of not spending time with her. In a few weeks she'll be at school full time.' She let out a sigh. 'And I'll feel positively ancient.' She looked out at the passing view of Lamlash. 'Where are we headed anyway?'

Logan couldn't stop smiling. Ancient. She looked anything but. And it certainly wasn't one of the adjectives he'd use to describe her. 'We're going to Blackwaterfoot at the other side of the island. We have a satellite clinic there, and there are a few of the bigger farms that I want to point out to you en route.'

'How often is the clinic open at Blackwaterfoot?'

'Only once a week. It's about a thirty-minute drive. But it's a nice one—right around the coast.'

'Are we going to stop there today?'

Logan held up a set of keys. 'Sure. Luckily enough, it happens to be right next to a fish and chip shop, so I might introduce you and Isla to some of the local cuisine.'

Gemma raised her eyebrows. 'You already promised that—and reneged.'

Logan shook his head with embarrassment. 'The strawberry tarts. Yeah, I'm sorry. I was on call last night and was up half the night.'

'What happened? And what happened to "You won't be called out much"?'

He shook his head. 'Bad luck, I guess. One of my old farmers has a really bad chest. I had to admit him to Angel Grace Hospital and start him on IV antibiotics, some nebulisers and some oxygen.'

'Was he okay?' She sounded genuinely concerned. And it was nice. Past experience of some of the locum doctors had proved that most of them didn't really care about any of the older patients. They just did what had to be done and moved on. Maybe Gemma would be different?

There was definitely something in the air between them.

Gemma was easy to be around. She'd proved herself professionally competent the day before and he'd been more than a little relieved. The help at the practice would be a real weight off his shoulders.

Isla was chattering away in the background, talking between her ponies and occasionally asking questions of both her mother and Logan. She was a confident child and obviously intelligent.

Something gave a little twist in his gut. His self-protection mechanism. A fleeting memory of his ex Zoe and her son Ben. Gemma was a work colleague—nothing else.

So why did he find it so easy to flirt with her? And why did she seem to find it easy to respond?

He did his best to show her around the island, pointing out some of the almost hidden track roads to the farms that were hidden from view. Gemma took a few notes and asked a few questions. It didn't take them long to turn up at the farm of the old man he'd admitted to hospital the night before. He pulled up outside the stables and opened the door to let Isla out.

'Is this it?' she asked excitedly.

He nodded.

Gemma gave him a strange look as she climbed out of the car. 'Why do I get the feeling we would have been coming here whether Isla liked ponies or not?'

He lifted his hand. 'Guilty as charged. I promised Fred I'd put out some food for the ponies. It will only take a few minutes.' He gave her a wink as he settled a hand on Isla's shoulder to guide her. 'And, wait and see, I'm about to become your favourite friend.'

Gemma smiled and followed them, her hands on her hips. 'If I didn't know any better I would have thought you'd planned this. But since you didn't know Isla was coming, I guess you're just lucky.'

He led them over to a field where three Shetland ponies were waiting. They were obviously used to contact and nuzzled into his hand straight away as he filled up their water trough and put out some good-quality hay. He lifted up Isla and carried her over next to them. 'Would you like to touch the ponies?'

She nodded, her excitement clear.

He took her over to the oldest one. 'This is Skylar.' He put Isla down, sheltered between his legs, and helped her pet the quiet animal. The other two ponies came closer and she got to touch them too. He kept his voice low and whispered in her ear, trying to stop her squealing with excitement.

Gemma stood with her arms leaning on the fence. She seemed happy to let him take charge of Isla under her watchful gaze. He waited for around ten minutes, ensuring the ponies were happy, before he led Isla from the field.

'Did you see, Mummy? Did you take a picture with your phone?'

Gemma looked over and gave Logan a grateful nod. 'Thank you,' she whispered, then knelt down next to her daughter. 'Of course I took your picture, Isla. We'll print it out when we get home. She looked up at Logan. 'What happens tomorrow? Will someone else take care of the ponies?'

He nodded. 'I've spoken to one of the neighbouring farmers. He couldn't come over today but will help out the rest of the week. It won't take long.' He opened the car door again. 'Now, can I interest either of you ladies in some finely caught Arran fish and chips?'

Both of them nodded. It was nearing lunchtime and he could almost hear the rumble from their stomachs. 'Jump in, then. We'll have a quick visit to the surgery then get some fish and chips.'

Half an hour later they were sitting on a bench, looking out at the sea at Blackwaterfoot.

'So, tell me, Dr Scott, do you do this every day that you come down to cover the Blackwaterfoot surgery?'

He tapped the side of his nose. 'Aha. That's a state secret. A doctor on a diet of fish and chips. What would the patients say?'

Gemma grinned and glanced back to the chip shop. 'Maybe I should just ask the owner?'

'Oh, no. You don't want to do that.' He turned his head towards her, leaning forward a little. Gemma was only inches away. For a second it seemed as if they were the only two people in the world. All he could see was her dark brown eyes, and he could have sat there for ever and just watched them. It was like an addiction.

'Mummy, I'm finished. What do I do with the paper?'

Isla's voice broke the spell and made him start and pull back. Gemma's eyes lowered and he could see her take a deep breath before she held out her hand. 'Give it to me, honey. We'll find a wastepaper bin to put it in.'

What was that? He hadn't imagined it. He stood up quickly. He'd almost forgotten Isla was there. And that embarrassed him. 'Let's go, ladies. Time to head back.'

Gemma took Isla's hand and they all walked back to the car together, Gemma and Logan averting their eyes from each other. The journey home was swift, Gemma's eyes fixed on the landscape and the conversation neutral, with Logan pointing out a few more farms. Isla chattered merrily in the back seat, oblivious to the sparks of tension in the air.

When they reached Gemma's house she got out swiftly, helping Isla out and bending back into the car.

'Thanks for that, Logan. That was helpful. Hopefully I'll be able to be more of a help now I know where I'm going.'

'No problem.' He kept it brief. He was trying to stop his eyes fixating on the fact her dress was gaping slightly and revealing the tiniest hint of cleavage.

Their eyes met just for a second before she straightened and closed the door.

He watched her retreating back as she walked up the path, opened the door to her house and gave a final little wave. His mobile started to ring almost immediately. For a second he was annoyed as he'd been lost for a few seconds, daydreaming about the latest woman to spark his interest. There was more to Gemma Halliday than met the eye.

She was gorgeous. Curvaceous figure, big brown eyes and dark wavy hair. Once word got out about her he could almost write a list of the local single men who would turn up in the surgery. But the truth was on Arran just about everyone he knew would immediately peg her as his latest conquest.

And he wasn't sure he liked that. Because the one thing that was clear to him was that Gemma Halliday sure as hell wouldn't want to be known as that.

She intrigued him. He was going to have to put out some feelers.

It wasn't like him. He should have done it before she'd arrived. But Sam had been in charge of her recruitment and he trusted him. He had no reason not to.

He had more than a few old acquaintances working in and around Glasgow. Someone was bound to know about the beautiful young paediatrician who was a single mother. They might even be able to shed some light on why she'd decided to up sticks from the city and move to an island. It was more than a little unusual. And Gemma appeared to be holding her cards close to her chest.

It was the weirdest thing. But the barriers he'd kept firmly in place these last few years about dating women with children didn't seem all that rigid any more. He could almost imagine Isla telling him exactly what she thought of that idea. She was every bit as feisty as her mother and just thinking about her brought a smile to his face.

He glanced at the screen as he pulled up his phone. Claire. His sister.

Strange. She never phoned him in the middle of the day because she always knew he was busy with work.

'Claire? What's up?'

He could hear the wavering signal—an occupational hazard on Arran—and one that drove him nuts.

He strained to hear again. He could hear some background noise but no one talking.

'Claire? Are you there? I can't really hear you.'

Then he clicked. The background noise was that horrible sound. The sound of someone struggling to breathe because they were holding back their sobs. It was almost a regular occurrence for a GP. He just didn't expect it from his sister.

'Claire? What's wrong? Are you hurt? Do you need help? Where are you?'

He could barely hear her words through the sobs. 'It's the adoption agency…they just phoned.'

'And what? What's wrong?' His brain was racing. After seven years of IVF and other treatments, Claire and her husband had finally applied to adopt. The process was gruelling and not for the faint-hearted, but Claire was determined she wanted to be a mother.

'We failed the first assessment.' Her voice dissolved into another fit of sobs.

'You what? What do you mean, you failed the assessment? Why on earth would they fail you?' He was incredulous. This was his sister. He couldn't comprehend for a second why they would fail the assessment process. Sure—she'd been a little frail lately. But anyone who had been through what she had would be exactly the same. It was hardly a surprise.

'Well…it wasn't us that failed. It was me.'

He sagged back into his chair. A horrible sensation was sweeping over his skin. The hairs on his arms were pricking to attention.

His voice automatically dropped. This wasn't a time to shout. This wasn't the time to be angry. This was the time to be Logan Scott, brother to Claire. 'Why, Claire, what did they tell you?'

Her voice was all over the place. One minute up, one minute down. 'They said…they said…I wasn't stable. I needed some time.'

It was the most horrible sensation in the world. Tiny spots that had been sitting in different parts of his brain instantly having all the dots joined. He had been worried about Claire—she'd been under an enormous amount of pressure. And at times he'd worried about her mental health.

But he was her brother. Not her doctor.

And that churning feeling in his stomach was telling him just how much he'd failed her. Some stranger—in a room somewhere—had done an assessment on his sister—and had seen the current underlying issues. Said the words that no one else would say. Questioned her current mental health.

He could have stopped this. He could have stopped her having to go through this.

If only he'd had the courage to sit her down and tell her to wait a while—to take some time.

Instead, he'd seen his sister, who was so desperate to be a mother she'd just moved on to the next option. The next rational possibility for her, without taking time to ascertain if she was ready for it.

He couldn't have failed her more if he'd tried.

'Where are you, Claire?'

Her voice wavered again. 'I'm at home.'

He stood up. 'Stay where you are. I'll be there in ten minutes.'

He was instantly angry.

Angry with himself. And angry with those around him.

He should have spoken to his sister. He should have seen how everything had affected her.

Instead, he'd spent the last few days focusing on his latest colleague. Thinking about the snatched glimpse of satin underwear. Thinking about long brown curls and a curvy frame. Thinking about the joy on his mother's face as she got to experience being a surrogate gran.

He shook his head. That made his gut twist.

He didn't have time for Gemma.

He had to focus on his family.

He had to focus on the needs of his sister.

Because right now they were the most important thing in the world.

CHAPTER FIVE

IT WAS ALMOST embarrassing how early they were.

Gemma glanced at her watch—just after eight. Please let Mrs Scott be up already.

Isla was adjusting her bag of goodies in the seat next to her. Her array of toys that she'd decided to bring along today.

Getting Isla organised in the morning was usually like a military operation. It didn't matter how much she'd arranged the night before. One shoe was always missing and Isla always wanted to change her outfit at least three times. At least she used to.

Getting ready to go to Mrs Scott's seemed to take her all of two minutes. Hence the reason they were so early.

She pulled the car up outside the house and Isla opened her door and shot outside before she had a chance to speak. In two seconds flat she'd knocked on the door and opened it, shouting, 'Hello, Granny Scott,' at the top of her voice.

Gemma followed her through to the big kitchen, the heart of the family home. Mary was baking—already—and Isla was tying her apron around her waist as they spoke.

'Good morning, Mary. I'm sorry we're so early. I

thought it would take longer to get Isla organised in the morning.'

Mary smiled and nodded towards the garden outside. 'No matter, Gemma. You're welcome any time. Go outside and say hello to my daughter Claire. There's a pot of tea and some toast out there. Help yourself.'

Gemma smiled and glanced at her watch. Surgery didn't start until nine-thirty. She had lots of time to kill and meeting Logan's sister would be nice.

She walked out into the back garden. The early summer sun was already filling the sheltered garden with warmth. It really was a beautiful setting with the rich smell of Mary's multicoloured rose bed filling the air.

She was always a little nervous meeting new people, which was strange for a doctor as she met new people every day. But professional and personal were very different. The last few years had made her guarded about revealing too much of herself to people she didn't know.

'Good morning,' she said, holding out her hand. 'I'm Gemma Halliday, the new island paediatrician. I'm working with your brother Logan.'

The young dark-haired woman shifted in her seat at the sound of her voice and turned to meet her. She stood up and took Gemma's hand. 'Oh, how lovely to meet you. I'm Claire. My mum has told me so much about your daughter Isla.'

She lifted the teapot and gestured towards a cup. 'Would you like some tea?'

Gemma nodded gratefully and sat down.

'Thanks, Claire. That would be lovely.'

She was struck by how pale Claire was. Maybe it was that her hair was so dark, but her skin seemed rather washed out. Maybe belying some underlying condition?

She couldn't be much younger than Gemma was herself, but Claire was quite thin, with dark circles visible under her eyes. And there was something else. Something she couldn't quite put her finger on.

'So, what brings you to Arran, Gemma? And you'd better get used to answering that question, we're a nosey bunch over here.'

Gemma laughed. She wasn't quite sure how to answer the question without giving too much away. 'I wanted to get away from the city. Isla's about to start school and we lived in a really built-up area. I guess I decided that's not where I wanted to bring up my daughter.' She looked around the beautiful garden and shook her head. 'We didn't have anywhere like this to sit back home. It was time for a change.'

Claire took a sip of her tea. 'You timed it well. Isla will make lots of new friends, starting school here.'

'I hope so.' She watched as Isla appeared at the back door, carrying a pile of washing that looked suspiciously like dolls' clothes. There was a little rope strung between two trees and she took great care in pegging her washing to the line. She smiled. 'Your mum has been a real blessing in disguise for me. My mum and dad died years ago and, to be honest, I didn't really appreciate what Isla was missing out on. She was practically skipping this morning at the thought of spending time with your mum.'

There was a sad flicker across Claire's eyes, her voice wistful. 'My mum will be a wonderful grandmother. It just hasn't happened yet.'

And she didn't need to say any more. Because the look on her face said it all. That's what it was. The sadness around Claire. The periphery of a dark cloud sitting on her shoulders. Gemma recognised it so well. It had been the look of her friend Lesley for years and years.

Guilt twisted at her stomach. The permanent reminder of what she'd done.

This was bringing back painful reminders. She hadn't been able to bear Lesley looking like this. The stress, the not eating, the weight loss, the depression. She hadn't been able to bear the river of tears that Lesley had cried every month when, again, she hadn't been pregnant. And the accumulation of all those things had resulted in her making the biggest decision of her life—offering to be a surrogate.

It was odd. She hadn't been around anyone in the same position since. And the overwhelming rush of emotions at Claire's predicament seemed to flood her. She had to be calm. She had to be reasonable. Most importantly, she had to be supportive.

She sipped her tea. 'Well, give it time, Claire. You're still a young woman. There are lots of options out there.'

Claire nodded and started spreading some butter on the toast, handing a slice over to Gemma. 'Arran's a fabulous place to bring up children. I hope you'll like it here. How's your house?'

'Honestly? Better than I could have hoped for. I didn't even view it before I bought it—except online, of course. It suits me and Isla perfectly. I've always dreamed of having a house that looked over the water. I can't actually believe I've got it, I have to keep pinching myself.'

Claire smiled. 'I took all those things for granted for so long. As a teenager I couldn't wait to get off the island. But after a few years on the mainland I couldn't wait to get back. I couldn't see myself getting married and living anywhere but here.'

'Is your husband an islander?'

She nodded. 'And I hated him all the way through school. The frog took a number of years to turn into a prince.'

Gemma threw back her head and laughed. She liked this girl. She really did.

'So what does he do?'

Claire rolled her eyes. 'Oh, you'll meet him at some point—everybody does. Danny's the manager of the island bank.'

'And are you working right now?'

Claire nodded. 'I'm lucky. I do accounts. So most of the time I can work from home and do things online.'

'That's great. But I guess just about everyone that knows you wants a little advice for free.'

Claire nodded. 'Oh, yes, just like everyone who meets you will tell you the list of symptoms they've got, usually as you're buying a drink at the bar or just about to eat dinner.'

'Have you been camping out in my life?'

She shrugged. 'Happens with Logan all the time. It drives me nuts.' She topped up the tea. 'Do you read, Gemma? Fancy joining a book club?'

Gemma felt her heart flutter. She'd spent the last few weeks focusing on settling in. She hadn't had much of a chance to meet other women—except at the surgery. 'I love reading. I was part of a book group in Glasgow.'

Gemma nodded. 'The book group in Brodick is a real mix. We range in age from twenty-two to eighty.'

'Wow. How do you pick your books?'

'We all just take a turn. You're never going to please everyone. So we just ask that people pick something that they couldn't put down.'

'Sounds fabulous. What do I need to do?'

'Not much. We meet every fortnight at someone's house and...' she nodded at Isla '...kids are welcome. There's always someone to play with. When it's your turn to host you just supply the wine and the cakes.' Claire leaned across the table. 'I'll let you into a secret. I never bake. Mum makes me something when it's my turn. I just buy the wine. I'll bring you the book list and you can order online. The next meeting is a week on Thursday. Don't worry if you've not had a chance to read the book—just come and drink the wine.'

At last. A chance to meet some female friends on the island. She didn't care what age they were. She just wanted to have people she could have a laugh and a conversation with. And Claire seemed like one of those people. Even though she had a sadness around her eyes, she was trying to get on with things.

She could see her watching Isla from the corner of her eyes. But it was nice. She obviously appreciated the relationship her mother had with the little girl and could see that it benefited them both. Thank goodness.

Claire was still smiling at her. 'Think you're up to it? A hard night's reading?'

Gemma laughed. 'I think I'll cope.' She reached over and gave Claire's hand a squeeze. 'Thanks, Claire.'

She was taking the first steps towards making some new friends on the island. And it felt good.

Gemma stared at the screen. Twenty-five patients this morning already. And that was before she'd even had a chance to look at the list of emergencies added on at the end.

She straightened up and stretched her back. If she

could grab a quick cup of coffee, it might give her some energy for the next onslaught of patients.

In some respects Arran was working out better than she could have hoped for. The island was beautiful, the people warm and friendly. It was inevitable that some would be a little set in their ways, but that was to be expected.

Isla loved it here. And she especially loved Logan's mum. Her excitement was almost palpable in the mornings when she was dropped off, and she spent most of the evening telling Gemma everything that she and Granny Scott had got up to. Mrs Scott had introduced Isla to another couple of little girls who would be starting school after the summer and they had become instant playmates.

If only she could make friends so easily.

For the last fortnight it had been clear that Logan was avoiding her. The strawberry tarts had never appeared and, unless it was to do with work, their conversations were short and stilted. Surely he couldn't be annoyed about having to do some extra on-calls? If she hadn't been here, there would have been no one to help out with the surgery, which would have put even more pressure on him.

Yesterday she'd gone to ask him something about a patient and he could barely look her in the eye. It was as if all the slightly flirtatious behaviour had disappeared in a big puff of smoke. What on earth could she have done to offend him?

She grabbed some coffee from the staffroom and went to the reception desk to speak to Julie. 'How many extras do we have?'

Julie glanced over her shoulder into the waiting room. 'There's only an extra five patients so far. But Logan still hasn't finished his surgery. He's actually running a bit behind and still has three more to see. Then he's got the home visits too.'

'That's fine. I'll take them all.'

'Are you sure?'

Gemma nodded. 'Unless there's any patient that would rather see a male GP then I'm happy to see them.'

Julie nodded. 'That's great. I'll put them on your list and you can pull up their files on your computer.'

Gemma took a quick gulp of coffee and headed back to the surgery room. Logan's door was still firmly closed. Two bouts of tonsillitis, one episode of gout and what looked like a slipped disc later, she only had one patient left to see.

She pulled up his file. David Robertson, twenty-six. No previous medical history to speak of—in fact, the guy never usually set foot in the surgery. She stepped out to the waiting room to call his name.

It was clear exactly who David Robertson was. He was the only male left in the waiting room, with an anxious-faced female holding his hand.

'Hi, there. I'm Dr Halliday. Would you like to come through, David?' she asked.

She watched as he grimaced as he stood up and gave a slight stagger. She was at his side in an instant. 'Are you okay?'

He nodded through gritted teeth and walked slowly through to the surgery room, easing himself into a chair.

He had a glorious tan. But his complexion was almost grey. This young man was clearly unwell. 'Can you tell me what's wrong?'

'We've just come back from our honeymoon,' his wife said quickly, her eyes shining with tears.

'Where were you?' Gemma's brain was whirring, trying to decipher what could be wrong with this young man. *Please, don't let it be some weird and wonderful tropical disease she'd never heard of.* The crossover into GP land had been a little easier than she'd expected. Lots of conditions that affected kids also affected adults, making her breathe a sigh of relief and not feel so out of her depth.

The young woman spoke. 'We were in Egypt. We just got off the plane at Glasgow Airport and got the boat home. David has been sick the whole way.'

Egypt. Her brain clicked into overtime. Were there any specific diseases from there?

'Vomiting or just nausea?' Could he have picked up some weird stomach bug on holiday?

David had closed his eyes. He seemed happy to let his new wife do all the talking. Another sign of how unwell he was feeling.

'Both. He started feeling really dizzy and sick then he started vomiting on the plane. He said his joints were all sore.'

Gemma had lifted her pen and was noting the symptoms as she watched her patient. She didn't like this. She didn't like this at all.

At first glance it was a list of indiscriminate symptoms that could be related to almost anything. But the patient was sitting right in front of her and he was the sickest person she'd seen since she'd got here.

'Were either of you unwell while you were on honeymoon? Did you have gastric symptoms?'

The young woman shook her head. 'I know lots of people say that's normal if you go on holiday to Egypt, but we were both fine. It was literally just as we got on the plane that David started to feel unwell.'

'Any injuries on holiday? Bumps, scrapes, bites or falls?' She was trying to cover all her bases here. Could he have picked up some kind of infection or blood disorder?

But both husband and wife shook their heads.

What she really wanted to do was look up bugs and insects and see what kind of things the ones in Egypt carried. Tropical diseases. That's what she'd need to study tonight. The variety of things in GP practice was going to make her brain explode.

Gemma pulled out her stethoscope and BP cuff. She took a few seconds to wrap the cuff around his upper arm, noting him wince as she touched his elbow joint. He hadn't even opened his eyes.

'This will just take a few seconds, David.' She inflated the cuff and watched the figures on the digital monitor. His blood pressure was quite low, but that couldn't account for all his symptoms. She put her stethoscope in her ears. 'David, if you don't mind, I'm just going to have a listen to your chest. Can you sit forward for me?'

He gave a little groan and sat forward. She pulled up his shirt a little to get a look at his skin and see if there were any strange rashes. Nothing obvious. Just more of the glorious tan.

'This isn't like him at all. David's never unwell. He's as fit as a fiddle. I don't understand what's happened.' His wife couldn't stop talking, her nerves obviously getting the better of her.

Gemma gave a little nod of her head and then gestured towards David's chest. 'Can you give me a sec to listen?'

His wife blushed then looked as if she was about to burst into floods of tears.

Gemma frowned. She couldn't quite decipher what she was hearing. One part of his lung sounded as if it wasn't inflated properly. Could he have a pneumothorax? And why on earth would a fit, healthy young man have a collapsed lung if he'd had no injury? Could it be undiagnosed TB or some other kind of chest condition?

He started to move, scratching at his skin, first lightly and then with more venom, as if the itch was getting worse. She was missing something here.

She pulled over the oxygen saturation monitor and put it on his finger. His level was way too low. Instantly she pulled over the oxygen cylinder that was kept in the room. 'No history of asthma or chest conditions as a child?'

It would be dangerous to put pure oxygen on someone with asthma.

David gave the slightest shake of his head. She turned the oxygen on full and slipped the mask over his face. 'I'm just going to try and make your breathing a little easier. Rest back in the chair.'

The truth was she really needed a chest X-ray to get a clear picture of what was happening. But that would involve transporting David over to the hospital—and, to be honest, he didn't look fit for that.

Then again, maybe he would be better over at the hospital?

Panic was starting to fill her. Her inexperience in general practice was starting to feel like a weight around her chest. She was used to paediatric emergencies. They were part and parcel of her previous life. But this was entirely different.

All her paediatric emergencies had been dealt with in

a hospital environment, with a whole host of equipment, drugs and other staff to help. As an experienced paediatrician, even when chaos was erupting around her, she was confident in her abilities to deal with the situation. Right now she had no idea what was wrong with this young man. But he was looking sicker by the second.

Maybe she should go and see if Logan or one of the other partners was around?

Logan. She really, really wanted to talk to him. She was starting to feel a bit sick herself right now. But she pasted a composed smile on her face.

'Mrs Robertson, can you tell me more about your holiday? Did you take part in any unusual activities? Eat anything different? Get bitten by an insects?'

Her questions were starting to sound desperate. Just like the way she was feeling.

Mrs Robertson looked a bit confused for a second. 'Well, we went on a camel ride one day. And we ate out in the desert one night at a special restaurant.'

'Any unusual foods you haven't eaten before?'

She shook her head. 'I don't think so, and call me Pam. I can't get used to Mrs Robertson.' She lifted her eyes, clearly racking her brain for the rest of their activities, as her other hand anxiously twisted the new wedding ring on her finger. 'We did a tour inside the pyramids, oh, and I bought David some diving lessons. He did them too.'

Diving. Her brain started to go mad. She'd been reading all about this just the other day. 'When was the last time he dived? Was it a few days before you came home?'

Pam shook her head again. 'Oh, no. It was just a few hours before we got on the plane. He had three lessons to fit in, and we'd been so busy that it was the only time he could fit the last one in.'

No. It couldn't be. The thing she'd researched just the other day because she didn't know a single thing about it. But all these little symptoms were starting to look horribly familiar.

'Let me just check with you. Nausea and vomiting. Joint pains. Dizziness. Itching. Anything else you can think of?'

Her head was adding in the clinical symptoms she was seeing. Hypotension. Low oxygen saturation. The strange-sounding lungs.

She was trying to remember the recommendations for flying after diving. Was it wait twelve hours after a single dive and eighteen hours after multiple dives? There had been so much information she couldn't recall all the details.

But there *had* been a checklist of symptoms and a neurological assessment.

She crossed over to the computer and checked her browsing history, pulling up the pages she needed.

Her heart was starting to race. One thing was clear. She needed to act quickly or this young man could die. The diving lessons his new wife had bought him could be the death of him.

Logan. She needed to speak to Logan.

'Can you excuse me both a second?'

Hoping her face wasn't betraying her and her demeanour was remaining calm, she crossed over to the door. The waiting room and surrounding area was empty. The door to Logan's door was open with no one around.

Julie was in the staffroom, her sandwich just heading to her lips. 'Where's Logan?'

Her eyes widened. 'What's wrong?'

'Is he here? Are any of the other partners here?'

Julie shook her head. 'Logan's on his way to Short-bank Farm, Mr Gallacher's got some kind of injury—and that's out of range for the mobile. I can't even phone him for you.'

'Is anyone else around?'

Julie shook her head. 'Dr King is away to the mainland. He had a hospital appointment in Glasgow this afternoon.'

Gemma couldn't help the words that streamed out of her mouth.

Julie put down her sandwich and stood up. 'What can I do to help? Is it David Robertson?'

Gemma took a deep breath. Julie hadn't exactly been over-friendly before, but she could obviously be counted on in a moment of crisis. She'd worked in the surgery for a few years, so must have a good handle on how things were dealt with in an emergency.

'I think David Robertson is showing signs of decompression sickness. He was diving just before getting on the plane. But I haven't done the neurological assessment yet, so I'm not entirely sure.'

Julie shook her head. 'Time is what matters here. I'll page the consultant at Aberdeen and you can speak to him while you do the assessment on the patient. He'll arrange the emergency transport and getting the hyperbaric chamber at Millport ready.' She waved her hand at Gemma. 'I'll put the call through as soon as I get him, and I'll keep trying Logan on the other line.'

'Has Logan treated a patient with decompression sickness before?'

Julie's nose wrinkled. 'I'm not sure. But he did some specialist training over at the hyperbaric chamber last year. So he'll be able to tell you everything you need to know.'

Gemma felt a tiny glimmer of relief. She went back through to the consulting room. It was obvious that there had been no improvement.

She sat down beside Pam and reached over and touched David's hand. 'Okay, the signs and symptoms that you're showing, David, are causing me some concern. I'm wondering if there's a connection between you diving and then flying quite so soon afterwards. It can cause something called decompression sickness and I'm just going to run through a checklist. There is a specialist who deals with this condition and I'm waiting for him to call me back, so I might have to talk to him as we are doing this.'

Tears started to fall down Pam's face. 'Decompression sickness? Isn't that what the people who do diving for a living get? The nitrogen bubbles floating around their body?'

Gemma nodded as she started to quickly fill in the form that appeared on her screen, Name. Age. Date. Gas used...

'Do you know any details of the dive?'

David shook his head. Pam's eyes widened. 'What do you mean?'

'The type of gas used? How deep it went? How long the dive was?'

Pam was starting to sob now. 'I don't know any of that. David just did the same as everyone else that was there. It was a dive school in Egypt. I'd bought the package online.'

Gemma nodded. 'Can you remember the name of the

company? I might be able to contact them later and get some details.'

Pam pulled a bent card from her purse. 'I picked this up in the office when we went to book the lessons.'

At least it was something. She could deal with that later.

'Can you remember how long the dive lasted?'

Pam took a deep breath. 'Over an hour? Maybe an hour and a half?'

Gemma kept quickly typing. David wasn't talking right now. She was going to have to keep getting all information from his wife. 'Do you know if David stopped on the way up?'

Pam shook her head.

'And how many dives did he do? Was it three?'

She nodded her head.

Gemma checked the last question. 'This is really important. Can you remember when the last dive finished?'

Pam checked her watch and screwed up her face. 'Our time or theirs?'

Gemma reached over and gave her hand a squeeze. 'I'll work out the time difference. How long ago was it?'

'About ten hours?'

Gemma noted it on the record and turned back to face David just as the phone rang. It only took a few moments to introduce herself and the background of her patient to the hyperbaric consultant. She gave the signs and symptoms she'd already noted, the dive details and his blood pressure, oxygen saturation and current treatment.

On his instructions she started to run through the neurological exam. Asking David his name, the day, the date and asking him to follow certain instructions. It was a complicated process, with her relaying all the details to the experienced consultant at the end of the phone. David barely responded to some of the questions, mumbling at best. It took the consultant only a few minutes to decide to arrange transport for David to the hyperbaric chamber in Millport and issue a few other instructions that Gemma noted down. Even though this was a critical time, she couldn't help the surge of relief that was flowing through her.

She'd followed her instincts. And she wasn't crazy. For a few seconds she'd felt totally out of her depth. The long hours of research she'd put in over the last few weeks while Isla had been sleeping had been a lifesaver. Literally. 'Do I have to do anything else?'

'Just monitor him. If he maintains consciousness, try and encourage some fluids. Don't worry. You'll be met by the specialist team at Cumbrae as soon as you land.'

She finished the call and took David's BP and saturation levels again. He was still giving her cause for concern. Julie appeared at the door. 'I've called the ambulance.'

She must have taken in the confused expression on Gemma's face. She reached over and touched her shoulder, giving David and Pam a reassuring smile. 'The helicopter's landing bay is at the hospital. The ambulance will get you there in two minutes. I've also arranged alternative transport for Pam.'

'I won't be able to go in the helicopter?'

Julie shook her head. 'I'm sorry. There's only room for one other person...' she nodded towards Gemma '...and that has to be Dr Halliday.'

Gemma could hear roaring in her ears. She had to do the transfer in the helicopter?

Heaven help her. She'd never been near a helicopter in

her life, let alone ridden in one. 'Did you manage to get Logan?' *Please let him appear. Please let him be the one to go on the helicopter.* But she didn't even have time to think about it. Julie had pushed a wheelchair next to the door and was escorting Pam to the door. She was being much more help than Gemma would have expected. It was only at the last second she saw a little mad panic on her face. 'I'm sorry, Gemma, I couldn't get hold of Logan at all. I've left about four messages on his mobile,' she hissed.

Gemma gulped. She would have to do this all on her own. But she didn't have time to let it terrify her. She had a patient to look after.

She put her arms gently on David's shoulders, careful not to hurt his shoulder joints. 'David?' She spoke quietly. 'I know you're sore, but I need you to get in the wheelchair. We need to get you to the helicopter.'

For the first time in the last ten minutes he opened his eyes. It had been clear during his neurological exam he was starting to become a little muddled. 'What's happening?' The confusion was written all over his face.

Gemma took a few moments to kneel in front of him and touch his hand. 'We think you've got decompression sickness, David, caused by flying too quickly after your multiple dives. It's likely that the pain in your joints is caused by nitrogen bubbles. It can also be the reason you're feeling a bit disorientated and your skin is itching. We're really lucky—Millport is only a few minutes away in the helicopter and there will be a team waiting to treat you in the hyperbaric chamber.'

There had better be. Because she didn't have the expertise to deal with that.

'I'll be with you for the transfer and get you settled.'

'What about my wife?' His voice was weak, his throat sounding dry—probably from the high-dose oxygen. She lifted a glass of water and moved the mask to put it to his lips, letting him take a few sips. 'We're making arrangements for Pam, don't worry. She'll be with you.'

There was a flash of green beside her—a paramedic suit. He raised his eyebrows at her. 'Are you ready, Dr Halliday? We've already had radio contact with the emergency helicopter. It's on its way. ETA is ten minutes.'

'That quick?' She was surprised.

He gave a little shrug. 'Once it's taken off from Prestwick it covers the miles really quickly. Our weather conditions are good so there'll be no problems with landing.' He gestured towards the door. 'Okay if I take our patient?'

She nodded and grabbed her jacket, stopping at the door and putting her hand on Julie's elbow. 'Thank you so much, Julie. I don't know what I would have done without you.'

For the first time ever, normally frosty Julie gave her a smile. 'That's what I'm here for. And to tell you the truth, it's the most exciting thing that's happened in ages. Logan will be sorry he missed it.'

She felt a little lurch in her stomach. She almost wished that *she'd* missed it, and Logan had been here to deal with everything. Hopefully—whether he was in a mood with her or not—he'd sit down later and do a debrief with her and talk her through anything she might have missed.

She rushed out the door and jumped into the back of the ambulance. It took less than five minutes to reach the landing pad in the hospital grounds. The paramedic opened the back doors of the ambulance and looked up at the sky. 'I'm just going to do a few observations on David while we're waiting.'

Gemma nodded. Something was pressed into her hand. She looked down. Ear defenders. She hadn't even considered the noise. Then again, she'd never been around a helicopter before.

David was lying back again with his eyes closed. He was still unconsciously scratching at his skin. Was it wrong to pray for the helicopter to get here quickly?

After a few minutes she could hear the thump-thump of the spinning blades. It seemed only seconds before the speck in the sky was getting closer and closer.

She put the ear defenders on. The noise was incredible. As she jumped out of the back of the ambulance and stood at the side of the stretcher used to transport David, her hair was flying backwards and forwards—across her eyes, in her mouth. It was freezing. The glorious sunny day was no match for the helicopter blades.

After a few seconds there was a shout. The helicopter had touched down safely and the side door slid back.

She didn't know which was louder, the sound of the helicopter blades or the sound of her too-fast heartbeat in her ears. She'd forgotten her jacket—it was still lying in the back of the ambulance—and it felt as if any second now her shirt would be ripped from her body. Sure enough, one of her buttons pinged off and disappeared into the wind. She didn't have time to make a grab to cover herself. The stretcher was already being run towards the helicopter.

The transfer was seamless. The ambulance team pushed the stretcher towards the helicopter and the legs automatically collapsed underneath it as it slid easily on board. A hand stretched out towards her, ready to pull her in. The helicopter was higher than she'd thought, but someone gave her a boost from behind and a new pair of ear defenders was placed in her lap. She swapped them over, handed the first ones back. The door slid shut and seconds later they took off.

She didn't have time to think about the flight. Or the turbulence around them. It was almost like being in a bit of a bumpy car ride. The noise was still incredible, but her reactions were automatic. Years of being in emergency situations seemed to stand her in good stead and she helped the paramedic attach David to a monitor and set up an IV line, all with a series of hand signals.

Eventually she got a sign to strap in as they prepared for landing. She almost couldn't believe the time had passed already. Millport—or the Isle of Cumbrae—was smaller than Arran with a similar old-style hospital. Walking into the unit with the hyperbaric chamber and state-of-the-art equipment was almost like walking into a space station. From the outside you would have no idea all this was here. Thankfully, another doctor and nurse were waiting. They took her paperwork and started making calculations quickly. One grabbed the card for the dive school from her hand and walked through to an office, quickly picking up the phone. It literally took minutes for them to reassess David's neurological status and set him up to go in the chamber.

It was fascinating. The specialist consultant was on video call with them the whole time. He even took part in the conversation with the dive school in Egypt. Learning foreign languages was obviously part of his skills. And the whole scenario was something so specialist it was totally out of her realm of expertise. Another call came in for the emergency helicopter—a climber injured in Fort William—and before she could even think they were gone.

A nurse appeared at her side and touched her elbow. 'I'm Jill, can I get you a coffee to tide you over before you head back?'

Back. It hadn't even occurred to her. Not for a second. The helicopter was gone. How on earth was she going to get back to Arran? She looked around her—she hadn't even taken her handbag from the surgery.

Jill smiled. 'Stop panicking.'

She shook her head. 'I don't have my bag. I don't have any money. I have no idea how to get from Millport to Arran. What on earth happens now?'

Jill laughed and waved her hand. 'Don't worry about any of that. Logan Scott has already phoned to say he'll pick you up.'

She frowned. 'But how can he pick me up?'

Jill raised her eyebrows. 'In his boat?' It was obvious that Gemma wasn't proving to pick things up very quickly. Everything had happened at such a pace she hadn't considered any of these things. 'Come on. I bet you missed lunch. You can have something free of charge in our canteen. It's not every day the emergency helicopter lands.'

'Isn't it?' The way the staff had acted she'd thought this was a routine occurrence. 'How often do you use the hyperbaric chamber?'

'It varies. Anything from around ten to twenty divers a year need treatment here. Not all get transferred by helicopter, some come via the lifeboat service.'

She steered Gemma into a similar canteen to the one in Arran hospital. It was smaller but she was able to grab some soup and a sandwich and take a seat at the window for a moment to try and catch her breath.

Wow. Helicopter trip. Hyperbaric chamber. And a think-outside-the-box crazy diagnosis.

A smile crept across her face. When she'd told her colleagues in Glasgow that she was moving to Arran, some of them had told her she'd be bored.

If anyone had told her three weeks ago that this was how life would pan out she wouldn't have believed them.

And now Logan was coming to pick her up. Logan, who had hardly been able to look her in the eye for the last two weeks. What on earth was going on with him? And why did the thought of being confined to a small space with him make her stomach do flip-flops?

How long did the sail between Arran and Millport take? She had no idea at all. At least an hour or more.

She and Logan in a confined space together?

She hoped they would both survive it.

There was a buzz in his pocket that quickly cut off again. Darned reception. Shortbank Farm was in one of the only valleys in Arran, which made it difficult to get a signal. Old Peter Gallacher had managed to take a huge chunk out of his leg this morning and Logan was going to have to get the district nurse in for the next few weeks, along with a supply of antibiotics.

The phone buzzed again and cut off. Someone desperately wanted to get hold of him. Was it work, or was it personal?

Could it be Claire in a crisis? Surely not—she was supposed to be spending the day with his mother and little Miss Dynamo—his latest nickname for Isla. Or could it be Gemma at the surgery?

He blew his hair off his forehead. Things would have to be really bad for Gemma to phone him. He'd barely been civil to her over the last few days.

It was ridiculous behaviour and he knew it.

He just couldn't help it.

Everything about her drew his attention. He'd found himself thinking about her during the drives to patients' homes, or when he'd been having a conversation with someone else. None of which were good signs.

He couldn't understand why this tiny brunette, with her even tinier red-haired child, was invading his thoughts so much.

He didn't really have time for it. It wasn't to say he didn't want children. Just not right now. Especially when things were this way with Claire. It would be insensitive, to say the least.

He was already cringing at the thought of Claire appearing at his mother's one day when Isla was there. Neither he nor his mother had mentioned the fact she was looking after Isla three days a week during the summer holidays. The immediate, temporary solution of childcare for Gemma was now feeling like an elephant sitting on his back. More so because Isla and his mother appeared attached at the hip. They were both relishing the other's company.

At first he'd thought it was nice. And he would still think it was nice if he wasn't worried about the impact it might have on his sister.

The phone buzzed again. He was starting to get a bad feeling about this. He pulled it from his pocket. As he'd suspected—one intermittent bar that seemed to vanish and reappear before his eyes.

'Pete, can you excuse me? Someone's been trying

to get hold of me. I'm guessing it's kind of urgent.' He looked at Pete's temporarily patched-up shin on the little footstool. 'Once I get a better signal I'll get the district nurse to pick up some antibiotics for you and come and do a proper dressing.' He glanced around the farmhouse. 'I'll make you a quick cup of tea before I go. I don't want you to move until she gets here.'

Pete gave a little nod of his head and rested his head back on the chair, folding his arms across his middle and closing his eyes. He needed to rest. He'd had a shock that morning after the accident and had been lucky his intermittent mobile call had gone through to the surgery. Pete's own regular phone line had been down for months and the phone company had left him with a mobile phone that resembled a brick. Logan would need to try and talk to someone about that too.

It only took a few minutes to make the tea and leave it, with a supply of biscuits, next to Pete.

Logan jumped into his car and put his foot to the floor. As soon as he got out of the valley he would start to get a better signal and find out what was going on. It only took a few moments, but as his car climbed the hill the phone started to go crazy.

He had hands-free in his car, but that only worked properly for real calls. If he wanted to know about texts and messages he still needed his phone in his hands.

As he reached the crest of the hill he pulled over. Six missed calls and three messages. Oh, no.

All of them from the surgery—none of them from Claire.

For a second he felt a tiny, selfish surge of relief. His family was okay. But almost instantaneously guilt descended. He was a professional. While his family was okay, someone else's obviously wasn't.

He listened to the first message. It was Julie, asking frantically for him to call back. He pressed for the second. Julie again, this time to say Gemma really, really wanted to talk to him. Third message, and this one sounded a little garbled, they'd had to phone Aberdeen, something about a patient with decompression sickness. Really?

He couldn't believe it. Part of him was annoyed he hadn't been the one to see the patient and make the diagnosis. He'd spent a few days last year doing in-depth training but since then had limited contact with the staff at Millport and the hyperbaric chamber as their patients came from all over the west coast of Scotland.

He pressed the button to call the surgery back, and almost immediately became aware of the drone above him. The emergency helicopter. Things must have been really bad.

The phone was just ringing out—and he knew exactly why. All the surgery staff were dealing with transferring the patient for the pick-up. Had he been there, he would be doing exactly the same.

Poor Gemma. She was relatively inexperienced in GP land, but if he was honest, he was secretly impressed. What a call to make! She'd only told him the other week that she didn't know that much about diving ailments and she'd have to read up on them.

She'd obviously meant it, otherwise she would never have been able to make the diagnosis. He placed his phone on the passenger seat and put his foot to the floor. His colleague had obviously been looking for support. And had he received the call he would have given it to her.

She didn't have a clue what was going on in his family.

She had no idea how much she'd invaded his thoughts. Sure, she'd responded to a few casual flirtations, but she wouldn't have any idea why he'd been so abrupt lately.

As the helicopter swooped above him he did the only thing he could. He accelerated even more and tried to make it back in time to help out.

CHAPTER SIX

IT WAS A calm, easy sail. He'd almost been glad of the excuse to take the boat out.

Almost.

As soon as he'd heard the helicopter coming in to land he'd realised there must be something serious going on. But by the time he'd finally got hold of Julie and found out what had happened he'd felt sick. He could only imagine how out of her depth Gemma must have felt. Would he have recognised the signs of decompression syndrome? Would he have asked David Robertson the right questions to determine what was wrong with him? He wasn't sure.

But Gemma had. The woman who'd only been on the island for three weeks and had admitted to knowing nothing about hyperbaric chambers had come up trumps.

Thank goodness.

And now, as a means of apology for not being there to help her when she'd needed it, he was picking her up in Millport.

Julie had been talking at a hundred miles an hour when he'd got back to the surgery. Bill, the local paramedic, had been much more sensible—and very complimentary about their new doctor.

But give praise where praise was due. Gemma had

done a good job and by the sound of it Julie had been there to assist. When her mind was on the job she could be excellent.

She'd nearly burst into tears when she'd realised Gemma had forgotten her bag in the rush to leave the surgery. And when she'd remembered she hadn't given Gemma any instructions for getting back...

But it was fine. He was here now and it should be a good sail home.

He climbed the steps at the harbour. Gemma was sitting waiting for him in a nearby café. Someone had obviously dropped her off after he'd phoned to say when he would be arriving. He could see her through the glass. Her long brown hair was swept back into a ponytail and she was studying the paperwork on the table in front of her intently.

She jumped as he opened the café door. 'Oh, Logan. I'm sorry. I should have been watching out for you.'

He crossed the small space easily. 'That's okay. I'd no idea what time I'd actually get here. Sailing isn't an exact science.' He couldn't help but smile as he said it. It was one of the few things in life that gave him pure pleasure.

The feeling of freedom out on the open water. Shaking off all the usual responsibilities, with no other demands on his time. Just him, and a world of blue for as far as the eye could see. A chance to escape the world around him. And, as much as he loved them, a chance to escape his family and the reminder about how much he'd failed them in the last few weeks.

Gemma was smiling nervously at him, her hand holding her shirt closed. He squinted at her. 'Is something wrong?' Her hair was looking a whole lot more dishevelled than it normally did. Of course. The helicopter.

Someone had obviously given her a rubber band to pull it back from her face.

She gave a little shrug. 'Wardrobe malfunction. Old shirt versus shiny helicopter blades with huge wind sheer. I lost one of my buttons.'

He couldn't help but laugh. 'Just as well I brought you this.' He held up the heavy waterproof jacket. 'Julie mentioned you hadn't taken a jacket with you.' He looked across the harbour. 'And while the sun is shining out there, it's definitely a bit colder and choppier out on the water.'

A look of relief crossed her face. She stood up quickly, taking the jacket. Letting her shirt go to slip her arms inside the jacket, he had a quick glimpse of pink satin and lace at the little gap in her blouse. Was that the matching bra to the underwear he'd seen a few weeks ago?

She bent and zipped up the jacket—all the way to the neck. No chance of any further glimpses. And that was probably for the best.

'I thought I might have found you out at Crocodile Rock.' He waved his hand across the harbour to the popular tourist attraction.

Gemma gave a wide smile. The large crocodile-shaped rock was painted black, white and red, giving the appearance of a crocodile's mouth and eyes. Over the years thousands of visitors had had their pictures taken standing on crocodile rock. It was almost an unwritten rule that every tourist who visited should stand there.

Gemma shrugged and laughed. 'The wardrobe malfunction wouldn't let me risk it. I really have to bring Isla back to see this. She would love it. I didn't even know it existed.'

Before he could help it the words were out of his

mouth. 'Why don't we bring her over one weekend? It won't take long to sail over in the boat. She'd love it here.'

What had possessed him?

He'd spent the last two weeks avoiding her completely. Which was kind of difficult when Gemma was under his nose three days a week. But he couldn't afford distractions. He had to concentrate all his time and energy on his sister Claire and her worsening mental health.

Why hadn't he noticed earlier? It seemed the decision by social services on the adoption assessment had escalated everything. And while he hated to admit it, it was obviously the right decision.

Claire would be a wonderful parent. But right now she needed some time out and some support.

But instead of acting rationally, her behaviour was becoming slightly manic. She couldn't eat, she couldn't sleep, she couldn't think rationally. And she *certainly* couldn't take any advice from her brother.

Although he hated doing it, he'd asked one of his other colleagues to go out and visit his sister at home. He couldn't treat her, or prescribe anything for her. But they could. And maybe she would respond more positively to someone else. Because right now Logan felt about as much use as an inflatable dartboard.

Gemma straightened up in the seat. 'I'm sorry, Logan, I'd offer to buy you a coffee but I don't have my purse. I had to borrow some money from one of the staff at the hospital.'

He looked around. 'Don't be silly. Do you want something to eat before we get on the boat? I do have some supplies on board, of course.'

This time her smile reached up to her eyes. 'What kind of supplies?'

'Oh, all the kind I shouldn't have. Chocolate. Crisps. A bit of wine. And beans, lots and lots of tins of beans.'

She laughed. 'What's a "bit" of wine?'

He shrugged. 'The odd unfinished bottle that might have the cork back in it.'

'Should you have alcohol on a boat?'

'Should you question the man who's about to see you safely home?'

She shrugged. 'Fair point.'

He held out his hand towards her. 'Let's go.'

Something had happened. The wall he'd erected around her had disintegrated. This was all about him. He'd been deliberately avoiding her and, if he could get away with it, ignoring her. All because of this. All because of the strange sensations of being around her.

After a few short moments in her company it was apparent that Gemma had no problem with him. She was smiling again. That light floral scent of hers was pervading his senses again. One of these days he'd actually find out what that was.

Her small hand slid inside his larger one. He couldn't control his automatic reaction. He closed his hand around hers and pulled her up towards him. His pull was a little stronger than he thought—or maybe Gemma was lighter than he thought. But she ended up just under his chin. Just as well the thick jacket was in place to stop any body contact.

She lifted her head and looked up at him with those big brown eyes of hers. His breath caught in his throat. Up close and personal. He could see the smattering of light brown freckles across the bridge of her nose. Had they been there a few weeks ago? He wasn't sure.

She blinked, then the corners of her mouth turned up

and she whispered, 'I think we'd better move. We're attracting attention.'

He looked around quickly. Gemma would probably attract attention wherever she went, but the two island doctors standing so close in the village café was bound to be a talking point. Just as well they weren't on Arran. The knitting needles would be clacking as they breathed.

He pulled her towards the door and then out along the harbour. There was a short ladder to get down to the landing platform and he hesitated at the top of it.

'What's wrong?'

He wrinkled his nose and pointed to her skirt. 'Sorry, I brought you a jacket but I didn't think to bring you some trousers.'

It was cute. A little flush appeared in her cheeks. 'What's the problem? I'll go first.' She made to turn around and put a foot on the ladder.

His hand touched hers again, and he tried to ignore the current he was feeling. 'Best not. The platform moves. With those shoes you'll probably end up falling over.'

She shot him a fake scowl. 'Don't be so sexist. I can take these off.' She bent to take off her heels.

'Or you can just let me go first.' He winked at her. 'Don't worry, I'll catch you if you fall.' He swung onto the ladder, going down a few rungs and then jumping the last few to land on the platform, which bobbed under his weight.

She leaned down towards him. 'Who says I need catching?' She turned to put her foot on the ladder and then stopped. 'Wait.'

'What is it?'

She waggled a finger at him. 'You need to look elsewhere.'

He rolled his eyes at her. 'Oh, come on, I'm a doctor!' He lifted his hands from the bottom of the ladder and held them out.

'And I'm a colleague who'd like to keep her dignity intact.'

'I need to avert my eyes? Really?' He was teasing her, he couldn't help it. This seemed to be the natural way for them to be around each other. A bit of flirting, a bit of teasing.

She put her first foot on the ladder, one hand holding the edge, the other still grasping her skirt.

He couldn't wipe the grin from his face. 'Go on—just tell me.'

She poised in mid-air. 'Tell you what?'

'Is it a matching set?'

The expression on her face was priceless. It took her a couple of seconds to recover. Then, as quick as a shot, she climbed down a few rungs and jumped the last few like he had, landing in front of him.

She drew herself up to her full five feet three, squarely in front of his chest. She folded her arms across her chest, smiling but giving him a narrow gaze. 'Well, I guess you'll never know.'

It was a challenge. She was throwing down the gauntlet. And it was one he was more than willing to take.

He held out his hand to her again to lead her down towards the boat. 'I guess we'll need to see about that.'

Being in a boat was more comfortable than Gemma had expected.

Being in an enclosed space with Logan Scott? Definitely not.

She knew none of the intricacies of sailing but for Logan the boat seemed like his second home. It was larger than she'd expected, and although the sea was a little choppy in places it wasn't as rough as she'd feared.

Being sick over the side of a boat with a colleague could never be a good look.

After he'd navigated out of Millport harbour and set them well on their way he invited her down into the galley. It was cosy but certainly big enough for two people and a few kitchen appliances. He put the kettle on straight away.

'You're making me tea? I thought you promised me wine?'

'Yeah, about that. Can't get you drunk the first time you're on my boat. I haven't found out if you're a good sailor yet.' The kettle was already boiling and he was pulling teabags from a cupboard.

First time on the boat. Did that mean there would be a second? And, more importantly, would she want there to be?

'How long do you think it will take to get back?'

'A couple of hours. I've checked all the tide tables. We shouldn't have any problems. Oh, and I phoned my mum to let her know what had happened. She's happy to keep Isla until we get back.'

'Thank goodness. I don't know what I would do without your mum. She's been a massive help.'

Logan shrugged as he poured the boiling water into the cups. 'She likes it. She and Isla are good company for each other. I think she'd been getting a little bored lately. Isla's given her the spark of life that she needed.'

Gemma paused for a second. 'I met your sister the other day.'

He almost knocked over the cups. 'What?'

'Your sister Claire. She was at your mum's house when I dropped Isla off.'

He hesitated, lifting a cup and handing it to her. 'How did you find her?'

'What do you mean?' She looked up. She hadn't been paying attention. It was clear from the expression on his face that he was choosing his words carefully.

'Did she seem okay with you?'

What should she say? Was there really any point in tiptoeing around the edges? She took a deep breath. 'I liked her. She's a nice girl. But she did seem a little sad.'

Logan nodded slowly. 'Anything else?'

Gemma shook her head. 'Not really. She mentioned the fact she'd like a family and it hasn't happened. We didn't go into details. She invited me to join her book group.'

'She did?' He seemed surprised. His eyes fixed on the water outside. 'That's good. Claire hasn't been very sociable lately.'

Gemma shrugged. 'She was okay when I was there, but that's the first time she's met me.' She hesitated. 'And she seemed to like Isla. I was glad. I didn't want her to feel put out that her mum was watching my little girl.'

Logan gave a half-smile. 'I'd been a little worried about that too. But it seems to be fine.'

Gemma leaned back in her seat. 'They are good company for each other, aren't they?' Should she mention the one thing that bothered her? Now was as good a time as any. 'The thing is, Logan, your mum, she won't let me give her much for minding Isla. I'm not paying her the rate I would elsewhere. Could you persuade her to let me pay her some more?'

He raised his eyebrows. 'Seriously? You have met my mother, haven't you?' He shook his head firmly. 'She won't take any more and if you keep on about it, you'll only offend her—so don't.'

Gemma shifted in her chair. 'I feel a little as if I'm taking advantage.'

Logan handed her a cup of tea and sat down next to her. 'Like I'm taking advantage of you?'

They were close together. If she turned her head any more their noses would almost touch. She could feel her cheeks start to flush. What did that mean? Was this about the flirting?

After a few awkward seconds he broke in, obviously seeing that her mind was racing. 'I mean, with the surgery and everything.'

Of course. Idiot.

'Yeah, the surgery.' She rested her tea in her lap. 'You were pretty pushy about that.'

'I was desperate.'

'Obviously. But thanks for that.'

He lifted his hand, 'No. No. I didn't mean it like that.' Then he caught the expression on her face and realised she was teasing him again. 'Oh, stop it.' He rested his shoulders back. The bench seat they were sitting in was snug. With his shoulders back like that, she would almost be more comfortable in his lap. He grinned at her. 'Obviously I was desperate. Within two minutes of meeting you I'd glimpsed your underwear and started unpacking your daughter's clothes for you. I can assure you that's not a normal day for me on Arran.'

She started laughing. 'Really? You seemed such a natural.'

He looked a little startled. 'At seeing women's underwear?'

She shook her head. The temperature in this confined

space was definitely rising. Or maybe it was just the sparks flying between them.

This wasn't the first time they'd experienced them. But this was the first time they hadn't been surrounded by other distractions. There was nowhere else to go here.

'No,' she said quietly. His blue eyes were staring straight into hers. And even though her brain was telling her to look away, she just couldn't do it. 'At unpacking.'

His hand brushed against hers.

Her first instinct was to move it. But she wasn't going to. Instead, she gave him a wary smile. *Was there a chance she was reading this all wrong? It had been so long there was every possibility.*

'So, Logan. Other than with professional duties, how often do you glimpse women's underwear?'

Talk about a loaded question. But she had to ask. She had to know if he was the local Romeo. Someone who should clearly be avoided. Her throat felt instantly dry and she willed herself not to go red from her toes to her forehead.

Playing cool, calm and collected was difficult for her. Mild flirtation she could handle easily. Being one to one on a boat in the middle of the sea? Not so much.

A lazy smile spread across his face, along with the glimmer in his eye that showed he knew exactly what she was getting at. 'Now, Dr Halliday, is that a question you should ask your colleague?'

Had he just moved a little closer? Or was she imagining it?

And he certainly hadn't wasted any time in asking her if she was a single parent. She ran her tongue along her dry lips. She could play this game. She might be out of practice but she could pick up the skills with the best of them. 'Probably not, Dr Scott. But then again I'm not normally marooned at sea with a close colleague.'

The little lines appeared around the edges of his eyes as his smile grew wider. 'How close a colleague would that be?'

His hips turned towards hers and his hand settled on her hip. Her reaction was automatic, her hips turning a little, edging round to face his. She wanted to put her tea down, but anything that was going to make them break this stare or positioning was a definite no-no.

The air around them was practically sizzling. All of a sudden the thick, waterproof coat felt as if it was stifling her. Her lips were dry again. This time when she wet them with her tongue she was aware that he couldn't take his eyes off them.

'How close a colleague does he want to be?' Her voice was barely a whisper.

He took the cup from her, setting it down then reached up his hand and ran a finger down her cheek lightly. 'This close?'

She could barely swallow. She shook her head. 'Closer.'

He moved forward, his lips brushing against her ear. 'This close?'

She shook her head again, her hand reaching up and catching his.

His head moved, his lips hovering just above hers. 'How about this close?' he whispered.

'I think so,' she whispered, as her lips reached up to meet his.

Wow. No nudging of lips or gentle persuasion. This was a very definite full-on kiss. Logan was obviously a take-charge kind of guy, kissing her so thoroughly she was breathless. Then, as his lips finally released hers, he didn't hesitate. He moved on to her neck, right at the sensitive spot beneath her ear. How did he know just where to kiss her? Just where would drive her absolutely crazy?

One hand unzipped her thick jacket. It was a relief. The temperature was rising considerably in this compact cabin and she managed to shrug the jacket off without breaking contact.

Her hands were itching to touch his skin. Her eyes were itching to *see* his skin. He might have had the pleasure of seeing glimpses of her that he shouldn't, but she'd never had the same luck.

His jacket was already in a heap on the floor. He wasn't wearing his usual work garb, he must have changed before he'd come to collect her. It made it so much easier for her to slide her hands underneath his T-shirt onto his bare skin and up over the planes of his chest.

She could feel the muscles rippling beneath her fingertips, feel the curly hair on his broad chest. His fingers were moving in return, unbuttoning her more sedate blouse—or at least the buttons that were left. He smiled as he pushed it open and looked at her pale pink satin and lace bra. 'Now, there's a sight for sore eyes.'

He started walking her backwards, pushing her back onto the thinly padded bench they'd been sitting on. The breadth of her slim shoulders filled it completely. He leaned backwards, his eyes still focused on her breasts. 'You've no idea how many times I've seen these in my head.' His voice was low, husky and she liked it that way.

'And is the reality better or worse?' She couldn't help but arch her back a little towards him. Her breasts were probably her favourite part of her. Slightly bigger than average for her small frame—even more so since she'd had Isla.

'Oh, the reality is much better.' He ran his hands over her breasts, first cupping them and then concentrating on her nipples. She moved beneath his touch.

He gave a low, lazy smile. 'I wondered if you were a matching underwear kind of gal.'

'Your whole plan for seducing me was to see if I wear matching underwear?'

'I seduced you?' The tone in his voice had risen playfully, then he shook his head, 'Oh, no, lady, you seduced me.'

'I did not.'

He mouth hovered just above her breast. He had a teasing glare in his eye. 'How about this close?' he murmured.

Her hands were already cupping his bum in the well-worn jeans and her natural instinct was to move them around to the front. If they'd been lying in a bed his legs would have been on either side of hers. But the narrow bench didn't allow for that. Instead, he had one knee between her legs and his other leg still planted on the floor. This could get awkward.

His hand moved around to her back, ready to unsnap her bra. Her fingers poised at the button on his jeans. She couldn't think rationally any more.

She wasn't thinking about Isla. She wasn't thinking about living on a small island. She wasn't thinking about the fact he was one of her work colleagues. All she could think about was the electricity in the air between them. The way that things had just combusted in an instant. If this was what his kisses could do to her, how much better could this get?

It was like being a teenager all over again. Six years of virtual celibacy. With a few lousy dates and even lousier kisses somewhere in the middle of it all.

Before she'd got pregnant with Isla she hadn't had a steady relationship for months. And she wasn't the kind of girl who did casual sex. Well, not usually.

She couldn't wait. She couldn't wait any longer. She flicked the button—just as the biggest surge of waves hit the boat.

For a moment she was shocked. She'd almost forgotten they were on a boat until a huge swell tumbled them both unceremoniously to the floor.

Their positions reversed in mid-air and Logan landed on her with a thud. However many stones of powerful muscle and sinew pushed the wind clean out of her.

She started to cough. A reflex from the pressure currently on her lungs. He moved sideways, letting her draw in a breath and putting his knee on the floor next to her as he pulled himself up. Without a word, two hands appeared under her arms and lifted her back onto the bench. 'I'd better get out there,' he muttered, grabbing his jacket and opening the hatch door to let in an icy blast of sea air.

The hatch banged closed behind him.

Gemma's chin was struggling not to bang off the floor. Her knuckles clenched the edge of the bench as the boat continued to roll from side to side.

Her heart was clamouring against her chest. Was she relieved? Or disappointed? Could she phone a friend? Because right now she didn't have a clue.

Her finger touched her lips. If there had been a mirror in front of her she was sure they would be swollen. A chill swept over her skin and she instantly pulled her shirt together, fastening the buttons as best she could.

What would have happened if the boat hadn't hit some rough water?

She couldn't even think about it because she had no doubt about what would have happened.

Logan appeared to have walked out without a second thought. She pressed her nose up against one of the portholes but she couldn't see a thing out there. She had no idea what part of the boat he'd gone to. And it wasn't as if she could be any help. All the information she knew about boats she could have written on the back of a postage stamp.

She picked up the jacket and pulled it back on. Should she go out there and offer to help? She had a sneaking suspicion she would end up as more of a hindrance than a help.

She let out a groan. Logan had said that she'd seduced him. And he was right. She had.

Or at least she'd tried her best to.

Her hands covered her face. She was mortified. This was hardly her normal behaviour. But the building flirtation between them, followed by the crazy silence for the last few weeks, had driven her crazy.

Then, when he'd almost teased her to act, she'd been unable to help herself.

Thank goodness she didn't play poker. She would be bankrupt in five minutes.

The door opened and Logan stuck his head inside. 'Gemma? Are you okay?' He smiled when he saw she'd replaced her clothes. 'Yeah, you obviously are. Pity. I think I preferred you the other way.' He lifted his hand. 'Look, I can't come back in, I need to stay out and keep on top of things.' His eyes sparkled and he shook his head a little. 'That would be boat things.'

She nodded. She couldn't find a word, and she'd been too shocked to pick up on the innuendo there. Logan appeared completely at ease. Was he sorry they'd been stopped? She felt the tiniest bit reassured.

'Listen, we'll hit calmer waters soon, but by then we'll just about be back at Arran.'

The implication was clear. No more horizontal games. Not now, anyway.

'Okay.' It was the only word she could find.

'Come out in a bit if you feel okay.' He gave her one last smile before he ducked back out and closed the door.

She could still feel her heart thudding. This was for the best.

Really, it was.

If anything else had happened, how could she have looked her colleague in the eye?

Plus she had no idea what it would have meant.

She wasn't ready to introduce her little girl to any potential boyfriends—no matter what kind of pictures Isla drew. They hadn't even truly settled in yet. They still had to get through the summer and get Isla settled into school.

Anything else would have to wait.

Except the skin under her shirt was still burning from his touch. Her lips were aching.

But it was a good ache, not a bad one. To say nothing about the other parts of her body.

What she couldn't figure out was if this was just a reaction to him, or if this was just the reaction of woman who hadn't been touched in so long she was practically crazy.

It wasn't as if there hadn't been a whole host of boyfriends in her time. And, sure, there had been a few that had set her heart a-flutter.

But no one who had set off reactions like this in her.

Maybe Logan was just too good at this. Maybe this was how every woman who came into contact with Logan felt.

She winced. *Please, no.* That would be too embarrassing for words. Plus she couldn't bear to think that way.

She picked up the cups and took them over to the tiny sink to wash them. Anything to stop the thousands of thoughts flicking through her mind right now. Anything at all to distract her.

She caught a glimpse from the porthole. Logan was right. Arran was coming into view. She felt a little surge of something. It was home now. And there was some comfort in seeing it.

Logan had said he loved being surrounded by the sea. Gemma wasn't so sure. She didn't mind being out on the sea as long as she could still see a piece of land somewhere. It gave her a grain of comfort.

If the boat capsized right now she would have probably no chance whatsoever of being able to swim ashore. But at least now she would know what direction to swim in. She'd be able to try and swim home to her daughter.

The door swung open. 'Fancy coming up and watching us sail in?' He still had that glint in his eye, but was it for her or was it for the sail? She wasn't entirely sure.

His hand reached down and grabbed hers to help her up the steps. It was warm. It was comforting. And as soon as she reached the top of the steps he slung an arm around her waist and spun her around to face the sea again.

'Look at that. The sun's beginning to go down. Look at the colours across the water. Isn't it beautiful?'

He was right. It was beautiful. It was just too early for a sunset. But the colours in the sky had deepened slightly, sending some violets and blues across the darker sea.

She nodded and gave a little smile. 'Sunsets must be beautiful out here.'

He smiled. 'They are.' He leaned over and gave her a kiss on the forehead, before turning back to adjust the sails on the boat as they headed closer to Arran.

Her stomach gave a little flip. That had been his chance. That had been his opportunity to invite her back out on the boat. And he hadn't.

She took a deep breath. Trying to figure out Logan Scott was probably more trouble than it was worth.

And right now—with the way she was second-guessing every word and every touch—she just didn't stand a chance.

CHAPTER SEVEN

THREE DAYS. IT had been three days since Logan had kissed her. And almost a month since she and Isla had moved to Arran.

The summer had well and truly started here. The surgery was bursting at the seams. It seemed as if no one came on holiday with a prescription for their medication. She'd reached a stage that she and Julie had actually worked out a system to make the whole process a little easier. Julie contacted the patient's own surgery beforehand to verify their medical history and prescription, and Gemma then only saw the patient if they were unwell. Otherwise she spent the best part of an hour confirming them as a temporary resident on Arran and issuing a prescription.

She'd been on call last night and had been out twice when the doctor in A and E had been overwhelmed. It wasn't as bad as she'd feared. Isla had been virtually undisturbed. Gemma had just lifted her from her bed and bundled her into the car. When they'd reached the hospital one of the staff had a little room set aside that Isla could sleep in while Gemma was tending to patients. It wasn't ideal, but it certainly hadn't been as disruptive as she'd feared.

The doorbell sounded. Gemma let out a sigh. She'd just opened a bottle of wine and put her feet up.

Logan was standing on the doorstep with a box in his hands and a sheepish look on his face.

'What are you doing here?'

He held up the box. 'I think I might be a little late with these.'

Gemma took a sip from her wine glass. 'Only three weeks. That could be a world record.'

Logan leaned against the doorjamb. 'I get the feeling you're going to make me suffer.'

She turned on her heel, leaving the door open for him to follow her as she shouted over her shoulder, 'I'm a woman. It's my job.'

Gemma settled back on her sofa, tucking her bare feet under her. She waved her hand as Logan came into the living room. 'You'll need to get yourself a glass in the kitchen.'

She was trying to be cool, calm and collected. She was trying not to think about the last time she'd felt Logan's skin in contact with her own.

The truth be told, she was a little annoyed at him. And maybe the wine was making her feel a little less afraid. Logan seemed as laid back as ever. He put the box down on the table in front of her and shed his jacket, leaving it on the armchair. She heard him opening cupboards in the kitchen until he finally found her three remaining wine glasses, then she heard the fridge door open and close.

She waited until he'd settled on the sofa next to her, a glass of wine in his hand. 'That seems a mighty big box for two strawberry tarts.'

'Yeah, well. I figured I should pay with interest. I wasn't quite sure what Isla liked so I brought pineapple tarts and chocolate éclairs as well.' He looked around him. 'Where is she anyway?'

Gemma lifted her wine glass. 'She's having her first sleepover on Arran with one of the little girls your mum introduced her to.'

He looked surprised. 'Which one?'

'Adele. She seems fine. They both stayed here last night, and tonight they're staying with Adele's mum and dad. The other little girl who plays with them is away on holiday with her parents in Spain.' She shrugged. 'I didn't want Isla to feel left out.' She didn't tell him it had taken her around three days to be persuaded to let Isla have an overnight stay, plus practically getting a reference for her parents from Logan's mum.

Logan rested back on the sofa. 'Seems like a good idea. It's good that Isla's making friends.'

Gemma gave a little smile. 'Actually, it was your mum's idea. If I had my way I'd have Isla wrapped in cotton wool and permanently attached to my hip.'

'Aha.' He raised his glass. 'Single-parent syndrome?'

She straightened, immediately on the defensive. 'What does that mean?'

He shook his head at her changing stance. 'Only that you feel permanently responsible and on duty.'

'Oh.' Her shoulders rested back again. 'Okay. You might be right.' It made sense. She'd just never heard it expressed that way before. She did feel totally responsible for Isla—of course she did. But, then, she'd had a set of exceptional circumstances that most people hadn't. She found it harder to let go. She found it harder to trust people with her pride and joy. She was almost automatically on the defence.

He turned a bit more towards her, his broad shoulder

slipping underneath hers. 'So, how does it feel, being home alone?'

She could hear the tone in his voice. It was just like being back on the boat with him. Did he think he could just show up, snap his fingers and she would come running? She couldn't help but feel indignant. Trouble was, no one had told her body to act that way. Her hairs were already standing on end.

'It feels weird, being home alone. I'm not used to it. And because I'm still getting used to the cottage and the weather outside, I can hear every creak and groan. Every gust of wind makes me think someone is in the house with me. Every squeaky floorboard makes me think Isla is walking down the corridor towards me, even though I know she's not here. I love the cottage, I really do. I'm just not quite there yet.'

Logan leaned forward and set his wine glass down. 'Sounds to me like you're in need of some distraction.'

There was no way she was letting him get away with that so easily. She pointed at the TV. 'And I've got it, courtesy of Mr Indiana Jones.' She couldn't help a smile forming on her lips. 'What more could a girl want?'

'What indeed...' he leaned forward. She knew he had every intention of kissing her. Every cell in her body screamed out for it. But her brain just couldn't let her go there. She reached up, placing her hand on his chest and stopping him just before he reached her.

'How about a guy who can be straight with her? How about a guy who doesn't blow hot and cold?' Her voice was low, almost a whisper, but she knew that he could hear every word. She could feel him bristle under her touch for a second then feel the deep intake of breath into his lungs.

'Is that what I do?'

'You know it is.' There was silence. She wanted to kiss him. She really did. But not like this. Not because it was convenient. Not because there was a gap in his schedule. She couldn't afford to have a casual fling with a colleague. She had Isla to consider.

She saw him hesitate. There was something behind his eyes. Was it pain? Or was it something else?

'I've...I've been distracted. Personal issues. Family stuff.'

She knew instantly what it was. 'Claire?' Had something changed? She'd gone along to book group and met the other women. It had been fun.

Claire had been a little quiet. But Gemma had decided not to interfere or ask any difficult questions. She barely knew Claire and wanted to give her some space.

He nodded. His eyes fell and his fingers ran around the rim of the glass. 'It's nothing anyone can help with.' He leaned back against the sofa, pulling away from her hand. 'I'm sure you already know. Claire's been trying for a family for the last seven years. She's gone through ICSI, IVF—all unsuccessful. After a while she—no, they— decided to apply for adoption. The IVF had taken its toll on her both mentally and physically. I guess I just didn't realise how much.'

The tone of his words made a shiver creep down her spine. 'What do you mean?'

He gave the biggest sigh she'd ever heard. 'I mean that Claire got turned down for adoption a few weeks ago. She's totally distraught.'

'What? Why did she get turned down? She never mentioned it.' Gemma was more than surprised.

'How much did Claire tell you?'

She shook her head. 'Not much. But I didn't ask her any questions.' Her eyes met his. 'I'm sorry, but I just didn't think I knew her well enough to pry.' Now she was feeling guilty. Should she have asked Claire some more questions?

'It's not your fault, Gemma. It's mine. The social workers picked up on something that I should have picked up on long ago.' He sounded angry and his whole body had stiffened, his muscles tensing.

She shook her head. 'What do you mean?'

He clenched his fists. 'I mean I should have realised something was wrong with Claire. I should have intervened long before she applied for the adoption. I had no idea things had got so bad.' He stood up and started pacing about. 'I'm supposed to be a doctor. I'm supposed to look after people. But I couldn't even sit my sister down and ask her what was wrong.'

Everything started to fall into place. 'Is she depressed?'

He ran his fingers through his hair. 'That's just it. I'm not sure. I think so. Her mood has been low. But then again, she gets herself whipped into a frenzy with her latest idea and she seems a bit manic. She won't discuss anything with me. Just tells me "You're not my doctor" and storms off.' She could practically see the frustration emanating from his pores. 'Her mental health has slowly been deteriorating with every failed attempt at ICSI and IVF. I just didn't realise by how much.'

Gemma took a deep breath. 'I know it's difficult, Logan, and it's hard for me to comment. I certainly haven't seen any signs of her being manic when I've been with her. But it is obvious that her mood is low. I just assumed it was a result of her longing for a child.

I'm not an expert on mental health, so I probably couldn't be much help.'

Gemma stood up next to him and touched his arm. 'Is that what's been wrong these last few weeks? Why didn't you say something?'

He threw his arms up in frustration. 'Because it's not really my business to share. I asked Hugh Cairney at the surgery to see her.' He waved his hands a little. 'I didn't know what else to do. Claire gets on well with him and I thought she might talk to him. He's also known her for years and would be able to judge her change in mood.'

She reached up and touched his face. 'And you feel guilty?' Her voice was quiet, understanding.

His arms dropped down. 'Yes. Of course I feel guilty. I've let my sister down.' He paused. 'And it's not the first time.'

'What does that mean?' She kept her hand where it was, feeling the warmth of his skin through the palm of her hand. He was hurting. His eyes looked like a wounded soldier's. She was so close she could feel the rise of his chest as he took a deep breath.

'My dad. He died on the golf course on Arran when I was an SHO in Glasgow. I wasn't here.'

She nodded slowly. Understanding how he felt. 'What happened?'

'He had an AA. One minute he was fine, the next... he was gone.'

'Oh, Logan.' She ran her fingers through his hair. 'You know that's one of the hardest things to diagnose. Some people don't have any symptoms at all. There was nothing you could have done.'

His eyes met hers. The blue was even darker, full of despair. 'But I think I could. If I'd been here I might have picked up on something—anything—even minor, that meant he would have got checked out.'

'You can't know that, Logan. And you can't beat yourself up about that. You didn't let your family down then, and you haven't now. We've spoken about this before. Sometimes it's easier for someone on the outside looking in to see what's really wrong.'

He nodded his head slowly. 'I know. But it doesn't make me feel any better.' He sagged back down onto the sofa. 'And there's more. I can't interfere because Claire's seeing Hugh. But she's still not thinking rationally.'

'What do you mean?'

His head shook slightly. 'She's started ranting on about wanting to hire a surrogate. Hire someone else to have her baby. That's the last thing she needs to be doing.'

Gemma felt her stomach twist in a horrible knot. The very last thing on earth she wanted to talk about. The one thing on this planet she wanted to avoid.

But she couldn't. Particularly not now.

There was a roaring in her ears. Part of her was horrified. Part of her was indignant.

Her voice was wavering. 'Have you spoken to her about it? Maybe it's the natural next step for her—once she's well, of course.'

He looked aghast. 'How can it be the next step? She needs to get herself straightened out first before she even considers any other option. And certainly not that one.'

She felt herself stiffen completely. 'Maybe you should find out a bit more about it before you stand in judgement. Lots of people have babies using surrogates.'

'You think that's what I'm doing—standing in judgement?'

'Absolutely.'

'And what makes you the expert?'

She took a deep breath. Nightmare. If she dodged this question now she could never look him in the eye again. And she didn't want that. He would find out sooner or later anyway. Best just to get it over and done with. No matter how much she didn't want to go down that path.

She might be a lot of things, but a liar certainly wasn't one of them.

She couldn't hide the tremble in her voice. 'I've been a surrogate.'

Silence. Ticking past. Seconds feeling like hours.

His eyes had widened, as if he was trying to process what she'd just said. 'You...what?' His brow wrinkled, deep furrows appearing across its length and between his eyes.

This time her voice wasn't shaky. This time her voice was definite. 'I've been a surrogate.' She had to be confident. She had to let him know she wasn't ashamed of her actions.

'But why? When?' He looked totally stunned.

This was where it started. The multitude of questions. The expectation that she explain herself. All the things she detested.

'I did it for my friend Lesley and her husband Patrick. Lesley and I grew up together. She was like your sister, infertile. Even when she tried IVF the quality of her eggs meant that she didn't have a lot of viable embryos. It was always unsuccessful.'

'But I don't get it. What on earth made you offer to do that?'

'I cared about her. The whole situation was tearing her apart. I could see her collapsing in on herself before my eyes. Just like your sister, Logan. When I first met

Claire a few weeks ago I recognised some of the things I'd seen in Lesley. The low mood, the weight loss. And I was with Lesley constantly. I cried the river of tears along with her every month when she realised she wasn't pregnant again. I couldn't watch my friend being destroyed by something that was totally out of her control. I decided to do the one thing I could do to help.'

Logan was shaking his head. 'That's a mighty big favour.'

Gemma bit her lip. She'd told him now. She couldn't take the words back. But how would he react when he knew the truth?

Logan hadn't stopped. He was still shaking his head. 'So, how did Isla fit into all this? What did she think about you giving away her baby brother or sister?'

Gemma froze. He hadn't clicked. He hadn't realised. Her mouth was so dry. Licking her lips did nothing. Only emphasised the sandpit in her throat.

'Isla didn't know.'

'How didn't she know? Did you hide the pregnancy from her?' He frowned. 'Or was this before you had her?'

She had to say it. She had to put him right. 'Isla is the baby.'

'What?' His head spun around. 'Isla is the surrogate baby?'

She nodded.

'But that means…you stole your friend's baby?' He was astounded. But it was the only natural conclusion to reach.

'Isla is *my* daughter. She was *my* baby. It was my egg.'

He looked endlessly confused. 'So, you offered to have your friend's baby. You donated your egg, then you kept the baby. What about the father? Didn't he get a say in any of this?' He was still shaking his head in disbelief.

Patrick. The one person who could make her skin creep with no explanation whatsoever.

But Logan wasn't finished. He was pacing again. 'Didn't you have a legal agreement about all this? How on earth could you steal your friend's baby?'

'Stop it, Logan. Stop it. Isla is my daughter. My baby. She didn't belong to Lesley, she belonged to me.' She shook her head. 'We didn't have a formal agreement. We looked into it but Lesley—she was desperate. And as soon as I offered she just wanted us to get started straight away.' She knew how desperate this all sounded. She also knew how foolish this made her and her friends sound.

But, as far as she knew, Logan had never experienced infertility. How could he understand?

And even now, after everything that had happened, Gemma realised how lucky she was that they hadn't had a formal agreement in place. In the end, that had saved her and Isla.

Somewhere in his brain she could see the penny drop. He lifted his finger. 'You. You're the *bad surrogate*. You were all over the news. There was a court case.' Then a flicker of recognition came across his face. 'You. It was you. You put this idea into her head. How could you? You know how vulnerable she is right now.'

She cringed. Of course he would think that. It was a natural conclusion to jump to—even if it wasn't true. 'I swear to you I didn't. I've never mentioned surrogacy to Claire. I wouldn't…I couldn't.'

The bad surrogate. The label the press had given her, along with every unflattering picture they could take. Finally. The thing she'd absolutely dreaded. As soon as anyone realised she was the woman from the papers they all had to have an opinion. An opinion they intended to share with her. And Logan was going to be no different.

She gave a sigh. This was all going horribly wrong. 'There was a court case. It lasted five years. I came here to get away from all that. I came here for a new start.'

But he wasn't listening. He was fixating on one thing. 'I don't get it. Why didn't you have a proper agreement?' Bits of the case were obviously sparking in his brain. 'You're a doctor, for goodness' sake. You should have known better.' He let out an expletive. 'Or, more importantly, *they* should have known better.'

She shook her head. 'I won that court case, Logan. The court agreed that Isla was my daughter. That Isla should stay with me.'

'And that makes you feel better? How on earth could you look your friends in the eye?' He started pacing around the room. 'You swear you've never told Claire about this?'

She shook her head.

'No wonder. You stole your friend's baby. Why would you tell anyone that?' It was obvious his mind was jumping from one thing to another. One second it was on Claire, the next it was fixating back on her.

She sagged back onto the sofa. 'You have no idea what you're talking about. I did what I had to do. I did what was right.' It was pointless trying to explain. She already knew he was never going to understand.

'How is stealing your friend's baby "right"?'

She put her head in her hands. She'd had this conversation so many times, with so many people. But she'd never been so in fear of someone standing in judgement of her.

For some reason it seemed so important that he

understand why she did it. She wanted to persuade him that she wasn't the worst person to walk the face of this earth. Even though that was the way the press had portrayed her.

Then again, the press hadn't known the full story. Because she'd always left part of it out. It had been so important at the time. But it wasn't rational. She had no evidence. So her lawyer had told her not to breathe a word in case it harmed her case.

But the case was over. Now she could say whatever she liked.

She looked at Logan. His hair was rumpled from where he'd run his fingers through it, his pale denim shirt pushed up around the elbows. Just looking at him made her heart beat faster. But the expression on his face was anything but understanding. Why had this conversation even started? Things would have been so much easier if she'd just let him kiss her. Just let herself be lost in his touch. But she'd started now and there was nowhere else to go. She had to finish.

She sucked in a breath. 'Everything was fine to begin with. Patrick and Lesley were delighted. But as my pregnancy progressed things started to change. Patrick, he started to get really odd, really possessive. He told me to give up work. He started trying to tell me what to do about everything.'

'Maybe he was just concerned about his baby?'

'No. It was much more than that. He was *controlling*. It was a side of him I'd never seen before. I started to feel really uncomfortable around him. He was turning up at my flat unannounced, sometimes with a list of instructions in his hand.'

'Did you consider he might just be anxious?'

She let her head sag. 'I considered everything. Because Lesley was one of my best friends,' she said sadly.

Logan's brow furrowed. 'How did you get pregnant in the first place? Did you do it…the old-fashioned way?'

Gemma was horrified. 'Sleep with my friend's husband? Absolutely not. I used a turkey baster. It worked first time.'

'And you just decided not to give them the baby?'

She let out a sigh of exasperation. 'I can't explain it properly. I had a really bad feeling. The more Patrick's behaviour began to alarm me, the more connected to Isla I started to feel. I'd never thought of her as anything other than Patrick and Lesley's up until that point. But as I started to get bigger, as she started to grow and move I felt more and more uncomfortable around Patrick. She started to feel like my baby and I started to feel like a mother who had to protect her child.' She shrugged her shoulders in frustration. 'I had a hunch.'

His voice rose. 'You had a *hunch*? You based your baby's future on a *hunch*?' He was incredulous and she couldn't blame him. It sounded awful.

It didn't matter how futile things sounded. She had to try and explain. 'Don't make it sound crazy. We base our clinical decisions on hunches all the time. We just feel something isn't right but we can't explain it. Look at the assessment the health visitor does on families for child protection. She's allowed to give marks based on her "health visitor hunch" when she knows something isn't right but she can't put her finger on it.'

Something else sparked in her brain and she didn't hesitate to use it. 'Look at the clinical symptoms for an aortic aneurysm. One of them is "a feeling of impending doom" by the patient. There's no rational explanation for it. But it happens so often it's now considered an evidenced based clinical symptom.'

She could see the recognition on his face but he just kept shaking his head. She could see the pain on his face at her using the condition that had killed his father as a way of explanation. 'You're being unfair. Medicine isn't an exact science—we know that. But you didn't have any evidence. How on earth did you win the court case?'

For some reason she was determined to try and make him understand. 'It was more than that. One day I was with Lesley and I noticed she had a bruise on her thigh. It was unusual—in a place that no one would normally see—and I only glimpsed it while she was getting changed.'

'What did she say?'

'She gave me a reasonable explanation of what had happened.'

'And you didn't believe her?'

'At first I did. But then there was a mark on her shoulder—a scrape. Something else that would normally be hidden. It started setting off alarm bells in my head.'

'Did you ask your friend if she was being abused?'

'I tried to. I asked if there was anything she wanted to tell me. But she made a joke out of it—as if I was being ridiculous—and cut me off. It was almost as if she knew what I was going to ask.'

Logan shook his head. 'So what did you do?'

The big question. The one she still asked herself when she lay in bed at night.

Her voice was quiet. 'That's just it, Logan. What could I do? Lesley wasn't telling me anything and I didn't know—not for sure.' She looked him in the eye. 'I didn't have any evidence. And if I'd tried to report it…' Her voice tailed off for a second. 'I was worried. I was worried people would say I was making it up to try and discredit them. Try to keep my baby from them. So I didn't say anything. My job was to protect my daughter. I just said I'd changed my mind and wanted to bring Isla up on my own. She was biologically my child. We didn't have a formal agreement. The judge found in my favour.'

The frown lines in his forehead were deeper than she'd ever seen them. It was clear he was trying to understand, even if he didn't really. 'I just don't get it. Why didn't you try to prove there was a risk?'

'Because my lawyer told me not to. It would have been my word against theirs. Lesley was an adult. If there was abuse in the household, it was up to her to report it.'

Silence, as he contemplated her words. Was he trying to rationalise her actions in his mind?

He moved over towards the wall, leaning against it and folding his arms across his chest. 'So, why did you tell me?'

His voice was quiet. He couldn't hide the air of exasperation in it, but it was obvious he was curious as to why she was sharing something with him that her lawyer had told her to keep quiet.

She met his gaze. There was none of the compassion or desire that she'd seen before. He looked angry. He looked as if he didn't understand any of this. It seemed as though all the underlying sizzle and attraction had been snuffed out in an instant—ruined by her being honest with him.

'Because I wanted to tell you the truth.'

He didn't say anything. She could see him take a few steadying breaths. The rise and fall of his chest was calming. She rested back against the sofa, her hands in her hair. 'Do you think I really wanted to have this conversation with you, Logan?'

He looked at her again, and her heart ripped in two because it was almost a look of disgust.

Anger started to build inside her. This was pointless. He was never going to understand. He was never going to *try* to understand. Why was she even bothering?

'I can't believe this. I can't believe you would do something like this.' He'd started pacing around her living room, the glasses of wine, box of cakes and almost-kiss long forgotten. 'It sounds to me like you just got cold feet. You started to connect with the baby and you were just looking for any excuse.'

He stopped at a photograph of Isla with her red bouncing curls and pale skin. 'Isla—she doesn't look like you at all. Is she like her father?'

A horrible tremor crept down her spine. She loved her daughter with her whole heart. But Patrick's genetic traits were there for all to see. Her brown locks and sallow skin were nowhere in sight. She gave the slightest of nods. 'He has red hair too.'

Logan held his hands up. 'So what do you tell her? Does she ever ask about her father?'

Gemma felt as if a fist was currently tightening its grip around her heart. 'Of course she does.'

'And what do you tell her?'

She could feel the tears start to pool in the corners of her eyes. 'I tell her as much of the truth as I dare. I tell her I was originally having a baby for my friends but I loved her too much to let her go.'

Logan stayed silent for a few seconds, his eyes still on the photograph of Isla. 'Does she ever ask to see them?'

Gemma walked over and touched the picture with her

finger. Thank goodness Isla wasn't here right now. Thank goodness she hadn't witnessed any of this.

'She's asked to see photographs and I've showed her some. I told her that they'd moved away.'

His face turned towards hers. 'Is that true?'

A tear slipped down her face. It was like he was exposing every lie she'd ever told. And there was no excuse for lying—even with the best of intentions.

She shook her head. 'No. No, they haven't. As far as I know, they're still in Glasgow.'

'Patrick wasn't granted access rights?'

She looked him in the eye. 'Absolutely not. Patrick was the issue.'

His eyes narrowed. 'But you didn't tell anyone that. So how did you manage to get him denied access?'

Gemma could hardly focus. 'The judge decided the whole case was too emotive. He said it was better for Patrick not to be involved—to give everyone a fresh start.' She put her hand on her chest. 'My job was to protect my daughter. In the end, I had a really bad feeling about Patrick. I heard him one day in the hospital, being short with some kids in A and E. It made my blood run cold. And I didn't have a doubt I was doing the right thing.'

'Because the guy had a bad day?' He made it sound so ridiculous, so flimsy. She could feel her anger bubbling up inside.

'Don't say it like that. Isla is my daughter. *My daughter.* It's my duty to protect her. It was his manner with those kids. He looked over his shoulder to make sure no one could hear him. He didn't realise I had just walked up. Then he snapped at the kids and threatened them— telling them if they didn't behave he wouldn't treat their mother. As soon as he realised I'd appeared, he was all nicey-nicey again. There was no way I was handing my daughter over to man like that. How could I be sure how he'd be behind closed doors? I already had a bad vibe from him.'

Logan threw his hands up in the air. 'I just don't get it, Gemma. Part of me can't believe you agreed to do this in the first place.' He ran his fingers through his hair. 'How could you have even contemplated being able to give a baby away?'

His words brought tears to her eyes instantly. 'Because of people like Claire, Logan. Because of what infertility does to them. My friend Lesley was just like Claire. I went through it all with her. I wanted to help. I wanted to help my friend.'

He shook his head. 'But you didn't.' He took a deep breath. 'I get what you're saying about Patrick and Lesley. I get that you might have thought your baby was at risk. I'm just having a hard time dealing with the fact you were prepared to do it in the first place.'

The tears started to drip down her cheeks. She pressed her hand to her chest. 'But I didn't know. I didn't know how I would feel in here. I didn't know I would become so attached. I didn't know that every breath that I took would be about Isla. Would be about how much I loved my daughter.'

He dropped his eyes. 'And that's just it, Gemma. Do I believe all this? Or do I just believe you didn't want to give your baby up? Do I just believe you became attached and couldn't give her away? Maybe none of this is true. Maybe it's convenient to turn things around and put a shadow of doubt over Patrick.'

'No. No, Logan. I wouldn't do that.'

'Wouldn't you? What do you expect me to say? My sister is virtually having a breakdown over people like you.'

'People like me? Don't say that.' She pointed at his chest. 'You have no idea what's going to happen with your sister. She might get a surrogate and things will work out fine.'

'And how could I support my sister in that decision when there's people like you about? People who agree to do something then change their mind? Can you imagine what that would do to her? That would destroy what tiny part of her is left!' It was frustration. It was pure frustration and she knew it.

She could feel her whole body start to shake. She knew he believed what he was saying. She knew he felt so guilty about his sister right now that it could be affecting his reactions. She couldn't blame him. She couldn't blame him at all.

Because it was all true. She had no contact with Lesley any more. She'd all but destroyed her best friend and it was a horrendous truth to have to bear.

And even though she hated it, there was a real thread of reality to his words. She was the worst example of a surrogate. Her press coverage alone must have put hundreds of people off using the surrogacy route, and that made her feel so sad.

It made her feel guilty. It made her feel responsible.

But deep down she didn't doubt she'd made the right decision—even if she couldn't prove it. She and Isla were happy. If she could go back and have her time again, no matter how much she regretted the overall outcome for Lesley, she couldn't ever regret having Isla.

It didn't matter that the thought of Patrick sent shivers down her spine. She hadn't always felt like that towards him, obviously, or she wouldn't have agreed to the surrogacy. But even if Patrick had been perfect, would she have started to have doubts about giving away her baby?

Would she have become so attached to Isla and broken the hearts of her friends anyway?

Her brain couldn't even go there. Guilt had consumed her for so long that she couldn't afford to spend any time or energy thinking about all the what-ifs. Dealing with the consequences of the reality was hard enough.

Arran had felt like a safe haven. A little piece of quiet in this noisy world.

What would happen when the news started to spread about her? Would people not want to see her in the surgery? Even worse, would parents not want her to treat their children?

All she wanted was to do her job, have a quiet life and have a happy home for herself and Isla.

Logan Scott had complicated all that. Logan had started to make her feel things that she hadn't felt in years. His flirting and attention had made her start to consider the other possibilities out there. Made her start to think that she could find something else other than a life for herself and Isla.

But that was finished just as quickly as it had started. Nothing could be clearer.

She took a deep breath. 'You're not being rational, Logan. I know you're upset about your sister. But you're right. You can't let my example influence how you feel about surrogacy. You have to help your sister make the right decision for her.' She lifted her eyes to meet his. 'And who are you to judge me? Who are you to make judgements on actions and decisions I made five years ago? We didn't know each other then. But even if we had, my decision would stand.'

His blue eyes were nearly hidden from her, his pupils had widened with anger, their blackness almost taking over his eyes. He held up his hand. 'Don't, Gemma. Don't ever try and tell me something about my sister. And don't dare give me advice on surrogacy. Stay away from my sister. I don't want you anywhere near her. She has enough to deal with, without finding out what you've done.' There was a finality about his words. 'As for who am I to stand in judgement of you? I'm your work colleague, Gemma. And that's all I'll ever be.'

And with that he turned on his heel and stormed out of the door.

All the pent-up energy and frustration that had been holding Gemma together disintegrated in an instant. Her legs turned to jelly and she collapsed on the sofa, sobbing.

Things couldn't be any worse. How on earth could she and Logan work together now?

And how on earth would she survive on Arran once word got out?

CHAPTER EIGHT

'MUMMY, WHAT DOES "belt up" mean?'

Gemma choked on her cornflakes and milk spluttered everywhere. A fit of coughing followed and Isla calmly walked around the table and started hitting her on the back.

After a few seconds the coughing stopped. Gemma stood up and walked over to the sink, grabbing a glass for some water.

'Where on earth did you hear that, Isla?' She was horrified and racking her brains to try and think who had spoken like that around her daughter.

Isla was back to solemnly spooning her cereal into her mouth. Sometimes she seemed so much older than five. 'Granny Scott said it to Logan. He's her baby, you know,' she added with a nod of her head. She was crayoning with her other hand, concentrating fiercely on her drawing.

Gemma tried not to smile. 'Yes, I did know that.' She sat back down at the table. Why on earth would Mary be speaking to Logan like that? She chose her words carefully. 'Did she actually say those words to Logan?'

Isla nodded. 'Why, Mummy?' Then something obviously dawned on her and her eyes widened. 'Is "belt up" a swear word, Mummy?' she whispered.

Gemma took a sip of her tea. 'Not exactly. But it's not something I'd like to hear you say. It's definitely not a very nice thing to say to someone.'

Isla nodded. 'Logan wasn't happy with his mum. He stomped around the house and slammed the door.' She rummaged through the box for another crayon.

Gemma winced. The last thing she wanted was for her daughter to be exposed to any family arguments.

'His mummy told him he was being stupid.' Isla was saying it matter-of-factly as she finished her breakfast and her drawing.

Gemma bit her lip. She should cut this conversation dead—she knew she should. But curiosity was killing her. 'Why did Mrs Scott say he was being stupid?'

Isla shrugged. 'Not sure.' Then it seemed as if a little brainwave hit her. 'She called him something else too. Ir-irr-national.'

Gemma smiled at the mispronounced word. 'Irrational?'

Isla nodded. Gemma could feel her heart rate quicken. Had they been discussing her? Had Logan told his mother about her? She cringed. And if he had, would the news travel? Would people start treating her differently?

Isla finished her drawing. 'There. It's for Logan. Do you think he'll like it?'

She started. 'You did a drawing for Logan? Why did you do that?' She stared at the picture. Logan on his boat. Her cheeks flushed—automatically going to her last memories of being there.

She swallowed, despite the huge lump in her throat. Isla was smiling at her picture. 'I think he'll like it. He read me a book the other day about ten little tugboats. I think it's my favourite now.'

Gemma tried not to grimace. She knew that Logan would see Isla at his mother's house. But it was obvious that he wasn't letting their fallout affect his relationship with Isla. In a way she should be happy. He was interacting with her daughter. He was forming a relationship with her and Isla obviously liked him. But she couldn't bear the thought of them talking about her. She'd experienced that enough for one lifetime. And here it was, starting all over again.

It didn't matter that it sounded as though Mary had tried to talk some sense into her son. Had told him he was being irrational. Mary had the same loyalties and ethics that he did. Claire was her daughter, just like she was his sister. But Mary obviously had the ability to step back and see the wider picture.

It was just a pity that Logan didn't.

Gemma finished rinsing the plates and turned to face Isla. 'Mum's off today. Fancy going down to the beach with your fishing net and we'll see what we can catch in the rock pools?'

'Yeah!' Isla jumped off her seat and scurried off to find her shoes. Gemma grabbed her jacket. She was determined to hold her head high. She'd made the right decision. And it was no one else's business but hers.

Heaven help anyone who tried to tell her differently.

The tension in the air could be sliced through like a thick, double chocolate cake. But a big piece of chocolate cake would be much more enjoyable than this. It was affecting everything and everyone around them.

Julie was running around in the surgery like a headless chicken. She jumped every time he asked her to do something and barely looked him in the eye. Even his usual patients, who normally wanted to spend half their day in his consulting room, seemed to be catapulting in and out of the surgery. What on earth was going on?

He knew that Gemma was meeting today with Mags, the health visitor, and Edith, the midwife, to discuss some patients there were concerns over. But he hadn't seen her at all today so had no idea what was going on.

He walked down the corridor to the staffroom, where he could smell the coffee brewing. The smell of coffee brewing in this place was like the Pied Piper with his magic pipe, usually luring all staff members out from their offices.

But the staffroom was empty as he walked in. Milk was sitting on the counter, along with a number of freshly washed cups. Someone had just been here.

He heard the low mumble of someone singing as he opened the cupboard in the search for some biscuits. Two minutes later the singing got a little clearer as Gemma walked in. She was wearing a red summer dress, a pair of flat sandals and her hair was loose around her shoulders.

Her whole body stiffened as soon as she saw him. 'Oh, sorry, Logan. Didn't realise you were here.'

Tension again. All around them. He eyed the packet of biscuits in her hand. 'I was searching in the cupboard for something to eat—I see you were doing the same.'

Why had he felt the urge to fill the silence around them? Because, like it or not, and whether he understood her or not, he was drawn to Gemma like a magnet. It was driving him crazy. And probably making him unbearable.

He hated things that weren't rational. He hated things that couldn't be explained logically. Was it any wonder his friends nicknamed him Spock?

He'd spent a good part of the day with Isla yesterday.

She was delightful. She was gorgeous. And she was getting under his skin every bit as much as her mother.

It didn't matter that he'd been down this road before. It didn't matter that he'd had a child torn away from him before. No one could help but enjoy her company and she was a happy, well-adjusted, sociable little girl.

If only he and her mother could be happy, well-adjusted, sociable adults.

Gemma gave a little nod and walked over to the counter, putting the biscuits down between them.

She looked gorgeous, and until she'd realised he was there, she'd looked calm and relaxed at her work. No. Happy. She'd looked happy at her work.

He watched as she filled a coffee cup and topped it up with milk. Yet again, he couldn't take his eyes off her.

He wanted to. He wanted to just walk out and not look back. But his eyes were drawn by the curves in her dress and glimpse of tanned leg. She put the milk back in the refrigerator with a bang and spun around. 'What? What is it you want, Logan? Is it to give me another lecture about a subject you know nothing about?'

He was taken aback by her venom. He'd been staring. He'd been following her every move and she'd noticed.

She tilted her chin and straightened her shoulders. 'What do you want, Logan, because I'm sick of the atmosphere in this place.' Her words were definite. It was clear she wasn't going to move until this was resolved.

He filled up his cup slowly, trying to choose his words carefully.

The last few days had been a nightmare. He'd discussed with his mother his concerns about Claire. He'd almost fallen off his chair when she'd said that she thought the surrogacy option was worth looking into.

He couldn't believe it and he'd exploded and ended up telling his mother all about Gemma and Isla.

He knew he shouldn't have. It was Gemma's business. And she probably hadn't wanted to tell him in the first place. Now he looked back on the conversation he realised she'd probably felt backed into a corner and had had to speak.

And his reaction hadn't been the best.

With hindsight, most of it had been shock value. And he hadn't felt ready to sit down and be rational about it all. He still had so much guilt about Claire that he couldn't even think straight.

But his mother had been blunt and to the point. 'I don't know what you're getting so worked up about.' She'd pointed to her chest. 'I'm Claire's mother. I'm the one who should have realised she needed some time out and some help. You hardly see her. I see her every few days. If anyone should have noticed that something was wrong, it was *me*.'

And then he'd felt even more guilty about putting the burden of responsibility onto his mother. None of this was working out how he wanted.

Here he was, stuck in a kitchen with a woman who looked ready to kill him, and all he could think about was running his fingers through her hair or touching the tanned skin on her shoulders.

He took a deep breath. 'Things aren't great, are they?' It was a simple enough statement. Acknowledging that something was wrong but not pointing the finger of blame anywhere.

Gemma thumped her coffee mug down, sloshing coffee all over the worktop. 'And that's your fault, Logan. You've been walking about here like a bear with a sore head, snapping at everyone who talks to you. It's as if there is a permanent black thundercloud hanging over the top of your head. You're the one that's created an atmosphere.'

'What?' Of course he'd noticed the oppressive atmosphere. But he hadn't realised that he was the cause. 'I have not,' he said, automatically on the defensive as he tried to remember the last few days.

Hmm. He might have been a little short with Julie. And he might have been a bit snappy with some of the rest of the staff too. Not deliberately. But just because his mind was so full of other things.

Other things like Gemma Halliday.

'Do you know what? If you're mad at me then be mad at me.' She waved her arm. 'Don't be mad at everyone else. They don't deserve it.' She frowned at her cup, noticing the spilled coffee all over the worktop, then fixed him with a steely glare. 'And to be frank, I don't think I deserve it either.'

She turned, her red summer dress sweeping around her, and flounced out of the kitchen, coffee and biscuits abandoned.

Logan shook his head. He hadn't even realised he was being short with everyone. Oh, he knew he was using definite avoidance tactics when it came to Gemma. But he hadn't been aware of the impact on everyone else.

He cringed. How embarrassing. There had already been a few whispers, a few knowing stares around him and Gemma. He might as well have put a sign above their heads. People must surely be wondering what had happened between them now. And it was clear it wasn't good.

This was unprofessional. For them and for their patients. And this was his fault.

What he needed to do was sit down and have a reasoned, rational conversation with her.

But it was difficult to concentrate around her. She didn't seem to realise the effect she had on him. It was almost magnetic. And when she was at her most angry, most emotional, she was even more gorgeous than usual and he just couldn't think straight.

It was time to get himself in order. It was time to think about what he was doing.

Not being around Gemma was killing him. Not being able to touch her was keeping him awake at night.

He was going to have to come to terms with what she'd done, and fast.

Otherwise he might as well just set sail off the coast and never come back.

'Are you in a better mood, or are you still grumpy?'

'What?' Logan was startled by the little voice. But then again, why should he be? Isla seemed to be a permanent fixture at his mother's kitchen table. She was beginning to feel like part of the family. And, to be honest, it didn't give him the usual *run, run as fast as you can* thoughts.

He glanced around and caught sight of his mother in the back garden, hanging out a load of washing. Isla pushed the seat out from the table. 'Do you want to see my new school uniform, Logan? My mum picked it all out for me. Granny Scott says she's going to take the hem up on my pinafore.'

Isla jumped down from the seat and stood in front of him, twirling around as only a little girl in new clothes could. She looked adorable. It was almost as if the bright

green of the school uniform had been made entirely to
suit her colouring.

Her curly red hair was tied neatly back with some
matching green ribbons. She had on a grey pinafore and
bright green school jumper, with a white polo shirt collar
showing around the neckline of the jumper, along with
highly polished—clearly never worn—school shoes. She
pointed to the door handle, where there was a hanger with
a green and white school summer dress.

'My mum got me one of those too, in case it's too
hot when I start.' She twirled around again. 'But I like
my jumper.' She jumped back up on the chair, standing
precariously on tiptoe and looking at herself in the mirror above the fireplace. 'I think I look *much* older in my
school uniform. What do you think?'

Logan couldn't help the smile on his face. There was
no getting away from it, Miss Five-Going-On-Eighty-
Five was just adorable. 'I think I would like you to stay
five for as long as possible, Isla Halliday.' He picked her
off the chair and put her back on the floor.

'But why? I want to be a big girl.' She settled back
down at the table. 'And when I grow up I want to have a
house just like Mummy's.' Her eyes stared off into the
distance. 'Or maybe a house like the castle on the hill.'

Brodick Castle. Logan stifled a laugh. It almost
wouldn't surprise him if Isla *did* have a castle when she
was older.

He looked around. 'Do you have a school bag yet,
Isla?'

She shook her head and looked a little sad. 'I wanted
a proper satchel. Do you know what a satchel is?'

He nodded. 'I think so.'

'But Mummy can't find one anywhere. She had one

when she was a little girl and started school. I wanted a bag just like hers.'

Logan smiled. This would be easy. He could finally do something that felt right. 'Was it made of leather?' He pulled over the tablet his mother frequently used, typed in a few words and pulled up a picture of an old-fashioned-style leather school satchel.

Isla let out a squeal and jumped up. 'That's the one. Exactly like that. That's the one I'm looking for.' Her hands were jittery with excitement. 'Can you tell Mummy?'

Logan shook his head. 'Let's not tell her yet.' Then he frowned at his own words. The last thing he wanted to do was tell a child to keep a secret from her parent.

He pulled up a website. 'I have a friend who makes these. Do you want a brown leather one like Mummy had?' He clicked onto another page. 'Or do you want a coloured leather one?' He pointed at the screen. 'You could get a green one to match your school uniform.'

'Wow,' said the little voice beside him. 'That is so-o-o pretty.' She touched her matching school jumper then pressed her fingers on the screen. 'I like the green one, but I think I'd like the one that looked like Mummy's best.'

Logan nodded. School satchels. He blinked at the price. No wonder his friend could make a living from this. The nostalgia bug was obviously alive and kicking.

Then he noticed something else. Four- to six-week delivery time. There were only two weeks until Isla started school. Just as well his friend owed him a favour. He scribbled down the phone number; he'd call him today.

'I tell you what, Isla. If Mummy says she's going to buy you a bag for school, tell her that Logan and Granny Scott are getting one for you. How's that?'

Isla nodded. 'Okay.'

Better. That was a much better solution. And Gemma might not object so much if she thought Logan's mother was helping get Isla her bag for school.

Isla had picked up her crayons and started drawing. 'Don't you like us any more, Logan? You haven't come to visit.' Her face was solemn. 'And you haven't brought cakes.'

Logan felt his insides squirm. Gemma obviously hadn't mentioned his last visit and it was probably for the best. 'I like you and your mummy very much. Sometimes grown-ups get a bit busy. I'm sure I'll come and visit soon.'

Was he wrong to tell a deliberate lie? After their last confrontation the chances of he and Gemma being in a room together were slim.

But there was something else ticking away at him. The time factor. It seemed like he'd worked a million hours this week. And his dad had done this job before him.

How had he managed it? Because Logan's overwhelming memories were of a dad who had always been there and always had time for him. Could he ever fill shoes like those?

If he got his act together and contemplated being around Gemma and Isla, would he be fair? Would he have the time to invest in a relationship the way he should? The last thing he wanted to do was be unfair to the little girl who now wanted the tugboat stories read to her five times a day. He'd created a monster. And it was all his fault.

He wrinkled his nose. 'Why have you got your school uniform on anyway?' School didn't start for two weeks.

Isla gave him a smile. 'It was a practice run today. Do you know it takes much longer in the morning to get ready for school than it does for an ordinary day?' She fingered her little red curls. 'It took ages to do my hair.' Her little face was solemn again. 'And that was without Mummy making me a packed lunch for school.' She shrugged her shoulders. 'I've still to pick a lunch box. I can't decide which one I want.'

He couldn't help the smile that spread across his face. He'd noticed a plastic bag in the corner of the room. 'Isla, are you supposed to keep wearing your uniform all day?' He couldn't imagine for a minute that Gemma wouldn't have sent a change of clothes.

Isla looked a little sheepish. She stared down at her uniform again. 'I like my uniform,' she whispered. 'I don't want to take it off.'

He stared at the books on the table—recipe books with photographs of a whole variety of cakes, biscuits and tray bakes. Isla was obviously supposed to pick whatever they would bake today. He could see her little blue pinafore hanging on a peg next to his mother's. Looking as if it was supposed to be there.

Something curled inside him. A realisation.

He *wanted* it to be there.

He almost couldn't believe it. Logan Scott, island bachelor, was once again picturing a woman in his future, and not only that but a woman with a child. Thank goodness he was sitting down.

Isla flicked through the recipe book until she found a picture of a rainbow-coloured cake. 'Ooh, this one looks pretty. Do you think Granny Scott will let me make it? It might cheer my mummy up.'

He straightened in his chair. 'Why would you need to cheer your mummy up?'

She tilted her head to one side. 'Because she's sad. She thinks I don't know, but I do.'

Logan wanted to ask a million questions. He wanted to know exactly why Isla thought that. But he knew better than to question a child. It would be an invasion of Gemma's privacy. She would eat him alive if she found out he was questioning Isla.

And the truth was he didn't need to ask any questions. Children were much more perceptive than adults gave them credit for. And it didn't surprise him that a bright little girl like Isla had picked up on something at home.

'Do you think Granny Scott will let me make the rainbow cake?' Isla asked again.

He nodded. 'I think she might. On one condition.'

Isla looked at him suspiciously. 'What?'

He pointed at the bag. 'That you change your clothes. You don't want to get your brand-new school uniform all floury.'

Isla seemed to take a few seconds, trying to decide if it was a reasonable trade-off.

She jumped up from her chair. 'Okay, then. I'll do it.' She grabbed the bag and scurried off to the bathroom. 'But only if you stay to taste my cake. I need it to be perfect for my mummy.'

Logan leaned back in his chair and put his feet up on the other under the table. He might as well get comfortable. Looked like he could be here for quite some time.

Then again, it could give him some thinking time.

Thinking time to figure out how he could sort out this mess he had created.

Because the truth was he had no idea how to start.

CHAPTER NINE

THERE WAS A knock at the door. 'Come in.' Gemma was just finishing typing up the last of her notes on the patient who had just left.

Julie stuck her head around the door. 'Gemma? Edith is looking for a doctor, she's got some concerns about a patient. Are you free?'

Gemma nodded. 'Of course. Who is it?'

'Lynsey Black.'

Gemma typed in the name and quickly pulled up the file to give herself some background on the patient. Lynsey Black, thirty-eight. Twin pregnancy and currently thirty-two weeks. Booked in to see the obstetric consultant on the mainland in a few weeks. Apart from a sore back, there was really nothing significant in her notes. She'd had a few antenatal scans and they'd all looked entirely normal.

Strange. They'd had a chat the other day about any antenatal patients that Edith was concerned about. Lynsey Black hadn't been one of them.

Gemma stood up and walked through to the other consulting room, pushing the door open and walking over to the sink to wash her hands. 'Hi, Edith, hi, Lynsey. I'm Gemma Halliday, one of the doctors here.'

She could tell straight away that the normally unflappable Edith was unhappy. A foetal monitor was attached to one side of Lynsey's abdomen, giving little blips, and Edith was listening with a stethoscope on the other side. She was obviously trying to monitor both babies.

Edith looked up. 'Lynsey phoned in to say she'd had some PV bleeding and some sharp abdominal pain. She only lives a few minutes away and was already on her way in when she phoned.'

Gemma nodded. 'How much bleeding?'

Lynsey's voice was shaky, she was obviously terrified. 'Quite a bit. I've had to change my pad twice.'

'And what colour is the blood?'

'Bright red.' Not a good sign. Gemma walked over immediately and glanced at the pad Edith had wrapped up in tissues. Lynsey was right. It was bright red.

Edith had stopped listening with her stethoscope and started winding a blood-pressure cuff around Lynsey's arm. 'Any back pain? Abdominal pain?' she asked.

Lynsey spoke in guarded breaths. 'My back's always sore these days. And my tummy just feels hard.'

Gemma could feel the hackles rise at the back of her neck and she daren't look at Edith. A hard tummy, along with the PV bleeding could mean placental abruption. That's what it sounded like. And it was serious. Sometimes deadly.

Gemma started checking off Lynsey's risk factors in her head.

Multiple pregnancy. Check. Over thirty-five. Check.

She glanced at Edith's notes on the desk in front of her. Lynsey was a smoker. Check. Maternal smoking was associated with up to a ninety per cent increased risk.

She walked over to the side of the examination couch.

'Lynsey, if you don't mind, I'm going to have a little feel of your abdomen.'

Lynsey nodded and Gemma placed her hand on Lynsey's stomach. It was rigid, masking the signs of further bleeding taking place.

Edith was making a few notes on a chart and Gemma glanced over her shoulder. Both babies were starting to show signs of foetal distress. They had to act quickly.

Lynsey's colour was pale and she was slightly clammy. All further signs of placental abruption and associated hypovolaemic shock.

Gemma moved quickly, grabbing a tourniquet to wrap around Lynsey's arm. 'Lynsey, I'm just going to see if we can get a line in to allow us to get some fluids into you.'

'What's happening?' Her voice was shaking. Inserting the line literally took seconds. Gemma was used to dealing with babies with tiny veins so an adult was much easier.

She sat on the edge of the examination couch. 'I'm concerned about the bleeding. I think your placenta could be separating from the uterine wall. We're going to arrange to transfer you to the mainland.'

'How?'

Gemma didn't hesitate. 'By helicopter.'

Tears started to roll down Lynsey's cheeks. She knew exactly how serious this could be. Anyone who lived on Arran knew that the helicopter was only called for real emergencies.

'But it's much too early. I'm only thirty-two weeks. My babies will be far too small. How will they survive?' Her voice was beginning to break.

Gemma touched her hand. 'We don't know everything yet, Lynsey. Give us another few minutes. But I can assure you that babies at thirty-two weeks can live. We can also give you some steroids to try and aid the development of their lungs before delivery. But we'll cross that bridge when we come to it.' She took a deep breath.

'Edith, I'm going to get the ultrasound machine.' Gemma walked quickly across the hall to the other room and wheeled the portable machine across. It was vital she act quickly, but she also needed to know exactly what she was dealing with.

She plugged the machine in and switched it on, spreading a little gel across Lynsey's stomach. She swallowed, trying to keep her voice nice and steady. 'When was the last time you felt the babies move, Lynsey?'

'I was up most of the night, between them and my backache.'

Backache. Was it really backache, or was it something else? She felt Edith's hand rest gently on her shoulder, letting her know she was just as concerned.

Gemma swept the transducer over Lynsey's abdomen. 'And since then?'

'They've been quieter. They're probably having a sleep.' She let out a nervous laugh. 'But they're usually quieter at this time of day so I wasn't worried—not until I saw the bleeding anyway.'

Gemma was keeping her expression as neutral as possible. Her heart gave a little leap as she found the first baby's heartbeat and pressed a button for a little trace. She sent a little silent prayer of thanks upwards. In cases of placental abruption around fifteen per cent of babies died.

She swept the transducer over to the other side of Lynsey's abdomen. Thankfully she found a heartbeat there too, but this time the reading gave her cause for concern. Edith was instantly at her elbow, watching the printout on the machine. This baby was showing signs of foetal distress. They had to get Lynsey to the maternity hospital as quickly as possible.

Gemma had one final sweep of the abdomen. It was difficult to visualise the placenta with two babies fighting for space in there, but she could see some signs of where it had separated from the uterine wall. Time to act.

As Gemma stood up Lynsey clutched her abdomen. *'Aaawwww.'*

'What is it, Lynsey?'

Her face was deathly pale. 'Oh, no, I think that was a contraction.'

Edith was already pulling out some other equipment, designed to monitor women in labour. Gemma didn't have a single doubt. Class two placental abruption. They had to act quickly.

'Is there someone we can call for you, Lynsey?'

She nodded. 'My mum. Callum's out on the fishing boat. He won't be back until after two.'

Edith handed Gemma a piece of paper with a number on it. 'This is Lynsey's mum. Can you ask Julie to phone her and I'll wait with Lynsey while you make the other arrangements?'

Gemma nodded. Thank goodness for Edith. Her experience, knowledge and calm attitude were just what was needed in a situation like this.

She walked out the door to make the call for the emergency helicopter, crossing her fingers that it wouldn't already be on callout somewhere else. Placental abruption could be serious for both mother and babies. In some cases the babies could die.

Lynsey seemed to have a mixed abruption, which meant that some of the bleeding was evident, and some was hidden internally, with the blood trapped between the placenta and uterus. Chances were the babies would need to be delivered—and soon.

She glimpsed the broad span of Logan's shoulders from the other end of the corridor. It didn't matter that he could barely talk to her or look her in the eye. All that mattered now was the patient.

'Logan? Can you hang about a bit? I've got a problem with a patient who will need to be transported off the island.'

For a second he looked as if he was about to say something else. But whatever it was, it vanished in an instant. Logan was the consummate professional. 'Who's the patient?'

'Lynsey Black. Pregnant with twins, possible placental abruption.'

Logan's face paled but Gemma held up her hand. 'It gets worse. She's starting to have contractions.'

Logan pointed towards the phone. 'Make the call, Gemma, and I'll stay with the patient.'

She breathed a sigh of relief. She'd known if it was a matter of a patient Logan would be fine. He was always professional at work. His patients always came first.

In a way it was reassuring. She knew she could always depend on her colleague.

Too bad that only related to work matters.

Gemma appeared back in the room in minutes. She walked over to where Logan was monitoring Lynsey's contractions. Her voice was low. 'There's a problem,' she whispered in his ear.

He turned his head away from Lynsey, who was deep in conversation with someone on her mobile phone.

'There are no neonatal beds at the local maternity hospital. The helicopter is going to have to take us to the Princess Grace Maternity in Glasgow.'

Logan resisted the temptation to let out a curse. 'Can they give us an estimate of how much time that will add onto the journey? I have to tell you that now she's started having contractions, things are moving quickly. We don't have a lot of time here.'

'I know that. The helicopter will be here in the next ten minutes. But they've asked for two doctors—one for each potential delivery.'

Logan nodded. Of course they had. Their paramedic would have to deal with a mother who was potentially haemorrhaging. It made sense to have two other professionals to deal with possibility of two premature babies.

He put his hand on her shoulder. Gemma looked ready to burst into tears. She'd already had to make a transfer in a helicopter, and he knew she hadn't enjoyed it. This journey would be longer, and fraught with even more danger. Three lives were at risk here.

'I'm happy to come along, Gemma.' Then he added, 'And I'm even happier to have an experienced paediatrician on board. You might need to give me some tips.' He wanted to give her a little confidence and some professional reassurance. Personally, he wanted to wipe the look of terror out of her eyes, which she was obviously trying to hide.

He should have sat her down and talked to her the minute she'd come in this morning. The trouble was, he still didn't really know what to say to her, or how to say it. So, as usual, he'd been waiting for an opportunity to present itself. Too late.

She shook her head and put her hand up over his.

There was a tremble to her hand. This was freaking her out more than she would ever let on.

'What about Edith? Can we take the midwife too?'

Logan shook his head. 'It will be a tight fit as it is. There will only be room for you, me and the paramedic. As it is, you might have to sit in my lap.'

He was deliberately joking with her. Trying to take some of the tension out of the air. He needed her to be calm. He didn't doubt her professional capabilities for a second. But he could almost sense her fear.

He gave her hand a squeeze. 'Don't worry, Gem. We're in this together.'

Her brown eyes met his. There were grateful tears in the corners of her eyes. It didn't matter what he thought about her history. It didn't matter about the fights they'd had. Deep down, he knew Gemma was a good doctor. A good person. Even if he didn't understand her reasons, she'd been right about one thing. He had absolutely no right to stand in judgement of her.

She was his colleague and they had to work together to try and keep this patient and her babies alive.

But it was so much more than that.

Gemma Halliday and her beautiful daughter had got under his skin. When he heard a little girl laugh, he automatically looked over his shoulder to see if it was Isla. And even though he tried to fight his own thoughts, Gemma was permanently among them.

Edith signalled to them. She was holding the bag of IV fluids in one hand and gesturing to a stretcher with the other. 'Bill is here to transport us over to the landing pad. Are we ready to go?'

Gemma had already turned back round, her professional face once more firmly in place. 'Let's go,' she said, as she headed towards the door.

Logan smiled. He picked up her bag from the floor and her jacket from the peg behind the door. 'Gemma? Forgotten something?'

'What? Oh.' Her face flushed red as she ran the few steps back and grabbed her bag and jacket. 'Thanks.'

Her hand brushed against his again. 'No problem.'

She was gone in an instant and he was left staring at his hand, at the skin she'd just touched.

There it was again. No matter how much he tried to deny it, there was no getting away from the effect Gemma had on him. It was electric.

The journey was a nightmare. By the time they'd arrived at Grace Maternity one baby had been delivered and the second was well on its way. Lynsey had been haemorrhaging significantly and they'd ended up with two lines in her veins, both pumping fluids into her.

Logan had never been so relieved to see the delivery team waiting for them as soon as they'd opened the doors of the helicopter. Lynsey was swept away on a stretcher, with an incubator and neonatologist waiting for the first baby. The second incubator was raced along the corridor after Lynsey's trolley and disappeared into the nearest theatre.

Logan stared down at his gloved hands. Even though he'd pushed his shirtsleeves out of the way they were still stained with blood. Lynsey's haemorrhaging had been severe. He only hoped this second baby could be delivered safely.

He pinged off the gloves into the nearest clinical waste bins. One of the staff at Grace gestured him towards a trolley. 'You'll get a scrub top in there. Showers are just along the corridor on your left if you want to get yourself tidied up.'

'Thanks.' He grabbed a navy scrub top and started down the corridor in the direction he'd last seen Gemma heading. They would need to make arrangements to get back to Arran. He didn't want her to think he'd just disappeared.

She was standing with her nose pressed up against the glass in the theatre door, watching the proceedings from a safe distance. She jumped as he placed a hand on her shoulder.

'Logan! Sorry, you startled me.'

'How are things going?'

She pointed through the door, 'They've already got her on a rapid transfuser. She's lost a lot of blood.'

'And the second baby?'

'Just about to be delivered.' She glanced down, first at his shirt then at her own blood-splattered one. 'Can you show me where you got that? I think I need to change too. Then I'd like to stay long enough to make sure Lynsey and the babies are okay.'

'No problem. Why don't we get changed then go for a coffee?'

She held up her bag. 'I can pay this time. Someone reminded me to bring my bag.'

They showered and changed quickly, their dirty clothes stuffed into a patient clothing bag and stored behind the reception desk to be collected on their way out.

As they made their way back along the corridor they could hear some raised voices. 'I want to see her. She's my wife. Let me in.'

Someone was speaking in a calm, quiet manner. 'I'm

sorry, sir, your wife is currently being assessed by the doctor. If you take a seat in the waiting room, someone will come and get you in a few minutes.'

Gemma froze, her steps halting in the long corridor. Logan's arm had been behind her body and it knocked into her backside. She didn't even notice. She looked shocked.

'You're not listening to me! I want to be there when my wife is being assessed. Don't you know who I am?'

Logan bristled at the angry voice. All patients' relatives could become anxious, but this was getting ridiculous. He could glimpse the older woman, who was tiny, squaring up to the large red-haired man.

'I know exactly who you are. That's why I'm telling you now to have a seat in the waiting room. If you don't do exactly as I say I'll have you removed. Have I made myself clear?' She was obviously used to dealing with difficult relatives and her diminutive size strangely only seemed to make her a more formidable force.

Logan's feet carried him closer. The man was shaking with rage. If he was going to take a swing for the nurse, Logan wanted to be ready to stop him.

The man's face was almost the same colour as his hair. After a few tense seconds he stomped down the corridor, still ranting under his breath.

Logan shook his head. 'What a prat. I bet his wife doesn't even want to see him.' He turned back to Gemma. She looked scared. She looked in shock. 'Gem? What's wrong?' He walked over and put his hands on her shoulders.

His touch seemed to spur her into action. Her legs moved quickly, pacing up the corridor and staring through the gaps in the curtains surrounding the cubicles.

She was like a woman on a mission. What on earth was she doing?

She searched through four empty cubicles then another three with patients she obviously didn't know. He could tell immediately when she'd found who she was looking for.

'Lesley!' She disappeared at once behind the curtains. A chill swept over his body. It was the way she'd said the word. She'd sounded almost...haunted.

Realisation was sweeping his body, making every tiny hair stand on end. Lesley. The friend she'd been a surrogate for.

That's why she'd stopped in mid-step in the corridor. The boorish redhead must have been Patrick. But this was a maternity hospital and Lesley couldn't have children. Did she work here? Gemma hadn't mentioned anything on the flight here.

Logan was torn. This was the thing that had pushed them apart. But no matter what his feelings on the matter, his only concern here was Gemma. He'd seen her face. He needed to be sure she was okay.

He stood at the gap in the curtains. Lesley was lying on a trolley, her face badly bruised and swollen, her abdomen revealing a pregnancy. Logan's first reaction was horror at the wounds inflicted on the pregnant woman. His second, surprise that Gemma's friend was pregnant in the first place. He'd thought she couldn't have kids.

Gemma was over in an instant, her arms wrapping around her friend's neck. 'Lesley, are you okay? What happened? Are you hurt?' She hesitated then put her hand gently on Lesley's. 'You're pregnant.' He could hear the surprise in her voice. But there was real and absolute concern in her voice. He didn't doubt how much she cared about her friend, even if they had been estranged.

Lesley didn't answer. She was sobbing. Logan turned away, not wanting to invade either of the women's privacy but wanting to make sure he was close enough to support Gemma if needed.

After a few minutes Lesley lifted her head. Her lips were burst, her nose looked as if it was broken. Purple livid bruising was appearing across her face, the tops of her arms and...around her throat. *He'd tried to strangle her?*

Logan's hands clenched into fists. His pregnant wife. And he'd tried to strangle her. It didn't matter to him that he didn't even know this woman. How dared a man do this to his wife?

His stomach curled. Gemma had been right. She'd been so right. Logan couldn't bear the thought of what Isla might have been exposed to if Gemma had handed her over to this couple.

Gemma was cradling her friend's head, slowly stroking the back of her tousled hair. 'Lesley, I'm so sorry.' She bent a little lower, shaking her head. 'Obviously, I'm happy that you're pregnant, Lesley. And I'm praying that your baby is safe. You have to tell me, is this the first time Patrick's done this?'

Lesley's sobs got louder as she shook her head. 'It's been worse since I've been pregnant. He can't stand the fact that there are things out of his control.' She put her head in her hands. 'After all those years, all those treatments, I just fell pregnant out of the blue. Then Patrick started questioning if the baby was his.'

Logan could see Gemma's shoulders start to shake. Was she going to start crying too?

Then he noticed her stance, how she was holding her body. No. Gemma was mad. Gemma was enraged.

'Have you reported him to the police, Lesley?'

'No! I can't. He's my husband. What would people think?' She shook her head fiercely. 'He's a doctor. He can't have something like this on his record.'

Gemma's voice was shaking. 'Lesley…' she pointed at Lesley's abdomen '…you have a baby to protect from a violent man. You owe it to your child to report Patrick's actions.' She lowered her voice until it was almost a whisper. 'What if he's harmed your baby, Lesley? You've waited such a long time for this. You *can't* let him harm your baby.'

There was another burst of sobs. 'They've scanned me. They think the baby is fine but I've to stay in for other treatment.'

Well, that much was obvious. The maternity staff would be determined to keep her and her baby safe. They would want to give her time to consider what had happened. They would want to give her options. It was a sad fact of life that for a lot of women domestic abuse was much more prevalent during a pregnancy.

But Lesley was still clearly trying to work through things. 'It isn't the baby he wants to hurt, Gemma. It's me. He won't touch the baby once it's here.'

Logan could see the rage build in Gemma's face, although to the outside world she appeared icily calm. Her professional demeanour meant she could say the words she should, he only hoped her personal feelings wouldn't take over.

'You don't know that for sure. Lesley, as a paediatrician, I need to tell you that your child is at risk. By raising his hands to you today he put the life of his child in danger. This is a child protection issue. The staff at this hospital will already have reported this incident to the police.'

'They need my permission!'

'No. No, they don't. They consider you, and your child, vulnerable. They have a responsibility to report this.' She placed a hand over Lesley's. 'It's time, Lesley. It's time to tell the truth about Patrick. It's time to realise he can't do this and to protect your baby.'

Her face crumpled and she knelt beside the trolley. It was clear she would try anything to get through to her friend.

'I'm sorry, I really am. But you've got to look after yourself. And you've got to look after this baby. Do you have somewhere safe you can go? Could you call your mum? I'm living on Arran now—if you want to get away from everything, you can come and stay with me.' Logan flinched at her words. Gemma had a bigger heart than he could ever have expected. She was willing to open her door to her friend in her time of need. Even though she knew it would be hard. Even though she knew that Isla would meet the woman who had been meant to be her mother.

He could hardly imagine anything more difficult. But for Gemma it seemed more important to keep the baby and Lesley safe. He shouldn't have expected anything less.

Lesley dissolved into a fit of tears, shaking her head, her hands wrapped across her stomach. 'I don't know, Gemma. I just don't know. How can I get away from Patrick? You know what he's like. I'm surprised he hasn't busted the doors down to get in here.' She started to shake. 'What if he hurts my baby, Gemma? What if he hurts my son?'

'A boy? You're having a boy?'

Lesley nodded as Gemma enveloped her in a hug. 'I am so happy for you.' She knelt beside the bed. 'Let me help you. Please, let me help you keep that baby safe.'

Her hands stroked her friend's hair. Her eyes met his. 'I have a friend with me, Lesley. A friend who will help. If we can get you the all-clear, we can whisk you out of here tonight. Take you back to Arran with us. You can have a few days to decide what you want to do.'

Lesley's voice was shaking. 'I think I want to go home. I think I want to go home to my mum in Uist.'

Uist. One of the other Scottish islands. She'd need to try and get her a flight from Glasgow to Benbecula. It would take some organising.

Gemma nodded and took a deep breath. 'Then come home with me. I'll arrange your travel.'

Lesley was shaking. 'What about Patrick? What about my things?'

Gemma shook her head. 'There's nothing you can't replace. We'll get your things. Just not right now.' She gave her friend another hug. 'Let me go and speak to the sister. Let me try and find out what's safe for you, and for the baby.'

She turned towards Logan and walked towards him. He could tell by the expression on her face that it was taking every ounce of self-control she had just to hold herself together.

She could have said so much more. She hadn't even mentioned Isla. She hadn't even mentioned the fact that five years before her friend had contemplated taking her baby into an environment where Isla could have been at risk. He could only imagine how much was circling around in her brain right now.

Lesley was the victim here. They both knew that.

But even Logan couldn't hide his feelings of anger at what Isla could have been exposed to. It made his blood run cold. He didn't know Lesley. He hadn't been her friend. But if it had been Gemma lying on that bed, could he have been so rational and self-contained?

Not a chance.

He admired her self-control.

He took a few steps backwards down the corridor and held out his arms to her as she almost collapsed into them. He moved her further along the corridor, away from Lesley's cubicle and into one of the side rooms.

Her whole body was shaking. She couldn't stop it.

Logan was consumed with guilt. She'd been right.

The hunch. The bad feeling. The uncomfortable vibes.

Every instinct of hers had been correct. Why had he ever doubted her?

Logan settled at the edge of one of the chairs in the room and just let Gemma sob. Stroking her hair, just the way she'd done for her friend a few moments before. After a few minutes she lifted her head. He couldn't help it, he acted on instinct. He dropped a gentle kiss on her lips.

But he'd mistimed it. He'd totally misjudged the situation. What he'd meant as a sign of comfort hadn't been perceived that way. She looked mad. Logan could practically see the sparks jump from her eyes.

'Isla could have been there. Isla could have had that life.' Her whole body was shaking with rage. Her mind was totally focused on one thing, and one thing alone.

The truth was he couldn't blame her. He could almost imagine feeling exactly the same way.

He nodded. 'I know, Gemma. You were right. You were right to take her away. You were right to fight. I should never have doubted you.'

He lifted his hands and touched her shaking arms, trying to calm her, trying to stop the surge of adrenaline that was coursing through her body. The pain in her eyes was torturous.

'But you've no idea, Logan. No idea how much I doubted myself. No idea how much I struggled over that decision. Even when we fought the other week— you made me feel I had been wrong. I was doubting myself all over again.' She was starting to panic.

He gripped her firmly by the shoulders. 'But you weren't wrong, Gemma. You weren't. And I shouldn't have doubted you.'

She could hardly get a breath. He looked around the room. Should he try and find a paper bag for her to breathe into? 'Take it easy,' he said quietly, 'take some slow, deep breaths.' He kept his voice steady, calm, willing it to have an effect on her.

He was watching the rise and fall of her chest beneath the thin scrub top she had changed into. He lifted his hand from her shoulder and placed it on the side of her cheek. He could feel the pulse throbbing wildly at the side of her neck. Her heart was racing.

'Look at me, Gemma.' She was all over the place right now, and he had to calm her down. Get her back to him.

Their eyes met and he nodded then took a long, deep breath. 'Watch me, Gemma. Breathe with me. Slowly. In, out. In, out.'

For a few seconds her breathing continued in the same

manner, frantic, panting, then she eventually started to follow his lead. In. Out. In. Out. Slow. Steady.

Her eyes were still fixed on his, her hand lifting and covering the hand he had at the side of her face.

Everything he'd said had been wrong. Everything he'd done had been wrong. But being here, now, with Gemma was everything that felt right.

Nothing could be clearer in his mind. He didn't ever want to be without her.

Something flitted across her eyes. Her breathing had calmed, her pulse had stopped racing. She started to shake her head. 'I'm so angry at her, Logan,' she whispered. 'I'm so angry that she was going to take Isla into that environment and say nothing—and do nothing to protect her.' Her voice was trembling again. 'How could she? How could she let that happen?' Her voice started to break. 'And I can't say that to anyone, can I?'

But Gemma couldn't stop. 'I know she's the victim. I know that.' She pressed her hand to her heart. 'So why am I so annoyed with her?'

Logan nodded. 'You can say it. You can say it to me between these four walls. And then I want you to lift your head up and walk down the corridor with me and we'll both do what we can to help your friend. You've got to put this aside. She's taken the first step to leave an abusive relationship and protect her child.'

He twisted his fingers in her hair. 'It makes perfect sense to you and me. But it's hard for her. And we can't do anything to upset her.' He cradled her head against his chest. 'You're not the only one who's angry. The thought of Isla being exposed to that…' His voice tailed off and he took a deep breath. 'Right now, I could easily go to the waiting room and knock Patrick into next week. And if he gets in our way—I might.'

Gemma lifted her head and nodded it slowly. It was clear she was struggling so much with this. Her sympathy for her friend was being overwhelmed by her own mothering instinct to protect her child and keep her safe. Lesley had threatened that for her. And right now it was obviously too much to handle.

He pulled her a little closer towards him. 'What do you say we go and check on Lynsey and her babies? We need to phone home to Arran to let Edith know how things are. Once we've done that we'll speak to the sister here. If we can magic Lesley out of here tonight, we should.' He wanted to get her out of here. He wanted to get her away from this. The last thing he wanted was for her to come face to face with Patrick. He couldn't be responsible for his actions then.

'Home,' Gemma repeated. She still sounded a bit detached. Her hands came up and rested on his chest. He thought for a second she was going to wrap them around the back of his neck, but instead she pushed him away. 'I don't know if Arran can be my home.'

'What do you mean?' The words shocked him. Gemma and Isla had seemed to settle on the island so quickly. Where had this come from?

Everything about her seemed a little different. Her whole persona seemed detached. As if this was the only way she could deal with all this. 'I don't know how I feel about that any more. I don't know if we can keep working together, Logan. You didn't believe me. You judged me. I'm not prepared to be judged. Not by you, or anyone else on the island.'

She was upset. He knew she was upset. 'Gemma, I

said I'm sorry. I know I was wrong. Don't make any hasty decisions. Isla loves the island. She loves my mum—and my mum loves her. Don't uproot her because we've had a fight.'

Gemma shook her head. 'It's not just you. Arran's a small island, and word spreads fast. I have no idea how people will react when they find out the truth about me and I just don't feel the urge to defend myself at every turn. I don't think I should have to. What if they're like you? What if they think I was wrong?'

He tried to wrap his arms around her again but she shook her head.

A strange sensation was sweeping across his chest. He was starting to feel desperate. An experience that was all new. Because even in the midst of any emergency Logan Scott was always calm.

This was a whole new range of emotions for him. He'd been frustrated about his sister. Frustrated that he hadn't recognised her deteriorating condition first and acted on it. But he'd never felt like this. Never felt as if he couldn't breathe. Never felt as if everything was out of his control.

'Gemma, wait. Don't be hasty. There's only one more week to go. After that Sam Allan should be well enough to take up some duties again and you can reduce your hours at the surgery. You can start doing the paediatric job you came here to do.' He held his hands out towards her.

'You've already met some of the children that you'll need to see. You know how much we need a paediatrician. Don't think about walking away. Isla's just about to start school. She's excited already. She's got her uniform and her school shoes. I've bought her the school satchel she wanted. It should be here any day now. She's met her teacher and made some friends who'll be in her class.' He shook his head fiercely and pressed his hand against his chest.

'This is my fault, Gemma. *My fault.* Not yours. Not Isla's. Patrick's already destroyed your friend's life. Don't let him destroy yours too.'

He couldn't say out loud what he desperately wanted to. Every cell in his body was screaming 'self-preservation' at him, and the only way he could do that was to keep the feelings that were bubbling over in his heart to himself.

He couldn't tell her he would be devastated if she and Isla left the island. He couldn't tell her how much he would miss them. He could only hope she would see, and feel, what was bubbling under the surface.

But Gemma still had the strange detached look on her face. And he recognised it as her own self-preservation mode. 'Leave it, Logan. Leave me alone. I need some time to think. I need some time to decide what to do.' And she turned and walked away.

Logan was shocked. They were in the middle of Glasgow, miles away from Arran. Was she even going to come back?

He should have said it. He should have said the extra words. *Patrick's already destroyed your friend's life. Don't let him destroy yours too.* And don't let him destroy mine. Because I don't know how I can live without you both. I love you, you and Isla.

But he hadn't. He hadn't said it out loud.

He lifted his finger to his lips. Had that been the last kiss they would ever share?

CHAPTER TEN

SHE PUT THE phone down as an email pinged into her inbox. The last patient had just left. Only two emergencies today. Maybe she would get the chance to do some referral letters and review some test results. She hadn't been expecting a quiet day so this was perfect.

She leaned back in the chair. She was starting to calm down again, relax. Meeting Lesley again—and seeing what Patrick had done to her—had been an absolute shock to her system. Bringing Lesley back with her had been harder than she could ever have imagined.

Both of them had struggled with it. Lesley had spent most of the time in tears. And they hadn't talked—not properly. They probably never would. It was hardly the time to vent her hidden anger at her friend for hiding the abuse and protecting Patrick for so long.

She'd learned a hard enough lesson and Gemma couldn't add to it.

By tomorrow Lesley would be gone. Logan had offered to drive her to Glasgow Airport and wait with her until she boarded the flight to Benbecula. It was only eight miles away from Uist and she would be home. Safe, with a family who would protect her.

What had surprised her most was how angry she'd felt

about it all. How angry she'd felt with Lesley—the victim—for not taking steps to protect herself and her baby. Even thinking about it sent a cold shiver down her spine.

That could have been Isla. That could have been her baby. A defenceless child in an environment with…goodness knows what. She hadn't slept a wink that night. She hadn't slept a wink because of the sea of what-ifs that had floated around her head.

'What if' she'd been overcome with guilt and handed Isla over? 'What if' she'd then had concerns and hadn't been able to do anything to protect her daughter or her friend? 'What if' something had happened to either one of them? No wonder she'd spent the whole night tossing and turning.

And the only person she felt as if she could talk to about it all was the one person she'd taken her temper out on. Logan may have judged her, but he'd admitted he hadn't understood the circumstances. He'd apologised. And he'd tried his best to support her that day.

He'd arranged transport for them all back to Arran. He'd practically carried Lesley from the hospital and into a waiting car to drive them back to Ardrossan. He'd arranged for some policemen to go to her home and pick up some of her things. All without saying a word to her.

But she'd pushed him away. She had been unable to deal with the pity in his eyes, or the way he'd looked as if he'd wanted to protect her. All she had been able to think about had been her own failings. How many things she could have done differently. Ways in which she could have done something to support the friend she'd more or less abandoned.

That first night, after she'd finally got home to Arran and she'd settled Lesley in, she'd brought Isla into her bed and just held her all night. It was something that rarely happened. Usually the only time Isla ended up in bed with her was if she was sick. But Gemma had just felt the need to hold her that night. To hold her and never let her go.

The last two nights she'd spent a few minutes watching her from the corridor as she'd slept. Her little chest rising and falling peacefully, without a care in the world. Logan had been right. Isla loved it here. And she was thriving.

Her relationship with Mrs Scott was priceless. They were like two identical personalities at opposite ends of the age spectrum. She'd had a few doubts about staying here on that day. She'd been scared. Scared that people might judge her like Logan had.

But she had to think positively. She was looking forward to starting her paediatric hours soon. Sam Allan would be returning to the practice, and Harry Burns would be well enough in a few weeks to decorate her house.

And the house? The house was perfect. She could spend a lazy evening looking out over the Firth of Clyde and drinking a glass of wine. It might be a little lonely at times, but she had no idea what would happen in the future.

She ran her hand along her arms. Her hairs were standing on end, and she knew exactly why. Logan. He'd just appeared in her brain and her body was having an instant reaction.

Logan Scott. The island bachelor. Would he ever look for something else?

The connection between them felt so real. So instant. So alive.

Isla talked about him all the time. They seemed to

have made an easy connection. Could she hope for anything else?

She'd seen Claire again yesterday. She'd been at Mrs Scott's house when Gemma had gone to pick Isla up. She'd told Gemma about being turned down by the adoption agency.

It had been heartbreaking. Gemma had seen the longing in her eyes as she'd watched Isla play with her mother. But when she'd asked a few questions about how she was feeling and her mood, Claire had been quite open to Gemma's suggestion that they talk some time.

So maybe things would work out for Claire. And maybe Logan's guilt would finally be appeased.

Gemma lifted her nose in the air. She could smell coffee. And scones. She'd need to be quick. These things never lasted in a busy practice like this.

She turned back to face the screen and clicked open the email. Her friend Lottie. She'd marked it urgent. Odd. She hadn't spoken to Lottie in the last few weeks.

Gemma's heart fell as soon as she saw what it contained.

No. Please, no. She put her hand over her mouth. She felt sick.

Not now. Not this. Just when she'd finally thought she could relax and draw breath.

It seemed as if life on Arran had just slipped out of her grasp.

Logan finished his run and headed towards the shop. He didn't like to break his routine. After an on-call last night when he hadn't got a wink of sleep, this was a precious morning off. He still hadn't slept, though.

By the time he'd finished at the hospital the early

morning sun had just been rising above the waves. It was a perfect time for a sail. Two hours out on the open sea followed by a run along the nearby beaches and main road.

It was supposed to be a chance for him to get his thoughts in order. To plan an approach to Gemma and what on earth he was going to say.

His feet slowed as he approached the newsagent's. The morning paper and some fresh rolls and he'd be all set.

He noticed straight away that something was wrong. The local Scottish red-top was missing from the stack of papers lined up on the shelves. Sometimes there were problems with the deliveries to Arran, it wasn't that unusual.

But what was unusual was that every other paper was up to date and on the shelf.

'What's wrong, Fred? Delivery not arrived yet?' He picked up his usual paper and a bag with four rolls and set them down on the counter.

Fred looked as if he'd swallowed a rat. His face was twisted and fierce. He folded his arms across his chest. 'Best not to sell it today.'

Logan looked up. He hadn't really been paying much attention, but now his interest was definitely piqued. Fred, in protest about something? Seemed unusual.

'Why not?'

Fred screwed up his face even further. His head gestured with a nod to the pile behind the counter at his feet. 'Don't want to upset the new doc.'

Logan's eyes widened and he reached down behind the counter and grabbed the nearest paper.

Oh, no. He let out an expletive.

Bad surrogate in emergency visit to her pregnant ex-best friend.

He couldn't believe any journalist had actually got hold of the story. That had been a few days ago.

He scanned the rest of the article. No mention of Lynsey Black and her babies. They obviously hadn't made the connection with the helicopter. Thank goodness. But someone had made the connection between Lesley, Patrick and Gemma.

There was even a picture—albeit a pretty fuzzy one that didn't really capture Gemma's true beauty. But it did list a lot of information about her. Like the fact she was Arran's new paediatrician, and that she had moved to the island with her daughter Isla, and the fact she was working in the GP practice on the island. How on earth had they got all that information?

Logan could barely read the rest, and it was just as well as it made his blood boil. The tear-jerking story of Gemma stealing Patrick and Lesley's baby—with no mention of the fact she was Isla's biological mother.

Then a further huge story about Lesley's 'miracle' pregnancy, and the minor 'incident' that had caused Lesley to end up in hospital and Patrick led away in handcuffs. Funnily enough, there was no picture of that.

Or of the damage to Lesley's face and throat, or the potential damage to the unborn child. Worse than anything, it mentioned some vague remark about Lesley being 'elsewhere'. Logan fumed. It wouldn't take a genius to work out what that meant—especially when they'd given so much other information about Gemma.

If she'd been feeling unsure about staying on Arran before, how was she going to feel about this?

Logan's stomach churned. He had to speak to her. He

had to warn her. Fred had been kind enough to hide the papers, but not every newsagent on the island would do that, and word would spread quickly.

Logan threw some coins on the counter. 'Thank you, Fred. Thanks for this. I'll go and speak to Gemma now.'

He jogged along the seafront towards the surgery. There was no time to go and get changed. He couldn't even think about that right now. All he could think about was getting to Gemma and warning her. Getting to her and letting her know that all the partners in the practice would support her—no matter what the press said.

He jogged inside, walked over to Gemma's room and gave a little knock on the door before entering.

Gemma didn't even notice him. Her eyes were fixed on the screen in front of her and tears were pouring down her cheeks. It didn't take him long to notice that the front page of the red-top in his hand was currently showing on her screen.

He sat down next to her and pulled his seat closer, his hand reaching over to encompass hers. Her hand was freezing, so he lifted it from the desk and rubbed it between his own. 'Gemma, are you okay?'

Her mobile was on the desk next to them and it buzzed. He looked down. Unknown caller. His heart lurched. Undoubtedly it would be the press. Without even waiting for her response, he pressed reject. Ten missed calls and twenty-two texts.

She wasn't moving. Oh, she was breathing, he could see the rise and fall of her chest. But she looked as if she was stunned.

He spun her chair round so she was facing him, then lifted his hands to either side of her face. He hated to see her like this. 'Gemma?'

She blinked. More tears flooded down her face. 'What if someone says something to Isla?' she whispered.

And that was why he loved her. Even in the midst of all this, her thoughts were for her daughter. She was her first priority. Just as it should be.

'You're finished for the day here. Let's go home. Let's go home to Isla.' He leaned over and switched off her computer, taking her hand and pulling her up towards him.

She noticed the paper in his hand. 'Is that why you came here?'

He nodded. 'I wanted to make sure you were okay.' He wrapped his arms around her, pulling her closer to his chest. 'You know, Gemma, Fred Jones wouldn't even put the papers out to sell. You're just here and there are already people on the island who feel protective towards you—who look at the rubbish printed in rags like this and know without a doubt that it won't be true.'

He felt her give a little sob as her head rested against his chest. 'This was supposed to be a clean start for me and Isla. I knew eventually that people would find out, I just didn't expect it to be so soon.'

His fingers ran through her hair. 'How did you find out? Did someone call you?' It hadn't looked as though she'd answered any of her calls or texts.

She shook her head. 'One of my friends emailed me with the link to the press story. It was apparently re-leased in the early hours of the morning. She wanted to forewarn me. She saw the way I was treated last time, and wanted to make sure I didn't answer my phone this morning to some reporter.'

'You should have phoned me.'

She lifted her tear-stained face towards his. 'Why? So

you could tell me that the patients wouldn't want to see me? So you could tell me it would be better if I didn't do any hours at the practice?'

'Is that what you think?' He shook his head fiercely. 'Gemma, don't doubt for a second that I'll stand behind you all the way here. So will all the partners in this practice.'

The phone started ringing and he picked it up immediately. 'What? Where? You're joking. At Gemma's house? Call John Kerr.' He grabbed Gemma's car keys from the desk.

'What? What is it?'

He shook his head. 'It's Patrick. He came over on the first ferry. Someone who did read the paper this morning recognised him. He's headed to your house.'

'Oh, no. Lesley.'

Logan's feet were already running through the surgery and pounding across the car park. He couldn't depend on the local policeman getting there in time. For all he knew, John Kerr was on the other side of the island. He flung open the door and jumped inside, Gemma throwing herself into the passenger seat. He gunned the car, and it screeched out of the car park.

Thank goodness Isla was safely out of the way. She was at his mother's.

Five minutes. That's all it would take to get to Gemma's house.

He just hoped they wouldn't be too late.

The door to Gemma's house was lying wide open. One of the local taxi drivers was standing in her driveway, looking aghast. He held up his hands. 'What's going on? He just shot straight into your house.'

But Logan was already in front of her, thudding up the corridor in the direction of a loud, piercing shriek.

Patrick hadn't even reached Lesley. She'd dropped the cup she'd been holding as he'd burst through the kitchen door. Logan barrelled into him from behind, taking him unawares and dropping him in a rugby tackle.

Legs and arms flew. It took Logan a few seconds before he could finally land a punch. Gemma winced as she heard something crack. She rushed over to Lesley and pulled her from the kitchen and back towards the front door. 'Come with me.'

'But Patrick…' she started. Her eyes were wide with fear. She was terrified. It was clear she'd never thought he would find her. And he wouldn't have, if the press hadn't put it in the papers.

Patrick's face was getting redder by the second. 'Don't you dare move!' he screamed at Lesley as he wrestled with Logan.

They rolled, and for a second Patrick was on top of Logan, almost escaping from his grasp as he dived towards them. But Logan wasn't letting go. He was holding on for all he was worth, the veins in his neck standing out as his knuckles turned white.

Gemma didn't think twice. She picked up the vase of flowers from the hall and smashed it over Patrick's head.

For a second there was silence. The taxi driver had tentatively ventured his way into the house. 'Thought you might have needed a hand, Doc. But it seems like Doc Gemma's got it all under control.' He held out his arms towards Lesley. 'Come with me, love. Let's get you out of here.'

Lesley nodded numbly, taking his hands and following him outside.

Gemma started shaking. She dropped to her knees and put her hand to the side of Patrick's neck. His pulse was there. His chest was rising and falling with his breathing.

Logan rolled out from under him, pushing himself to his feet and wrapping his arms around her. 'Remind me not to get on the wrong side of you,' he whispered in her ear.

She couldn't stop the tremble in her hands. 'I didn't even think. I just acted.'

Logan looked down at Patrick on the kitchen floor. Luckily, he'd almost landed in the recovery position. 'He's not going anywhere right now. Once the police arrive we'll check him over at the hospital. Come on, Gemma. Let's sit down.'

Fifteen minutes later everything was under control. Patrick had been removed by the police to the local hospital and Lesley was being checked over by Edith.

Gemma sat on her doorstep with her head in her hands. She still hadn't stopped shaking.

Logan put his arm around her shoulders and edged onto the step next to her. 'It's fine, Gemma. It's over. Take a deep breath.'

She shook her head. 'But it's not over. Look what was in the paper about me today. Even those that didn't read it…' she held out her hand '…will hear about this. What are people going to think about me? I came to Arran to get away from all this, not bring it with me. I should have known something would happen.' She winced.

'Isla's just about to start school. You know how cruel children can be. Can you imagine what the other kids might say to her?' He could sense she was getting agitated as she started to talk quicker and quicker. 'She's so excited about school. She's got her school uniform and everything. Now I should probably take her away. Go somewhere else where people won't associate us with the news. The last thing I want is for Isla to be bullied because of my actions.'

Logan took a deep breath and pressed his hands down on her shoulders. He couldn't even compute the thought of Gemma and Isla moving away. He would do anything to stop that happening. He had to make her see sense.

'Gemma, stop it. None of this is your fault. You're not going to go anywhere. You're going to stay here on Arran, with me. You've already moved Isla once. She's started to settle on Arran. She's met new friends, and she loves her new house. You can't disrupt all that for her again. No one's going to bully her at school. I'll speak to the headmistress. I'll make sure.'

Gemma looked up at him. There was confusion in her dark brown eyes.

'What? What is it, Gemma?'

'What do you mean?'

'Mean about what?'

'You just said…you wanted us to stay here…with you.' Her eyes were wide.

He felt his heart jump. He'd said the words out loud without even thinking twice. There hadn't been a second's hesitation. He lifted his hand up and stroked his finger down her cheek. 'I mean it, Gemma. I don't want you and Isla to go anywhere. I want you both to stay here, on Arran, with me. If you want to, that is.'

'I don't get it, Logan. Since when did you want this?'

He gave her a smile. 'Oh, since I caught a glimpse of some pink satin underwear.'

Even in the midst of the tensest moment he wanted to

see her laugh. He wanted to see her smile. The corners of her lips moved up by the tiniest amount.

He could tell she still wasn't convinced.

'Gemma, I don't want you to go anywhere. I don't want Isla to go anywhere. I've never enjoyed being bossed about by a woman so much in my life!'

This time the corners of her lips definitely turned upwards. 'She does like to be in charge.'

'She certainly does.'

Gemma shook her head and held her hands up. 'How can I stay now? I know I'm only supposed to cover here one day a week. But look what's happened.' She held up her hands and used an age-old Scottish expression. 'I'll be the talk of the steamie.'

He smiled and held up the red-topped paper that was lying crumpled next to the doorway. 'This, Gemma? This is tomorrow's fish and chip paper. And as for the steamie? I've been the talk of it for years. I'm glad of the company.'

'But what about the patients? Some of them might not want to see me. And that could harm the smooth running of the practice.'

Logan took a deep breath. 'Gemma, do you think for one minute that every patient who comes into the surgery wants to see me?' He shook his head firmly. 'Julie knows the people who don't want to see me. Some—because they've known me since I was a boy. Some—because I'm a male. And some because they just plain don't like me. And that's fine. That's general practice for you.' He laughed.

'One woman doesn't want to see me because she says my signature is like a five-year-old's! We all have circumstances like these, Gemma. And it works both ways. Sam Allan has a list of patients he doesn't *want* to see!'

Her eyes widened. 'You're joking, right? You're just saying that to make me feel better.'

Logan shook his head. 'Go and ask Julie. I guarantee you, she'll tell you the same thing.' He pulled her closer. 'This will all pass. Today is just the worst day. Tomorrow it will get a little better.' He pulled her even closer, running his fingers through her hair, 'By next week it will mostly be forgotten.'

Her head turned towards his touch. He couldn't let her go. He just couldn't.

'Do you really think so?'

'I really think so. Please, don't even think about leaving. I've only just started to get to know my new family.'

Her head jerked upwards. 'Your what?'

He smiled. 'My new family.' He bent down and whispered in her ear, 'Between you and me, I think they're currently auditioning me, and my family, to see if we'll be a good fit together.'

'What are you saying, Logan?' She smiled up at him, her brown eyes looking reassured for the first time.

'I'm saying that I want to audition.'

'For what role?'

He ran his finger down her cheek. 'For the boyfriend role...' his finger caught a lock of her hair and he twirled it around his finger '...maybe turning into a fiancé.'

She hesitated. 'And what else?' He could tell her voice was about to crack.

'For a potential dad—only if I come up to scratch, of course, and then eventually, maybe, a husband. And a shot at being a dad again if it all works out.' Then he dropped his head and whispered in her ear again, 'Providing, of course, Isla lets us. Because we both know who the boss is.'

He could see the breath catching in her throat. He wasn't letting her go. It had been hard enough to say the words, he definitely wanted to see her response.

His breath was caught halfway up his chest. His whole life rested on these next few moments.

Gemma blinked. He could see the hesitation in her eyes. 'Why me, Logan? Why us? You've been a bachelor for years. What's changed?'

His hand cradled the back of her head. 'Who says I wanted to be a bachelor? Up until six weeks ago I just hadn't met the right woman.'

'And now you have?'

He nodded. 'And now I have. Better than that. I've met two of them.'

'How do you know, Logan?' She wasn't going to make this easy for him. And so she shouldn't. She had a little girl to think about. And he knew that Isla was the most precious thing in the world to her.

He smiled. Nothing was more important than saying the right words. It was time to lay his heart on the line. Something he'd never done before. He'd never had reason to. Not like this.

He took her hand and pressed it against his chest. 'I know because I wake up in the morning and you're the first thing I think about. It doesn't matter that I've spent most of the night dreaming about you. You're still the first thing on my mind. I know because every time I have a conversation with Isla she reminds me so much of you. Every word, every characteristic, every expression.'

Gemma looked surprised. 'Really?'

He nodded. 'Really. She's a complete hybrid. Like a cross between you and my mother. A lethal combination!'

Her brown eyes fixed on his. 'And you want to take that on?'

He put his hands on her shoulders. 'I want to take you *both* on. If you'll let me.'

Gemma started to smile again. 'Isla's had a lot of change in her life recently—a new house, new friends, a new island. And she's just about to start school. It's a lot for a little girl.' She let out a sigh. 'I'm just thankful she missed out on everything today.'

He nodded. 'So am I. And we'll take things slowly. That's why you should let me audition. You can both decide if I should get the role.'

Gemma heaved in a huge breath. He understood. He really did. After everything she'd been through she needed to feel in control. And that was fine with him.

She looked up at him through her dark lashes. There was a twinkle in her eye, as if she was finally satisfied with his words. Her arms wound up around his neck. 'And what happens if I agree to let you audition?'

He smiled. 'In that case, there are certain things we should start practising right away.'

'Such as?'

'This,' he said, as he bent to kiss her.

EPILOGUE

'ARE WE READY, Mummy?'

Isla was jumping up and down, her three-quarter-length dress bouncing around her ankles.

Gemma took one last quick glance in the mirror. Veil up or veil down? She still couldn't decide. She pulled it back again at the last minute. She wanted to look Logan straight in the eye as they said their vows. There should be nothing between them.

Except, of course, a small bump, currently hidden behind a pale green sash around her cream gown. The colour had been picked by Isla, her dress the same colour as the sash. She was the only bridesmaid after all.

Two years. That's how long she'd made him audition for. She glanced down at the diamond on her hand. It hadn't taken him long to give her an engagement ring, but extending the house for them to stay in, along with the extra rooms they'd now need, had taken a little longer.

The doorbell sounded. They weren't doing things the traditional way. She and Logan had decided to travel to the church together, with Isla, as a family.

She opened the door nervously, wondering what Logan would say. But his face was a picture and he swept her up into his arms instantly. 'You look gorgeous.' He bent to kiss her.

'Careful, Logan, you'll spoil Mummy's lipstick.'

He leaned back. 'Well, we can't have that, can we?' He picked up Isla. 'Shall we go out to the car together?'

'Is it a big car?'

He opened the door. 'The biggest.'

Gemma smiled and picked up her bouquet of cream roses and pale green leaves. The church was so close they could have walked, but Logan had insisted they go in the 'wedding car' for Arran. An old Bentley owned by one of his patients.

It only took a few minutes and on this beautiful summer's day it seemed as if half the population on the island had made their way to the local church.

Gemma stepped out of the car and gave a quick hug to Claire, her soon-to-be sister-in-law. She was so much better now and ready to start to explore the surrogacy option of having children. She already knew about Gemma and Logan's little secret and had been delighted for them both.

Lesley was standing near the door, holding the hand of a chubby toddler. By her side was her soon-to-be husband. A definite improvement on Patrick.

Logan was by her side as friends and family shouted greetings to them as they walked towards the church. Everything was just perfect.

He turned around and held out his hand. 'Ready, Mrs Scott?'

She smiled at his joke. 'Ready, Mr Halliday,' she countered, as she put her hand in his and walked towards her future.

* * * * *

RETURN OF
DR MAGUIRE

BY
JUDY CAMPBELL

Published in Great Britain 2014
by Mills & Boon, an imprint of Harlequin (UK) Limited,
Eton House, 18-24 Paradise Road, Richmond, Surrey, TW9 1SR

© 2014 Judy Campbell

ISBN: 978 0 263 90764 3

Harlequin (UK) Limited's policy is to use papers that are natural,
renewable and recyclable products and made from wood grown in
sustainable forests. The logging and manufacturing processes conform
to the legal environmental regulations of the country of origin.

Printed and bound in Spain
by Blackprint CPI, Barcelona

Dear Reader

Sometimes our first impressions of people are wrong! I have jumped to conclusions too soon about people I've met in the past, and I thought it would be interesting to explore my heroine's initial response to Lachlan and her gradual understanding of his character because of his past history.

I've set this story, as I do many of my books, in Scotland—a place I love—and I hope you like the setting. It was fun to write—I hope you enjoy it too!

Best wishes

Judy

Dedication

To Donald, patient and long-suffering
when the muse deserts me—my very own hero!

CHAPTER ONE

'I JUST DO not believe it!' muttered Christa Lennox. 'What the hell is that man doing?'

Titan, the Border terrier, lying at the foot of Christa's desk, sprang up and looked at her enquiringly with head cocked to one side.

'Don't bark, Titan!' she warned him sternly.

She opened the window and leaned forward to get a better view of the opposite wall, squinting through the dancing shadows of the trees nearby. Her gaze was riveted on a man perched precariously at the top of a ladder, hacking away at the guttering and filling a sack suspended from a rung.

Yet another thieving toerag trying to take what he could—and in broad daylight too! Well, she'd darned well show him he wasn't going to get away with it—two burglaries in a fortnight were two too many! On top of the tragedy of dear Isobel dying so suddenly three weeks ago, it was just all too much...

Christa swung away from the surgery window and raced through Reception, closely followed by Titan. She ran towards the ladder at the side of the car park, her auburn hair escaping from its clips and springing out in a mad bob. No point in ringing the police on a Sunday—it would take hours for them to come.

She and Titan skidded to a halt at the bottom of the ladder.

'If you're trying to nick lead from the roof, you're too late—it's all gone!' she yelled up at the man. 'Get down now, or I'll call the police!'

Titan joined in by barking ferociously and adding an extra growl or two for good measure. The man twisted round and looked down, frowning. He had tied a large handkerchief round his lower face so that only his eyes were visible. Trying to remain anonymous, thought Christa scornfully. 'Titan! Titan! Be quiet!' she commanded.

The dog lay down, panting with its tongue lolling out, and watched her adoringly. The man's glance flicked over to Christa, slowly taking in her angry upturned face and sweeping over her indignant figure.

There was a pause before he said rather irritably, 'Well—what is it?'

Christa, put her hands on her hips. 'I want to know what on earth you're doing up there!'

He raised an eyebrow. 'Excuse me?'

'Could you tell me why you're on the roof?'

The man leaned on the ladder, a flash of annoyance in the clear blue eyes that met hers, then whipped the handkerchief from his face, revealing tanned good looks and an irritated expression.

'Not that it's anything to do with you, but I'm examining the guttering—it looks as if it's on its last legs.'

Christa wasn't to be put off. 'Examining the guttering, my foot!' she said angrily. 'Come down now!' she ordered. 'I can't carry on a conversation when you're up there!'

He shrugged, half-amused. 'Oh, for God's sake...of all the bossy women...' He descended the ladder, leaping lightly down the last three rungs, and the little dog sprang up and would have thrown himself at the man's legs if Christa hadn't grabbed his collar.

'Don't worry, Titan—I can handle this...'

Titan sank back unwillingly and Christa turned back to the man and demanded peremptorily, 'Well? What have you got to say for yourself?'

He leaned against the wall in front of her with hands stuffed into his pockets, his eyes narrowed, ranging coolly over her. 'Do you always sound like a headmistress? Now just what's bugging you?'

A moment's doubt—could this guy *really* be a thief? He seemed so assured, so...brazen. Surely a thief would have taken off by now? He stared at her boldly, and she decided that he was just bluffing it out, conning her into thinking he was a legitimate builder.

Christa drew herself up to her full five feet six inches and said majestically, 'I want to know what excuse you've got to give for this daylight robbery—taking a chance because it's a Sunday and the place is empty, I'll bet!'

He laughed out loud and Christa blinked. He didn't seem a whit worried by her threat to call the police or her accusation—in fact, he looked totally relaxed, in charge of the situation, no sign of being intimidated. She glared at him, looking him straight in the eye, and he stared impudently back at her, making fun of her. The cheeky bastard!

She shouldn't have looked at his eyes—massive error! She was taken aback by their compelling shade of deep, clear blue, fringed with black lashes and…well, they were incredibly unusual…even sexy—which, of course, was nothing to do with the situation whatsoever, she thought irritably.

The man had a tall, spare figure, dressed in faded shorts and a ripped shirt, revealing a muscled torso. He could have got a job playing the lead in a James Bond movie or doing ads for some exotic men's shaving lotion, reflected Christa… And for a split nanosecond she felt an unexpected flutter of excitement somewhere in the region of her stomach.

It took her unawares, made her cross because after her experience with Colin Maitland, she was off all men for a very long time, wasn't she? She crushed the desolate, empty feeling that seemed to be a reflex action whenever she thought of that unmitigated rat, and told herself to stop reacting like a teenager being turned on by some celebrity just because the man in front of her was reasonably good looking.

She cleared her throat and said sternly, 'If you're not pinching lead, who gave you permission to look at the guttering—if that's what you were doing?'

'I don't have to ask anyone's permission—I own the house.'

She stared at him witheringly. 'You *own* the house? Don't be ridiculous! How can it belong to you? Dr Maguire only died three weeks ago and probate can't have been granted yet.'

He said quietly and without apparent emotion, 'Isobel Maguire was my mother. She left me Ardenleigh in her will.'

'Oh, my God…' Christa's hand flew to her mouth, her eyes wide with embarrassment. 'I'm really sorry—I didn't realise…' Her voice faltered, and she gazed at him in a stunned way. So *this* was the mysterious son, Lachlan, that Isobel had rarely mentioned, and who, as far as she was aware, had never visited his mother…

'Perhaps you should make sure of your facts before making accusations,' the man suggested coldly, an edge of sarcasm to his voice.

'I had no idea who you were. If you'd let us know you were coming I wouldn't have leaped to conclusions when I saw you with a handkerchief over your face on the roof,' she protested, slightly stung that he was putting all the blame on her for not knowing who he was. 'We've had such a spate of burglaries I thought you were yet another thief.'

He nodded rather wearily, pushing his spikily cut thick hair back from his forehead. 'The handkerchief was to protect my lungs from the showers of dirt I was disturbing—but, yes, I guess you're right. I should have told the practice I was coming. It's all been a bit of a rush.'

Her tone softened. 'We knew Isobel had a son, but we had no idea where you lived…'

'I flew in from Australia on Friday and came up from Heathrow yesterday. I stayed in a pub last night, but tonight I'll stay here if there's a habitable room.'

'You couldn't make it to her funeral?'

'No,' he said curtly. 'It was too late by the time I was contacted by her solicitor—I didn't even know she'd died until a few days ago.'

Christa bit her lip. How could she have been so tactless? It was shocking that no one had known how to find him to tell him about his mother. He must feel terrible about that.

'I'm so sorry…' she repeated, and her voice trailed off,

but the man had turned his attention back to the building. Christa looked at him more closely. Now she knew who he was, she saw the family resemblance to his mother, who had also been tall and with those clear blue eyes. There was no doubt he had inherited the good looks that ran in the Maguire family.

The man looked sadly at the vast untidy lawn, the dense undergrowth beneath the trees at the end of the garden. 'Everywhere looks very neglected... When I was young the garden was always immaculate, and that little copse well managed. I guess my mother had no interest in the place.'

'She was too busy,' said Christa defensively. 'Isobel's work meant everything to her—and being on her own, of course, it can't have been easy, having to look after everything.'

'I don't suppose it was easy, but frankly it looks as if it's falling down. I can't believe she left it in such a state...'

'I know she kept meaning to have things done. There never seemed to be time...'

'A great pity,' observed the man with some asperity.

He didn't seem to have much sympathy for his mother, reflected Christa, even though Isobel had been alone and had worked so damned hard that it had probably contributed to her death. There was something rather...well, callous about his attitude.

'It may have been that latterly she wasn't feeling very well and hadn't the energy to turn to domestic matters,' suggested Christa rather coldly.

Lachlan nodded. 'Maybe you're right,' he conceded. 'But just look at the state of those windows and wood-work... I used to escape through that window when I was a kid and was about to get a belting for something I'd done—I think it would fall out now if I opened it!' He turned and held out his hand, saying briskly, 'Anyway, it's about time we introduced ourselves. I'm Lachlan Maguire...and you are...?'

'I'm Christa Lennox, and I am...or rather was...your mother's colleague, her junior partner in the practice.'

The expression on Lachlan's face changed subtly from pleasant to wary, the blue eyes widening slightly. He repeated tersely, 'Christa Lennox? You worked with my mother?'

'Why, yes...' Christa looked at Lachlan, puzzled. 'Is there something wrong?'

'No...no, of course not.' Then he added casually after a pause, 'I used to know a man called Angus Lennox—are you a relation, by any chance?'

A look of wry amusement flickered across Christa's face. 'Ah...the black sheep of the family...wicked Uncle Angus,' she remarked. 'How did you know him?'

Lachlan idly kicked a stone away from his foot. 'Oh... he used to come to the house sometimes...' He looked up at Christa, a spark of curiosity in those clear blue eyes. 'And do you know what he did to deserve that reputation?'

Christa shrugged. 'Oh, I don't know all the details and it's a tragic story. I know that he left his wife and child and my father was so outraged by his behaviour he wouldn't speak about him, then Angus was killed in a car crash—a long time ago now.'

Lachlan nodded sombrely. 'I remember that happening...as you say, it was a long time ago.' He smiled. 'Anyway, enough about your wicked uncle—tell me how you came to work with my mother.'

'My own mother was ill some years ago and I was desperate to get a job here as my father had died, and Isobel offered me one. I loved your mother very much—she was a sweet woman and was extremely kind to me over so many things...' Christa's voice faltered slightly and she swallowed hard. 'I was devastated when Isobel collapsed and died so suddenly—I couldn't believe it. It'll be very difficult to find someone to replace her—we shall all miss her so much.'

Lachlan took a rag out of his pocket and wiping his filthy hands remarked, 'You won't have to look far if I take on this place.'

'What do you mean?'

For the first time a fleeting look of sadness crossed Lachlan's strong features. 'My mother left me a letter—you will have known from the post-mortem that her heart had been very damaged, and I think she knew she was on borrowed time. Amongst other things, she wanted me to take over the practice, and it's something I will have to think about very carefully. It's a big decision to make. The house needs such a lot doing to it, and the surgery at the side is rather the worse for wear—it's going to eat up money.'

Christa only heard the first part of his reply and stared at him with her mouth open in astonishment and shock.

'I beg your pardon? You would take over the practice?'

'My mother obviously wanted me to—and, anyway, what would be the point of having the house without a job up here?'

'And did she have any other wishes I should know about?' asked Christa tartly. 'You say she mentioned other things in this letter?'

Lachlan Maguire hesitated then said crisply, 'Nothing of consequence.'

Christa took a deep breath and swallowed hard, trying to compose herself. 'I suppose it had never occurred to me that I wouldn't become the senior partner after Isobel retired—we'd never really discussed it. Perhaps having worked here six years I assumed I'd earned that right...'

Lachlan looked thoughtfully at Christa. 'It must be a shock, but having started the practice and built it up, perhaps she had the right to say whom she would like to succeed her.'

'Isobel didn't build the practice up on her own—I think other people came into it too,' said Christa sharply, a slight flush of anger on her cheeks. 'I rather take exception to someone just waltzing into the practice without any discussion and...'

Lachlan held his hand up. 'Whoa! Keep your hair on! I haven't decided to take it all on yet—it's a big decision, leaving my job in Australia.' He flicked a quick glance at her flushed face and said lightly, 'Perhaps we can discuss this over a drink and not in the car park?'

She nodded coolly. 'A good idea—when do you suggest?'

'This evening about six? Come to the house and I'll see what's been left in the drinks cabinet.'

'Come on, then, Titan, we'll be going.' Christa bent down to ruffle the dog's head, and he leaped up and trotted at her heels towards the little terraced house she owned on the village green.

Lachlan watched her slim figure striding away and grimaced. Of all the people his mother had had to choose to be her colleague, he could hardly believe that it should be Angus Lennox's niece! It was extraordinary that Isobel should have picked Christa, of all people, to work with her. And now there was this poignant letter, Isobel's dying request...

Lachlan felt his throat constrict as he reread it in his mind's eye, urging him to take over the practice. That was a reasonable enough wish and one that left him with a mixture of emotions—a poignant regret that they hadn't talked about it before her death, and pride and relief that Isobel must still have loved him enough to want him to carry on her work.

It was her other bizarre suggestion that had floored him—it was ridiculous, almost cheeky! Perhaps it was even a joke—but for some reason he was pretty sure his mother had meant every word, he could even hear her voice with that soft hint of determination in it.

He shook his head tiredly. He couldn't think about it now, his brain was a jumble of contrasting thoughts. Lachlan turned abruptly back towards the house and went in, slamming the door irritably behind him.

'How could she do this to me—never warning me that Lachlan was her preferred choice for senior partner?' muttered Christa angrily, as she opened her front door and went into the kitchen to make a cup of restorative tea.

A torrent of aggrieved feelings had been building up inside her as she'd walked home, a bitter sense of injustice mixed with bewilderment that a good friend like Isobel should apparently want a son she hadn't seen for years to take over the practice. Isobel had always said how she hoped that Christa would remain there when she retired, and from that Christa had assumed that she would take the surgery over. How wrong she'd been, she thought sadly.

Christa gazed out of the window at the people crossing the green towards the church, a peaceful scene in the mellow late afternoon light, and gradually she began to calm down. She didn't want to allow this to colour her view of Isobel, who had been so incredibly kind to her, not only when her mother had been ill but also when Christa's affair with Colin had disintegrated. Whatever had happened, Isobel had shown Christa that there was life after a broken heart, and had encouraged her to seek new interests, given her more responsibility in the practice. Christa would be forever grateful for that.

And after all, it was natural for Isobel to leave the house to her son despite their distant relationship—she must still have loved him very much and maybe she felt the job went with the house. Even so, Christa wasn't about to hand control of the practice to this Lachlan—she didn't know him, didn't have an idea of his work or how they'd get on with each other. And one question that persisted—why had he never been to see his mother or, to Christa's knowledge, had any contact with her for so many years? It was a very hard thing to understand—Christa couldn't imagine severing contact with a mother, however difficult relations between them might be.

A sudden image of Lachlan's strong face and unusual eyes floated into Christa's head—he had a tough, rather exacting look about him, a look that indicated he wouldn't suffer fools gladly. The kind of man who got what he wanted. She imagined that he could be manipulative—just like many a good-looking man—and probably thought he could talk Christa round to anything with his flattering tongue and celebrity looks.

Well, she was prepared and she'd jolly well show him she wouldn't be pushed around by another man in a hurry! She certainly deserved just as much say in the running of things, having worked for Isobel for six years.

She scribbled down some bullet points that she would put to him—she wouldn't simply step meekly aside.

'I've got to be firm, Titan,' she informed the dog.

Titan looked up from his comfortable basket and thumped his tail sleepily in agreement.

Lachlan Maguire towelled himself down vigorously after his shower in the tepid water, the hottest temperature he could raise from Ardenleigh's antiquated boiler. The whole place needed gutting—a fortune would have to be spent on it. He looked round at the cracked plaster and suspicion of damp on the walls, the stained bath and peeling lino floor. It was basically a handsome house, but where to start?

Years ago, before he'd left home, the house had been beautifully kept—light, bright chintzes in the sitting room, an airy dining room with lovely old furniture and a huge bay window that looked over the garden. Now there was an unkempt and uncared-for feel about the place—it felt sad and neglected.

Lachlan wound the towel round his waist and started to shave, peering into the dim mirror, and his bleak reflection stared back at him. A mixture of regret and sadness washed over him as he thought of the naïve judgemental youth he'd been, blaming his parents totally on the break-up of his family, impulsively moving as far away as he could.

Once he'd loved them dearly—a love that over the years he'd thought had turned to hate. Even now, years later, he could feel the resentment and despair he'd felt as a young lad when his world had seemed to collapse around him.

What an irony it was, therefore, that Isobel had left him the house—and perhaps by way of an apology, or some form of restitution, written that emotional letter, hoping Lachlan would take over her beloved practice. His mother had shown him that she still loved him, and had had faith in him. With a sudden and overwhelming feeling of guilt and sorrow, he realised that it was too late now to tell her that, despite everything, he had still loved her, had still missed her and had often longed to come home and see her again. How stupid he'd been to let his pride get in the way!

Could Lachlan fulfil his mother's last requests? Surely a sense of obligation at least would mean that he should take over the house and the practice. But the other bizarre wish? That might be more difficult to contemplate! Then he grinned wryly as he splashed cold water on his face and patted it dry with one of the cardboard-like towels he'd found in a cupboard. He considered the situation.

Lachlan flicked a hand through his thick, spiky hair to try and tame it and dabbed at a cut on his chin with the towel. He did have some sympathy with Christa— he would probably have felt a good deal of resentment if a strange guy had appeared out of the blue to take over the practice.

She wasn't the kind of girl to accept things meekly, he reflected. He recalled her angry-looking figure at the bottom of the ladder that afternoon, commanding him to come down! He grinned. For some reason he'd rather enjoyed seeing her sherry-coloured eyes snap and sparkle at him when she'd been annoyed.

Christa had no idea of the connection between their

two families—and perhaps it was better to keep it that way, although the truth had a habit of coming out when you least expected it.

Then suddenly a wave of exhaustion overcame him. He stretched and yawned. The last few days had been a complete blur. The time from learning that his mother had died to getting a plane from Sydney to London and then eventually arriving in Inverness had seemed endless. When he'd finally arrived in Errin Bridge and seen the solicitor, jet-lag had begun to catch up on him.

Lachlan wandered into one of the bedrooms, stuffed with heavy dark furniture and a huge sagging bedstead. In his exhausted state it looked quite inviting and he flung himself onto it. Just a little kip for a quarter of an hour would do him the world of good. He lay back on the musty pillow and fell into a deep slumber.

Through a fog of sleep Lachlan heard the doorbell ring. He stirred restlessly, trying to ignore it, then heard a dog barking. With a muffled oath he sat up and swung his legs over the side of the bed. The doorbell rang again— whoever it was couldn't wait.

He padded downstairs wearily and opened the front door, realising too late that he was still only dressed in a small towel wrapped round his waist. Christa was standing there, with Titan standing guard by her side.

They stared at each other, his eyes sweeping over her slim figure, elegant in jeans, long black boots and a warm, close-fitting red biker jacket with a black scarf casually looped round her neck. He clapped a hand to his forehead.

'Oh, God! Sorry! I fell asleep after my shower...forgot you were coming.' His austere expression changed to a

wry grin. 'I'd have put something on to hide my modesty
if I'd known it was you.'

Christa flicked a glance over the lean and athletic
body before her. Good God, was ever a man in such su-
perb shape! She wondered crossly why the sight of his
bare chest should affect her when it was something she
saw routinely in the surgery—but, then, of course, not
many of her patients had torsos like Lachlan Maguire!

She tore her glance away and said blandly, 'Don't
worry, I've seen it all before... If it's inconvenient, I'll
come back another time.'

'No time like the present...' He held the door open
and motioned her in. 'If you'll wait in the kitchen I'll put
some clothes on—won't be a minute.'

He stepped away as Christa passed him and she
caught the faint fresh smell of soap and shaving lotion.
She watched as he bounded up the stairs, holding onto
the towel, and grimaced to herself when she remembered
the way she'd harangued him about being nothing but the
scum of the earth! That was the last thing he looked...
he had to be the sexiest male on two legs that she'd seen
for a very long time. Not, she reminded herself sharply,
that she was at all interested in sexy males—they were
too sure of themselves, too confident by half and far too
duplicitous.

She sat down in the ramshackle kitchen with Titan
curled up on an old rug under the window. There were
ancient cupboards with broken hinges, an old-fashioned
stove on four cast-iron legs and a few dusty shelves with
bottles and jam jars jostling for space. Isobel had been a
lonely person, living on her own in this big house, and
patently had had no interest in cooking if the look of the
kitchen was anything to go by. It was almost shocking

that she had allowed the house to get into this state—odd, too, when she had been a well-organised and efficient doctor.

If Lachlan was married and came to live in Errin Bridge, how would his wife take to living in a time warp like this? Indeed, would she relish the thought of leaving Australia and coming up to a Scottish backwater?

Engrossed in her thoughts, Christa didn't notice Lachlan at first when he appeared at the door. She was gazing out of the window, her shiny bob of auburn hair framing a profile of a determined little chin and a tip-tilted nose. She was feisty with decided opinions—rather like he was, he acknowledged. He guessed she wasn't about to defer to him in any discussion about the practice.

'I've looked in the drinks cupboard,' he said from the doorway. 'All I can find is whisky and more whisky… Would that be OK?'

Christa jumped with surprise and looked round at him, relieved to see that he was now more modestly attired in jeans and a T-shirt under a corduroy jerkin. 'Yes, please, with a splash of water.'

She watched him as he poured out the drink, his movements neat, unfussy. He handed her a tumbler and she twirled the amber liquid around in her glass, watching the light catch it, and then looked at him warily.

'So. When are you going to decide on whether or not to follow your mother's wishes?'

'I've almost decided, although I do have some matters to discuss with the solicitor,' he admitted. 'If those matters can be resolved and I can find a way to pay for the repairs to the house, then I'm tempted to come back.'

'That's a big decision—to give up your life in Australia,' commented Christa. 'Did you like it there?'

'Certainly I did…' A slight change in expression flickered across his face. 'But I've been there a good while and perhaps it's time to come back to my roots.' He looked across the rolling fields to the side of the house and the sea beyond, lacy with white breakers, and smiled. 'Who wouldn't want to live in the beautiful surroundings of Errin Bridge?'

'And are you married—would your wife mind you moving away from Australia?'

Lachlan laughed. 'No—I've no ties, I'm entirely free… And you? Are you someone's wife or mother?'

Christa took a gulp of the whisky and it trailed fire down her throat. 'Oh, no,' she said airily. 'I'm not into commitment—far too much to do with my life first.'

'How very wise,' he murmured.

Christa changed the subject abruptly—she certainly didn't want to dwell on the past, especially her relationship with Colin Maitland. She drew out her list of bullet points from her bag and looked at Lachlan challengingly.

'Now, can we get down to business? I have to say bluntly I'm not happy that you can just leap into the practice here as senior partner—I can't believe that Isobel wouldn't understand how I'd feel about it all.'

Lachlan put his hands up. 'Hey! Not so fast! You have a habit of jumping to conclusions, don't you? I'm certainly not proposing to leap into anything, but if I'm to have full responsibility for the buildings, I need to have at least an equal say.'

'Fair enough…but, to be blunt, I'd like to know what experience you have. I know nothing about you.'

'Of course!' The austere face broke into a grin. 'I've been with the Flying Doctor service in Australia for a few years, and I'm quite brilliant at small ops…a dab hand at dealing with every imaginable situation, from snake bites and childbirth to extracting teeth and acute dehydration...'

Christa couldn't resist smiling at him, her cheeks dimpling. He certainly had all the Maguire charm of persuasion, and underneath that sometimes dour expression he seemed to have a sense of humour. But there were still questions as to why he'd leave his life in Australia so easily.

'You have an interesting job there—why give it all up, even if your mother has left you Ardenleigh?' she asked curiously.

He swirled the whisky round in his glass, the smile fading from his face. 'Time to move on, I guess. I'd been thinking of leaving for some time—it was a great life, but it wasn't Errin Bridge. I think I always hoped to come back here some day.'

But not while your mother was alive, thought Christa, puzzled as to why that should be. She tapped her fingers on the table thoughtfully. 'We'd have to get on with each other...'

A raised eyebrow. 'You're bound to be able to get on with an easygoing guy like me!'

She looked at Lachlan sardonically. 'You think? Suppose we don't, and incredibly I find you're impossible to work with? I'm certainly not going to be the one leaving the practice.'

'Let's give it six months—if the incredible happens and you find you can't work with me, then I shall go!' He took another swig of his drink. 'I'll give you the e-mail address of my boss near Sydney—I can guarantee he'll give me a good reference.'

Christa nodded coolly. She wasn't about to go over-

board and welcome him with open arms yet. 'I imagine
it will be very different from the Australian Outback.
You ought to know something about the practice here…"

'People still have the same illnesses, I suppose. What
about local hospitals?'

'St Luke's, about eight miles away, is the nearest, but
we have a small cottage hospital in the town, mostly
for post-operative use when patients living in outlying
districts have no one to look after them. And we have a
minor injuries unit at the surgery.'

'Sounds good. Anything else?'

'You'd have to be good at walking up mountains.
We're the back-up team if things go wrong up there—
and you'd be amazed how often that happens in the summer with the tourists.'

He raised an impressed eyebrow. 'You're a Jill of all
trades, then. I remember going out to help before I went
to medical school. I enjoyed it, so you can count me in.'

'You sound as if you've made up your mind!'

'I suppose I have,' he said cautiously. 'A germ of an
idea came to me when I was resting upstairs about how I
might raise some money to restore Ardenleigh House—
and that makes me feel quite excited about the future
here.'

'So that's a yes, is it?'

He nodded and smiled. 'Probably. As I said, there are
just one or two things I need to clarify, but I think they
can be resolved.'

'Then we'll need to hammer out some sort of an agreement for the partnership…' A moment's misgiving as
Christa flicked a glance at his self-assertive face—she
could imagine he'd want his own way on quite a few

matters, and she certainly wouldn't give in easily! 'When can you start? How much notice do you have to give?'

'I'm due a few weeks' holiday—I'll use that in lieu of notice.'

'What about your stuff—won't you have to go back and pack?'

He shrugged. 'I travel light so I've brought all I need. I've a friend who'll arrange to have things shipped out if I need them.'

Christa bit her lip. Was she being foolish, leaping into work with someone she knew nothing about? Then she gave a mental shrug. The man was here and available and she was desperate for help, and in any case how could she stop him? She'd just have to hope he was efficient.

'I'll see you, then, in a week, with the proviso of a six months' probationary period to see if it works, and that we'll be equal partners. I'll put it in writing.' She looked at her watch and stood up. 'I've got to fly and see my mother. I usually pop in on a Sunday evening.'

'Your mother still lives in the area?'

'Oh, yes. She has a little flat near me and she loves it there. She's made a good life for herself since my father died.'

Christa got up and Lachlan went with her to the door. It was getting dark now and the courtyard light made deep shadows against the walls. Drops of rain had started to fall, and there was a soft, sweet smell of damp earth on the cool air. Autumn was on its way, and soon the soft purple heather and greens of the glens would be replaced by sparkling frost and snow on the hills.

He'd missed those definitive seasons, and although he'd had a ball in Australia, there had been times when a certain tune, the waft of scent of the sea, or a Scottish voice passing him on the street, would stir a longing in him to be back in Errin Bridge. He should have come back before, he thought sadly, and not allowed his stubborn nature to dictate his life.

Titan, standing beside Christa, suddenly stiffened, the hackles on his neck rising. Then he gave a low growl before breaking into a cacophony of barking.

'What is it, old boy? Calm down…'

Titan took no notice and suddenly darted across the yard, still barking at full pitch.

'There's someone there,' said Lachlan in a low voice, putting a restraining hand on Christa's arm. 'I wouldn't be surprised if this turns out to be one of your pesky thieves.'

CHAPTER TWO

THEY STOOD FOR a moment on the doorstep, looking towards the barns, the outside light from the surgery casting a beam across the courtyard and the ladder that Lachlan had been using. It was raining heavily now and the sound of it drummed on the roof and made huge puddles across the yard.

Then above that sound there was a muffled crash as if something heavy had fallen. A scream came from one of the outbuildings, and a hooded youth ran out into the beam of light, the raindrops silver as they landed on his frightened face. He looked wildly around and then darted back into the building. Titan barked excitedly and rushed after him.

Christa drew in a sharp breath. 'I know that boy—it's Carl Burton. He's a patient! What's he doing in the barn?'

'I'm not waiting to find out,' growled Lachlan. 'Is there a torch anywhere?'

He ran quickly across the yard and Christa flew to the surgery, scrabbling round in a drawer to find a torch, and instinct telling her to grab the emergency medical bag she kept locked in a cupboard by her desk. She was back in the barn inside two minutes.

The light in the outbuilding was dim, but in the torch's

beam they saw a boy lying on the floor, ominously still, his legs splayed at an awkward angle. His face was so pale that the large gash over his forehead looked as if it had been painted on. A piece of wood had fallen from the roof and was wedged above him at an angle. Carl Burton crouched by the victim's side and he looked up at Christa and Lachlan with a mixture of fear and bravado on his face.

'Bloody hell,' muttered Lachlan, darting forward and pushing Carl out of the way. 'Let me see what the damage is.'

Carl backed away from the victim. 'Is he dead?' he said, his voice cracking. 'Has he been killed?'

Lachlan put his fingers on the boy's neck to feel his carotid artery. He raised his eyes to Christa's questioning look and nodded. 'He's still with us…better get some help, PDQ.'

'It wasn't my fault,' Carl blurted out. 'Greg saw that ladder. I told him not to climb on the roof, but he did. He was being stupid, standing on one foot and waving his arms about. Then he…he…dropped, like a stone…' He stopped, putting his hands over his face.

'That's why he's got to be treated as quickly as possible.' Lachlan's voice was brusque. 'It's lucky we were here.'

Christa pulled her mobile out of her pocket and flicked it open, punching out numbers. She walked over to the doorway as she spoke, glancing back at Lachlan bent over the victim's body. Christa felt an almighty surge of thankfulness that she wasn't alone in having to cope with things.

'Ambulance and the police services, please—Dr Lennox here from the Ardenleigh Practice in Errin Bridge.

I need the air ambulance for a serious leg, head and possible spinal injury to a youth who's fallen from a roof just by the practice. My colleague and I will try and stabilise him, but he needs hospitalisation without delay. If you could inform St Luke's to have an orthopaedic surgeon and anaesthetist on standby, please.'

'We'll have to do our best until they get here,' observed Lachlan. He pulled back the upper lids of the boy's eyes. 'Pupils dilated,' he murmured to himself, then examined the victim's body, checking his head and other visible injuries. 'He's not bleeding too much from this head wound…'

'That's good, isn't it?' Carl looked up at Lachlan hopefully.

'I'm afraid it's not the same as just banging your head on a cupboard. Hitting your head at speed can give rise to arterial bleeding, and he's had a tremendous crack to his forehead, besides his possible back and neck injuries and a broken leg.'

Christa bit her lip. Had the boy's spine survived the impact of falling from the roof? Could they keep him alive until the paramedics arrived with their specialist equipment? She looked closely at the young boy's face, where a bruise was developing around the gash on his forehead.

She drew in her breath. 'Oh, God, I know this guy too…he's Gregory Marsh, aged about sixteen.' Her eyes met Lachlan's. 'Are you thinking acute subdural haematoma?'

He nodded and bent low over the boy, saying clearly, 'Do you know where you are, Gregory?'

After a few seconds the boy whispered, 'I'm in the barn, aren't I?'

'That's right, Gregory, well done. Now, where does it hurt? Can you tell us?'

The boy's eyes fluttered open, his breath rasping, his face contorted with pain. 'My leg…bloody hell, it's my leg,' he muttered.

'You can feel your leg, then?' A measure of relief in Christa's voice.

'Of course I can feel my effing leg…' he croaked. 'It's agony…'

'Let's look at this leg,' said Lachlan briskly. 'Can you cut his jeans?'

Christa used a pair of scissors from the bag to cut the leg of the jeans very gently from the distorted leg. They both looked down at the limb, which was gashed and swollen. Protruding through the gash was a white piece of bone.

Christa grimaced. 'A compound fracture, not very nice…'

'Poor blighter—it needs splinting.'

'That's OK. We've got some we use for the mountain rescue work. I'll get them.'

'Give me your bag of tricks and I'll put some sterile dressings on these open wounds, and give him a ten-mil shot of morphine for the pain.' Lachlan looked down reassuringly at Gregory and laid a comforting hand on the boy's shoulder. It was a gesture not lost on Christa. Physical touch was an incredibly important and soothing thing, and reassurance could reduce the severity of shock—it was as important a medical tool as any conventional treatment.

'Don't worry, Gregory, you're in good hands and we'll soon have you in hospital.'

Christa went to get the collapsible splints and returned

swiftly, snapping the splint joints into place and laying them out. The two doctors worked as gently as possible to immobilise the leg by strapping the limb to the splint, but Lachlan kept flicking a wary look at the beam above them, jammed across most of Gregory's body. Christa heard him suck in his breath.

'Bloody hell—can you hear that beam creaking?' he muttered. 'The whole damn thing could fall on top of us. It has to be moved.'

'I don't know how…' began Christa.

He turned to Carl, watching them mutely, his face as white as a ghost's. 'I tell you what, Carl—you can help me try and push it out of the way.'

'Don't even think of doing that!' Christa's voice was sharp. 'The helicopter will be here soon—'

'And that could be too late. If I could get underneath it, I could lift it out of that gap in the wall and with Carl's support we could push it to one side.'

She stared crossly at Lachlan. 'Suppose you get crushed?'

'If we wait for that damned air ambulance to come, the boy will need more than a spinal brace and a leg splint.'

Christa got up from Greg's side and pulled at Lachlan's arm. 'Do you want there to be two casualties, for heaven's sake?'

He shook her arm away irritably. 'I'll be OK. We haven't got a choice—look, it's swaying again…'

For a second they looked at each other stubbornly then Christa shrugged, acknowledging that Lachlan was right. They couldn't just ignore the situation—something had to be attempted. She looked around the barn desperately. There were some old packing cases and dust sheets by the wall near Carl. She began dragging them across to Gregory and shouted to Carl.

'Come on! Help me get these over Gregory to protect him before you start tampering with the damn beam— put the sheets over him and then the packing cases like a cage. It might just take the shock if the beam falls.'

'Why can't we just pull him away from it?' asked Carl.

'Because,' said Christa in a low voice, 'we don't know what damage Gregory's done to his spine. If he's damaged it in the fall, we could sever it.'

They worked feverishly to construct some sort of barrier between Gregory and the chunk of wood wedged over him, then Lachlan slid his body underneath it to the side of the injured boy, so that he could try and shift the beam from where it was so precariously perched. There was a tense silence: Gregory's eyes fluttered open again and he focussed them on Christa.

'What's happening?' he whispered.

Christa's voice was calm. 'Nothing to worry about, Gregory, just making sure the beam's secure. Everything's under control.'

She hoped devoutly that that was the case, and indeed something told her that if anyone could handle an emergency like this, Lachlan Maguire could. She watched him tensely as he manoeuvred the beam, calm but concentrated, no sign of panic. Perhaps she shouldn't have been surprised by his competence—someone who worked with the Flying Doctor service had to be able to think on his feet, quite an asset for someone she was going to work with.

Lachlan pulled the rag from his pocket and wound it round his hand to try and get more purchase. 'Come on, Carl—I know you're in shock, but you've got to help me, for your mate's sake.' His voice was tough, uncompromising. 'Give me a hand to try and shift this. While I push it up, get your arms round it to pull.'

Both men grunted with the effort of trying to shift the wood away from over Gregory's body, and eventually, with a final push and a shout of warning from Lachlan, it fell harmlessly to one side.

'Thank God,' whispered Christa, blowing out her cheeks and closing her eyes in relief. Lachlan climbed stiffly to his feet with a relieved grin and dusted his hands together.

'There you are—nothing to it!' He went across to Carl. 'Thank you for helping there,' he said quietly. 'I couldn't have done it without you. Now, tell me how all this started.'

Carl hung his head and muttered, 'We…we were trying to get at the guttering—we saw the ladder and Greg thought it would be easy. I told him not to, but he started pretending he was a high-wire act and just fell from the beam up there.'

'Were you trying to nick the lead?'

'We didn't think nobody would miss it. We didn't mean any harm, we just needed a bit of cash…' The boy started to shake at the memory of the accident, wrapping his arms round his thin body, rocking slightly on his heels.

Lachlan looked at Carl's white face. 'You feel all right?'

The boy shook his head helplessly as if unable to express just how he felt. 'I…I just can't believe it… Seeing it happen…'

His voice petered out, not equal to describing what he'd just seen, and Lachlan nodded, recognising all the signs of violent emotional shock in the boy. What Carl had witnessed had happened with appalling swiftness, with no time for him to prepare or adjust to the situation. His senses were stunned by the events and Lachlan recognised all the signs of 'onlooker reaction'. He put his arm round Carl's shoulder and drew him to the wall.

'I want you to sit down here. Your body's got a touch of shock, just as much as if you'd had a physical injury. After a nice hot cup of sweet tea you'll feel much better.'

The boy's face relaxed slightly. He hadn't been expecting any kind words, but they helped to calm him, bring back something of normality to his fractured emotional state. There'd be plenty of condemnation later, thought Lachlan wryly.

Christa attached an oximeter peg to Gregory's finger to get a readout of his vital signs.

'What's it like?' said Lachlan.

Christa grimaced and murmured, 'BP's low, eighty over fifty. Not surprising, and his pulse is thready. How's the pain, Greg?'

The boy stirred slightly but didn't speak, and Lachlan looked at his watch.

'How long are they going to be?' he growled.

Then through the beating of the rain on the roof there was the sudden clatter of a helicopter's rotors overhead, the sound increasing in volume as it descended somewhere near the surgery. Christa sent up a silent prayer—they'd arrived just in the nick of time.

'Where will they land?' asked Lachlan, as he and Christa exchanged relieved glances.

'There's a field beyond the woods at the end of the garden, they'll put down there. It'll only take them a few minutes to get here now.'

Lachlan got to his feet and went to the door to meet them, and very soon three men in bright orange outfits and luminous jerkins with 'Doctor' and 'Paramedic' labels across them came running across the courtyard. Lachlan gave a quick résumé of Gregory's visible injuries and what he and Christa had done so far to stabilise him.

'He'll get a full body scan, and the theatre's on standby,' said the doctor accompanying them. 'He was damn lucky that he had you two near him when he decided to do his sky-walking exploits.'

The paramedics set up a drip and strapped a spinal board on Gregory, with an oxygen mask over his face, and Carl started to sidle surreptitiously towards the door. One of the paramedics stopped him, looking at his pale face and trembling hands.

'Have you hurt yourself?' he enquired.

'No. I'm OK.' The voice was sullen, uncooperative.

'Why don't you come with us for a check-up, eh?'

A vehement shake of the head. 'I'm OK, I tell you. I'm going home.' He jerked his head in Gregory's direction. 'He'll be OK now, won't he? You don't need me.'

'Oh, yes, we do, my friend.' A burly policeman had appeared at the barn door and stood in front of the boy. 'We need a few names and addresses, young man. A little bit of information as to how this happened, if you please.'

He led Carl out of the building. The boy looked pathetic, shoulders drooping, and his jeans hung so low around his hips they were barely able to stay up. He looked back at Lachlan and muttered, 'Will Greg be all right?'

'Hopefully, but he won't be climbing around on roofs for a while,' remarked Lachlan drily.

* * *

The emergency services had gone and it had stopped raining as Christa and Lachlan walked back across the yard, Titan trotting proudly beside them, as if aware that he had been the first to alert them to the emergency. Lachlan stretched, flexing his stiff lower back, which had taken the strain of him pushing the beam away, and took a deep breath of the clear air. The velvety night sky had cleared of cloud and was twinkling with a tapestry of stars. In the distance was the sound of the sea, whooshing in and out on the beach.

'God, that smells good. How I've missed that special Highland tang,' he murmured. 'I'd forgotten just how intoxicating the air can be in this little corner of the world.'

'How many years since you've been here, then?'

A short silence, then he said roughly, 'Too many...but it's good to be back.'

Christa looked at the bleak expression on his face, and felt a moment's impatience. If he had missed home so much, why hadn't he come back occasionally to see his mother, a woman on her own? Christa was tempted to ask outright what had kept him away, but she sensed that that would be a question too far at the moment.

She pushed that thought to the back of her mind. So much had happened in the last hour and she should have felt drained, but instead she felt the kick of adrenalin after a job well done. Together they'd managed to keep Gregory alive, to retrieve a situation that had looked almost impossible.

She was profoundly grateful that Lachlan Maguire had been there—almost unwillingly she admitted that he'd been pretty impressive, efficient and reliable. Just the kind of person one would want in an emergency. She flicked a glance at his tall figure beside her—perhaps, after all, she was prepared to believe that he was as good as he said he was at his job!

'I…I'm glad you were here. In fact, if you hadn't been, I think the ending could have been very different. Thank you,' she said.

'Do you think our young friends are the culprits who've been nicking stuff from here?' he said.

'Could be… They're both patients but I haven't seen them for ages. From his odd behaviour on the roof I wonder if Gregory's on something Anyway, they'll do plenty of tests at St Luke's.' Christa sighed. 'I'll bet his parents don't know what he's up to—or are turning a blind eye to the situation.'

'They're going to find out soon,' said Lachlan grimly.

'God—it was a bit scary, like being back in A and E again. I thought we'd lost him, and he had so many injuries…' Then she puffed out her cheeks, laughing up at Lachlan, her amber eyes dancing with relief. 'But it was a great feeling that we kept him going till the paramedics came, wasn't it?'

He looked down at Christa's dust-covered face turned up to his, and a feeling of affinity with a colleague after a job well done intensified into something else—the treacherous flare of sexual attraction. For a second his eyes roamed over her heart-shaped face and wide eyes, as if seeing her properly for the first time, and he sucked in his breath. Good God, she was absolutely ravishing… and desirable.

Almost absent-mindedly he touched her cheek, wiping away some mud and allowing his finger to trail down her jaw. He smiled at her, then without warning he bent his head down and brushed her lips with his, slowly, deliberately, fiercely.

'You shouldn't look so bloody beautiful,' he whispered against her ear.

Christa remained motionless for a second then touched her lips where his had been. They felt full, tingling and soft, and for a second she was bewildered. Where the hell had that come from, or had she just imagined it?

Then a feeling of outrage swept through her—Lachlan Maguire had the cheek of the devil!

'What the hell do you think you're doing?' she demanded icily.

He laughed. 'Come on—you've got your headmistress look on your face again! It was just an expression of thanks for a job well done. Am I to sit on the naughty step?'

'Don't be ridiculous.'

'We seemed to work rather well together, that's all! A spur-of-the-moment thing!'

'You took a damn liberty!'

He looked rather penitent, but his blue eyes danced at her mischievously, and he gave his most disarming grin. 'It was just a little gesture of, er, thanks,' he protested. 'I didn't mean to offend you—it was a sort of compliment!'

Christa opened her mouth to say something cutting then shut it again because for a minute Lachlan looked so like a naughty schoolboy that, despite herself, she felt an urge to giggle. Obviously the impulsive kiss that had sent her reeling meant absolutely nothing to him—just a bit of fun.

And yet, she admitted to herself, the truth was that every single nerve in *her* body had seemed to respond with a longing for something more, something much more intimate, something that would repeat the fireworks that had seemed to explode so suddenly around her as his mouth had plundered hers. It was as if a switch had been thrown, and something that hadn't worked for a long time had been kicked into action.

She pushed these thoughts to the back of her mind and decided the best response was to try and treat the episode with dignified aversion.

She buttoned up her jacket, and said rather pompously, 'Don't expect a repeat performance, Lachlan—I took you on as a work colleague, not a rake!'

He burst into laughter. 'Come on...it doesn't suit you to take life so seriously, Dr Lennox! I thought you secretly wanted to press your lovely body close to mine...'

This was a little too near the truth. Christa flushed and said indignantly, 'Don't be silly!'

Lachlan assumed a more contrite expression. 'Don't be cross. I'm sorry if I took you by surprise, but I know we'll make a very good partnership.'

Those amazing eyes danced winningly into Christa's, almost like a caress in itself, and although she was really mad at him, she couldn't help smiling back. They were going to have to work together amicably, she told herself, so there was no point in maintaining a frigid atmosphere. She'd just have to be on her guard in the future. After all, wasn't it typical of some males to take relationships as casually as picking sweets from a jar?

Then, dangerously, the thought echoed in her mind that if one kiss could practically send her into orbit, making her heart clatter in her chest and a thousand butterflies seem as if they were fluttering somewhere around in her stomach, what would it be like if they made real, proper love?

Titan whimpered and Christa bent down to ruffle the little dog's head, grateful of the distraction to her thoughts. 'Poor old Titan, you want your supper. In all the fuss I'd forgotten that. Come on, then—home time now.' She turned to Lachlan and said lightly, 'See you soon.'

As she walked home through the still night Christa's heart beat a tattoo against her ribs, and even her legs felt slightly wobbly. It had been so long since any man had caressed her or kissed her—so long since she'd fancied anyone enough to do so. But out of the blue, out of no-where, had come a man she didn't know at all, sending her into a spin! She came to her front door and her hand trembled slightly as she tried to put the key in the lock.

'What's the matter with me, Titan?' she asked the little dog. 'Have I gone completely mad?'

Lachlan closed the door, leaning against the wall for a minute, and took a deep breath, reflecting on the effect two soft full lips could have on a man when they were pressed to his mouth. He hadn't expected his body to respond so urgently, and wondered what on earth had possessed him to kiss Christa after a mere afternoon's acquaintance. Then he grinned to himself—because she was so damned beautiful, of course, and didn't the thought of shocking that rather prim, headmistressy personality rather appeal?

He was used to casual relationships—never commit yourself because they never lasted, was his mantra. Take your pleasure where you could. He wasn't going to make the same mistake his parents had—get married, suppos-edly for life, and then destroy the family with a bitter and cruel break-up.

Perhaps he'd gone a step too far with Christa Lennox,

expecting her to take his kiss as casually as he had—but life was for living and having fun, wasn't it? Except, of course, he'd forgotten that one person he should keep at arm's length was someone from the Lennox family. And neither had he bargained for the fierce longing he now had to kiss Christa again—and more.

'Isobel's *son*? I don't believe it!' Alice Smith's large blue eyes looked at Christa in amazement, and she paused in mid-action as she pulled open a filing-cabinet drawer. 'He's a bit late, isn't he? Isobel's funeral was a week ago!'

'Nobody knew where he was, and he only heard she'd died a few days ago,' explained Christa.

Christa and the two receptionists, Alice Smith and Ginny Calder, were having a quick cup of coffee before the Monday morning surgery, and Christa had been re-galing them with the previous day's events in the barn. Both girls goggled in disbelief at Christa.

'Where's he been, then, all these years?' asked Ginny, the elder of the two receptionists, her eyes popping with surprise behind her thick-lensed glasses.

'He's been working in Australia—it took a time to find out where he was.'

Alice stuffed some papers into the files and said thoughtfully, 'It was sad, wasn't it—to stay away as long as he did. I wonder what happened.'

'I remember him,' recalled Ginny. 'He was a hand-some lad, and I know he was the apple of his mother's eye. She was so proud of him.'

'Well, what went wrong?' asked Alice bluntly. 'How come she never spoke about him?'

Ginny shook her head. 'No one knows, except that Isobel's husband left her around the time that Lachlan went off to college—and, of course, Lachlan was never seen again. How long's he staying?'

Christa put her cup of coffee down on the desk. 'Actually, it's not just a flying visit—he's going to work here permanently. Isobel left him a letter saying that she wanted him to take over the practice. And he's decided to do that. She's left the house to him.'

'What?' Alice closed the filing-cabinet drawer with a crash and turned to her in amazement. 'But…but I thought you would be taking over… It doesn't seem fair.'

'It's OK, Alice. We've talked it over, and he's coming in as an equal partner. He understands that, at least for a trial of six months. And anyway we need another doctor, that's for sure. Even before Isobel died we were pretty stretched.'

'Since Colin Maitland left, I suppose… I hope Lachlan's nothing like *him*,' said Ginny sharply, then watching Christa's face she grimaced and clapped her hand over her mouth. 'Oh, I'm sorry, love, I shouldn't have brought up the subject. But you're over Colin now, aren't you?'

Christa smiled brightly. 'Of course I'm over him,' she said robustly. 'I can assure you I won't be taken in by any other con men, however charming!'

'And *is* he charming, this mysterious Lachlan?'

Christa shrugged, trying to look as casual as possible. 'He wasn't so charming when I thought he was a burglar—he was up on the roof inspecting the gutter, and I shouted at him. I got a frosty reception, I can tell you!'

'We want more information than that!' protested Alice. 'Is he single or married, good looking?'

'Now, why do you want to know that?' teased Christa. 'You've got a lovely boyfriend. But for general information, yes, he says he's single, and I suppose some people would say he's not bad looking. Not that I find him attractive,' she lied.

Of course the truth was that she'd found it difficult to get that mind-blowing kiss from the night before out of her head. To him it had been just a casual brush of flesh on flesh, but in her imagination she could still feel the imprint of that sensual mouth on hers, and the feeling of exploding stars and fireworks it had produced! She took a deep slurp of coffee, hoping the girls wouldn't notice the blush she was sure was spreading over her cheeks.

'Ah!' Alice said with satisfaction, her eyes meeting Ginny's with meaning.

'What do you mean, "Ah"?' Christa looked sternly at Alice and Ginny. 'I can assure you both I'm off men for good, however eligible. I can promise you that if George Clooney were to go down on bended knee and give me a million pounds to marry him, I'd send him off with a flea in his ear! I've no ambition to have a wedding ring on my finger!'

A discreet cough from the doorway and they all whirled round. Lachlan was standing there, a suspicion of laughter in his startling blue eyes, but the expression on his face was impassive.

Christa's cheeks crimsoned, and she jumped up in a flustered way, swallowing whole the biscuit she was eating. Had the darned man heard her inane comment about marriage as he'd stood there?

'Sorry to interrupt you all,' he said smoothly. 'I know I'm not starting work until next week, but I just wanted to know if you'd had any word about how that young boy is from last night's accident...'

Christa rearranged her features quickly from shock to welcome. 'Oh, Lachlan, it's you!' She turned to Alice and Ginny and cleared her throat. 'This is Lachlan Maguire—Isobel's son. Alice and Ginny are the backbone of the practice, Lachlan. We couldn't work without them.'

He looked like someone out of central casting for the lead in a medical drama, she thought, noting irritably how Alice goggled at him with frank admiration. He unleashed a charming smile.

'Then I must keep on the right side of them!'

'I was telling them what happened yesterday,' she explained, then felt her heart begin to race as she remembered just what *had* happened between them after attending the accident.

Lachlan grinned, his eyes holding hers rather too long. 'Plenty happened, that's for sure! I was pushed in at the deep end all right.'

Christa looked away hastily and added some more sugar to her coffee, stirring it vigorously. Alice looked at Lachlan rather like a puppy given a special treat.

'I believe you're going to be working here with us permanently,' she enthused.

'Yes, that's right. I know it'll be a steep learning curve, but I'll do my best. I look forward to getting to know you all.'

He smiled urbanely at them, and Christa could see Alice melting under his easy charm, although Ginny looked more wary. Perhaps, thought Christa, she was a little more cynical than Alice, wondering just why a son should lose touch with a lovely woman like Isobel, then suddenly appear out of the blue after she'd died.

'A cup of coffee?' enquired Alice, still staring at him as if mesmerised.

'Thank you, just a quick one. I guess you're pretty busy and I don't want to hold you up. As I say, I just wanted to find out about the young lad who was injured last night.'

Christa nodded. 'I rang the hospital a few minutes ago. He's injured vertebrae in his back, and he's being operated on this morning for his leg—he'll pull through, though.'

'That's the good news I was hoping to hear before I see the builders this morning. There is one more thing, however. I wondered if it would help if I started on a part-time basis this week—I could get to know the ropes, and if I came with you on one or two visits it would familiar-ise me with the area again, after so long away.'

Of course it would help. Christa had been sleepless for many nights, wondering how she could cope with the work that was piling up. But she wasn't so sure that being close to Lachlan Maguire was a good thing so soon after her experience with him the night before. She'd rather have liked that episode to fade into the past.

'Oh, I don't think there's any need to—'

'I think that's a great idea,' interrupted Ginny. 'You've been working yourself to a frazzle over the past weeks, Christa. You accept any help that's offered!' She turned to Lachlan. 'Visits are usually done around midday to two o'clock after morning surgery.'

Dear Ginny—she was like a mother hen where she, Christa, was concerned, and she'd been marvellous when Isobel had died, staying late to reorganise surgeries, bringing Christa meals to eat at the surgery. But some-times she was just a little too fussy!

'Right!' Lachlan said briskly. 'I'll be back, then. See you later.'

When he'd gone, Alice turned to Christa and said

accusingly, 'You misled us there! You said he wasn't bad looking…'

'Well?' asked Christa innocently.

'You ought to go for an eye test…he's absolutely *gorgeous*!'

'Beauty,' said Christa grimly, as she picked up a pile of blood results and went towards the door, 'is in the eye of the beholder!'

'Quite so,' agreed Ginny tersely, as she reached out to answer the phone.

'Will you listen to yourselves?' demanded Alice in disbelief. 'I can tell you, that man's made my pulse go into overdrive! You two must be made of stone!'

Lachlan stood for a moment before he got into the car and looked back towards the surgery, amusement flickering across his face. So Christa Lennox wouldn't get married for a million pounds—even to George Clooney! What the hell had brought that on, a bad experience perhaps?

He grinned to himself. It was a delicious irony that she should say that she wouldn't marry at any price, when one of his mother's ridiculous suggestions in her letter to him had been that he should get married. And that, of all people, Christa Lennox should be the bride!

Well, that was one proposition that wouldn't be ful-filled! He was damned if he'd be manipulated by his mother from beyond the grave, however much he regret-ted her death and wanted to atone for his quarrel with her.

CHAPTER THREE

'COME ON, TITAN! In you get!'

Titan sprang into the boot of the car and stood up with his front paws on the back seat, looking around eagerly.

'He seems to enjoy going out on visits,' remarked Lachlan as he folded himself up to fit in Christa's little car.

'Oh, he's spoilt rotten—all my regulars seem to love him, especially at our first port of call. Fred was a shepherd and misses his sheepdog dreadfully. She died only a few months ago, so he loves to spoil Titan.'

Christa started the car and it did its usual little jumps and jerks to get going. She felt self-conscious and tense boxed up in this small space with Lachlan, extremely aware of how close he was to her, exuding sex appeal. The faint smell of shaving lotion and the warm tweedy smell of his jacket drifted over to her.

'Have you had this car serviced recently?' asked Lachlan, rubbing his knee as it hit the dashboard sharply and brushing his hand against Christa's as she changed gear. She inhaled quickly as something like a little electric shock of excitement flickered through her at the unexpected touch.

'Er, what?' she said, flustered. 'Oh, no, it hasn't

been serviced for a while—I keep meaning to make an appointment. It's something to do with the clutch, I think—sorry about that.'

She glanced at Lachlan's long legs doubled up in the cramped space of the passenger seat. Her car certainly wasn't designed for a hunky guy of over six feet! In fact, the space in the car seemed to have diminished since he'd got in. She'd slept fitfully the previous night, her mind racing over the dramatic events that had taken place, but the thing that stayed with her in 3D clarity, and much to her irritation, was her reaction to Lachlan's kiss. Like the rerunning of a recording, she went over and over it in her mind, reliving the total surprise of it all and the heavenly sensation of his firm mouth on hers, the odd feeling of something interrupted when she'd pulled away from him.

She turned on the car radio to distract herself, irritated that her mind seemed to be fixated on the man, then turned it off again when all she got was loud static and a humming sound.

'You won't get good reception in these hills,' commented Lachlan. 'We'll just be forced to talk to each other, I'm afraid!'

Christa was aware that he had turned to look at her, a quirky smile on his lips. Perhaps, she thought with embarrassment, he could read her mind! She gripped the steering-wheel tightly and started to talk quickly.

'You said you'd had an idea to raise money to do up Ardenleigh. What was it?'

'It was just a vague idea—I've not thought it through properly, but it's to do with the fact that the place has so much land. It might be a good idea to make more use of it...'

'What do you mean?'

'I don't know if it will be feasible, but there's a hell of a lot of land attached to the house—land that takes in several fields down to the river, which I can't possibly look after. I wondered about developing it as a holiday complex and leisure centre. Perhaps a nine-hole golf course.'

'*What?*' Christa's head whipped round to gaze at him in horror, and the car swerved alarmingly.

'Hey...steady! You're driving a car, remember?' Lachlan looked at the sudden angry flush of her cheeks and raised his eyebrow. 'You don't sound very pleased. What's wrong with the idea?'

She knew she was being unreasonable. After all, Lachlan had only put the suggestion forward tentatively. But the very idea of him thinking of such a thing when he hadn't lived in the area for years, had only just arrived, was ridiculous. It would spoil the whole atmosphere of the pretty little village, and at the moment there was a beautiful walk over the hills that started through that very wood. Perhaps if he'd helped his mother more over the past years, Christa thought angrily, the house might not have deteriorated, and there'd be no need to spend so much money on it.

'What's right with the idea, you mean! I think it's totally mad—you can't just appear after years away and put a ghastly complex in the middle of this idyllic countryside. Hundreds of cars, concreting over beautiful fields... it...it's ridiculous!'

He laughed. 'I don't intend to concrete over the beautiful fields. There'll be some well-designed chalets in the woods, perhaps a really good gym and a small golf course. It'll bring some much-needed employment to the area.'

'But at what cost to the countryside?' protested

Christa. 'It'll change the whole character of the place. Besides which, I have a friend who runs a small gym in the village—it'll ruin Richie's business.'

He leaned back in his seat and shrugged. 'It's just a bit of healthy competition. I've got to raise money to do up the house somehow. It could solve a lot of financial difficulties, and give something more to the area that would help young lads like our friends Carl and Greg.' He looked at her sardonically. 'Perhaps you need to think about it.'

'I don't need to think about it. I know it stinks.'

His face hardened and he said drily, 'Fortunately, it's not your decision to make, and you can always object if and when the plans are put forward, but I'm pretty sure it has a lot to recommend it. And one thing I do know—although my mother and I had our differences, it was obviously her wish I have the house. I intend to abide by her wishes.'

All except one, he thought wryly—her wish that he should marry Christa was a step too far!

Christa flicked a cold glance at him. She guessed he was a man who got what he wanted—charming when he wanted to be but nevertheless a dominating character who could ultimately control a situation and steer things his way. There was an inner steel she detected about Lachlan Maguire, which probably brooked no opposition. On the other hand, she thought with spirit, she wasn't about to let him walk roughshod with his schemes without pointing out some of the disadvantages.

An icy silence descended between them, and both of them stared straight ahead. In two minutes the atmosphere seemed to have plummeted! Christa gritted her teeth, wondering how on earth two people with diverse opinions like they seemed to have could possibly work together.

She glanced at Lachlan's implacable profile and cursed her impulsiveness at agreeing in such a precipitate way to work with this man. Then she shrugged inwardly—the deed was done and they had to work together now. Of course she should have thought before opening her mouth. It was stupid to start off on the wrong note, and after all, she conceded, this development scheme was only an idea of Lachlan's at the moment.

They had come to a viewpoint on the road that showed the valley below with the inlet from the sea snaking into it and the majestic hills and mountains stretching far out into the distance. Christa skidded to a halt in the layby, the car facing the view. 'I'm sorry,' she said quietly. 'I should never have flown off the handle like that. But do look! How could you think of defiling countryside like that?'

Lachlan's expression softened and he smiled at her. 'Apology accepted,' he murmured.

He leaned forward and scanned the scenery. It was one of those nippy autumn days with a foretaste of winter, the sky a piercing blue and the trees turning into a magical kaleidoscope of reds, oranges and scarlet, interspersed with green.

'It all looks just the same, I'm glad to say,' he said softly. 'I can remember it all—that special magic and colour that the Highlands possess. Soon those hills will have a white cap of snow on them, and all the trees will have lost their leaves.' He turned to look at her. 'I promise you, Christa, I would never think of defiling the place.'

Christa raised her eyebrows cynically. Sincerity seemed to blaze out of his eyes. But she'd heard men make promises before when in the end they'd wanted their own way.

'I'll hold you to that,' she growled.

'Trust me, please. Now I'm back I realise how much of my heart is here, how many of my earliest memories remain with me. Why, I recall fishing in the loch some-where along this road when I was a kid. I don't want to change the place.'

He smiled beguilingly at her and Christa's irritation with his ideas began to fade, despite her misgivings.

'You'll be thinking of Loch Fean,' she said. 'It's up in the hills fairly near to where we're going.'

'My friend Colin and I used to go off for the day to-gether when we were kids.' Lachlan turned to look at her. 'Didn't Colin work in the practice for a time?'

Christa's foot hit the accelerator rather hard as she set off again, and they skidded round a bend on two wheels. Lachlan grabbed the dashboard as they missed the other side of the road by inches, and she wrenched the steer-ing-wheel back, wondering what on earth he thought of her driving.

'Sorry! Sorry! Foot slipped! Yes…' she said lightly. 'Colin worked for a while in the practice, but he left and works in a practice a few miles away.'

'I haven't spoken to him for years—I wonder what happened to him?'

'Oh, he got married…' Her voice was offhand.

'So old Colin got married—I never thought he was the type to make it to the altar! Was he at my mother's funeral?'

'Yes, he was there with his wife.' The familiar pang, mixed with sadness, fluttered through her when she recalled Colin standing with his beautiful pregnant wife at the funeral.

The car shuddered to a halt as she stopped at a crossroads, turning right towards her patient's home. She changed the subject from Colin and his wife to the patient they were going to visit.

'By the way, we're going to see Fred Logan—he's eighty-seven and lives with Bessie, his wife. She and Fred enjoy verbal scraps with each other, but both of them are very frail.'

Lachlan smiled. 'Ah, so Fred Logan's the shepherd you were talking about? He used to give us chocolate mints if he saw us fishing. He and his wife were very kind to us. I'd like to see him again. Is it just a regular check-up, then?'

'Lorna Storey, the community nurse, told me this morning that she didn't like the look of him when she checked him at the weekend after a fall he had. Like a lot of the independent souls around here, he refuses to believe or admit he's ill.'

'Is it his heart?'

'Partly—he has congestive cardiac failure for which he's on vasodilator drugs, but his immediate problem is his cut hand and she's worried it may become infected. I've brought some antibiotics with me to save Lorna coming out again. He hardly ever gets down to the village.'

'Does he have a family?'

'A son, Ian, who works in Inverness. He does his best, but his own wife works at weekends and they have two children, so it's difficult for him to get away. He'd like his parents to go and live nearer them, but being an independent couple they're resisting that. Lorna wants me to persuade them to have some daily help.'

She turned into a long, bumpy drive, with stone walls on either side and multiple potholes on the surface. At the end could be seen a small cottage with smoke curling straight up into the air from one of the chimneys.

'Here we are! By the way, take a few lungfuls of fresh air before you go in—Fred likes his pipe!'

Christa knocked on the door and then opened it, and Titan trotted in. It was cold in the room, although Fred was sitting by a peat fire, wrapped in an old shawl. He was wreathed in smoke from the pipe he was puffing, and Titan bounded up to him, putting his nose on the old man's knee.

'Ah, Titan, you wee thing—it's good to see you. Bessie! Bessie! It's the doctor—bring some treats for the dog now!'

A tiny little woman with the hunched back of someone afflicted by curvature of the spine came out of a back room, drying her hands on a towel and smiling a welcome.

'Ah—there you are, Doctor! It's good to see you, and little Titan. We've got his special dog biscuits in case he came.'

'No wonder he loves coming here,' remarked Christa as she watched Titan skid across the floor to Fred's wife and sit watching her patiently until she produced the longed-for treat. 'But I've not come so that Titan can be spoiled by you! I hear from Lorna that Fred's had a fall and cut his hand badly.'

'Aye, and he's in a bad mood today, won't have any breakfast. I tell you he'd rather have that filthy pipe than food! I've told him there's nearly fifty years of pollution in this house! Perhaps he'll take notice of you and stop smoking.'

'I doubt he will, Bessie, I've told him often enough. Anyway...' Christa drew Lachlan forward '...I've brought someone with me you may recognise—he says Fred used to give him chocolate mints many years ago when he was fishing in the loch. Lachlan Maguire!'

'Well, I'm damned,' quavered Fred. 'Can you believe it, Bessie? It's Isobel's son! We haven't seen you for many a year. I remember you when you were just a wee lad, fishing with your friend...'

Bessie beamed at him. 'You used to go past the cottage with your bikes!'

'And you used to come out with some shortbread—we loved that.' Lachlan smiled.

The old lady put her hand on Lachlan's sleeve and said gently, 'We were so sorry about your mother's passing, my dear, she was a very good woman. And I know she was so proud of you.'

'I think everyone around here was very fond of her,' said Lachlan. He looked down at the carpet, bunching his fists in his pockets, and Christa wondered how difficult it was for him to meet the local people who remembered him and his mother in happier times.

Fred looked at him over his glasses. 'And where did you get to all these years?'

'In Australia with the Flying Doctor service.'

Bessie looked impressed. 'My goodness—so far away! And have you got a family of your own now?'

'I'm afraid not, Bessie—I don't think I'm the marrying kind!'

'Nonsense!' said Bessie firmly. 'There'll be someone in this world just waiting to meet you, somewhere! You young people probably think it will never happen, but it will!'

'That's nice to know, isn't it?' He grinned. 'Although I have heard it said that some single people around here wouldn't get married for a million pounds!' For a second Lachlan's dancing eyes locked with Christa's.

So he *had* heard what she'd said to Alice and Ginny, thought Christa. A blush of embarrassment flooded her cheeks, and a sudden nervous urge to giggle overcame her, which she disguised by blowing her nose.

Fred drew on his pipe and looked at Lachlan keenly under his bushy eyebrows. 'Bessie and I thought it was cut and dried that you were going to join your mother when you'd qualified, and then you disappeared...' he growled.

'I suppose it was a sad time for the lad—he needed to get away...' interspersed Bessie.

Christa flicked a covert look at Lachlan. She was learning quite a few tantalising things about Lachlan's background!

Lachlan shook his head and said lightly to Fred, 'My plans altered. But I could never forget the folk around here that I grew up with, I assure you, Fred.'

'Aye, well...have you come back for good?'

'I hope so, Fred, for the time being at least. I'm going to be working with Dr Christa.'

Fred grinned, showing a mouth missing several teeth. 'She's well worth coming back for, a bonny lass like her! You're a lucky young blighter, aren't you?'

'Hush, Fred!' admonished Bessie. 'You let your tongue run away with you.' She smiled at the two doctors. 'Now, I'm going to get us some tea and a little bit of the short-bread you like while you look at Fred, Dr Christa.'

'A cup of tea would be lovely, Bessie.' Christa sat

down beside Fred. 'Right, Fred, first of all, what have you been up to with your hand?'

Fred looked down at his bandaged hand as if he'd forgotten about it. 'This? Och, that nurse of yours did it up for me, but she's always fussing about. I cut it on a piece of glass when I was pouring myself a wee dram. The tumbler fell out of my hand and I fell, trying to pick it up.'

Christa took his gnarled old hand in hers, and undid the bandage. His fingers were misshapen with arthritis, but what worried her was the palm of his hand, swollen and red, with the danger that the infection might spread, leading to septicaemia.

'Lorna was worried that it might be infected, Fred, and I'm afraid she's right. You'll need antibiotics, and it's most important that you finish the course. I want you to take one tablet four times a day. Lorna will come in tomorrow to see how it's going on.'

The old man frowned and repeated slowly, 'One tablet four times a day? How can I do that? If I've taken the tablet I can't retake it!'

Christa laughed. 'You're right, Fred, I put it badly. I should have said take *a* tablet four times a day...'

Fred winked up at Lachlan. 'You've got to watch these lasses—she's trying to make out I'm doolally!'

'I'll put these tablets in the box divided up into sections for each day with all your heart pills.'

'I'll be like a rattle when I've finished,' Fred grumbled.

'Talking of food, Bessie says you haven't eaten today.'

Fred waved an irritable hand at her. 'Stop fussing, woman! Bessie's trying to force-feed me, and I'm not hungry.'

'And it's none too warm in here,' said Lachlan, going

to the door. 'You need some more peat on that fire, and I'm going to get some. I bet there's some already cut outside.'

Christa watched him go out and reflected that Lachlan Maguire had hidden depths. When she'd first encountered him he'd seemed brusque and impatient, and she would never have imagined he would have been the thoughtful and kindly man he appeared to be now with the Logans.

She took out her sphygmomanometer and stethoscope out of her bag, and started to check Fred's blood pressure, and then listened to his heart. As she'd expected, it sounded erratic and fast, labouring to circulate the blood round his body.

'Well, how is it?' demanded Fred. 'I'll bet it's racing with a lass like you so near me!'

'You're a wicked old man, Fred.' Christa laughed, putting away her stethoscope. 'But I really wish that you'd let us get you both a little bit of help—someone just to come in for a few minutes a day to give you a hand with things. It would help Bessie, you know,' she added craftily.

Fred scowled. 'Has my lad Ian put you up to this? He wants us near him in Inverness, but I'm not bothering them. Anyway,' he added half-humorously, 'my daughter-in-law's a real tyrant—I don't fancy being in her hands!'

Christa knelt down beside him, took his gnarled old hand in hers, looking into the faded blue eyes, and said gently, 'They're worried about you both being so isolated, Fred—we all are. Won't you try it for a little while, please?'

The old man sighed. 'Aye, lass, perhaps you're right. The two of us are getting no younger. I'm a stubborn old fellow, I know. But if you think Bessie needs help then you can go ahead and organise it—but just for a wee while, to tide us over.'

Lachlan appeared with a box of peat sods and put one of them on the fire, where it hissed and sent up a spiral of aromatic smoke.

'I see you've lost a few tiles from your roof, Fred,' he said. 'The winter's coming on and you ought to have them looked at.'

'Aye. I'll do it when I've time, lad.'

Lachlan laughed. 'I wasn't suggesting you should do it. I've got a builder coming to Ardenleigh and I'll send him up to do them for you.' He put his hand up to stop Fred's protest. 'And before you say anything, that's doctor's orders!'

Fred subsided back in his chair and shrugged. 'You're bullies, all of you!' he said gruffly, but Christa felt there was a certain relief in his manner, as if he'd realised that it wasn't such a bad thing to accept help—if only for Bessie's sake.

Bessie reappeared and handed round cups of tea in pretty little cups of bone china and a plate with warm shortbread covered with sugar. She wouldn't let Christa help her pour out the tea or distribute the food—however frail, she was determined to show the doctors that they could do things independently. Despite Fred submitting to help, it was going to be difficult for them to accept that someone would be coming in every day to keep an eye on them. They were so used to doing everything for themselves.

'When Lorna comes in tomorrow morning to look at your hand, she'll introduce you to the home help she'll put in place,' Christa explained. 'She's such a nice young girl and will do any shopping for you once a week—and if you need the bed changed or perhaps a casserole done, she'll do that for you…'

Bessie stood up and said indignantly, 'I certainly don't need anyone cooking for us—I hope I can still put a hot-pot in the oven!'

'Consider yourself told off!' remarked Lachlan with a grin as they left.

The car did its usual impression of a bucking bronco as they set off again towards the valley below the Logans' cottage, a rough, grinding noise coming from the engine.

Lachlan raised his eyebrows. 'It really might be a good idea to get this car serviced soon. It sounds very dodgy to me.'

'Oh, don't fuss, it'll be fine. It's never let me down yet.'

Christa put her foot on the accelerator and the car seemed to recover for a few miles, but after a renewed series of bangs inside the engine and one or two lurches it came to an abrupt halt.

They both sat in stunned silence for a second, then Lachlan laughed, 'Never let you down, eh?'

'It's Sod's law, isn't it? Blast the thing! Are you any good at mending engines?'

'I can have a go, but on the whole I'm more au fait with the human body. You'd better ring your rescue company.'

Christa scrabbled for her phone and scrolled down to the number. After a few seconds she looked at him quizzically. 'No signal,' she reported.

'I'd better have a look at its innards, then.' Lachlan climbed out of the car and opened the bonnet, peering into it with a frown, then scratched his head. 'As I said, I'm more familiar with human intestines than all these pipes and tubes in a car. Perhaps,' he said hopefully, 'the plugs need cleaning.'

He delved into the engine, took out the plugs and began cleaning them with his handkerchief, then examined the oil and water levels.

'See if that brings it back to life,' he said.

Christa turned the key. There was a spasmodic cough and a brief shaking, then silence.

'I don't seem to have cured it,' remarked Lachlan. 'We'll have to wait until someone comes along, I suppose.' He looked up at the Logans' cottage, high above them on a hill and the little spiral of smoke drifting over the roof. 'I could run back there and use their land line,' he suggested.

'It's miles away, and I'm sure someone will come along soon.' Christa gave an exasperated sigh. 'I should have had the thing serviced, I know—there just didn't seem to be a window of time, what with organising the funeral and trying to get a locum...' She flicked a guilty look at Lachlan. 'Sorry, I'm certainly not moaning about organising Isobel's funeral. It's just—'

'I know,' he said abruptly. 'It must have been difficult, and of course I'm very grateful to you.' He was silent for a second, looking down at the road, scuffing the dirt with his shoes, then he said roughly, 'Of course I should have been there to do that. If I'd known earlier that she'd died...'

'We tried to find you—her solicitor did his best. If you'd left a forwarding address...'

Was it guilt that made his expression change and harden? Whatever it was, Christa had touched a raw nerve. 'Well, I didn't leave a forwarding address,' he said tersely. 'It's too complicated to go into now, but if my mother hadn't been so damn selfish...'

Christa stared at him in surprise. How could he say that about his mother? Surely she had been the most gentle and kindly of people and not deserving the cold-shoulder treatment meted out by her son.

'Aren't you being rather harsh on Isobel?' she said coldly.

Lachlan scowled. 'You don't know the circumstances—you see her as a colleague, not as a mother who ruined her son's life!'

There was a shocked silence broken only by the bleating of sheep in a field across the valley.

'What on earth do you mean?' asked Christa bluntly. 'How the hell did she ruin your life? Isn't this all rather melodramatic? After all, you've had a good job in a wonderful country—all you had to do was send the odd e-mail...'

'Don't tell me what I should have done, please.' His blue eyes glared icily at her. 'I don't need lessons in how to be a good son. It's too late for that.'

Funny how the atmosphere between them had plummeted yet again in the space of half an hour! God, he was touchy! But, then, she might have known that someone like him wouldn't have taken the slightest hint of criticism. How typical that was of a man—from charming and gentle to hostile and angry!

'For God's sake, stop feeling sorry for yourself,' she snapped. 'It seems to me you punished a lovely, kind woman for no good reason!'

Steely blue eyes held hers. 'Then let me tell you the reason that I left this "lovely, kind woman", as you call her...' Lachlan's voice grated with emotion. 'I was

seventeen when I learned that my mother—the woman
I looked up to and revered—had been having an affair,
betrayed my father and me!'

Christa's jaw dropped and she stared at him in disbelief. 'Isobel had an affair?' she faltered. 'I can hardly
believe it!'

'My father was not an easy man, he had a quick temper, but he was devastated. She refused to end the affair,
and he left. The happy home life I'd thought we'd had
vanished. I couldn't believe a word she said and it was
as if the family had never been happy, never been a unit
at all. She had put her own selfish desires before that of
her young son.'

Christa was stunned into silence then said slowly, 'I
never knew that. She never talked about her life before
I came—just the odd remark about you and how well
you'd done at med school.'

'Then,' he said bitingly, 'you had no right to tell me
what I should or should not have done—you didn't know
the background. Just because you forged a close bond
with my mother, it doesn't mean to say that she was an
angel.'

'I'm surprised you came back at all if that is how you
think of her.' Christa glared at his mutinous face. 'Perhaps it was only the fact that the practice became available—is that it?'

'How dare you say that?' His voice was low and con-
trolled but she could see the fury in his face. 'I came back
because I loved my mother...'

Christa closed her eyes. 'Oh, God, I'm sorry, I
shouldn't have said that. I didn't mean to hurt you. Of
course you loved her.' As usual, she'd opened her big
mouth before thinking.

Lachlan pushed a hand through his hair wearily and kicked a stone roughly into the verge. 'Oh, what the hell, it's I who should be sorry,' he said quietly. 'I've been unforgivably rude—perhaps it's because I feel so guilty. Of course I regret like mad not being here when she died, not making my peace with her.'

Suddenly he looked worn and tired, something grief-stricken in his eyes as he gazed unseeingly over the valley, and Christa glimpsed something of his inner turmoil.

She looked at him quizzically and said gently, 'We seem to be apologising to each other rather a lot! Let's hope our working relationship goes more smoothly.'

'Of course it will,' he said firmly. 'I know we can work well together. I suppose I've still not come to terms with things.' He sighed, a sudden sweet smile lighting his face. 'Friends again, then?'

And because he looked so gorgeous and incredibly sad, Christa forgave him, pushing to the back of her mind that she could never have left her own mother in similar circumstances. She smiled back at him, putting her hand up to pat his cheek comfortingly. 'Of course we'll be friends,' she said gently.

He caught her hand and squeezed it. 'Friendly colleagues, a good idea,' he murmured.

BODY SWAP?

CHAPTER FOUR

A GUST OF wind with a cold bite to it swirled around them, and a last bright shaft of light from the sun made the loch glitter. The blue skies were disappearing and dark clouds were coming up fast over the hills, changing the scene very quickly from benign to a dramatic, brooding intensity. Christa shivered and hugged her arms round her body, and Lachlan took off his jacket and put it around Christa's shoulders.

'Hey, you're cold. Look, put this jacket on.'

'I don't need it, I'm fine!'

He pulled the jacket round her and said firmly, 'You're not fine, you've gone blue! I don't want you going down with pneumonia before I've even joined the workforce.'

'I'm made of hardier stuff than that!' she protested.

He pulled the jacket further around her. 'Listen to me—I'm a doctor. I can tell when someone's getting hypothermia without having to take their core temperature.'

Lachlan's blue eyes danced mischievously into hers, and Christa looked away hastily. She wanted to be friends with him—but not too friendly! She stepped away from him, confused by her mixed emotions. One minute she was enraged by him and his plans to raise money for the house, and the next minute she was filled with sympathy because he obviously felt the loss of his mother so acutely, and the fact he'd missed her funeral. And now he was flirting with her. It was like being on a roller-coaster!

Lachlan's sexiness and cheeky smile, and the nearness of him, triggered a powerful memory of how it had been when Colin had been near her. She felt a longing to be held and loved again. In her imagination she could almost feel Lachlan's demanding firm mouth on hers, passionate, urgent, and his muscular body crushing her close to him. A little trail of fire ripped through her body, and for a second she closed her eyes, leaning provocatively towards him. That long-forgotten sensation of desire flickered through her again, bitter-sweet.

She couldn't encourage him like this—hadn't they just agreed they'd be 'friendly colleagues'? She stepped back from Lachlan abruptly and gave an involuntary shiver as if, having stepped to the brink of an abyss, she'd saved herself in the nick of time.

'There you are!' he said triumphantly. 'You're shivering. I know you're freezing!'

She looked at him mock-sternly, trying to keep things on a light level. She had to make it clear once again that their friendship was to be a strictly business arrangement, with positively no flirting! Wasn't that how her relationship with Colin had started—a little mild flirting?

'I'm actually feeling quite warm.' She smiled, shrugging off the jacket he'd put around her shoulders and handing it back to him. 'If you live around here long enough you become quite tough.'

'I think I guessed that...' He grinned down at her. 'I knew from the moment I first saw you yesterday that you were one feisty girl.'

'What on earth makes you think that?'

'Oh, I've gleaned quite a bit of knowledge over the past twenty-four hours to realise that you're something very special.'

Those blue eyes were flirting with her again, and she bit her lip. It could be Colin speaking, just the kind of thing he would say, and she was damned if she'd be hoodwinked by that any more! There was something chancy about Lachlan Maguire when he wasn't in a sombre mood, she concluded—that teasing manner combined with eye-catching looks spelt danger with a capital D!

She shook her head and said in a brisk, no-nonsense voice, 'You don't know me at all—just as I know nothing about you. It's going to be a learning process for both of us over the next few months, and I'm looking forward to a very good friendly working relationship from now on.'

A smiled touched Lachlan's lips at her formal tone and the slight emphasis she'd put on the word 'working'.

'Of course,' he said urbanely with a little bow of his head.

Perhaps, thought Christa nervously, the penny would drop now that she was only interested in him as a colleague and nothing else—no dangerous flirting! She stole a glance at him, his long, lean body now leaning against the car and his thick hair being blown casually over his forehead. Yes, it was definitely safer to make it quite plain from the outset that their relationship had to be purely professional—friendly maybe, but purely professional!

The sound of a car changing gear as it came up the steep hill floated towards them, and Christa went to the other side of the road to wave it down. Lachlan watched her wryly. They'd crossed swords twice in one afternoon, but he knew there was a spark between them. How

sensible, then, that they'd agreed to be friendly colleagues
and nothing more—keep that spark at a distance!

Of course it was a relief to him that their relationship
should stay at that level, he thought. The truth was that
he deeply resented the fact that his mother should try
and manipulate his life even from the grave—how dared
she suggest he marry Christa Lennox just because she'd
formed a close bond with the girl? How did Isobel know
the kind of girl he wanted?

In another time and place perhaps Christa would have
been the sort of girl he would have gone for. He sighed.
And if she hadn't been Angus Lennox's niece… But that
was a subject he was better off keeping to himself.

'So this guy's on top of the roof and I'm shouting at him
to come down—and guess who he turns out to be?'

Christa and her mother, Pat, were sitting in Pat's little bright kitchen, having a quick cup of coffee before
Christa went back to afternoon surgery. Titan was lying
contentedly by a radiator, half-asleep. Christa cradled her
mug of coffee in her hand and her mother leaned forward,
her bright, dark eyes, so like Christa's, alive with interest.

'I can't imagine who it would be. Brad Pitt perhaps?'

Christa laughed. 'I wish! Of all people, he's Isobel's
son. Lachlan Maguire!'

Pat Lennox stared at Christa in astonishment. 'Isobel's
son?' she repeated. 'Lachlan Maguire? He's turned up,
after all this time—I never thought we'd see him again!'

'I know—it's incredible, isn't it? He didn't know Isobel had died until after the funeral. He's been working
in Australia.'

'But what was he doing on top of the roof?'

'That's what I wondered. I thought he was filching

lead, but it turns out he was just inspecting the guttering. The place is very neglected, and his mother's left it to him. You do remember him, then?'

Pat took a sip of coffee and replaced the mug precisely on a mat on the table. 'Yes,' she said rather abruptly. 'Of course I remember him—he used to run home through the village from school, and your father supplied any drugs the practice needed.'

'Well, as I said in my text to you on Sunday, explaining that I wouldn't be able to pop in and see you, there was an incident with two youths in the big barn and luckily he was there to help.'

Pat got up from the table and went over to the coffee jug, her back to Christa. 'Sounds as if he came in the nick of time. Another cup of coffee? I'm having one…' Her voice was light, inconsequential, and she turned back to Christa with a bright smile. 'Fancy him being found. Sad that he missed Isobel's funeral, though. How long's he going to be here?'

'That's the thing, he's decided to leave Australia and he's going to come back to the practice. At first I wasn't sure about it but, actually, it's a relief that I've got someone.'

'You mean he's going to be working with you?'

'Well, yes. Apparently he's been pining for Scotland.'

'Did…did he say why he left, or at least stayed away for so long?'

'It's extraordinary—he told me he found out when he was just about to leave school that Isobel had had an affair when he was younger. That's why his father left. Lachlan blamed his mother for the break-up of the family, and I guess that's why he and she had a falling out. He didn't go into detail.'

Pat put her hands round her coffee mug as if to warm them, and gazed ahead of her as if looking into the past.

'But that was many years ago...' she said softly, and shook her head. 'All this time and never a word from him.' She focussed back on Christa. 'You'll be working closely with him, then, won't you? Probably get to know him quite well.'

A little nervous tremor passed through Christa, the doubts she was having about not allowing herself to get too involved with this man surfacing yet again.

She shrugged, trying to appear casually indifferent. 'Well, as colleagues we're bound to see each other quite a lot.' She looked at her mother more closely. 'You OK, Mum? You look a little pale.'

Pat Lennox stood up and moved restlessly to the window, twisting her hands together. 'I'm fine... It's just, well, you seem to be irretrievably bound up with the Maguire family, always working with them. Couldn't you get someone else...someone who has nothing to do with them?'

Christa looked taken aback. 'But surely you liked Isobel, Mum?'

Pat's lips compressed slightly and she said briefly, 'She offered you a job near me when I was very ill, and I was grateful for that—although perhaps I didn't find her as...congenial as you did.'

'I never knew you thought that,' said Christa in some surprise.

Pat picked up the mugs and stacked them in the dishwasher, then shrugged. 'It's of no consequence—one can't like everybody,' she said offhandedly. 'Tell me, is Lachlan's family going to join him soon?'

'Oh, he's no wife or children...and he can start straight

away, thank goodness. Frankly, I'm finding it pretty hard going at the moment and I can't wait for him to start properly next Monday.'

Pat turned round, leaning against the machine, her eyes studying Christa intently. 'You will be careful, won't you, darling, working closely with another single man...?'

Christa laughed. 'Oh, for goodness' sake, Mum. Just because I fell for that rat Colin when he was working at the practice, it doesn't mean that every single man I work with is going to break my heart! I'll be extremely careful who I fall for another time. I've learned my lesson. He may be reasonably good looking and have a bit of charm, but it's mixed with a short fuse. No—it'll be strictly business from now on, I can assure you.'

She met her mother's searching look almost defiantly, because she meant every word, thought Christa fiercely. She'd made it clear to Lachlan the other day when the car had broken down that there was no way she would allow relationships to get in the way of work. Yes, she admitted he was one sexy guy and that kiss had set every erogenous zone in her body buzzing and kept coming back to haunt her. But liaisons of any sort with him were quite definitely not on the cards. Once bitten, twice shy.

'Well, if you're happy to be working with Lachlan and he's a good doctor, I guess that's fine.' There was a terse note in Pat's voice and she softened it by smiling down at Christa lovingly. 'I...I just don't want you hurt again, darling, that's all.' She paused and sighed. 'What I really want is for you to meet a nice reliable man who won't let you down.'

Christa got up and gave her mother a hug, grinning. 'God, you sound as if you want me to marry Mr Dull-as-

Ditchwater… Anyway, you're looking very glam today—I like that tweed jacket. Are you off somewhere exciting?'

Pat laughed, suddenly looking very like her daughter, although her hair was white now.

'If you call going out with Bertie to the pub outside the village for a meal exciting!'

'Good for you!' Christa looked teasingly at her mother. 'You know, I don't know why you and Bertie Smith don't move in together—he only lives in the next flat. You might as well be married!'

'Oh, no, I value my independence too much. Besides…' Her mother's voice was brisk, devoid of self-pity. 'The thing is, I'm very fond of Bertie, but I made one lot of vows once, and I'm not inclined to make the same ones again.' She glanced at the kitchen clock on the wall. 'Aren't you going to be late? It's nearly two o'clock.'

'Oh, God, you're right…I'll have to fly!' Christa blew a kiss to her mother as she dashed out. 'See you soon—enjoy your meal… Come on, Titan, back to work!'

Friday night and a chance to wind down in the local little gym after a gruelling week. The surgery seemed to have been crammed with patients needing urgent referrals, and more than the usual amount of visits, and however ambivalent Christa was about Lachlan joining the practice, she couldn't wait for him to start work on Monday and take some of the load from her.

She really enjoyed her weekly workout at the gym, which her friend Richie had converted from one of the little warehouses off the main road. She admired Richie so much—he had been a ski instructor in the Cairngorms during the winter, but after a bad accident had had to give that up. After that he had trained to become a personal trainer, and had set up this small business. Gradually he was building up his clientele.

'Now a final exercise for those abdominals!' he shouted. 'Touching the floor with the heels as you air-bicycle for twenty... Good, good—and stop! Now a good stretch against the bars and then you can put the kettle on!'

Eight pairs of legs collapsed back on the floor and there was a general gasp of relief.

'You worked us hard tonight, Richie,' protested Christa, wiping her forehead. 'I'm so out of condition!'

'That's because you've missed a few weeks,' said Richie mock-sternly. 'I know you've been run off your feet, but no excuses now because I hear you've Isobel's son to help!'

'Yes, thank God. He starts properly on Monday—such a relief.' She smiled at Richie and looked around the gym, which seemed quite crowded. 'You seem to have more people here since I was here last. Things going well?'

Richie pulled a face and rotated his hands. 'So, so. At the moment I feel I'm just about making a breakthrough. But I've heard rumours about a new development...'

'When did you hear that?' asked Christa, amazed that what had apparently just been an idea of Lachlan's should be almost common knowledge so quickly. Hard to keep any secrets in a small place like Errin Bridge!

'The builder who adapted this place for me said that all the land around your medical centre could be sold off for a leisure centre and holiday complex, even a golf course! Can you imagine what that could do to a little place like this? I've invested quite a bit of money in it...' His voice trailed off, but Christa got his drift.

She looked at Richie's worried face with concern. 'It's not set in stone, is it, though?'

'Hopefully not. But I couldn't possibly compete with that sort of thing so close.' He sighed heavily. 'It's not something I want to think about, especially now Ruth is expecting our first baby.'

Christa was filled with sympathy for a guy who had tried so hard to turn his life round after his accident and the numerous operations he'd had to mend his hips. She tried to think of some positives. 'But surely that sort of place would be much more expensive than coming here. The subs would be huge.'

Richie shrugged. 'I've no doubt they'd hold out a carrot for a special opening offer. Anyway…' he straightened his shoulders and gave a wan smile '…I'm damned if I'll give in—I'll just have to try and attract more people somehow!'

'Good for you, Richie. I'll certainly try and get my friends to come, and some of my patients could definitely do with the exercise! It may never happen anyway.'

Christa went into the changing room, feeling slightly depressed for Richie and more than ever determined to try and convince Lachlan that his plans could adversely affect a great many people in the village.

She slung her old warm jacket over her shoulders and changed her shoes, deciding that she'd have a shower at home as there was a queue to use it in the cloakroom. She flicked a look at herself in the mirror and pulled a face— hair like a bird's nest and a face like a tomato! What a marked contrast to the photos round the walls of various celebrities apparently having just finished a punishing routine and looking neat and glowing.

Alice, one of the practice receptionists, had also been

to the class. She saw Christa glancing at the photos and grinned. 'There's been a bit of airbrushing on those photos! How else do you think the girls in keep-fit DVDs manage to look so cool and glamorous after forty minutes' punishment without some digital tweaking?'

'I need more than digital tweaking.' Christa laughed. 'I just want to get home before anyone sees me in this disgusting state. See you on Monday.'

She pushed through the door and barged heavily into the muscular arms of a tall guy walking past.

'Whoa, there! In a hurry?' The man held her at arm's length, then raised his eyebrows in surprise. 'Well, hello there! Dr Lennox, I presume. Getting your stress levels down?'

Lachlan Maguire was looking down at her with amused eyes, and she got a quick impression of a strapping, well-honed, muscular figure in Lycra shorts.

'Something like that,' she gulped, making a grab at her coat to conceal her perspiring, out-of-condition body.

The coat slipped from her shoulders onto the floor, and she stood before him feeling hot, dishevelled and purple-faced. She tried to disregard the fact that in gym attire Lachlan Maguire was the sexiest man that she'd ever seen.

'What are you doing here?' she enquired, trying to control her ragged breathing to something slower than if she'd been running a marathon.

'Trying to keep in good condition, like you!' Lachlan said, his eyes twinkling as they swept over her beetroot face. 'You've obviously upped your heart rate—keeping your body in good shape!'

Christa wasn't sure if there was a double meaning to

his remark. Was he referring to her admirable training regime or was he being more personal?

'I try to keep healthy,' she rejoined.

'I approve of that.'

He stepped onto the treadmill and started off at a brisk jogging level on tanned muscular legs, grinning cheerfully at her as he settled into a steady rhythm, increasing to a faster pace with seemingly little effort.

Christa clutched her coat firmly round her top. 'I thought you might be coming to suss out the competition,' she said lightly, mindful of their mutual pact to be friendly colleagues.

He flicked a puzzled look at her then his face cleared. 'Oh, you mean the leisure centre? I told you, it's only an idea yet.' He added rather offhandedly, 'But I don't suppose what I have in mind would have any effect on this place. I imagine we'd attract different clientele.'

'In what way? You'd be offering fitness classes and machine work. Where's the difference?'

He shrugged, still pounding away easily on the machine and scarcely out of breath. 'I imagine this gym would be cheaper and with less commitment. Here you can just pop in without joining for a minimum time...'

'But you can see how it would compete directly with Richie's little business.'

'I don't agree—I don't think he's got anything to worry about.'

Christa warmed to her theme. 'And what about the local people who benefit by Richie's gym—all the people popping into the little café over the road for lunch after they've exercised? I bet you'll have a plush coffee place under the same roof.'

Lachlan decreased his speed and stopped the machine,

before jumping off, barely panting and breathing with remarkable ease. He put out his hand and brushed some of Christa's dishevelled hair from her forehead, his eyes travelling down to her cleavage where a little bead of perspiration was making its way between her breasts.

'For God's sake.' He grinned. 'You're in headmistress mode again! If I did go ahead—and I repeat "if",' there's plenty of room for both businesses and more jobs to spread around as well.'

Then he got onto the rowing machine and started rowing with powerful strokes that looked effortless. He was the picture of athleticism, the merest sheen of perspiration on his forehead. The Australian way of life had obviously suited him, thought Christa, aware that she was still puffing and out of breath from her exercise class.

She dragged her eyes away from his impressive physique and said in her most reasonable voice, 'But it'll change the whole character of the village. Don't you agree?'

'Not sure I do,' he said lightly, upping the speed of his rowing.

Christa gave a snort of exasperation and stood looking at him with her arms folded. He stopped rowing and got off the machine.

'Got another point to make about the gym?' he asked impishly.

She shrugged. 'No—I've said all I want to about that, for the moment!' She turned to go out then stopped. 'Oh, by the way, I forgot that I haven't shown you your room at the surgery yet. If you come round tomorrow morning at about 11 o'clock I'll show it to you and give you a rundown on the computer system.'

Lachlan nodded. 'Good idea. I'll be there.'

He watched her as she marched out of the door, and grinned to himself. Little Miss Bossy, he thought, but, wow, what a figure, and how bloody sexy she looked in that far-too-tight Lycra costume! It was rather a pity that he'd sort of promised not to be anything but a friendly colleague, because he was going to find Christa's proximity extremely tempting…although, of course, just because his mother had said he should marry the girl made Christa the last person on earth he'd ever have an affair with. It was out of the question.

'So this is it. It was your mother's room, and we haven't really had a chance to clear it yet, but perhaps you're the one who ought to sift through things anyway.'

Christa watched Lachlan as he walked to the window, pulling aside the blinds and looking at the view. Then he turned back, surveying the room rather bleakly. That familiar fleeting expression of great sadness crossed his face and there was almost a little-boy-lost look about him. Suddenly Christa's arms ached to go round him, to comfort him, let him know that he wasn't alone in his grief.

At last he said haltingly, 'So this is where my mother worked, until about three weeks ago. It feels…rather weird.'

Christa said gently, 'It must do. No doubt you want to look at things quietly for a while. When you've finished, come through to the office.'

Lachlan nodded and sat down. The room was neat and tidy, very different from the house—it was almost as if this had been Isobel's real home, where she liked to be best. On the wall facing the examination bed was a large painting of the view over the hills from Errin Bridge— the sun was shining on heather-covered hills and the sparkle of the loch could be seen in the distance. He smiled. He knew that view so well, and he could guess just why she'd put it in that spot—so that nervous patients could look at it and be calmed.

He opened the drawers of the desk—they were empty except for a few papers and a brown envelope with some photos inside. He pulled them out and took a deep breath, staring at them as if transfixed. They showed a boy at various stages of his life—a toddler on a little tricycle, a young lad grinning into the camera with fishing rods in his hand, and a teenager with a sullen expression. They were all of him and written across the back of each were the words 'My darling son'.

Lachlan closed his eyes for a moment, overcome, then he put the photos back neatly in the drawer. The love he'd felt for his mother surged over him again and he felt torn by conflicting emotions—almost reluctant to accept his mother's legacy of the house if he could not in his own mind make amends in his heart by trying to fulfil her wishes.

'But you don't own me, Mum,' he muttered. 'You can't tell me who I must marry just because you liked Christa Lennox…'

CHAPTER FIVE

IT WAS THE weekly practice meeting, made more important because it was Lachlan's first official day at work.
He came into the room chatting to Lorna, the community
nurse, and Sarah Duthey, the part-time practice nurse,
whom he had met the week before. Christa was standing by the coffee machine, reading through the agenda.

'Are you coming or going?' enquired Lachlan, noting
she was still in her warm overcoat.

She looked up at him and dragged in her breath, swallowing hard. Holy Moses, he looked drop-dead gorgeous!
Until now she'd seen him in a variety of casual clothes,
from shorts to ragged jeans, but today he was in a dark,
well cut suit and crisp white shirt, which seemed to em-
phasise his tanned skin and rangy figure. He looked confident, relaxed and as if he could run the health service
singlehanded. Brad Pitt, eat your heart out, she thought
wryly.

She tried to ignore the double thump of her heartbeat,
and said smilingly, 'I've just got back from taking Titan
for a walk. He had a bust-up with a dog twice his size and
it took ages to catch him, so I've only just arrived.' She
waved a mug at him. 'What about a coffee?' she asked.

'That's a great idea. I haven't had any breakfast yet—

the kettle went on the blink and I forgot to stock up on milk…'

Christa smiled sympathetically and pushed some biscuits towards him. 'Perhaps these will help.'

'Thanks, they'll certainly keep me going.' He raised his coffee mug as if it were a wine glass and grinned at her. 'Well, here's to the first day of a happy working relationship!'

'I'll drink to that! By the way, before I forget, I'm having the director of information technology, Ahmed Kumar, round for supper on Thursday evening, and he wants to meet you. It's just a general discussion about networking the computer systems within the local hospitals and GP practices—not wildly exciting, I'm afraid.'

He grinned. 'On the contrary, fascinating stuff! No, seriously, I'm keen to be in on that, but more importantly a cooked meal would be a lifesaver! I seem to be on a restricted diet at the moment of a lot of ready meals in the microwave. It would be great to have some proper good food. It'll be the highlight of my week!'

'Don't be expecting a cordon bleu experience,' Christa warned nervously, suddenly wondering if her invitation for a meal was such a good idea.

Then Ben Conlan, the practice manager, came in and Christa introduced him to Lachlan. Ben had been on holiday for the past two weeks and hadn't met Lachlan before. He was a harassed-looking man who had a demanding wife and two sullen teenage children. Sometimes Christa thought he came in early and stayed late to get away from his family!

'How was the holiday, Ben?' she asked.

He groaned. 'We spent two weeks prising the kids out of nightclubs late at night, or going round the resort trying to find them, wondering what they were getting up to. I tell you, I'm glad to be back at work!'

They all laughed, and even Ben smiled. 'Good to meet you,' he said to Lachlan. 'We were all so fond of Isobel and it's great to know that you're carrying on the family tradition. I'm afraid my holiday came at totally the wrong moment, leaving Christa to try and find a replacement, so I'm so pleased that you arrived in the nick of time.'

Lachlan smiled around pleasantly at them all. 'I'm glad to be here. My mother obviously had a place in everyone's hearts at the practice, and I hope I'll be able to fill her shoes adequately and that I can give good service in Errin Bridge. However...' He paused for a second and the others looked at him questioningly. 'I have to say I'm a little dismayed at the state of the place—no need to point it out really...'

'You're right,' agreed Ben. 'Isobel had finally agreed to at least do up this part of the building that housed the practice, but sadly she died before we could get around to it.'

'Well, I intend to put things right. I'm planning to have the place reroofed ASAP, and when I've got the money together to do the rest.'

'Word's got out about your plans to sell some of the land for a leisure and holiday centre,' admitted Ben, adding cautiously, 'If the plans go through, I can imagine there'd be quite a lot of interest.'

Lachlan grinned. 'I'll have to be careful of any secrets I have in future! Why, I hardly know what the plans are myself yet!'

Christa bit her lip—better not to stir up a hornet's nest at Lachlan's first meeting.

Then, as usual at the meetings, there were discussions

about the budget, and individual patients and those who were housebound and had special needs.

Lorna, the district nurse, a pleasant-faced, motherly woman, explained to Lachlan how she and another community nurse in the area took it in turns to see their more outlying patients and that there was a rapid response team to step in for emergency care. Once a week a minor surgery clinic at the local cottage hospital offered treatment for removal of warts and moles and the different GP surgeries in the area took it in turns to man it.

'It's supposed to be for minor surgery,' said Christa, 'although some of the patients use us as a drop-in centre for a good chat! But it does have an X-ray unit and other back-up.'

'I'm all for that,' said Lachlan enthusiastically. 'Having worked in the Flying Doctor service I've got used to spreading myself over the whole area and not being confined to one surgery—keeps you in touch with the hospital as well. And I can tell you I'll be pleased not to work in forty-degree temperatures!'

Christa had a sudden image of Lachlan in shorts and a bush hat, leaping on and off aeroplanes and striding out with boundless energy over the Outback to get to his remote patients. It was rather an exciting thought...

Lorna's voice cut into Christa's reverie. 'Then I'll put Lachlan down for next week's stint, shall I?' she asked. 'I should think Christa could do with a break!'

'I look forward to it—I want to get into the swing of things as quickly as possible.'

Ben put his hand up. 'Just before we break up the meeting, don't forget the village dance next month to raise money for the new scanner at St Luke's. I said we'd take a party from the practice, so put it in your diaries. And I expect everyone to come!'

He looked sternly at them all, and Lorna giggled. 'Is it a three-line whip, then?'

Christa's heart skipped a beat. Every year the village held a dance for a good cause. Two years ago she'd been with Colin, and that had been the night that he'd told her their affair was over. It didn't hold good memories for her, and even if she wanted to go there didn't seem anyone to go with. Unless... She flicked a quick look at Lachlan, lounging back in his chair and making notes, and looking incredibly dishy. Then she dismissed the notion as preposterous!

Her thoughts were interrupted by Ginny Calder putting her head round the door.

'Could one of the doctors come immediately? We've a young girl who's just come in, and I think she needs to be seen urgently. Her name's not on our list—she wouldn't give me any details anyway.'

Lorna grinned. 'Well, Lachlan, you wanted to get into the swing of things! Looks like your wish is going to be fulfilled. Do you want to take this one?'

Lachlan stood up. 'No time like the present,' he remarked. 'Would you bring her into my room, Ginny?'

She was only a kid, Lachlan thought, and very heavily pregnant. She slumped into the chair and bent over tiredly, allowing for the bulge of the baby. Lachlan ran a quick assessing eye over her—matted hair, dishevelled clothing and a greyish complexion. She looked uncared for, young and vulnerable.

He bent down beside her, noting that close to she looked even younger than he'd thought.

'Aren't you feeling well?' he asked gently.

'I feel dizzy,' she mumbled. 'Not myself. Weak, sort of…'

He looked at her thin face and stick-like legs. 'Have you had anything to eat today?'

'A bit of toast…'

'Well, let me just take a few details.'

A guarded look crossed the girl's face. 'What d'you want to know?' she muttered sullenly. 'I just want a bit of medicine—a pick-me-up.'

Lachlan guessed that it had only been because she felt so ill that she'd come to the surgery at all, and that she wanted to remain as anonymous as possible. He'd make a safe bet that she'd never been to an antenatal clinic or had any tests done.

'Look, it's only for our records. No one else will know,' he assured her gently. 'Your age and where you live. To start with, what's your name?'

'Lindsay Cooper,' was the muttered reply.

'And your age?'

She looked at him defiantly. 'Fifteen… And don't tell me to get rid of the baby,' she said fiercely. 'If I went home they'd make me have an abortion, and I won't do that.' She stared at Lachlan as if daring him to censure her.

Lachlan's face was impassive as he wrote down the information. 'Then we'll make sure you and your baby have all the support you need,' he reassured her.

Lindsay was a tough little cookie, he reckoned, noting the flash of obstinacy in her eyes. She wasn't about to be pushed around by anybody imposing their wishes on her.

'And do you live locally?'

'I'm…I'm living temporary, like…with an aunt. She

doesn't know I've come.' Then more belligerently, 'And I don't want anyone to know either.'

From that Lachlan surmised that the young girl's family had not been supportive of her condition.

'OK…can you tell me how many months pregnant you are?'

Lindsay shrugged. 'Not sure…a few months maybe.'

'Never mind—I can make a rough assessment and you can have a scan later. I'd like to take your blood pressure and get some blood from you. But I've got a pretty good idea why you're feeling so dizzy.'

He took her hand in his, holding it palm down. The nails were cracked and spoon-shaped, and together with her red-rimmed eyes were reliable signs of iron deficiency. No wonder she felt so exhausted.

She looked suspiciously at Lachlan as he started to wind a sphygmomanometer cuff round her arm, propping up the scale indicator on the cupboard by the bed. He watched the dial as he pumped air into the tube, and made a note of the result without comment, then leaned back in his chair and looked at her kindly. 'I think you need building up, and a course of iron tablets. And bed rest wouldn't come amiss either.'

Lindsay laughed scornfully. 'I won't get much of that at my auntie's. I have to give my bed up in the daytime to her daughter who works nights at an old folks' home, and there's four little ones running around all day.'

'I was thinking perhaps a few days' rest in the local hospital—just to keep a check on you and a scan to discover how many months you are. How about that?'

The girl started to protest, but in a muted way. It didn't take much persuasion by Lachlan to make her agree, and he sensed that there was relief after her show of reluc-

tance. The past few months had obviously been gruelling for her.

'So you've an auntie who's taken you in. What about
a boyfriend?'

Lindsay blinked rapidly, trying to hold back sudden
tears, and suddenly looked like the little girl she really
was. 'He...he's in hospital. He had an accident.'

'Does he know about the baby?'

''Course he does.' She took a grubby tissue out of her
sleeve and scrubbed her nose, sniffing. She twisted her
hands together, screwing up the tissue and looked mourn-
fully at Lachlan.

He smiled at her encouragingly. 'What's he done to
himself—and which hospital is he in?'

'He fell from a roof and he's...he's really badly hurt.'
She rubbed her eyes and whispered, 'We...we was living together. Then a week ago he was with a friend...
He was trying to earn some money, and it happened. I
only heard about it when Carl came and told me. I don't
know how Greg is or anything... I think he's in that St
Luke's Hospital.'

Something clicked inside Lachlan's head. He frowned
and leant forward. 'What did you say his name is, Lindsay?'

'Greg,' she whispered. 'Gregory Marsh. He said he
knew a place he could get lead and stuff to sell—off
someone he knew. He was doing it for me and the baby...'
She gave a hiccuping sob. 'But he might be dead now,
for all I know!'

Lachlan widened his eyes in surprise and smiled.
'Well, well, what a coincidence! I've good news for you.
Greg isn't dead, although he's badly injured. I'm going to
ask my colleague Dr Lennox to join us, because she may

have more information about him. You see, we both happened to be there when your boyfriend had his accident.'

Lindsay stared in a dumbfounded way at Lachlan as if trying to work out what he meant. 'What d'you mean, you happened to be there?' she said falteringly.

'Because he had his accident just across the courtyard here, in the barn. Luckily we heard him fall and were able to help.'

Lachlan didn't go into detail, or mention the dodgy circumstances that surrounded Greg's accident—that was for another time. He lifted the internal phone and asked Christa if she could come in for a moment.

Lindsay shook her head. 'I don't understand. I thought he was going to a metal dealer's,' she mumbled. 'The thing is, I couldn't go back to the place we was living, not by myself. It was just a derelict building, so I went to my auntie's. At least she took me in. But when Greg comes out, he won't know where I've gone. He'll think I've scarpered.'

Lindsay looked at Lachlan piteously and he felt saddened by the car crash of a life that she was having. 'You never know,' he said comfortingly, 'we might be able to get a bed for you in the same hospital.'

Christa came into the room, eyebrows raised in enquiry. 'How can I help?' she asked.

She'd discarded her coat and was in a smart taupe-coloured suit with a slimline skirt and fitted jacket that emphasised the curves of her neat figure. Her auburn hair was drawn into a neat chignon to the back of her head and she looked cool, efficient and absolutely delectable.

Lachlan, unprepared for the jolt of his heart at her appearance, took a gulp of air. God, she was a knockout— he wasn't used to being distracted at work by any girl,

however attractive, and it slightly baffled him. He liked
to be in command of himself, in charge of the situation,
like he had been in Australia. Plenty of pretty girls there,
but none of them had seemed to have this unsettling effect that Christa was having on him.

He pulled himself together and said briskly, 'Ah, Dr
Lennox. This is Lindsay Cooper—Lindsay, this is Dr
Lennox. As I told you, she and I were at the scene when
your boyfriend had his accident.' He turned to explain
the position to Christa. 'I think that Lindsay needs bed
rest and observation for a few days. Her BP's slightly
up and she has definite signs of iron deficiency. Do you
think there's any chance she could get a bed in St Luke's,
where her boyfriend is?'

Christa smiled at the apprehensive girl. 'I'll do my
best. Hello, Lindsay, so Greg's your boyfriend?'

Lindsay's voice cracked slightly. 'I want to see him.
I didn't know what had happened until Carl came and
told me the next day...'

Poor kid—she looked totally exhausted and bleak,
thought Christa compassionately.

'I can tell you that he's making good progress. He
cracked one or two vertebrae in his back and his leg's broken, but luckily these are all things that can be mended,
although they'll take some time.' She turned to Lachlan.
'I'll ring Mr Foster, the gynae consultant at St. Luke's,
now and ask for Lindsay to be admitted.'

'Don't tell my parents where I am. Not that they care.
They slung me out when they knew I was expecting anyway. They'll only make trouble for me and the baby.'

How could parents do that to their young daughter?
wondered Christa almost in despair. Her eyes met Lach-

Ian's in mutual sympathy for Lindsay, and he smiled down at the young girl and patted her shoulder reassuringly.

'We won't tell your parents if you don't want us to. But for the sake of your baby, you need help—you've done the hard part, coming in here. Now let the right people help you. I'll ask the practice nurse to help you onto the bed and then I can examine you.'

In a few minutes Sarah Duthey had helped Lindsay onto the bed and draped a towel over her lower abdomen to give an illusion of modesty. She stood by as Lachlan gently examined the high, firm mound of the girl's abdomen, and all the time he chatted to her, feeling the tension in her body gradually relax and watching her clenched fists slacken.

'Now I'm just trying to find out roughly how far on your pregnancy is,' he said soothingly. 'At the moment the baby feels fine, but Nurse here will take some blood from you so that we can run a few tests to see how well *you* are. Do you know what you want—a boy or a girl?'

A glimmer of a smile appeared on Lindsay's lips. 'Don't care, so long as it's not a garden gnome!'

The two doctors and Sarah laughed. Lindsay was beginning to trust them, and that had been achieved, thought Christa shrewdly, because Lachlan Maguire was pretty good with vulnerable, edgy people. Not everyone would have been able to get through the hedgehog prickliness that Lindsey used against the world.

'I think from your size, Lindsay, that you're probably seven or eight months pregnant—that means we've got enough time to improve your iron levels and feed you up before the baby comes,' said Lachlan.

Lindsay propped herself up. 'So what do I have to do now?' she asked.

'We'll get an ambulance to take you to the hospital, where you'll be able to put your feet up.'

Sarah tucked a sheet over her. 'How about a nice cup of tea, love, while you're waiting?' she said.

Lindsay smiled and nodded, then lay back on the bed and closed her eyes, looking as if she could drift off to sleep there and then.

'The poor wee lamb,' murmured Sarah as she passed Lachlan and Christa. 'All she needs is some TLC.'

Later, when most of the staff were having coffee after morning surgery in the little kitchen, Christa said to Lachlan, 'You did well to get Lindsay to agree to go to hospital. I never thought she'd go.'

He grinned and shook his head. 'I think she was secretly glad to be taken care of. She'd obviously been living rough at some point. But Mother Nature's curious—you can get a girl who takes tremendous care of herself, eats all the right things, doesn't smoke or drink and she can end up with all kind of problems. And here we've got young Lindsay, undernourished and in general poor health, and her baby seems to be developing normally and a good size.'

'Fancy Greg Marsh being her boyfriend. God, one trembles a bit for her, relying on him to help her.'

'I think she's pretty clued up—she had the good sense to go to her aunt's when Greg didn't come back to her after the accident. She's probably going to be the one looking after Greg!'

Alice Smith came in with a pile of files and said cheerily, 'You're getting a pretty good press, Lachlan. This morning several of the patients asked me if you were the hero who saved the day and moved a dangerous beam when that boy was injured. I think your surgeries are going to be booked up for months ahead! And I've had the local paper on the phone, wanting a photo of you both for their "People of the Month" slot—they're coming some time today to get it into this week's edition.'

It wasn't surprising that patients took to Lachlan, reflected Christa. That special blend of kindliness and authority that she'd seen him display with Lindsay reminded her poignantly of another medic she'd worked with, and that was Isobel Maguire, Lachlan's mother— the best-loved doctor in the district.

The next few days were busy but very satisfactory in that Lachlan seemed to gel into the practice well and Christa began to relax. They had no verbal spats, and the subject of the development didn't come up. The only worry was the supposedly delicious meal she was going to provide for Ahmed Kumar, the director of information technology, and Lachlan on the Thursday evening. Eventually she'd decided on some venison in red wine and juniper berries, in her slow-cook oven.

Janet, her next-door neighbour, who always took Titan for a long walk in the middle of the day, would switch it on and by the time Christa got home it would be ready! She imagined Lachlan's gratified and impressed smile when he took the first mouthful—hopefully so much more delicious than the ready meals he'd been microwaving!

She was surprised when she arrived home that evening to find that no tantalising smell greeted her as she went into the kitchen—just Titan galloping across the floor to give her his usual extravagant welcome. She lifted the lid of the casserole and dipped a spoon in to sample the gravy and the meat—stone cold! What had gone wrong with the blessed thing? Then she noticed with increasing horror that the light was out on the cooker. Janet must have forgotten to do it—or, more probably, Christa had forgotten to tell her!

'Marvellous!' she muttered, slamming the lid back on the casserole. 'What on earth shall I do now? They'll be here in half an hour!'

She peered hopefully into the fridge. Nothing much in it except for eggs, a few shrivelled little mushrooms and two tomatoes. Not enough for the banquet Lachlan must be expecting. She was pondering whether she had time to rush to the supermarket when the telephone rang. It was Ahmed on the line, sounding very weary and fed up.

'So sorry, Christa, I'm still at Heathrow. I was in London for a meeting and the flight's been cancelled. Can you believe it? I probably won't be home till tomorrow now.'

Of course she could believe it, thought Christa wryly— it was that kind of an evening! Any minute now Lachlan would call to say he couldn't come either, which of course would solve the dilemma she had of nothing to produce in the way of food! She commiserated with Ahmed and assured him that it didn't matter, then flopped down in a chair as she considered what to do.

Maybe, she thought hesitantly, she should ring Lachlan and say the evening was all off for now, and they'd arrange it for another time. A funny little feeling of disappointment niggled at the back of her mind—despite the fact that Lachlan coming to be fed that evening had worried her all day.

She brought up his number on her phone, but the only response she got was for the caller to leave a message and he would get back to her as soon as possible. He was probably on his way already, she thought in a sudden panic. She just hoped he liked omelettes!

Christa flicked a look at her watch—just time for a quick shower and a change of clothes. If she couldn't produce a good meal at least she could try and look fresh and less work-weary. She scrambled into a pair of jeans and a loose-fitting blue silk blouse, gave her hair a quick brush and her lips a quick slick of gloss just before the doorbell rang. Funny how her heart started hammering against her chest. After all, this wasn't a date. It was just an evening together to discuss practice affairs—nothing exciting at all. Titan bounded joyfully to the door. He liked visitors, and barked a welcome.

Christa gulped nervously and murmured to Titan, 'I should have put him off, shouldn't I?'

But, then, she said sternly to herself, this was purely a polite social evening for two new colleagues to get to know each other, and just because Ahmed couldn't come there was no reason why she and Lachlan shouldn't spend the evening together.

And then she opened the door and swallowed hard as she looked at Lachlan. She *had* done the right thing after all! The porch light threw a sort of halo around him, investing him with a bright glamour. Like her, he had changed into jeans, as well as a loose cream sweater over an open-necked shirt. Casual suited him so much—he looked younger, more relaxed, and that Australian tan made his eyes seem bluer, his teeth whiter. She took a deep breath. She had to put his good looks to the back of her mind because, of course, she had told him friendship was the only thing on the cards—nothing else. Madness to think otherwise!

She brushed a tendril of hair back from her forehead,

hoping she looked more composed than she felt, and said unnecessarily, 'Oh, there you are!'

He stood there, smiling engagingly, with a bottle of wine in one hand and a large box of chocolates in the other, his eyes lingering for a microsecond over her tall, slender figure.

'Hello, there, Dr Lennox! I've been dreaming of this meal all day. All through Mrs Phillip's description of the trouble she's been having with her haemorrhoids, and likewise Mr Burn's saga about his bad feet, my stomach's been rumbling with anticipation...'

Christa pulled a wry face. 'Oh, God. I'm awfully sorry, but I'm afraid your dreams of a meal are going to be dashed,' she said, leading him through to the little living room. 'Dinner's off, and I hope you're not allergic to eggs!'

CHAPTER SIX

LACHLAN THREW BACK his head and laughed. 'That's a great welcome! But an omelette would be fine—anything that doesn't come in a fast-food packet!'

'The thing is,' Christa explained, 'I forgot to tell my lovely neighbour to turn on the slow cooker, and then Ahmed rang to say he's stuck at Heathrow. The evening's been a disaster before it's even started!'

'Oh, I don't know,' said Lachlan, his eyes twinkling at her. 'I think we can manage without Ahmed or the full-blown meal. Tell you what—I'll uncork this wine and you start throwing the eggs in the pan. How about that?'

And that is what she did, and after a mushroom and tomato omelette and a bit of salad, along with two glasses of very nice Sauvignon Blanc, somehow the evening didn't seem such a disaster after all.

There wasn't a dearth of conversation—Lachlan had plenty of questions to ask about the practice, and although they talked about improvements to the surgery, the vexed question of the development of the land never came up.

The dining table was in an alcove in the little sitting room, and a wood fire burned in the grate—it all looked cosy and warm. Christa had decorated the walls in a soft cream and the sofa and chairs were covered in modern striped upholstery. Lachlan looked around approvingly, taking in the neat pine dresser against the wall and the little desk under the window—just the right size for the room.

'This is a lovely little place,' he said. 'You seem to have struck just the right note. Not too old-fashioned, and it looks bright and fresh. I'm at a complete loss to know what to do with Ardenleigh. The rooms are beautiful, but I've not a clue how to furnish them. I'd like a fresh start, I think.'

The wine seemed to have loosened Christa's tongue and she found herself saying brightly, 'Could I help at all? I rather enjoy planning the colours in rooms'

He pounced on the idea enthusiastically. 'That would be fantastic! Let's make a firm date for you to come and look at it all. The place is really far too big. I'm beginning to realise that, and yet, well, it's such a beautiful house, and although there's just me, it's always been a dream of mine to live in it again.'

'Your mother wanted you to have it, didn't she? She left it to you. And as for it being too big, you're bound to have a family eventually.'

Lachlan raised an amused eyebrow. 'Am I? I don't think I'm the type to marry, settle down and have children. At least, I've no plans in that direction. Keep your options open, I say!'

So just like Colin, then, play the field, never give yourself completely, thought Christa grimly. Love and commitment didn't seem to be in their vocabularies.

Lachlan watched her expression and said quietly, as if in explanation, 'Marriages that break down can have a devastating effect on a family—I know that. Never give promises you may not be able to keep.'

Christa bit her lip. He was probably referring to his own parents' marriage, and it certainly seemed to have affected him deeply, to the point of him leaving his home. Her own father had died some years ago, but he and her mother had had a very happy and loving marriage. Christa's childhood had been idyllic, and although it had been horrible when her father had died, her mother had borne her sadness with stoicism and had taken up new interests and made plenty of friends.

Lachlan rose from his chair and walked over to the fire, standing with his back to it.

'Talking of families—what about you? I can't believe that there hasn't been someone special in your life.'

He was bound to find out sooner or later, because Colin dumping her for someone else wasn't a secret. That was part of the heartbreak, it being so public. Everyone in Errin Bridge had known they were an item. And then everyone had begun to realise that he had been playing the field at the same time as dating her—everyone except her, of course, cocooned in her safe little world of romance and love.

'There was someone once, not any more.' Christa's voice sounded casual—too casual, as if she was making a deliberate effort to make a broken love affair sound of no consequence. Lachlan's blue eyes looked at her astutely.

'You had a bad experience, then?'

'Like loads of people, it didn't work out. End of story,' she said flatly.

'It's never the end completely, though, is it?' murmured Lachlan. 'Hard to switch off from loving someone with all your heart to feeling nothing at all for them.'

'Very perceptive of you.' She shrugged. 'I learned something from the experience, and I realise now that Colin and I wouldn't have been right for each other anyway.'

Lachlan frowned. 'Colin...?'

Christa shrugged. 'Colin Maitland—the one you used to go fishing with when you were a little boy. He worked at the practice for a while.' She added flippantly, 'He did a pretty good impression of a rat while I was going out with him.'

'He's always had a reputation,' growled Lachlan. 'Now, there's a man I thought would never settle down to marriage. You told me he was married now, didn't you?'

'Oh, yes.' Christa gave a mirthless laugh. 'He found her while he was going out with me—the word's "two-timing", I think.' She rose from the sofa and went over to Lachlan and picked up the photo on the desk. 'This was him on his wedding day.'

Lachlan took the photo from her and looked at it, then said slowly, 'Why did he marry this girl if he liked to "play the field", as you said?'

'Because Paula became pregnant, and she's the daughter of the MP for this area. As a local doctor Colin's name would have been mud if he'd abandoned her. But it was a shock, I can tell you, when I heard about the engagement from someone else—not from Colin!'

'What a sod. How long had you gone out with him?'

'About two years. I was mad about him—and I thought he loved me too.'

The words hung in the air, bleak and heartbreaking, revealing only too well the story of shattered dreams. Christa gave a shaky little laugh. 'I'll never be so naïve again!'

'Did you go to the wedding?' he asked softly.

'No. That was something I couldn't bring myself to do. So he sent me that photo.'

'As if to show you what you'd missed out on? What a bastard!' He frowned. 'Why on earth do you keep a photo up of the man on his wedding day?'

Christa looked at the floor, twisting her hands together, and whispered after a short silence, 'Because... because I needed to remind myself every day that he wasn't worth crying about...but it didn't seem to work...'

Something in the catch of Christa's voice made Lachlan look closely at her. She had bowed her head, but he could see a tear rolling slowly down the curve of her cheek, and then she put up a hand and brushed it away impatiently. In an instant his arm was round her shoulders, hugging her to his body and wiping away her tears with a handkerchief.

'Christa—sweetheart. I'm sorry, I didn't mean to hurt you, to stir up old memories. What a dolt I am!' He rocked her backwards and forwards as one would to comfort a child, stroking her hair gently. 'He's always been a selfish sod, out for his own pleasure, never mind who he tramples over. Perhaps that's why we lost touch.'

'It's not your fault I'm upset,' snuffled Christa, blowing her nose and shaking her head. 'I'm an idiot to cry over the man. The thing is, the week before he married Paula he came round and begged me to go back to him.'

'But he was engaged to someone else. How the hell could he do that?' Lachlan looked down at her, and a flicker of amused sympathy flickered in his eyes. 'Is that the reason I overheard you say you wouldn't get married for a million pounds?'

A wry smile touched Christa's lips. 'Can you blame me?'

'Of course I don't. And since then there's been no one?'

She shook her head and looked up at him with some spirit. 'Absolutely not! I can do without men and sex for quite a few years, thank you very much—too much hassle!'

He chuckled and looked down at her with dancing eyes. 'That's my feisty girl,' he murmured, giving her a comforting squeeze. 'But I wouldn't put a time limit on your celibate life, it's a hell of a long time to be lonely.'

She laughed back at him, with a sudden feeling of release in having told her sad little story. Lachlan was right, she couldn't condemn herself to singledom for years just because a man had hurt her in the past. She relaxed against him, and his arm around her felt comfortable, safe.

'Perhaps you're right…' she murmured. 'Maybe I should live a bit, play the field. Enjoy life!'

He stroked her soft cheek. 'You can't live in the past, Christa, or let the darned man ruin your future.'

In the background the wood fire crackled and Titan snored slightly in his basket. The atmosphere was warm and intimate, just the two of them together. They smiled at each other, then gradually something changed between them and the smiles faded. They were so close—standing hip to hip, her soft breasts pressed against his body, his face so near hers she could see the little grey streaks in his hair, smell the male smell of him, the clean, soapy freshness of his body.

Of course it wasn't the first time Christa had felt that dangerous thrill of attraction towards Lachlan Maguire—she'd tried to suppress it then, but now it was like a red-hot flame flickering treacherously through her body, unstoppable. And as he held her close with his arm around her, she was only too aware of how much he

wanted her as well. She knew exactly what was going
to happen—could see the dark need that mirrored hers
in his eyes.

Was she crazy to blank out the loneliness of the past
two years by making love to a man she knew wasn't in
the market for any emotional attachment, someone she'd
known for a bare two weeks, for heaven's sake? But, then,
she was under no illusions about Lachlan Maguire. He'd
told her he didn't believe in lasting love. She was going
into this with her eyes open. And, hey, she wasn't into
commitment any more either, was she? She just wanted
to be desired, to have fun once more.

He was still stroking her cheek gently and she put her
head against his chest. 'Lachlan…' she faltered. 'It's been
so long. I think I've almost forgotten how to…'

'Oh, no, you haven't, sweetheart,' he said huskily, and
lifting her face to his he brought his mouth down on her
full, tremulous lips, kissing them softly at first and then
more demandingly.

And whether it was the uninhibiting influence of the
wine, or because she had just unburdened herself to him,
Christa threw caution and sense to the winds, and it felt
natural and right that she should wind her arms around
his neck, arching her body against him in instant response, opening her mouth languidly to his. Her insides
liquefied with longing, her heart beating a mad tattoo in
her chest. Two lonely people and no strings attached, fulfilling a mutual need. Wasn't that what she wanted? The
bitter memory of Colin's betrayal faded into the background.

Lachlan gazed down at her in the half-light of the
room, examining her face—the black lashes fringing

those wide, amber eyes, her full, soft lips and the ten-drils of hair across her forehead.

'Christa,' he whispered raggedly, 'you are so bloody delectable. When I came back, I didn't expect to find someone like you around.' He wrapped his arms around her tightly and put his forehead to hers. 'You do know where this could lead, don't you? Do you really want this to happen? Will you be sorry later?'

And she almost laughed because surely it was too late to have second thoughts with his hard frame clamped around hers and every erogenous zone in her body de-manding release that very moment. She felt as if she were on a wave of euphoria, light-hearted, free of the sad thoughts that had plagued her when she'd thought of Colin.

'Of course I want it to happen. I want it very much.' She held back from him for a moment, her eyes dancing. 'Is this what you meant by being "friendly colleagues"?'

His face split into a grin. 'Certainly—if you want to interpret it like that,' he murmured.

Lachlan pulled her gently down onto the sheepskin rug on the floor and unbuttoned the silk blouse and the wispy bra she was wearing. Then he tore off his shirt, and his hard and demanding body was on her soft skin, his lips trailing down to the little hollow in her neck, his skilful hands exploring her most secret places, arousing her to fever pitch.

And suddenly Christa realised she hadn't forgotten what it was like to make love, and somehow it was more marvellous than she ever remembered. She ignored the tiny seed of doubt that hovered at the back of her mind—could she really live for the day, keep her feelings for Lach-lan as casual as he wanted to, after what was happening?

* * *

Afterwards they lay curled around each other, and Christa fell asleep in Lachlan's arms. He watched the embers of the fire flickering and their shadows on the wall, and the most incredible feeling of happiness swept through him. He looked down at her face against his chest. God, she was beautiful—her skin as soft as a peach and those large expressive eyes that were a running commentary on her feelings.

He'd certainly never led a celibate life—plenty of girls had given him every encouragement, but no one had awoken in him this strange and sudden tenderness he felt for Christa, or moved him like she had. Dammit, this wasn't supposed to happen, was it? This was meant to be a light-hearted romp, neither of them committing to the other...pure lust on either side. And yet it didn't seem to be working like that for him at all. What should have been a one-off, ships-that-passed-in-the-night scenario felt like just the beginning, the start of something precious and exciting.

Only a day or two ago he'd vowed that Christa was the last person he should become involved with—not just because of their families' entwined histories but because he wasn't going to be ruled by his mother's wishes and ever ask Christa to marry him. And he still believed that, didn't he? Then he thought of the photos he'd found in his mother's desk and their poignant words on the back: *My darling son.*

An ache for something once cherished and lost for ever overcame him. Perhaps after all his mother had only wanted the best for him—and yet he still shied away from that complete commitment to another person, was still sceptical of the 'Till death do us part' bit. He'd seen how breaking vows could lead to broken lives.

Christa stirred in his arms and opened her eyes, looking into his, and smiled sleepily.

'Hello,' she murmured. 'That was…wonderful, wasn't it?'

He held her close to him and kissed her tousled hair. 'Yes,' he whispered. 'Quite wonderful.'

It was late, very late, when Lachlan left. Christa walked slowly through the living room into her bedroom, her heart dancing with a happy excitement she hadn't felt for a very long time. She saw the photo of Colin on his wedding day, and picked it up, looking at it scornfully.

'I don't need the memory of you any more, Colin Maitland,' she said calmly. 'I've my own life to lead now, without your shadow hanging over me.'

She dropped it in the waste-paper basket and went to bed. Christa enjoyed the best sleep she'd had for many weeks.

Alfie Jackson sat bellowing loudly on his grandmother's knee in front of Christa. His eyes were round and frightened behind wire-rimmed spectacles and his mouth a large wide 'O'. He was three years old and dressed in a policeman's uniform, the helmet sitting crookedly on his head. He looked utterly adorable, and completely inconsolable, holding one hand tightly in the other.

'So what happened, Mrs Pye?' asked Christa loudly above the noise.

Mrs Pye, plump and flustered, said helplessly, 'I feel so guilty. I'm supposed to be looking after the little lad today—my daughter's got this interview for a part-time job this afternoon. I was getting Alfie ready for a party and he opened a cupboard to get something out and then slammed it on his finger! It looks so sore and I don't know what I can do…'

Alfie turned and buried his face in his grandmother's ample bosom, sobs shaking his little body. In between the sobs could be heard the words 'Not my fault…the door hurt me!'

'Of course it's not your fault, Alfie!' soothed Christa. She came round the desk and bent down beside him. 'Won't you just let me have a little peep at this poorly finger, sweetheart?'

Predictably, more screams and Christa sighed inwardly. It had been quite a gruelling day, including a quick dash over to see the old shepherd, Fred Logan, who'd developed a urinary infection and had been taken to hospital. He'd needed a lot of persuasion to do that! Dealing with a frightened child in great pain was going to be even more difficult. She pulled open a desk drawer and pulled out a small toy car, wound it up and placed it on the floor, where it proceeded to flicker and whirr, with lights flashing on and off as it whizzed round the room.

'Look at that, Alfie—look!' cried Christa, above the child's sobs.

A very quick peep from his grandmother's bosom, and then a more prolonged stare as the toy banged into the wall, somersaulted and started off again. In those few seconds Christa managed to prise Alfie's hands apart and saw for herself the little boy's blackened nail and swollen finger, incongruous on that small, chubby hand.

She winced. 'That is one sore little finger,' she said to Mrs Pye.

'I suppose it'll have to be drilled, won't it, Doctor? Oh, dear, I don't think I could bear to watch…'

'I can do something much more quickly and more accurately than that,' Christa assured her. She lifted the internal phone and pressed the button for Lachlan's room. 'Have you got a minute? And a match or a lighter?'

In the few seconds it took for Lachlan to appear Christa had taken a needle out of a packet and a pair of tweezers from a box in her drawer. Mrs Pye looked nervously at her.

'Wouldn't it be better to take Alfie to hospital and give him an anaesthetic?'

'If we can release the pressure now, before the blood begins to clot, it will be instant relief. By the time you get to hospital it would be too late to do much,' explained Christa.

Lachlan came into the room, his imposing figure somehow reassuring, his eyes taking in the scene at a glance then coming to rest on Christa. Their gazes locked for a heart-stopping moment, but even in that moment she could read the messages of desire and need in his eyes, the memory of Lachlan's body moulded to hers, his hands caressing her, bringing her to fever pitch coming back to her in graphic detail… What a difference a night had made! A rush of adrenalin flickered through her, made her pulse start to race.

She was brought back down to earth as Lachlan turned to Mrs Pye and Alfie, and said briskly, ''I thought I could hear a young man in pain over the intercom. What's happened?'

Christa pulled herself together, almost ashamed that she'd allowed thoughts of their lovemaking to intrude on her professional life.

'Alfie's got a subungual haematoma on his finger,' explained Christa succinctly.

Lachlan winced. 'Ooh, poor little chap, that's very nasty. But, as Dr Lennox has no doubt told you, we'll soon have him right as rain again. Here's the matches. I pinched them from the kitchen.'

'Now, Mrs Pye, I want you to hold Alfie very firmly,' instructed Christa. 'I'll hold his hand and if we keep it steady, it'll take literally a few moments.'

Mrs Pye gave a faint squawk of horror. 'I hope I don't faint,' she quavered, her eyes on stalks as she watched Christa strike a match and Lachlan hold the pin with the tweezers in the flame until the tip of the pin glowed red.

Alfie redoubled his screams, but Christa held his hand in a vice-like grip while Lachlan pressed the red-hot pin firmly onto the blackened fingernail. There was a slight hiss and a faint trace of smoke as the pin burnt through the nail and a tiny globule of blood appeared through the hole.

Christa bound the small finger with a gauze strip. 'I can guarantee that it's hardly hurting at all now. Am I right, young man?'

A few residual sobs from Alfie, and then he looked down at his covered finger. 'Is it better now?' he asked.

'It will heal very quickly. You can even go to your party now if you want to!'

'Well, I'm blessed!' murmured Mrs Pye in awestruck tones. 'Can you credit it, just a pin and a match!'

Christa smiled. 'We aim to please—but don't try it at home.'

Mrs Pye shuddered. 'Certainly not!'

The little boy slid off his grandmother's knee, his

policeman's helmet at a rakish angle over his brow, and
Lachlan crouched down beside him.

'You've been a very brave policeman,' he said. 'It so
happens we give medals for brave policemen, don't we,
Dr Lennox? You're a hero, Alfie!'

He reached into his jacket pocket and pulled out a
metal badge with 'Bravery Award' imprinted on the front
and stuck it on Alfie's little jacket. Alfie looked down at
it and then a beam split his round face.

'Am I?' he said, looking at Lachlan round-eyed, and
then turned to his grandmother. 'I'm a hero, Grandma!'

Lachlan ruffled the little boy's hair and smiled. 'Enjoy
your party.'

Mrs Pye smiled tremulously at the two doctors. 'Oh,
thank you so much, I'm really grateful. Come on, Alfie,
love.'

She took the little boy's hand and they walked out, an
incongruous couple—the large elderly lady and a very
small policeman, now chattering happily to his grandmother.

'A very different child from the one who came in,'
observed Christa. 'You've made a friend of that young
man!'

Lachlan smiled. 'It was a job well done,' he commented. 'They call it "trephining", don't they? A neat
little trick!'

'Did it on a short course called "Surgery on a Shoe-
string".' She grinned.

'Very droll…' He caught her arm as she went past
him to the desk and swung her towards him. 'Christa…
about last night…'

She gazed at him innocently, but a smile quivered at
the corners of her mouth. 'What about last night?'

He grinned and ran his finger down her cheek. 'Don't be a minx…and why do you look so unutterably gorgeous? You should look exhausted after what we did last night…'

'I slept rather well,' Christa said demurely.

'Well, among other exciting things, last night you said you'd help me with ideas for the house—don't forget about it! Perhaps you could come over one Saturday or Sunday and we could have a walk and eat a pub lunch after you've had a look at things?'

It sounded idyllic—so unlike the weekends over the past months, which, although there had been many fun times with friends, playing tennis or riding in the hills, had been without that thrilling excitement of being with someone who was the sexiest thing on two legs!

'I might be able to manage that,' Christa said gravely. 'I'll pop round with some sample pots of colour from the decorator's shop in the village.'

Lachlan's hand went behind her neck and he drew her to him, kissing her full on the lips. 'I look forward to it very much indeed…' He held her away from him, and his eyes twinkled at her. 'Don't let it be too long!' Then he left the room.

Christa hoped her flushed cheeks had faded and that Alice didn't notice anything untoward in her appearance when she came in a few minutes later with the post.

And then the phone rang, and it was the community nurse, Lorna, to say that Bessie Logan, alone in the cottage, had fallen after Fred had been taken to hospital, and although she was uninjured was finding it difficult to stand unsupported.

'Bessie managed to ring her son, Ian, in Inverness, and he got hold of the rapid response team from the hospital,

who came and got her up,' explained Lorna. 'She's adamant she won't go to hospital because she thinks Fred
will be back soon and she must be there for him.'

'I'll come immediately,' promised Christa. 'Surgery's
nearly over and Lachlan can cover for me.'

On her way through the hills, back to the Logans' for
the second time that day, Christa started singing, filled
with a joy of life that she hadn't had for so long. She'd
always loved her job—the variety of it, helping people
through the highs and lows of their lives—but the sadness of Colin's betrayal of her had tarnished that pleasure. How strange that a man she'd been determined to
dislike should have changed her whole perception of life
in a few hours!

She considered the Logans and the support they were
going to need. Christa didn't doubt that Bessie would not
be at all eager to go into a retirement home, and immediate plans for her future would have to be discussed very
tactfully when she arrived at Bessie's.

Bessie was sitting up in bed, sipping a cup of tea and
chatting with Lorna and three members of the rapid response team. Ian, her son, had also arrived, looking big
and brawny in the small room, his face creased with
worry.

'Good to see you, Doctor,' he said. 'Mum and Dad
have given us a bit of a fright today, what with Mum's
fall and Dad being taken in to hospital.'

Bessie looked frail and frightened. 'I'm sure they're
going to send me to a home, but I don't want to go, really I don't,' she said in a faint voice, her faded blue eyes
looking pleadingly at Christa. 'I'll be all right. I just took
a tumble, but I'll be fine.'

She looked anxiously from Christa to the team and

Christa went up and took her thin little hand, lying on the counterpane.

'Don't worry,' Christa said reassuringly. 'We'll sort something out, Bessie. Nobody's going to send you any-where—only if you need nursing for a little while. How is your walking?'

'I'm not too bad with a frame.' Bessie sounded rather defiant, as if to tell them all that she could manage very well.

'We think maybe she's not been eating, with worry about Fred, and that could be why she's a little weak,' explained Lorna.

'I think we'll take some blood for anaemia and thy-roid function,' said Christa.

Ian stood by, twisting his cap in his hands and look-ing frustrated. 'I'm concerned,' he said in a low voice to Christa. 'Mum being all alone in the hills here—it's not satisfactory. I'd really like her to come home with me.' He directed his words to his mother. 'It would just be for a few days, Mum.'

'But I need to be here for your father. He could come home any day.'

'I don't think he'll be back for a week at least,' said Lorna. 'It's going to take a bit of time to get on top of the infection he's got. Would you not go back with Ian for a little while?'

Bessie tried again. 'What about one of those disc things that you wear round your neck and can call some-one if you fall?'

'You're still a long way away in the middle of the night, Mum. Please, you know I'll worry so much if you're by yourself.' He turned to the others in the room. 'I'd come and stay here but I'm in the middle of a new job—I don't think it would go down well if I took time off.'

Bessie sighed. 'Well, perhaps for just a few days, then. Just to get my strength back.' She looked dolefully at Christa. 'That Shona of his—she's a bully, though!'

They all laughed, and Ian threw his eyes to the ceiling. 'You need looking after, Mum. You've been working so hard here, and a bit of care and feeding up is what you need, and Shona's looking forward to doing that!'

'Well, when you come back we'll put forward a plan for your needs,' said Christa. 'Hopefully Fred will be back then.'

Ian came out with Christa to the car. 'It's been difficult, Doctor,' he said wearily. 'I know she's a wonderful old lady, but she can be as stubborn as an ox! I really think my parents would be much safer in a retirement home.'

'No one wants to leave their own home, Ian—we can't force her. We'll assess their needs for long-term care when she's come back here. Who knows, in the end she may see for herself that life is going to be very difficult looking after Fred and herself out here. Why don't you and Shona start looking around homes to see what they're like? Just groundwork really.'

He nodded. 'Aye, we'll do that. Anyway, I'll bring her home with me now and I'll be in contact with you regarding Dad and his progress.'

It was practically dark by the time Christa returned home. She parked the car and as she fumbled for the key in her bag, the door opened in the next house and her neighbour, Janet, came out, with a bowl of flowers in her hands.

'Hi, Christa, I saw these on your doorstep when I

came back from taking Titan for a walk. I took them in, in case that cat down the road started playing with them. Aren't they lovely?'

Christa took them from her and buried her nose in the delicate arrangement of tiny tête-à-tête daffodils and freesias in a small blue pottery bowl.

'Mmm, they smell so fresh and springlike,' she said.

'Looks like you've got an admirer,' teased Janet.

Christa tore open the note that was stuck on the side. It said, 'Thank you for the most delicious omelette I've ever had in my life.'

She giggled, then grinned at Janet and stuffed the note in her pocket. 'Only a thank-you note for a pretty awful meal I made for the new partner in the practice,' she said lightly.

And although she glowed with pleasure as she put the little arrangement on the table, she told herself sternly that it was just a polite but amusing gesture of thanks, and that the evening had meant nothing more to Lachlan than a bit of fun between two people who were free agents.

Of course they were attracted to each other, but hadn't they agreed, as adults who knew their own minds, to keep it cool without commitment? She smiled wryly to herself. Deep down, didn't she yearn for more than that with Lachlan? Something that would involve a meaningful future?

CHAPTER SEVEN

Please be ready at seven-thirty tonight for a brain-storm meeting re work, etc., to expand on what we did the other evening. We need to discuss that thoroughly. We'll go to local restaurant. Lachlan.

CHRISTA GIGGLED. READING her e-mails at work was usually pretty routine, but this one gave her a jolt of delight. She wondered just how much work would be discussed at the 'brainstorm meeting'! The 'etc.' bit gave her a clue that there would be more to it than talk about the practice, and a lovely feeling of anticipation at meeting him later on kept shooting through her all day.

This was her first 'proper' date with Lachlan Maguire, but she was determined to take things slowly, stick to her airy intentions of keeping everything casual and emotionally detached between them. Well, she could try, anyway!

She sent him a reply. 'Look forward to discussing programme...'

Christa was ready hours before seven-thirty. It seemed like a family of butterflies was fluttering in her stomach, and as if this first proper invitation from Lachlan to go out with him was one of the most important dates she'd ever had in her life. She'd gone through every outfit in her wardrobe and discarded them all as unsuitable. During the past year, shopping for clothes had not featured much in her life. Finally she'd selected a pair of black trousers with a soft blue angora jumper that was warm without being suffocating.

She looked doubtfully at herself in the mirror as she brushed her hair. Was she looking too casual? Not casual enough? Then she laughed, wondering just why she was getting in such a spin. It was just going to be a normal, pleasant evening of chat, wasn't it? But it had been a long time since she felt this sort of excitement before a date. Had she really felt this pent up before going out with Colin? She bit her lip, remembering how she had sent caution to the winds and had had a wild affair with him that had all ended in tears.

She certainly wasn't going to be like that with Lachlan—however much she longed to. He wasn't for commitment and if anyone got hurt it would be her. If she'd learned anything from her past mistakes it was to be careful when it came to love. Just because she and Lachlan had had an unexpected fling one night, it didn't mean that was on the agenda for every date!

She peeped out of the window—the snow had started falling heavily and she suspected the wind would be as sharp as a honed knife. When it was cold in Errin Bridge it was really cold. She put on a coat her mother had given her, a long cream suede with a sheepskin lining, and plonked a Cossack hat made of fake fur on her head, then went to the door when she heard the bell.

Lachlan had on a large quilted jacket and fleecy hat with ear flaps, his clothes covered with a dusting of snow. He ran his gaze slowly over Christa, taking in the way the tendrils of her auburn hair curled round the white hat, the contrast of her flushed cheeks against the cream of the coat.

'Wow,' he said softly. 'You look like a snow queen…'

He leant forward and brushed her mouth with his lips, his cheek cold against hers. Christa felt herself go limp with desire—so much for keeping things light and casual! If he'd suggested giving up on the meal and going inside to make love, her good intentions might have floated out of the window.

'How gorgeous are you?' he whispered, drawing back and looking down at her with those sexy eyes of his.

'Well, you look as if you've just landed at an airport!' She grinned. 'Very macho and rugged.'

He grimaced. 'Thank you! Good job I kept this old hat—I used to use it when I was in the Flying Doctor service. It's come in useful for this weather, although I don't think it matches up to your outfit in any way. By the way, I hope you're hungry!'

Anticipation seemed to have taken away Christa's appetite. She'd been longing for this all day, and now the time was here she couldn't think of a thing she wanted to eat!

'Matelli's' restaurant was small and intimate and quite busy. There were red and white tablecloths gaily covering the candlelit tables, and on every wall were murals of sunny Italian scenes from the Bay of Naples to hilly views of Tuscany. In a corner a young man was playing Neapolitan songs softly on a guitar, and Christa felt that it was like stepping into another country after the wintry conditions outside.

Paolo Matelli, the owner, made a fuss of them as he

led them to a table in an alcove, talking in a strong Italian accent.

'Ah! My favourite doctors! My bad back ees completely better, thanks to you, Dr Maguire! I miss your dear mother very much—but you are taking over very well! And, Dr Lennox, you look after my wife so well when she had her last baby! Look! I show you how well the bambino does!'

He whipped out a little leather folder and opened it, revealing several photos of a bouncing baby boy. Then, as the two doctors admired the photos, he fussed around, putting napkins in front of them with a flourish, pouring water into glasses.

'He's beautiful, Paolo. What do you call him?' said Christa.

'Vincente. He's very good, the best baby in the world!' Paolo's eyes twinkled at them. 'I tell you, there is nothing like a happy family to keep you going, eh? I trust that, like me, you will be blessed too!'

'I hope I will, Paolo,' said Lachlan quietly. 'And you're right—everyone needs a happy family.'

Christa looked at him compassionately. You didn't have to scratch very much beneath the surface for the experiences in Lachlan's own family to be recalled in the flicker of sadness in his blue eyes, and a shadow passing over his face.

Paolo put menus before them. 'Well, take my advice, and don't leave it too late. You have to be young to cope with five of them!'

'Five children?' remarked Lachlan, his grave face breaking into a grin. 'I'd like children but I think five of them might test me a little.'

A little throb of longing lodged somewhere in Christa's

brain, the wistful thought that she would love to have his babies—any amount! She looked at his face as he gravely studied the menu. She'd seen him dealing with youngsters over the past few weeks and had thought what a great dad he'd make. Perhaps he'd be strict, but fun and loving, learning from what had happened in his own life.

For goodness' sake, what are you like, Christa? she thought wryly. You're only on a first proper date with the man and already you're making him a father!

Lachlan looked at Christa across the table. The light in the restaurant was muted, but in the glow of the candlelight her auburn hair looked lustrous and her eyes as warm as a summer's day. When she looked down, her thick eyelashes shadowed her peachy cheeks. God, she was perfect! He longed to kiss her full mouth, to run his hands over the light blue angora jumper she was wearing, feel the softness of her breasts underneath. The sudden heat of desire rushed through him—for the first time in his life he knew that he wanted more from a girl than a light-hearted liaison, but he didn't want to rush things. Christa had had her heart broken before, she probably wasn't ready for commitment yet! Paolo came up to him, holding a bottle of champagne.

'I hope you accept this from our family—just to help make the evening a happy one!' He popped the cork and poured the sparkling liquid into two fluted glasses. He beamed benignly at them both. 'There! You celebrate, yes?'

'Thank you, Paolo—we'll do our best! We've a lot to discuss.' Lachlan's eyes held Christa's, something very tender in their warm depths, and she felt her heart turn over with happiness.

She laughed as they chinked their glasses together. 'I

thought you wanted to have a "brainstorm meeting" to discuss work,' she said impishly.

'First things first—let's order some food. I'm starving! I believe Paolo's the best cook in the north east of Scotland.'

'I know what I'm having—scallops in wine sauce.'

'Make that two,' said Lachlan. 'And I think this bottle of champagne will go down well with that.'

Paolo bustled away and Lachlan picked up his glass. 'To us, sweetheart…' His blue eyes were warm and tender. 'I can't believe that only a short time ago I didn't know you…and now look where we are!'

They chinked glasses again, and then he leant forward and took Christa's hand. 'And now I want to know everything about you—why my mother took you on and when your friendship with Colin Maitland started…'

Christa swirled the champagne in her glass and watched the bubbles rise. She smiled and shrugged. 'Not much to tell, really,' she began. 'I'd been away for a long time, at med school and then doing my GP training. I returned to Errin Bridge because my mother had had a mastectomy and my father had died. I wanted desperately to be near her, but jobs for GPs weren't plentiful as there was only one medical centre in the village. I didn't want to work miles away, and in desperation I went to your mother to see if she needed anyone.'

Lachlan watched Christa intently. 'And? Did she take you on immediately?'

'She seemed a bit cautious at first. Said she'd think about it. I'm so glad that she did!'

'You obviously got on well.'

Christa smiled in reminiscence. 'Oh, yes! She had a great sense of humour—she was always telling me to find a man! And the irony was that four years ago she took on Colin Maitland.'

Lachlan nodded. 'Ah, the charming Colin—he pulled the wool over your eyes, then?'

'And some! Of course I fell for him completely—I thought the feeling was mutual. I made excuses for him when he didn't always turn up when he said he would, when he said he had to go off on long weekends… In short, I was a bloody fool! Gave away my heart too easily, I guess.'

'Still bruised by that?' commented Lachlan lightly.

She laughed and shrugged. 'I've certainly learned a few lessons…' Then she added softly, 'But it was Isobel who saved me. She was incredibly kind, told Colin he'd have to find another job. If…if it hadn't been for her, I don't think I could have coped.'

'Of course you would! My mother was obviously very fond of you too—I know she would be pleased that we'd got together.'

Christa grinned. 'Perhaps. On the other hand, she might have thought you were completely mad to start something with me!'

The scallops arrived, steaming and succulent in the light wine sauce, and suddenly Christa felt ravenously hungry.

She looked at Lachlan impishly. 'This looks better than omelettes,' she murmured.

'Nothing will ever outdo the omelette you made for me that night,' he remarked, his eyes twinkling. Then he added, 'By the way, you haven't forgotten that you offered to give me some ideas about doing up Ardenleigh. This weekend?'

'Of course—but not this weekend. I'm at a conference in Inverness on cardiovascular disease.'

'Sounds pretty riveting,' he teased. 'Come a week on Sunday, then. Would that be OK?'

'I'll be there,' she promised.

He leaned towards her, his hand behind her neck, and kissed her softly on her full lips. 'Something to look forward to then…' he murmured.

Paolo bustled up to their table solicitously, beaming at them both. 'Excuse me, *signor, signorina*, a little something from the sweet trolley now? Tiramisu, pannacotta or a delicious gelato perhaps?'

'Just a cappuccino for me,' said Christa. 'I couldn't manage another bite of food!'

'And then home…' whispered Lachlan.

Christa looked at him shrewdly—he had that mischievous twinkle in his eye that revealed what he was anticipating when they got home! And how wonderful it would be to tumble into bed with him and make love. Wasn't she longing for a rerun of the other night? Then that cautious inner voice warned her to be careful—was this going to become the norm, that after an evening out they went to bed together? That was how she and Colin had started—a mad affair that in the end had left her bereft. Surely she'd learned to tread more carefully this time…

She looked at him mock-sternly. 'Don't get too many ideas, Lachlan Maguire. That night we had together was meant to be a one-off!'

'Point taken,' he said, with a wicked grin. 'No harm in trying, though!'

And Christa surmised that he might be chary—not because he was afraid of a broken heart but because he didn't want things to get too serious—whereas she could feel she was already on the threshold of tipping into that thrilling roller-coaster of being headlong in love that she hadn't felt for so long…and it was wonderful.

Christa rested back in her chair and yawned after a busy afternoon dealing with everything from sore backs to chickenpox, and her thoughts drifted happily back to her evening with Lachlan at Matelli's. Despite the fact that she was sure Lachlan was a fair way off a long-term commitment in their relationship, she had a little bubble of elation inside her that made everyday irritations fade into minor blips.

She grinned when she recalled Ginny coming into her room that morning with a face like doom.

'Everything's happened this morning,' she'd intoned gloomily. 'The computer's crashed and the man can't come until lunchtime. We're going to be in chaos.'

Whereas normally Christa might have shared Ginny's frustration, somehow today it hadn't seemed to be such a disaster. 'Oh, well,' she'd remarked serenely. 'We'll just have to go by the manual diary until he comes.'

'And the cleaner's just walked out. Where on earth will we get someone else at short notice?'

'Don't worry!' Christa had said gaily. 'I'll ask my neighbour—she runs an agency. I'm sure she'll find someone.'

Ginny had frowned as if unconvinced and pursued her pessimistic theme. 'And this month's figures on non-attenders are worse than ever. What are we going to do about that? Ben wants to discuss it with you.'

Christa had smiled. 'Oh…we'll put a notice up warning people we may have to ask them to pay if they don't give us notice of non-attendance. We may not be able to carry it out, but it might frighten them!'

Ginny pursed her lips, looking at Christa suspiciously. 'You don't seem terribly bothered—it's not like you to take it all so well. Usually you hit the roof!'

'Oh, well—no good worrying, is it?' Christa had declared blithely. 'We'll work it out!'

Ginny had sighed heavily as if she couldn't understand Christa's casual attitude and had stomped out. She liked to keep on top of all problems! Dear old Ginny—she'd be having a good chunter with Alice about the doctor's irresponsible manner. But that's how being on the edge of love made you, Christa had thought—rather carefree—and after all the sadness of Isobel's death, it was lovely to feel that way!

Now, at the end of the day, Alice came in with a cup of coffee and glancing at Christa's happy expression said rather pityingly, 'I'm afraid I'm going to wipe that beaming smile off your face, Christa. You've got another patient to round off the day. Mrs Donnington, of all people. She's been slotted in this afternoon as an emergency—wouldn't you know it would be her?'

Christa took a grateful sip of coffee and said mildly, 'But that's what I'm here for, Alice! I'm her sounding board, you know. Mrs Donnington may be a pain in the neck sometimes, but part of her trouble is that she's lonely and has no one to talk to.'

Mrs Donnington was a widow, a 'frequent attender', convinced that she suffered from myriad health issues, continually worrying about her health but never with anything specific wrong with her.

'But she comes in nearly every week—she's taking up another poorly patient's place,' protested Alice.

'Even so,' said Christa lightly. 'I can assure you the one time we don't give Mrs Donnington an appointment will be the time she'll have emergency appendicitis. We ignore her at our peril!'

Alice grinned, unrepentant. 'Not much chance of ignoring her. I'm afraid she's got a complaint—other than her health, of course…'

Christa laughed. 'Well, what is it this time?'

'She feels she's been put to the back of the queue today—calls it "discrimination". She wanted to be fitted in this morning—she said an afternoon appointment was highly inconvenient and she'd miss a very important meeting. I offered her one tomorrow, but she said it was too urgent for that.'

Alice went out, clutching a pile of post, and Christa pressed the call system button that lit up the board in the waiting room, calling the next patient.

Amanda Donnington, elderly, but tall and imposing, came into the room and sat down heavily in the chair, pulling off her scarf and sounding rather breathless.

'At last, Doctor! I've been in such discomfort, and this seems to be the only appointment I could get today, although I wanted to come this morning.'

'Tell me what the problem is,' said Christa kindly.

Mrs Donnington fixed her with a steely glare. 'Of course the main problem is that this place is dangerously understaffed. Since Dr Isobel died it's been nigh impossible to get an appointment on the day one wants. It's been chaos!'

Don't I know it, thought Christa wryly. She smiled at Mrs Donnington pleasantly. 'At least you're being seen today, and you'll be pleased to know we've got another doctor in the practice now.'

'Ah! About time! Perhaps urgent cases won't be pushed to the back of the queue now! Do I know this doctor?'

'He's Dr Lachlan Maguire, Dr Isobel's son.'

Mrs Donnington's expression livened up. 'Really? So he's turned up after all these years. Funny how he left his poor mother so suddenly and never a word from him…'

Christa butted in hastily before her patient could give her thoughts about that. 'Please, tell me what's worrying you.'

'Oh, I suppose you'll say it's nothing to worry about—that's the usual response I get,' remarked Mrs Donnington rather sourly. 'I've been trying to cope with it for as long as possible, Dr Lennox, knowing how stretched you are, but eventually I've had to give in. Sleep has eluded me completely. I shall need sleeping pills.'

'Where is the discomfort, Mrs Donnington?' asked Christa patiently.

'It's this cough I have—all night, no respite.'

'How long have you had it?'

'On and off for a while. I didn't mention it when I came in last week because it wasn't so bad. But it's got worse. And I'm so sweaty at night. It's extremely uncomfortable.'

Christa looked at Mrs Donnington more closely. She certainly didn't look as robust as usual, paler and perhaps slightly thinner in the face. Somewhere alarm bells rang.

'Have you lost weight, Mrs Donnington?'

'I don't believe in this obsession with weighing oneself—but clothes do seem a little looser, I have to admit.'

'You aren't a smoker, are you?'

'Certainly not, a filthy habit. I'm afraid my dear husband was a chain smoker. I could never persuade him to give up.' A genuine look of sadness crossed Mrs Donnington's face. 'And of course he died of a smoking-related illness, a few years ago now.'

Christa took out her stethoscope. 'I think I'd better have a listen in to your chest.'

A few minutes later, with the examination done, Christa sat down in her chair and looked thoughtfully at her patient. She didn't want to alarm her unnecessarily, but for once Mrs Donnington's trip to the doctor's had been very necessary. The decreased breath sounds and unusual lung noises with areas of dullness in the lung were symptoms that could not be ignored.

Apprehension flickered across Mrs Donnington's face. 'Is something wrong, Doctor?'

'You've certainly got signs of loss of lung function—possibly an infection, for which I'll give you an antibiotic—but given your shortness of breath, night sweats and possible weight loss, I'd like to send you to the chest clinic at St Luke's Hospital.'

Mrs Donnington turned pale. 'The...the hospital?'

Christa leaned forward in her chair and smiled reassuringly. 'I want to make sure we cover every possibility, and I can't do all the tests here or give you a chest X-ray. But you've done absolutely the right thing coming to me...'

'You think I've got lung cancer, don't you?'

'Not necessarily. Your symptoms could have many reasons—but we need to cover every possibility. Of course it's my job to investigate your problem, and if I'm not sure of a diagnosis to send you to a consultant who specialises in everything to do with lungs. I'm sure you agree with me, don't you?'

Mrs Donnington suddenly looked smaller and frailer. Most of the many times she'd come to see the doctor her complaints had been trivial and her worries had always been allayed—now she was having to face the reality that she could be really ill.

Christa watched Mrs Donnington with compassion as the woman tried to assimilate the unexpected news that her complaint could be more serious than an irritating cough. There would be shock, physical as well as mental, a feeling of being out of control, even panic.

'I don't want you to think the worst, Mrs Donnington,' Christa said gently. 'More often than not these things turn out to be run-of-the-mill symptoms that have no sinister cause. Now, why don't you go and have a coffee with your daughter? Doesn't she live near you?'

Mrs Donnington got out of her chair slowly, clutching her enormous handbag, and gave a nervous laugh. 'Oh, I don't think so... Verity leads a very demanding life, you see, what with taking the children backwards and forwards and dealing with her horses. We don't seem to have time to see each other very often, and, as she says, the weekend is the only time she gets to herself.'

And that's one of the clues to the cause of Amanda Donnington's loneliness, thought Christa, looking at the sad expression on the woman's face and wondering how much the woman's grandchildren featured in her life. Without knowing Verity, Christa surmised that an elderly woman who might be bossy, interfering and possibly rather needy, could be sidelined from the daughter's life.

She smiled sympathetically. 'Well, treat yourself to something at the local café! I'm going to ask for an early hospital appointment, which should be in a few days. You won't have long to wait.'

Mrs Donnington nodded, her imperious manner diminished. 'Thank you, Doctor. Thank you for seeing me.' Then added with more spirit, 'I knew there was something wrong!'

And that, thought Christa wryly, was a very good example of why every patient should be listened to carefully. She wrote an e-mail to St. Luke's lung and chest department, asking for an urgent appointment for Mrs Donnington.

She closed down the computer and picked up her handbag, wishing like mad that she'd be seeing Lachlan that weekend, instead of sitting through two days of lectures on tackling cardiovascular disease.

CHAPTER EIGHT

AFTER THE STUFFY gloom of the lecture hall it took Christa a second or two to adjust to the bright light in the huge reception area. All around her people were jostling and chattering, relieved to stretch their legs after a long stint listening to the professor's rather expressionless voice expounding on the benefits of the early diagnosis of hypertension.

A small plump figure with blonde hair materialised in front of her, and a cheery voice said, 'I don't believe it. Christa Lennox! I never thought I'd see you here!'

Christa stared in surprise at the smiling face. 'Suzy Collins, as I live and breathe!' she gasped. 'I thought you were in Australia!'

'Not any more I'm not! I'm married and doing anaesthetics near Glasgow now.'

The two women embraced and Suzy stepped back and surveyed her old friend admiringly. 'You look better than ever, Christa—hardly changed at all after nearly ten years. I thought a few years in the hard world of work would age you!'

'Is it that long since we shared a house at uni?' Christa laughed. 'God, have we got some catching up to do! Let's have lunch and forget about hypertension and cardiac problems for a while.'

They made their way to the canteen and sat down at a side table.

'So,' said Suzy. 'What's it like, working up in the Highlands?'

Christa gave her a quick résumé of her life at Errin Bridge, and told her of Isobel Maguire's tragic death.

'Isobel Maguire?' repeated Suzy with a frown. 'Not Lachlan Maguire's mother?'

'You know him?' asked Christa in surprise.

'I met him in Sydney when we were first looking for jobs. We kept bumping into each other—he always had some glamorous bird in tow!'

Christa's heart did a double thump. 'I suppose he had lots of girlfriends,' she said lightly.

Suzy chuckled. 'You don't get a hunky guy like him being stuck for female company. But he was always very careful not to get tied down—you know what I mean? I knew him quite well and we used to have the odd coffee together—nothing romantic between us, I was otherwise engaged! He used to tease me, saying he couldn't understand people getting hitched for life—he liked to have variety!'

'Oh, he did, did he?' Christa forced herself to laugh, but Suzy's description seemed to be an accurate portrayal of what Lachlan had said, so it shouldn't surprise her.

'Too right! Many girls tried to catch him, but he wouldn't be tied down. So, honey, you be careful around young Maguire,' teased Suzy.

'I certainly will.' Christa smiled, but her casual words hid her firm intention to be very careful indeed when it came to dating Lachlan. Everything Suzy had said

seemed to confirm what he was like. Then she changed
the subject and they talked of the happy times they'd
had together as students, and what had happened to all
their friends.

'It's been so good seeing you,' said Suzy when they'd
finished lunch. 'Let's get together very soon. We mustn't
lose touch again. I'd love you to meet Pete, my husband.
He's looking after the kids at the moment, so I'll be dash-
ing off after this afternoon's stint.'

And for the rest of the weekend Christa seemed to hear
Suzy's words about Lachlan echoing round in her head.
'He couldn't understand people getting hitched for life!'
A gypsy's warning, perhaps?

Christa had barely seen Lachlan since their evening out
at Matelli's As they had arranged then, the Sunday following the conference she was to go over to Ardenleigh
with her ideas on decorating the house.

When the day came she was delighted to see that after
a week of dull, cold weather it was a beautiful sparkling
day. She pulled on a fleece over her T-shirt and jogging
pants, and Titan bounded up, full of joy at the anticipation of a long walk.

'Come on, then, Titan—we'll see Mum before we go
to Lachlan's.'

The little dog gave a bark of approval and trotted
cheerfully alongside Christa as she set off. The crisp air
was as heady as champagne, and she took deep breaths
as she ran along the lane towards her mother's flat, feeling the release of tension as she worked her body hard
after a week's arduous work. There was a light hoar frost
on the verges, and it clung to the trees and hedges, glit-
tering in the morning sun—everywhere looked magical.

Her thoughts went like a magnet to Lachlan. Indeed, it had been difficult to get him out of her mind since that magical night when he'd come over for a meal. In moments when she wasn't busy, her imagination worked overtime, feeling the firmness of his mouth kissing her lips, his skilful hands caressing her and the strength and warmth of his fit, lean body against hers. She'd almost come to the conclusion that she would never again feel attracted to any man. But after only a short acquaintance with Lachlan, everything in her body and mind was revitalised—she felt alive, energised and free of all the sad memories of the past.

She was tremendously happy—of course she was! She was going to be spending most of Sunday with Lachlan. He'd suggested lunch and a walk after they'd discussed the colour schemes and alterations he might try at Ardenleigh.

Christa tried to push to the back of her mind any possibility that she might be stupid enough to fall madly in love with a man who only wanted a brief encounter. Suzy's words still echoed in her head, and it would be a sure-fire way to having her heart broken again.

This heady feeling of happiness wasn't love—of course it couldn't be. She'd only known the man a matter of weeks. But it was certainly an overwhelming attraction. She was going to play it cool, make sure that the only exercise they did would be that brisk walk and forbid herself to think their relationship would go on for ever! She didn't want a rerun of her experience with Colin.

She turned into the drive that led to the block of flats in which her mother lived and knocked on the door, which was on the latch.

'Mum? Are you there?' she called. 'I've just dropped in for a moment to make sure you're OK.'

She heard the murmur of voices in the lounge and went into where her mother was sitting with Bertie, her friend from the next-door flat.

Pat came over to kiss her. 'Darling—how lovely of you to come over. Have you run here? How trim you look! I wondered if you'd have time to see me this weekend, you being so busy at the moment.'

Bertie, tall and military looking, bent down to stroke Titan. 'Grand little dog, this,' he said. 'If we weren't in a flat I'd have one just like him.'

'You can always borrow him.' Christa smiled. 'How are you, Bertie—your angina not troubling you at the moment?'

Bertie was a patient of hers and had had a few episodes of angina over the past few years.

'Absolutely fine. Those pills work a treat.'

'Well, don't forget to come in for your check-up soon. Are you off somewhere nice today?'

'We're just off to Marfield House—it's that stately home in the hills. We'll have a little walk in the grounds and a coffee. I'm so glad it's not raining, everything looks so much better in the sun.' Pat looked assessingly at her daughter. 'Talking of looking better, you look one hundred per cent less stressed and tired than the last time I saw you. This Lachlan Maguire must be pulling his weight. Is he proving an asset?'

'It's a tremendous help, having him there.'

'So you like him, then?'

Christa suppressed a giggle but kept her voice light. 'He's a good doctor—no worries about that.' She paused for a second and then remarked easily, 'Perhaps you ought to meet him some time.'

Her mother smiled. 'Maybe, one day—there's no hurry, I'm sure,' she said lightly. 'And you? What are you doing today? Having a rest, I hope.'

'Well, I'm on my way to see Lachlan, as a matter of fact. I said I'd help him with some ideas for doing up Ardenleigh. He says he hasn't a clue!'

Pat looked at her sharply and took a deep breath. 'Look, darling, I know you'll think I'm interfering, but it's just a bit of advice. Please, be careful, won't you? After your previous experience you must know that sometimes working closely with someone can lead to... well, you know, working with a colleague is one thing, but socialising is another...'

Christa sighed. 'I've told you, Mum, I shall be very careful. And I'm bound to see him outside working hours anyway.'

Pat shook her head and pursed her lips, and Christa said impatiently, 'Oh, for goodness' sake, Mum! What have you got against Lachlan? You don't know him! The episode with Colin is history now, anyway.' She looked at her mother's expression and frowned. 'Is it Lachlan or men in general you're not keen on?'

Pat looked flustered and rather forlorn. 'Darling... it's just that... Oh, dear, let's not come to blows about it. I shouldn't have said anything. You're a big girl now— I suppose I forget that sometimes!'

Christa gave her mother a quick hug. 'I know you do, Mum!'

But as she left the flat Christa recalled her mother's less-than-enthusiastic words about Isobel the other day. What was it about the Maguire family that made her mother uneasy? she wondered. Then she shrugged to herself—there had to be a reason for her mother's anxiety and one day she'd get to the bottom of it, but for the immediate future she had more interesting things to do. She felt a flicker of excited anticipation as she started running down the lane towards Ardenleigh.

Lachlan was hacking away at huge overgrown laurels by the front door, and for the first time in years the beautiful golden stonework was beginning to appear. His hair was dishevelled, and he was wearing an old tartan lumber jacket over battered cord trousers—he looked strong and utterly gorgeous, as virile as someone in an advertisement for an unbelievably effective tonic!

When he saw her, he flung down his secateurs and strode over to her, sliding his arms round her waist, his hands spread across her back so that she was imprisoned against him. Christa's vow to distance herself from him seemed to disintegrate like bubbles floating in the air, and she found herself winding her arms round his neck, desperate to be as close to him as she could, to feel him against her once again. He buried his face in her hair and kissed her neck softly.

'Mmm...you smell so sweet,' he murmured. 'I've nearly gone crazy waiting for you to turn up...wanting to hold you.'

His hand crept under her T-shirt, cupping her breast gently, and a whoosh of sensation thrilled through her. Any second now it would be a complete rerun of the other night!

With a tremendous effort of will Christa managed to disentangle herself from Lachlan and, half laughing, managed to gasp, 'Hey, not so fast, young man! And anyway,' she said primly, 'we agreed that what we did the other night, was just a bit of fun, a one-off, didn't we?'

Lachlan raised his eyebrows. 'Is that all it meant to you?' he said lightly. 'I obviously didn't make much of an impression! I'll have to make more of an effort next time!' he said with a grin.

She pushed him away with a giggle. 'We've got work to do! I've brought the sample paint pots.'

He looked down at her, surprised. 'The what? Oh...' He threw back his head and laughed. 'Good God, girl, I wasn't thinking about paint then. I was thinking... Oh, what the hell, come in and let's have some coffee while I tell you what I was thinking about!'

It was like an invitation from the spider to the fly, thought Christa wryly. There was no way she could regard him as purely a work colleague when the man exuded sex from every pore, and no way she could resist that invitation!

The percolator was already bubbling quietly away and there was a delicious smell of fresh coffee pervading the place. Lachlan poured some out into mugs for them both and put them on the table, then turned to her and put his hands on her shoulders,

'Now I'll tell you what I was thinking of...' he said with a cheeky grin, dipping his head to hers and brushing her mouth softly, then gradually his kissing became more demanding, teasing her lips apart, moving his hands over her body. With commendable willpower, Christa wriggled free of him for a second time and he stepped back, his blue eyes dancing with amusement.

'What's the matter?' he asked innocently. 'Am I doing something wrong?'

Christa tried to look severe, and smothered another

giggle. 'If you want me to help you with advice about the house, you'd better not do that,' she said crisply. 'It seems to drive any sensible idea out of my head!'

'You're so bossy,' grumbled Lachlan. 'But don't imagine it's out of the question that I won't try again!' He handed her a mug of coffee and they sat in a companionable way on the wooden kitchen chairs next to each other. 'So how was your conference—a lot of laughs?'

'I met an old friend of yours there.' She smiled. 'She told me all about you!'

Lachlan looked startled. 'Who could that be?'

'Suzy Collins—she knew you in Australia.'

'Ah, Suzy! Great fun...' He looked suspiciously at Christa. 'I hope she didn't give away any state secrets...'

Christa smiled demurely. 'Nothing I didn't know about you already!'

He laughed. 'Then I can relax. Let's get back to business. Tell me what you think about the kitchen, for a start.'

Christa looked around—he'd made an attempt to clear the place of all the old bottles and cans that she'd seen on the shelves the first night he'd arrived, and he'd stripped the floor of the battered linoleum that had been there before. The old green-painted doors on the cupboards had been taken off and were piled on the kitchen table.

'You've been working hard—it looks better already!'

'You should have seen some of the stuff in those jars! I think there was a good supply of penicillin growing on top of some of them!'

'So are you going to strip the doors or paint them again?'

'I don't know... What do you suggest?'

'I think I'd like to see the original pine or perhaps

spray them cream. Lighten things up a little.' She peered through a half-open door at the side of the kitchen. 'What's through there?'

'A very cold scullery with two sinks in it—I suppose it's what used to be called a wash-house.'

Christa went to inspect it and laughed. 'It's too tiny to be of much use—you could always knock down the wall and make the kitchen bigger. And then you could make a huge picture window here, overlooking a lovely view of the garden.'

Lachlan looked enthusiastic. 'Yeah, that would look great. I suppose we could even have huge glass sliding doors the length of that wall...'

Was it a Freudian slip that he said 'we could have'? wondered Christa wistfully. Then she told herself crossly that he had no notions of including her in his plans—he just wanted advice. He led her to the front of the house and into the drawing room.

'What about this room?' he said.

It was a magnificent room with two huge bay windows on either side of French doors, which flooded the place with light. But there was the musty, damp smell of a room never aired, never lived in. At one end of the room there was an enormous fireplace that cried out for a log fire on a winter's day such as this. In her imagination Christa saw the cheerful flicker of flames shooting up the chimney, could smell the sweet smell of applewood, picture the two of them in front of it, doing wonderful things to each other... She veered quickly away from that daydream—it was becoming almost a reflex reaction that when she thought of Lachlan she thought of making love!

'You need to warm this room up,' she suggested

briskly, forcing that image out of her mind. 'Have you any wood to make up a fire in that fireplace?'

'Plenty. I was cutting some from the front when you came. We'll do it later after we've been out.'

'And you know what? That peeling wallpaper should be easy to pull down, and it would look fabulous with a lovely soft green wash over the walls! And if you got rid of this old carpet and put down a new one—say, pale oatmeal, it would set off the lovely old oak furniture in here.'

Christa looked at the sagging and faded settee and matching chairs, and the curtains, sadly fraying, exposed as they were to the sunlight.

'And another thing,' she continued brightly, 'if you went to the country house sales around here, you could easily buy a new settee and chairs, and curtains, and if….'

Lachlan grinned and put up his hand. 'Whoa! Steady!' he remarked. 'We're talking serious money here. Remember, the stuff I'm short of?'

'I hadn't forgotten that. Talking of which…' She took a deep breath and said boldly, 'I suppose you haven't had second thoughts about the leisure development?'

He laughed. 'You don't give up, do you?' He leant against the wall, his legs casually crossed, hands in pockets. 'Actually, I've had a lot of interest and early signs are that the council isn't against it in principle.'

Christa's expression turned to one of determination. 'Well, when the planning application comes up, I can assure you that several of us will be objecting to that in the strongest terms.'

Lachlan looked at her from under his brow. 'Look, don't let's argue about it. Why don't we have that walk now while the sun's out? We'll go down to the beach through the woods and fields and I can show you exactly what the plan might be.' He stepped forward and put his arms round her, tilting her face to his, and said impishly, 'Who knows? Perhaps I can persuade you to change your mind.'

He smiled down at her, those blue eyes of his exuding sex. He took her face in his hands and kissed her lingeringly, and she turned her face away, half laughing, half irritated that he should joke about something so important to her.

'That's an unfair tactic,' she protested.

'All's fair in love and war,' he commented, taking her hand and going through to the kitchen, opening the back door and striding down the garden towards the woods and fields.

Titan bounded energetically before them, barking furiously at imaginary rabbits, and Christa felt a sudden surge of elation because she was alone with Lachlan on a beautiful day, and had a chance to get to know him better. Surely it was the start of a relationship that would go further than a light-hearted affair, and even if Lachlan protested that long-term commitment was not for him, perhaps one day he'd see some merit in it!

They came to the wood that bordered the fields and Lachlan stopped and put a hand on Christa's shoulders, pointing to a part of the wood that wasn't so densely treed.

'The company that wants to buy the land intends to have about eight wooden chalets here—and they'll be made Swedish-style with wood that blends in with the surroundings,' he explained. 'No huge buildings, and the minimum amount of tree felling.'

'And what about the leisure centre itself, with the

swimming pool and gym? That will be hard to disguise surely?'

'Same idea—a wooden structure on one floor and
to the far side of the wood, so it won't be seen from the
house or the road.'

He was good at the talk, thought Christa. He made
it sound as if no one would notice any difference to the
place at all, and indeed it didn't seem so very intrusive
despite what she'd imagined.

She murmured, 'I have no doubt it will be very
popular with holiday people—it's in such a beautiful
area. But you haven't quite convinced me yet.'

He grinned and bent down to kiss the nape of her neck.
'That's a challenge—I've every confidence I can win you
over!' He took her hand. 'Now, let's take Titan down to
the beach and you can look back at it from that angle.'

They walked briskly through the furrowed fields,
swinging hands, and came to the line of sand dunes that
marked the edge of the beach. It spread gloriously before
them, wide, empty and pearly pink, and the sun sparkled on the sea, millpond smooth but with little waves
like lace ruffling the shallows. Above them mewed the
seagulls, swooping and gliding before settling on the
water. To the right of the firth were the hazy outlines of
the Cairngorms, already white-tipped with early snow
against a wintry blue sky.

'Isn't this perfect?' Lachlan murmured, folding his
arms and standing in mute admiration of the scene for
a few minutes.

'Better than Australia, then?' teased Christa. 'What
made you go so far away when you love it so much here—
and for so long?'

'Good question.' He shrugged. 'Obviously it was an

adventure, a marvellous opportunity to see the world—
but would I have gone at that particular time if my mother
hadn't told me about her affair? I don't know… All I do
know is that I wanted to get as far away as I could from
my family.'

'You'd qualified by then?' probed Christa.

'Yes, thank God. At least I could earn my living at
something. And I loved it—the people, the country and
the experience. The variety of stuff I had to tackle was
like *Casualty* on a grand scale—snake bites, dysentery,
dehydration. It all made for a quick learning curve.'

She grinned cheekily at him. 'I'm surprised you can
contemplate coming back to work in the practice if you
loved it so much.' Then she added gently, 'But it must
have been a terrible shock when you heard Isobel had
died.'

His face shadowed sadly. 'I haven't talked about it before, but I admit it was a hammer blow.' He sighed and
bunched his fists in his trouser pockets, staring across the
firth. 'I'm ashamed to say that I actually felt resentful, as
if it was my poor mother's fault she'd died so suddenly
that I was unable to make my peace with her.'

Christa nodded. 'That's understandable.'

Lachlan shrugged. 'During the time I've been back
my feelings have changed—I feel guilty as hell that I left
it so long to come home. I'd kept thinking I should return, but I suppose I was too proud to meet my mother
again—apologise for what I had said to her. And now
it's too late…'

His voice died away, the sad words hanging in the air,
filled with poignancy. Christa reached for his hand and
squeezed it comfortingly, aware of the effort it was taking for Lachlan to admit his mistakes.

'I'm sure she forgave you, Lachlan, probably understood only too well why you left home. I'm sure she felt guilty too, breaking up the family.'

'Yes,' he said softly. 'She did forgive me—she left a letter with the solicitor that made it plain that she blamed herself for all that happened.' He was silent for a moment then looked bleakly at Christa. 'Now I realise that she was well aware that her time was short, and if I could only turn back the clock, I would. I regret so much not making it up with my mother. One thing I do know,' he added fiercely, 'is that I shall do everything I can to fulfil her wishes in that letter. At least I can do that!'

There was something heartbreaking about seeing his strong face etched with sadness and the remorse he felt about being too late to make amends with his mother. Christa put her arm around him and hugged him to her.

'None of it was of your making. You thought you had an idyllic family life with parents who loved each other. It must have shattered you when you realised that wasn't true.' She hesitated before saying diffidently, 'Did your mother's affair end when your father left home?'

'Her lover was killed in a crash on the motorway,' Lachlan said simply. 'I hoped it would mean she and my father would get back together but they didn't and he left the area.' He gave a short, bitter laugh. 'So much for that ridiculous vow to be together till death did them part.'

Was that shorthand for reminding her that he did not believe in commitment for life? wondered Christa wistfully. She remembered his throwaway remark: 'Marry in haste, repent at leisure.' Wedding bells didn't seem to be on his agenda!

He put his hands on her shoulders and smiled. 'God,

this is all about me, me, me! Now, let's get comfortable and tell me about your family—your mother…'

And by 'comfortable' he evidently meant that they should sit together on the soft sand in the dunes, one arm around her, hugging her to him. She snuggled up to him, loving the feel of his warm body against hers.

'Ah…Mum's one feisty woman,' she said. 'She was devastated after Dad's death, but gradually she's developed plenty of interests—and, of course, now she has her friend Bertie, the loveliest man from the next-door flat, and they do loads of things together.'

Lachlan grinned. 'A feisty woman, eh? You sound as if you take after her. I'd like to meet your mother. I take it your father wasn't a medical man?'

'No. He used to run a small business with my Uncle Angus, supplying drugs to medical practices, although sadly in later years apparently they didn't get on. But my father was lovely, great fun and I do miss him…'

'He was different from your wicked uncle Angus, then?' Lachlan said lightly. 'What happened to Angus's wife and child after he left them?'

'I believe she moved away down south and remarried. We never hear from her unfortunately. You said you'd met him—did he seem wicked to you?'

Lachlan hesitated for a second then said, 'He did have a reputation with women, I suppose…'

'How could you tell?' she asked, smiling.

He pushed his hand through his thick hair so that it stood up in little spikes, and looked at Christa quizzically. 'There's rather more to your uncle's story than you might imagine…'

She looked surprised and laughed. 'Oh? That's very intriguing.'

'Could be a bit of a shock.'

'Nothing much shocks me. Spill the beans, I'm a big girl now!' Fleetingly, she remembered that she'd said as much to her mother a few hours earlier.

Lachlan shrugged. 'Hell. You've got to know some time. Are you ready for this?' He paused as if weighing up how to tell Christa, then said, with a trace of bitterness, 'The fact is, the man my mother had an affair with was your uncle. Angus Lennox used to come to the surgery as a drug rep for his company—and that's how he met my mother. The rest is history. Then he was killed in a traffic accident coming to see her one evening, but by that time her marriage was over, and so was our happy family life.'

CHAPTER NINE

THE SMILE FADED from Christa's face and she gazed at Lachlan in complete amazement, her mouth an O of surprise.

'*What?* Isobel and Uncle Angus? You're kidding!' She pulled some long grass from the sand dune and pulled at it distractedly. 'I can hardly believe it. Isobel and I were so close, but she never gave a hint that she'd had an affair, let alone that it was with Angus...'

'Reopening old wounds, do you think?' suggested Lachlan gently.

Christa nodded. 'Perhaps... But it's such a shock.'

She bit her lip, suddenly realising just why her mother seemed less than enthusiastic about Isobel, and a relationship developing between her daughter and Lachlan.

So *that* was what had caused the huge rift between her father and his brother—brothers who had been so close before Angus's affair. That closeness had been severed for ever after he'd left his wife and had then died, and the unhappy memories of that time must still rankle with her mother.

She got up from beside Lachlan and walked over to the little stone breakwater at the edge of the dunes, and Lachlan stood beside her and put his arm round her. 'I'm sorry I had to tell you, sweetheart, but surely it's better that you know…'

'Of course I should know,' she said robustly. 'I can't imagine why Mum kept it to herself all these years—it certainly makes things a little clearer.'

'How do you mean?'

'I've always felt that she was never as, well, fond of Isobel as I was.' She hesitated before saying in a rather embarrassed way, 'And when I told her you were joining the practice she didn't seem exactly keen.'

He raised his eyebrows. 'But these things happened a long time ago, honey. Surely she's moved on from there by now?'

She sighed. 'Perhaps.' She looked at Lachlan with a frown. 'But you must have hated our family too. No wonder you seemed startled when you heard who I was—the niece of the man who had broken up your parents' marriage working with your mother! That's a big crumb to swallow.'

'It was a shock at first,' Lachlan admitted, then his deep blue eyes held hers and he said with a cheeky grin, 'Now I don't think that way at all, I can tell you—especially after that wonderful night we had together, sweetheart!'

He turned her round gently and tilted her face to his, then brushed her mouth with a feather touch of his lips, trailing kisses down her neck. It was unbearably sexy, sending sparks of desire through every nerve of her body, dissolving her legs to jelly, making her feel dizzy with desire—and it took every ounce of control for Christa to pull herself back from him, half laughing, half protesting.

'Oh, Lachlan—stop it! I just want you to understand how much that quarrel between my uncle and my father affected my family. I can see why Mum would resent any connection to the Maguires.'

'That's ridiculous!' The wind blew Lachlan's hair over his eyes and he brushed it away impatiently. 'Surely she doesn't harbour a grudge against me. After all, it wasn't *my* fault!' He looked down at her with a grin. 'Mind you, I won't deny it was a shock to learn when I arrived back here a few weeks ago that you were Angus Lennox's niece. I even felt a twang of jealousy that you and my mother had this terrific bond when you worked together. But it's history now...'

Christa looked at him levelly. 'I could never risk upsetting Mum, Lachlan. It's just been the two of us for so long and she sacrificed such a lot to get me through med school. Can you understand that? I need to tread carefully.'

'So what are you saying, Christa? That it affects your relationship with me?'

Lachlan's blue eyes glowered down at her truculently, and she was silent for a moment. Did it really make a difference to her relationship with Lachlan? Would she reopen old wounds of her mother's by going out with him? Perhaps it was better to put the brakes on a budding romance before it got too serious—on her side anyway.

'It changes things a little...' she said at last.

'But surely you're not going to be ruled by your mother all your life? Why should you be constrained by what she thinks?' He sounded exasperated.

Christa flushed. 'Because she *is* my mother! I just happen to care about her feelings—that's all.'

'I never thought of you as a mummy's girl,' he commented drily.

A cold wind blew across the firth and the temperature

between them seemed to drop as well—what had started out as a magical day suddenly seemed dark.

Christa's eyes flashed angrily. 'Don't be so ridiculous! I'm just saying that falling out with my mother is something I could never do!'

Lachlan's expression hardened and he said tersely, 'If that's supposed to be a sanctimonious dig at me and my relationship with Isobel, it's a cheap jibe!'

'You know I didn't mean it that way!' Christa stared at him coldly. 'I just want to sound the ground a bit... surely you can understand that?'

They gazed stonily at each other, their bodies tense, standing some way apart. Christa shivered, and not just because of the cold wind but because this silly quarrel seemed to have sprung out of nowhere—and it was horrible that one minute they could be so close and the next as if they were on different planets.

Lachlan bunched his fists in his pockets, appalled that the temperature between them had plummeted several degrees below freezing—and, in his view, over nothing at all! The wind had whipped Christa's auburn hair into a tousled halo and her eyes were bright with anger—and she had never looked lovelier. Lachlan's expression softened, and he stepped forward, putting out his arms and drawing her close to him.

'Come here, Christa. What are we like? Of course you care what your mother thinks, and so do I. Go and talk to her—tell her about us. She might not be so against it as you thought. After all, we're just...rather good friends, aren't we?'

Christa swallowed. Of course they were! She was making a fuss over nothing...

He smiled at her, his periwinkle blue eyes heartmeltingly rueful. 'I didn't mean to be so unsympathetic. We'll take things as slowly as you like. Am I forgiven?'

And Christa, nestled into the comfort of that warm body, shook her head, smiling remorsefully up at him. 'Don't be silly! It's my fault. I guess I went over the top a bit. You're right—who I go out with is nothing to do with my mother. But learning the truth about Angus was a tremendous shock. To think I worked all those years with Isobel and she never revealed it.' She dimpled up at him. 'There's no more little secrets you're hiding from me, are there?'

'Only a few,' he murmured. 'Now let me apologise to you properly…'

And apologising took quite a long time, because his lips were on hers demandingly, his hands caressing her body tenderly, and any thoughts she'd had about upsetting her mother seemed gradually to melt away. She would have a talk with her mother some time—that would be the best thing. If Lachlan could get over his aversion to the Lennox family, surely Pat could accept Lachlan.

A few huge drops of rain splashed down onto them and Lachlan glanced up at the sky. Dark clouds were massing over the firth and the wind was whipping up.

'Do you think we could go somewhere more comfortable?' he suggested mildly. 'It's bloody freezing out here and we're going to be soaked! We'll go back to Ardenleigh, and I'll light a fire in that big fireplace in the drawing room, like you suggested. It will be cosy and warm in no time.'

A sudden vivid vision of two bodies in front of the fire, warmed by its heat and entwined together, floated into Christa's mind, sending little sparks of excitement crackling through her body.

She laughed. 'Sounds good to me. But remember what we said about not rushing things…'

Lachlan grinned wickedly. 'I'll give it careful thought,' he said.

Neither of them heard Christa's mobile ringing at first, then Christa grimaced and pulled it out of her pocket.

'Wouldn't you know it—I thought I'd turned it off,' she said.

She held it to her ear and her expression changed. Her mother's agitated voice sounded in her ear. She mouthed to Lachlan, 'It's Mum—she sounds awful…'

'Christa? Oh, darling, something awful's h-happened,' Pat stuttered hoarsely. 'Could you get here as soon as possible? It's Bertie, he's, he's just collapsed with terrible pain across his chest. He says it's just a pulled muscle, but he looks very grey and his breathing seems so laboured…'

Christa's heart froze. Dear God, it sounded as if Bertie was having a heart attack. 'Have you rung for an ambulance, Mum?'

'Yes…then they rang back to say they'd come as quickly as they could, but they've been diverted because of a landslide through the Inchhill Pass. They told me to ring the GP and they'd be there as soon as they could—and to try and prop Bertie up. I've tried to but he's heavy… Oh, dear me…'

There was an edge of panic in her mother's voice, and Christa forced her own voice to be calm. 'I'm on my way now, Mum. Is he at your flat? I'll get in touch with the ambulance service again and see if they've got through the landslide. Don't worry—keep talking to Bertie, reassure him that help's on its way.'

'I get the drift,' said Lachlan, who'd been watching

her face intently. 'Come on—let's get your car and your
medical bag.'

They sprinted along the sands, the rain and wind beating into their faces.

'It's my mother's elderly neighbour...Bertie Smith,'
panted Christa, her words tumbling over each other as
she tried to explain what had happened to Lachlan as they
ran. 'She thinks he's had a heart attack, and the ambulance is stuck in the Inchhill Pass...'

Dealing with emergencies like this was something
GPs had to cope with, but Lachlan was well aware that
in a life-and-death situation it could be a blessing to have
another pair of hands.

'Have you got adrenalin and morphine in your bag?'

'Yes—and atropine.'

'What about oxygen?'

'Thank God I've got a cylinder in the boot. It's a spare
for a patient, but she's got plenty to be going on with.'

'Then while you're driving I'll get an update on the
ambulance's ETA.'

They picked up Christa's car and medical bag, and
she put her foot down, going as fast as she dared to her
mother's flat. Lachlan flicked a glance at her worried
face as they sped through the main street of Errin Bridge.

'You know this neighbour of your mother's?'

Christa nodded. 'Yes, he's a friend really as well as
being one of our patients. He's actually had angina for a
few years, but it seems to have been well under control.
He and my mother have been "going out" together for a
long time—he's wonderful with Mum and such a sweet
man.' She gripped the steering-wheel tightly and said in
a small voice, 'I—I'm glad you're here, Lachlan...'

'So am I—two hands are better than one in this case.'

'The truth is,' she said bleakly, 'this seems like a rerun of when your mother died. I was called out to someone who had collapsed at a farm in the hills, and I only knew it was Isobel when I got there. But I was too late...'

There was silence for a minute, the words 'too late' seeming to hang in the air.

Lachlan said softly, 'We can only do our best in these situations, you know—it doesn't always work.'

'I know, I know,' sighed Christa as she swung into the drive of her mother's block of flats.

Bertie was on the floor with a cushion half-propping him up against a chair, his head had fallen to one side, his skin grey and his eyes sunken. Pat was holding his hand and stroking his forehead, her head whipping round when she heard Christa and Lachlan come in.

'Thank God,' she whispered. 'I don't know if he's... It all happened so quickly—one minute we were discussing a holiday, and the next...' Her voice trailed off miserably.

Lachlan bent down by the stricken man and put two fingers on his carotid artery. His eyes met Christa's and he nodded. 'There's still a pulse...clear signs of coronary thrombosis. Have you heparin with you? I'll go and bring in that oxygen while you take over, Christa.'

Bertie's eyes fluttered open, and through purple-tinged lips he whispered, 'It's...it's the pain...'

Lachlan knew that the vice-like grip in Bertie's chest was all the man could think of, pain coursing through his neck and chest, and an increasing sense of losing touch with the world around him. He put his face close to Bertie's ear.

'Don't worry, Bertie—don't try to talk. We know

what's happened to you and we're going to sort you out. We'll give you something for the pain.'

His voice was crisp and authoritative, and Christa saw her mother put her hands up to her mouth, eyes wide with fright and riveted to the scene as she watched the two doctors trying to save the life of her friend.

'Will…will he be all right?' she whispered. 'He was fine when we went for our walk—seemed as right as rain. It all happened so suddenly.'

Christa didn't answer. Bertie might still be alive, but his life was on a knife-edge, with the grim prospect of a full cardiac arrest. She listened to Bertie's labouring heart through her stethoscope while she felt the weak, thready pulse on his wrist. Lachlan hooked a mask round Bertie's face and undid a valve in the oxygen cylinder to help the patient's breathing.

'He's bradycardic—heartbeat under sixty,' Christa said succinctly. 'I'm giving him one milligram of atropine to try and stabilise him and bring his heartbeat up, and five thousand units of heparin.'

She slipped off the cover of the syringe and tested it with a small spray in the air before injecting it into the man's arm. They watched him intently, and gradually the colour in Bertie's face began to change from grey to pink as his labouring heart found the capacity to pump blood more efficiently around his body.

Now a cuff was wound round Bertie's upper arm and Christa pressed a stethoscope to the skin below it, and after a few seconds the erratic beat of Bertie's heart began to steady.

She took a long breath and murmured, 'I think we're getting there…he's in sinus rhythm now.' She held Ber tie's hand and smiled down at him. 'You're doing well, Bertie—just relax until the paramedics get here.'

Pat watched them from the corner of the room and wiped her eyes. 'I…I'll just go and make some tea for us all,' she said in a trembling voice. She came over to Bertie and bent over him, squeezing his hand and saying softly, 'Don't you ever give me a fright like that again, Bertie Smith, or I'll not talk to you again!'

And Bertie, with his oxygen mask over his face, managed to mouth to her, 'I love you, darling…'

Pat bent down and kissed his cheek, her own cheeks wet with tears. 'I love you too, my sweet. Please…please get better for me.'

Over their heads, Christa and Lachlan's eyes met and held each other's gaze as they smiled at each other.

It wasn't long before the ambulance arrived and Bertie was taken to hospital, with Pat insisting that she go with him.

'I'm not staying here, and I'm not letting Bertie go alone in that ambulance,' she said firmly.

'We'll follow behind,' said Christa.

'No way!' declared Pat, with such a look of Christa's when she was in a bossy mood that Lachlan hid a grin behind his hand. 'I'll get a taxi back—you two need a meal. You've done everything you could—now the hospital can take over.'

'Promise me you'll ring me when he's settled, then…'

Pat held her hand up as if to stop Christa in full flow and said with dignity, 'I want to stay next to Bertie all night if need be—it's kind of you, but I shall come home by taxi and that's an end to it!'

Christa laughed. 'You win!' She looked from her

mother to Lachlan and made a quick decision. 'And, Mum, I haven't had time to introduce you to Lachlan Maguire. As I told you, he's working with me now.'

She watched her mother's face as she made the introduction. Pat hesitated for just a fraction of a second then put her hand out to shake Lachlan's with a smile of genuine warmth. 'I can't tell you how grateful I am—and pleased to meet you. Thank you so much for saving Bertie's life. I shall always be in yours and Christa's debt!'

The ambulance took them off and Christa and Lachlan were left standing together in the dark, watching the taillights disappear down the road.

'Well, well, what a wonderful thing love is,' murmured Lachlan. 'It looks as if your mother's found someone she loves very much.'

Christa took a deep breath and said softly, 'I'm sure Mum didn't realise that she loved Bertie so much until this happened. Seeing him at the brink of death made her suddenly appreciate what she might be losing.'

She shivered for a moment, and in the darkness Lachlan took her hand. 'You OK?'

'It was a bit stressful…' She squeezed his hand. 'But I'm so grateful you were here—it was wonderful to have your support. It's hard to be dispassionate when your own family's involved and I could see how upset Mum was.'

'When you think something's going to end, it makes you look at things differently. When we had our little tiff I think I realised just how much I cared for you, Christa. I hated arguing with you, especially over nothing at all! And now,' he said teasingly, 'we were rudely interrupted an hour or two ago. Can we resume what we were doing—start over again?'

'If you like,' she said, a little breathlessly, and a flicker of elation rippled through her—almost triumph that perhaps she'd cracked that aversion of his to long-term involvement. She smiled, her cheeks dimpling. 'If you really want to…'

So much for good intentions, she thought wryly.

'Hello, there! Come on, Sleeping Beauty—time to rise and shine!'

From the depths of the cosy duvet pulled up over her ears Christa heard a familiar deep voice. She pulled the duvet up further and pretended she hadn't heard, then there was a dirty chuckle and the duvet was rudely whipped from her.

'Don't do that!' she shrieked. 'It's freezing!'

Lachlan looked down at her, grinning impishly, holding a mug of tea in his hand. He was wearing boxer shorts and nothing else, slight stubble on his chin, thick hair ruffled. He looked dangerously sexy and incredibly hard to resist. Christa changed her mind about being cross that the duvet had been removed and stretched out provocatively on the bed, deliberately and mischievously tempting him.

'Why don't you get back in and warm me up again?' she suggested wickedly.

He groaned. 'God, don't tempt me. Like a flash I would! Only that might mean we'll be even later than we are already…'

Despite saying that, he sat down on the side of the bed and leant over her, running his hands lightly over her soft breasts and flat stomach. 'So beautiful,' he murmured.

'What did you say about the time?' said Christa, drowsy with contentment, winding her arms round Lachlan's neck, pulling him towards her.

'Only that we've got about ten minutes to get to the surgery...'

'*What?* You can't be serious!' Christa pushed her tousled hair out of her eyes, squinted at his watch on the bedside table and gave a little shriek, trying to sit up with Lachlan still on top of her. 'Oh, my God—it's after eight-thirty. How are we going to explain that to everyone?'

'I haven't a notion—possibly that it was a very busy evening, attending an emergency?'

'But the whole evening?'

'True... Perhaps we were discussing the patient's case afterwards?'

Lachlan's eyes twinkled into hers and Christa threw a pillow at him. 'Funny sort of patient conference,' she said, giggling, then put her hand to her mouth. 'Oh, God! Bertie and Mum—I should have rung first thing to find out how things are.'

'I rang about an hour ago while you were snuggled abed, snoring your head off. Bertie's in CCU and stable and your mother came home soon after he was admitted—he was asleep anyway. So you see, babe, no need to worry about anything.'

'Thank God for that,' she said.

Lachlan smiled, tracing his finger down her neck and into her cleavage, loving the tousled look of her, the soft, creamy texture of her skin against the sheets.

'Hell, if only it wasn't a workday. What wouldn't I be doing now?' he said longingly. 'It's only my magnificent willpower that's stopping me having my wicked way with you...' He got up from the bed. 'Anyway, there's steaming-hot coffee on the hob and plenty of toast downstairs. You need something to keep you going after last night.' He grinned cheekily.

Last night! Christa's heart did a loop the loop as she thought about what had happened in the space of a few hours. It had been so horrible when they'd quarrelled but after a wonderful night together it seemed they had moved to something more than light-hearted fun.

He looked down at her very lovingly and traced a finger down her neck. 'We could be doing this every night if you moved in with me...' he said softly. 'What about it? I don't like rattling around here by myself!'

A surge of joy rippled through her. At last he'd admitted that he felt much more for her than a casual dalliance! She laughed up at him. 'I thought we weren't into long-term pledges,' she teased.

'Surely we've gone beyond that now, sweetheart?' He brushed her lips with his. 'I know I have...'

And her heart nearly exploded with happiness. For the first time in many years the future looked wonderful. Her old friend Suzy Collins had been wrong about Lachlan!

She smiled at him. 'Perhaps that little disagreement was a good thing—it's made us realise how much we mean to each other. But I'm sorry I went over the top about it all.'

He stroked her cheek gently. 'Nothing wrong with being concerned about your parents,' he said rather sadly. 'I should have considered my own mother much more than I did.'

Christa smiled at him. 'She must have forgiven you. The fact that she left you Ardenleigh is proof of that,' she commented, sipping the refreshing tea Lachlan had brought her. She looked at him from under her eyelashes, her voice teasing. 'Supposing this scheme of yours doesn't materialise and you've not enough money to restore it?'

He went to the huge windows and pulled back the curtains so that the light flooded in, and gazed out at the wonderful view of the garden and woods and the bright sea beyond.

He turned round to face her and said simply, 'Then it may take longer than I thought, but if you're here to help me we can do it together.'

Christa lay back on the bed for a precious minute, smiling in tender reminiscence of the wonderful loving night she'd spent with Lachlan. How sweet it had been to nestle close to him on the sheepskin rug in front of the fire he'd lit in the beautiful drawing room. His strong face had looked down at her in the half-light as he'd gently undressed her in front of the flickering flames.

'This is what we were meant to do, sweetheart—forget the past and live our own lives!'

And later they had gone up to the bedroom with the old sagging bed and fallen asleep in each other's arms—and now he'd told her that he wanted to be with her all the time. Life was perfect!

'You've a huge backlog of patients,' grumbled Ginny to them both as they stood like recalcitrant schoolchildren in front of the two receptionists. 'The natives are getting restless.'

'Apologies,' said Lachlan with a charming smile at them both. 'If you knew what a night we've had!'

Christa stifled a giggle and the girls nodded sympathetically. 'Oh, yes—poor old Bertie Smith taken to hospital with a heart attack, wasn't it? You've had an e-mail from Coronary Care at St Luke's about him. You poor things, you must be exhausted!'

'Just a little,' remarked Lachlan lightly. 'So who's doing the clinic today?'

'Sarah's doing the BP clinic for the oldies, but the rep's cancelled his appointment.'

'Thank goodness for that,' remarked Christa, giving them all a sparkling smile. 'Now, let's get started, shall we?'

Ginny stared at Christa's retreating back. 'Well! She looks as if she's lost sixpence and found a pound,' she remarked to the room. 'I haven't seen her looking so cheery for ages!'

Alice glanced at Lachlan astutely. 'Are you taking anyone to the dance?' she asked cheekily.

'That would be telling.' Lachlan smiled, one finger tapping his nose, as he went out of the room.

'I'd love to know who he's taking!' said Alice in a stage whisper to Ginny when they were alone.

Ginny didn't believe in gossip. 'I've no idea who it is, Alice—that's his business,' she said loftily.

Alice took no notice. 'I bet you anything Christa and Lachlan are up to something! I mean, they came in to-gether this morning and I'd swear to it that Christa came across the courtyard from the house. I didn't see her come down the road. And did you see the way Lachlan looked at her?'

'Nonsense, Alice! Anyway, they bought separate tickets for the dance—if they were going as a couple, surely he'd have just bought two. And if she did come from the house this morning, it was probably because she'd been discussing Bertie Smith's heart attack last night.'

Alice giggled. 'I'm sure he wasn't thinking of Bertie

Smith's heart—just what his own heart was doing when he was near Christa!'

'Rubbish! What are you like?' said Ginny dismissively, but all the same there was a thoughtful look in her eyes as she went to the desk to deal with a patient.

CHAPTER TEN

CHRISTA RIFFLED THROUGH her wardrobe and threw the limited selection of evening wear she had onto the bed. Everything looked tired and dated. It was so long since she'd been anywhere glamorous that she'd forgotten what she had to wear!

She was beginning to panic about what she should wear to the dance in two weeks. She definitely didn't want to appear in the smart little black sheath dress she'd worn two years ago to the same event. It was the very one she'd worn the night Colin had so gallantly ditched her for someone else!

She threw it onto a pile of other clothes she had marked out for the charity shop and decided the only thing to do was to trust to luck and go shopping at the weekend in the little boutique in the village, and hope it would have something inspiring to wear. She wanted to look knock-out good for Lachlan!

Selina's was a busy little shop—the only dress shop for miles around—and was owned by Ginny's sister, a glamorous girl who had been a model in her younger days. She was a friend of Christa's, although Christa hadn't been in her shop for ages, because there'd been no occasion to dress up for.

'Hello, stranger!' Selina grinned. 'Can I guess you've come for something for the village dance?'

'I certainly have—the only possible thing I've got is two years old and I don't like it any more.'

'Well, long or short? I've some lovely maxi dresses in…' Selina gave Christa an assessing look. 'I think with your lovely creamy complexion and auburn hair, a soft apricot colour would suit you, and I've got the very thing.'

From the back room she brought out a dress and held it up to Christa. 'Wow!' she said. 'Put that on immediately before someone else nabs it! It's made for you.'

And even Christa had to admit that she looked good in it—a lovely column of the softest apricot satin that clung to her in all the right places and plunged at the back down to her waist, more modestly at the front.

'You don't think it looks a little…well, daring?' suggested Christa rather nervously. 'I mean, I'm hardly wearing anything at all at the back!'

'Rubbish! You're young and beautiful—wear it while you can. You'll have every male in the place salivating!'

There was only one male that Christa wanted to impress. She gave a little giggle at the thought of Lachlan's reaction. 'OK, Selina—you're a great saleswoman. I'll have it!'

She swung out of the shop happily. Next week she'd be in Lachlan's arms on the dance floor, and she could almost feel their bodies moving in harmony together to some impossibly romantic tune. Then she laughed to herself—it would more likely be a heavy metal number from the local group who thought they were in with a shout on *The X Factor*!

She hung the dress on the wardrobe door and flicked a duster round the living room with the radio belting out something cheery on the Saturday morning show. She hummed to the music. Lachlan was going to call for her on his way back from a run along the beach, and then they were going on a bracing walk through the woods to a local waterfall. She couldn't have been happier.

The front doorbell rang, and as usual Titan bounded to the door, growling ferociously.

'Don't you know me yet, Titan?' asked Lachlan, bending down to stroke the little dog. 'You're going to be seeing a lot more of me in the future!'

He had on old shorts and a battered sweatshirt round his shoulders, and as usual Christa felt that flip of excitement when she saw him.

'I won't kiss you.' He grinned. 'I need a shower first—you make some coffee at Ardenleigh while I'm making myself presentable.'

They walked back to the big house and Christa filled the kettle with water while he went upstairs. She wandered over to the table where a pile of old photographs was scattered—Lachlan had evidently been sorting things out. Christa leafed through them. Many were of Isobel and her husband with Lachlan as a little boy, and then when he was older, his arm around his mother. They looked a devoted little group, young Lachlan laughing up at them, his parents' hands on his shoulders. It revealed a window of happiness in his life, and emphasised the poignancy of how it had all been smashed so irrevocably.

From those old snapshots it was obvious that he had adored his parents, and how doubly sad it was that he'd gone abroad, cut off all ties from those he'd loved. No wonder now that he needed to assuage his guilt by meeting Isobel's requests—only then could he feel a sense of release from his guilt.

Then the kettle boiled and she made the coffee and poured out two mugs.

'God, that smells good,' said Lachlan, coming into the kitchen. His dark thick hair was slicked down across his head, and he smelled clean and fresh. 'First things first,' he murmured, and his mouth found hers, pressing her body to his hungrily.

Christa leant against him for a moment, loving the feel of his hard body against hers, then said gently, 'Those are lovely photos of your family, Lachlan—I couldn't help seeing them.'

He smiled wryly. 'I'm glad I found them. Shows that once upon a time I had a happy family.'

'We're going to look forward, remember?' she remarked. 'Lots of good times to come!'

He leaned against the cupboards and took a sip from his mug, looking at her over the rim. 'I can't think of anything better,' he murmured.

He poured himself some more coffee and said casually, 'What makes things even more wonderful, sweetheart, is that you are just the girl my mother wanted me to marry!'

She laughed. 'You don't know that!'

'I certainly do…'

'But the last time you spoke to her I was nowhere around!' she protested. 'For all you know, I might be the last person she would want. I doubt very much that she—'

Lachlan put a hand up as if to stop her talking. 'Will you listen for a second? I absolutely know that that is what she wanted—for you and I to be together…'

'How do you know for certain?'

'Because I have it from the horse's mouth!'

Christa frowned. 'I don't believe you! Anyway, we will never know what she really wanted, will we?'

'I can prove it to you.'

He went to the little dresser in the kitchen and opened a drawer and pulled out a letter. He unfolded it and gave it to her.

'Read it!' he said simply.

Christa recognised the writing immediately—a letter in Isobel's distinctive hand. She looked up at Lachlan.

'This is a private letter, Lachlan, from your mother—I don't need to read it.'

'Read it!' he repeated.

She shrugged and scanned the closely written page, feeling her eyes welling up as Isobel's voice came loud and clear through her writing. '"To my beloved son, Lachlan, I wish I could speak these words directly to you, but in case that doesn't happen, here are a few things I wish to say…"'

Isobel went on to write how she could completely understand Lachlan's attitude when his parents had broken up and why he'd felt he had to get away, and blaming herself entirely for everything that had gone wrong between them. She told him how she would love him to have Ardenleigh, the house he'd grown up in, and hoped he'd find happiness in it as he had when he'd been young.

'"And I want you to get married, my darling son, and have a happy family life—and I know exactly who I would like you to get married to! Christa Lennox has worked with me for six years and I have grown to love her like a daughter. I believe she would be perfect for you. She is fun, intelligent, kind and beautiful. I think I know her very well now, and I can think of no one better than

Christa to be my daughter-in-law! I would have been so happy to know she was your wife."'

Christa stared at the paper in her hand and swallowed hard as Lachlan stood watching her.

'Well?' he said. 'Do you believe me now?'

There was silence for a few seconds then she took a deep breath. 'Of course I do,' she said quietly. She turned the letter over in her hand rather distractedly, then put it on the table and said slowly, 'I suppose that's why you're keen to keep our relationship going—to fulfil your mother's wishes.'

Lachlan's mouth dropped. '*What?* Surely you don't really think that?'

'It seems we are both being influenced by our mothers,' she said in a tight little voice. 'I thought you were going out with me on your own account, not because Isobel said you should.'

He stared at her aghast. 'Don't be a fool,' he said roughly. 'That has nothing to do with it. I'd want to be with you, whatever my mother thought.'

'Would you?' she said sadly.

Christa felt cold, almost sick with remorse—what a blundering idiot she was! It was staring her in the face. Lachlan Maguire might be taking her out because he fancied her, but he'd been motivated by guilt and determination to do what his mother had wanted. He didn't really want to get married—he'd said as much once or twice, even her old friend Suzy Collins had known it—but the voice of Isobel came over powerfully in that letter. Lachlan would never have proposed marriage—if that was what it was—if his mother had not requested he do so!

Her eyes sparked with anger. 'Frankly, I'll be damned if I'm just going to be the means of assuaging your guilt about your mother, Lachlan—just fulfilling Isobel's wishes. I want to be the centre of your world, not part of a list you've ticked off of your mother's wishes: have the house; join the practice; marry me!'

He looked at her in disbelief. 'Come on—this is crazy! I only wanted you to know how happy she would have been! You and she were so close…'

'And what? Until now it's just been a bit of fun, a happy lark, which I suppose I went along with because I wanted so much to believe that you really loved me on your own account. But I was totally wrong, wasn't I? I'm just part of an arranged marriage—only I didn't know about the arrangement!'

Christa had never seen Lachlan so angry. A pulse beat on his forehead and his face paled, making his blue eyes seem even bluer. 'I don't know what the hell you're talking about—honey, I couldn't love you more if I tried. What makes you think anything else?'

'Why didn't you tell me?'

'Does it matter? OK, I didn't tell you at first because I thought you would think precisely what you've just said—that I was just doing what my mother wished. But I believed that now you'd only be thrilled that it was what she had wanted…' He came closer to her, holding her gaze. 'Surely you know that now I want you to marry me anyway?'

She took a deep breath and closed her eyes, then said bitterly, 'I don't know what I believe any more, Lachlan.'

Then, before Lachlan could stop her, she'd opened the kitchen door and was running through the courtyard and down the road to the village, with Titan bounding beside her.

Her head was spinning with conflicting emotions—

she'd fallen for Lachlan Maguire, she'd hoped he was falling for her too. But she was damned if she was just going to be the means of assuaging his guilt about his mother, just fulfilling his mother's wishes. She needed Lachlan to love her for herself alone, not because a voice from the grave had told him to! She reached her house and went in, slamming the door as hard as she could behind her. As far as she was concerned, she'd had it with romance!

Lachlan started after her, then gradually slowed down, watching her figure disappear into the distance. He shook his head in bewilderment.

'Well done, Maguire,' he muttered sarcastically to himself. 'You handled that very well—managed to make Christa feel really desired and needed.'

He drove his hands hard into his pockets in frustration. Why the hell had he shown her that letter now? He loved Christa, wanted to be with her always, wanted to show her that all men weren't feckless heartbreakers like that bloody man Colin, and all he'd succeeded in doing had been to make her feel she was just his mother's choice, not his. He'd been a complete and utter fool.

At first he had scorned his mother's wish that he should marry Christa. Now it seemed she was all that he wanted and more. After all these years of shunning close relationships, he'd found someone he loved and needed.

'I'm not going to let her go without a fight,' he told himself grimly. 'Somehow I'll get her back!'

It wasn't easy for Christa to maintain a natural atmosphere between the two of them at work that week. She took great care to keep her distance, and meetings were brisk and to the point. Often she would look across at

Lachlan covertly, and then think her heart would break because he looked so wonderful. But she'd done the right thing, hadn't she? He didn't really love her—he'd grow tired of her, just as Colin had done, and find someone else. She had to remember her friend Suzy's warning.

No, there wouldn't be any happy-ever-after and wedding bells. Lachlan Maguire wanted to settle down merely out of a sense of duty to his mother.

She took paperwork home with her rather than do it in the surgery after hours, as she used to do. She couldn't bear the thought of bumping into Lachlan when there was no one else there to dilute the meeting.

Towards the end of the week, while Christa and Lachlan were sorting out their mail, Alice said brightly, 'Looking forward to the dance? We've got a really big crowd coming this year.'

Christa felt, rather than saw, Lachlan glance towards her, then thought with spirit that she wasn't going to stay in because of her rift with Lachlan.

'Sure I am,' she said lightly. 'It'll be good fun!'

Lachlan flicked an intense glance at Christa. 'I can't wait,' he said grimly, 'I love dancing.'

Alice giggled. 'Well, I'm bagging you for a dance before you're killed in the rush!'

A tantalising picture formed in Christa's imagination of herself drifting across the floor with Lachlan, held close to his body, his cheek against hers, his heart beating close to hers... How wonderful that would have been, she thought wistfully, but now...

She couldn't avoid being alone with him altogether, of course. On the Friday before the dance Lachlan drove up beside her in the car park, and leaping out of the car barred her way as she tried to go up the ramp to the surgery.

'For God's sake, Christa, can't we talk to each other? This is totally ridiculous! If you won't answer my texts or e-mails then speak to me face to face! We are two adults after all.'

Christa shook her head, trying to ignore the effect that his powerful frame, so very close to her, was having on her libido. 'Lachlan, surely you don't expect me to keep seeing you when it's all about Isobel's wishes, not yours! A marriage based on that just wouldn't work!'

He seized her arm. 'You little fool, can't you see I love you? Nothing to do with that bloody letter or your damned uncle. Believe me, honey, when I made love to you I forgot all about any reservations I may have had to start with, or that you were a Lennox. Frankly, I couldn't give a toss—you are you, and that is all I care about.'

And for a moment perhaps she was tempted. There was something about the soft intensity of his voice, the look of yearning in his eyes that made her long to be held in his arms. And then she thought of her bitter experience before of a broken love affair. She swallowed hard, trying to suppress the tears that threatened to roll down her cheeks.

Several times she'd wondered if she should leave the practice and look for a job elsewhere, rather than endure this stilted relationship. Now she was sure she would have to do just that and try and start again. Her mother had Bertie and she didn't need her around any more—there was no reason to stay in the area.

She got into the car and drove off, leaving Lachlan alone in the car park.

Lachlan watched Christa go in despair, and yet he understood her reaction. He'd mishandled the whole situation and he just didn't know what to do next. He needed to talk to someone—someone with a bit of sense. He decided to ring John Davies, his solicitor—at least he'd listen, even if he couldn't advise!

A girl with a pram was crossing the drive. She was thin and shabbily dressed and vaguely familiar. She looked up at Lachlan and gave a sudden smile.

'Hello, Doc!' she said. 'I had the baby!'

Preoccupied as he was, Lachlan didn't recognise her at first. She grinned at him.

'Don't remember me, do you? It's Lindsay Cooper. I came into the surgery a few weeks back...you sorted me out.'

'Of course, I do remember you, Lindsay. You're Greg's girl, aren't you?' Lachlan sighed inwardly—he had to show interest, however depressed he was. 'What did you have?'

'A little lad,' said Lindsay proudly. 'I was going to bring him in to show you...wanted you to know what we'd called him!'

'And what have you called him?'

'We've decided on Lachlan—that's your name, isn't it? You helped save Greg's life and you helped me.' She smiled shyly at him. 'You don't mind, do you?'

Lachlan was touched. 'I'm honoured, Lindsay. Let me see your little son.' He peered under the hood of the pram at the baby, rosy-cheeked and sleeping with a dusting of blond hair. 'He's beautiful—congratulations to both of you. How is Greg?'

'They say he'll be out of hospital soon, and social services have found us a little flat.'

'So things are going well, then?'

Lindsay's thin little face lit up. 'Yeah—couldn't be

better! Will you let that other doc know—tell her thanks. If I'd had a girl I'd have called her Christa!'

'Yes. I'll tell her if I see her,' sighed Lachlan.

The village hall was an old square building situated at the edge of the village on a slight hill overlooking the sea. It had been dimly lit to make it look what was optimistically called 'atmospheric' by the committee of the annual charity dance. An attempt to make the place look festive had been provided by little paper lanterns hung across the ceiling, and a local DJ was testing the microphone, by intoning, 'One two, one two,' into it, his voice booming out over the hum of conversation.

The staff from the Ardenleigh Medical Practice were seated at a table in the corner, Alice sitting on the knee of her current boyfriend and Ginny next to her tubby little husband, Barry.

She should have been on top of the world, thought Christa sadly. Instead, she felt about as festive as a bear with a sore tooth, forcing herself to laugh at Ben's weak jokes and greeting all the locals with a smile.

It had been an ordeal to come, but she was determined that she was not going to do a rerun of her experience with Colin and opt out of everything when their romance had ended. Her heart might be broken yet again, but this time she was going to push it to the back of her mind, keep her life going, even though she felt on edge every time anyone fresh came into the hall, in case it was Lachlan Maguire. She half wanted him to come, to show him that she could do without him, and half hoped he wouldn't because she was afraid her heart would break when she saw him.

'You look fantastic, Christa—that apricot colour's just

gorgeous,' said Sarah, the practice nurse. 'I wish I could wear something like that—the trouble is, with my figure I'm limited to things that hide it rather than show it!'

'You look great,' protested Christa. 'I feel a little self-conscious really—there isn't much room for manoeuvre in this...'

'You don't need to do much manoeuvring,' said Sarah drily. 'Just stand there and look fantastic!'

There were so many people there Christa knew— Richie from the gym, John Davies the solicitor, friends from her running group. Soon she would have to give in her notice to the practice and all these old friends would know that she was leaving. She took a deep swig of the cheap wine that was on offer and hoped it would help to deaden the pain she was feeling.

By now the disco was blasting away at full volume and Ginny and Barry were doing a very stylish quickstep, with much twirling and sidestepping. Alice and her boyfriend were swaying together with their arms around each other, their eyes closed, oblivious to the rest of the room. Christa leant against the wall and put the cool glass to her hot cheeks, an oppressive headache starting to throb behind her eyes. She closed them tiredly.

The voice in her ear was so familiar, deep and resonant. 'Christa, I'm glad you've come. I wasn't sure whether you'd make it or not. But we need to talk, *please*.'

Her eyes flew open, and her heart lurched when she saw Lachlan standing in front of her, looking ultra-cool in a cream shirt, open to the neck, and navy chinos.

For a second speech eluded her, then she said tightly, 'We can't talk here, Lachlan—not in a crowded dance hall.'

'Then let's go somewhere else.' His eyes wandered

over her slim figure, the way her dress moulded to every curve and how the apricot colour enhanced her glowing skin. 'My God, Christa—I can't bear this,' he said roughly. 'You look quite…beautiful.' He hesitated and then said huskily, 'Please, let's have a dance together— just one.'

'That's not a good idea, Lachlan,' she said unsteadily. 'You…you don't need to have a duty dance with me.'

'For God's sake,' he said savagely.' His hand took her bare arm and she shivered, feeling the flickers of desire going through her like a hot knife through butter.

'If you don't trust me, if you really want us to part, think of it as a "last waltz". We can't end like this, with no communication at all!'

The words 'we can't end like this' echoed sadly in Christa's ears. She wanted him, oh, how she wanted him, longed for everything to be as it had been before when she'd thought he loved her for herself alone… Just one more time, then. She offered no resistance when he put his arm around her waist and pressed her body fiercely to his.

It was a kind of torture, reminding her of their love-making only a few days ago, when his body had locked with hers and they had been as one. He put his cheek to hers and she could smell the scent of soap on him, the slight roughness of his chin, feel his legs against hers as they moved in unison to the beat of the music.

It was as if they were welded together—and it was wonderful and terrible at the same time. Would this really be the last time she would ever be so close to him, ever feel his breath on her face, his lips tracing a trail of little kisses down her neck?

'Stop it!' she whispered fiercely in his ear. 'I don't

want to do this…it's not fair! People will see us and get the wrong idea!'

'Rubbish, the lights are too low for anyone to see anything.' He smiled, his arm tightening around her.

God, how beautiful she felt against him, thought Lachlan, an aching sadness somewhere around his heart. Her hair had a faint fresh smell, her body felt sexy and curvy under her silk dress, and he felt an indescribable longing for her. He'd been a bungling idiot, not realising how bruised and damaged she'd been after her experience with Colin Maitland. He looked down at her, seeing her long lashes lying against the curve of her cheek.

'Christa…Christa, darling, give me a chance to explain. Don't let us part like this.'

With a great effort she pulled away from him, suddenly unable to bear the paradox of being so close to him physically yet so distant from him in other ways.

'There's nothing to explain,' she said lightly. 'No hard feelings at all. And now, if you don't mind, I want to sit down.'

She sat rigidly in the chair, tossing back the rest of her wine, and he sat next to her—silence between them. Then eventually Lachlan got up and walked out of the room.

'Ah! Christa!' said a jolly voice. 'How about a turn on the floor? I'm not much good, but if you can put up with me?'

John Davies, the solicitor, was beaming down at her. She knew him quite well, having had to deal with him when Isobel had died. She smiled and jumped up, glad to take her mind off Lachlan.

They started off round the floor, John taking everything rather slowly and carefully and holding her as if she was made of delicate china.

Eventually he began to relax and said jovially, 'So what do you think of Lachlan's idea of putting Ardenleigh on the market?'

Christa stiffened with surprise and stopped moving, causing them both to stumble. 'Put Ardenleigh on the market?' she repeated in amazement. 'When did he tell you that?'

John looked flustered. 'Oh, dear. That was most indiscreet and unprofessional of me. I really thought you knew. He came to see me late this morning.'

'But…why does he want to sell it? I thought…I thought Isobel wanted him to have it?''

John looked embarrassed. 'You'll have to ask him the reason, my dear. I shouldn't have mentioned it at all.'

She stopped dancing again and looked imploringly at John. 'It…it's really important that I know just why he wants to sell Ardenleigh. I thought he loved the place and, of course, wanted to fulfil his mother's wishes.'

John shook his head and smiled. 'Christa, I'm not going to say any more. Lachlan's here—you go and ask him!'

Christa bit her lip. 'Oh, dear, the thing is, we've had a bit of a falling out…I don't know that he would feel like telling me.'

The elderly man looked at her shrewdly and laughed. 'Then go and make it up with him. I know this much— he adores you. I know he can't stop talking about you. That much I am allowed to say. Said he wished he'd met you ages ago!'

'Did he say that?' she said in a small voice.

John Davies smiled. 'He certainly did.' He looked at her, suddenly concerned by the expression on her face. 'Is something wrong, Christa?'

'I think, John, I've been very, very silly… Do you mind if I go and find Lachlan? I need to say something to him.'

'Of course, my dear. I'll see you later.' John gave a little bow and wandered off to the bar.

Was she too late? Had Lachlan gone home? Whatever happened, she had to see him that evening, tell him how very, very wrong she'd been. She'd been an impetuous fool, jumping to completely the wrong conclusions.

She dashed outside, hardly noticing as the cold air hit her body. By the wall of the car park stood a solitary figure, gazing out over the moonlit sea, watching the beam on the lighthouse across the firth swing over the water every minute or two.

How lonely and forlorn Lachlan looked in that setting. He'd had sadness in his life, admitted he made mistakes, and she had thrown everything he'd said back in his face.

Would he take her back, give them another chance? She ran up to him and touched his arm. 'Lachlan…' she said breathlessly. 'Lachlan, perhaps you were right. We need to talk…'

He whipped round with a start. 'What the…? Christa? I didn't expect to see you again tonight.'

'I've been such a fool. I've been speaking to John Davies. He told me you want to sell Ardenleigh! Is that true?'

His amazing blue eyes looked sadly down at her. 'I began to realise that without you it didn't matter a toss where I lived—and neither do I want to stay at the practice if I'm not with you.'

'But it's what your mother wanted. I thought you would do anything to keep it—sell the land for money…'

'She wouldn't want me to be unhappy, I'm sure.'

Christa's eyes filled with tears and put her hands on his shoulders. 'Don't say that, Lachlan—and don't leave me. I want you to stay.' She put her arms around his waist, looking up into his eyes, and said in a small voice, 'Darling Lachlan—I want you to forgive me. I've been such an idiot.'

He shrugged, his face shadowed in the moonlight. 'But no matter what I say, you don't seem to believe that I love you.'

'I was wrong,' she whispered, biting her lip. 'John Davies made it clear to me that you loved me, and I don't think I could bear it if you left...'

A flicker of amusement passed over Lachlan's face. 'So you're prepared to believe what John Davies says, even if you didn't believe me!'

She smiled up at him. 'Well, he is a solicitor...'

It was as if Lachlan was struck dumb for a moment, then he threw back his head and laughed. 'Good God. Haven't I demonstrated it most graphically?'

'Yes, you have, Lachlan,' said Christa meekly.

He encircled her with his arm and hugged her to him, cradling her head against his chest, a beaming smile on his face.

'Is this true, Christa? You finally believe me?'

She nodded, unable to speak.

Lachlan grinned a cheeky schoolboy grin. 'I didn't realise I was going out with an idiot, but it looks as if I am! I owe John Davies a lot!'

In sheer happiness he took her hands and whirled her round, then caught her in his arms.

'Perhaps now we can get on with the rest of our lives my love. We'll make a fresh start and buy a new home with our stamp on it—not with the ghosts of previous generations at our backs.'

Lachlan wiped away a tear that rolled down Christa's face and smiled. 'Are you beginning to regret coming back to me?'

'It…it's because I'm so happy,' she gulped. 'A few minutes ago I was beyond sad, and now I just can't describe how I feel!'

'I know one thing, you're freezing,' he whispered. 'And I know a very good way to warm you up, and it's even better than dancing. Let's go back to your house and I'll show you!'

He took her hand and they left the sound of the dancing behind them.

EPILOGUE

SPRING HAD COME late to Errin Bridge, but now, looking down the valley from the top of Errin Hill, one could see the fresh green mist of new leaves on the trees and a scattering of daffodils over the village green.

So much had happened in six months, thought Christa, looking around with pride at the old farmhouse that she and Lachlan had just bought. It was only small and a far cry from the grandeur and space of Ardenleigh, but it nestled at the side of the hill and commanded the most beautiful views of the countryside and the little village below. Ardenleigh had been sold and there were plans to make it into a retirement home—something that was desperately needed in the area.

In a few minutes guests for their house-warming party would be arriving, and Christa went into the living room and looked around doubtfully, wondering if all their guests would be able to fit into it!

Lachlan came in from the back, where a little copse of trees grew, and threw some logs on the fire—everywhere looked cosy and neat. He put his arms around her and nuzzled her neck.

'Glad we moved here, darling, and didn't stay at Ardenleigh?' he murmured.

She looked at him with a dimpled smile. 'This could be too small in a year or two—but of course I love it here!' she replied.

'Before everyone arrives, I've something for you, actually...a kind of moving-in present!'

'I like the sound of that!' She smiled. 'What is it?'

'Something to wear...but a little more permanent than a dress!'

Lachlan pulled a little box out of his pocket and gave it to her. 'Open it quickly before all our friends come,' he said.

She opened the lid and stared at the sparkling diamond ring that nestled in the white satin box, and then looked up at him in speechless amazement, her lovely eyes wide with disbelief.

He watched her with a wry smile. 'Well?' he demanded. 'Do you like it or not?'

'Oh, Lachlan...' she murmured. 'Of course I like it... it's beautiful!'

He tilted her chin towards him and his eyes were tender and warm. 'I think we've waited long enough for this, sweetheart. Will you marry me? It'll make me the happiest man on the earth if you will!'

A startled silence and then Christa gave a burst of laughter. 'And this from the man who said marriage wasn't for him!' she teased. 'What's brought this on?'

'After six months living together I thought you'd realise by now that my mother's wishes have nothing to do with us getting married! Now we're in our new home, starting a new life, it seems the perfect time. What do you say, sweetheart—ready for the final leap?'

She put up a hand and stroked his wonderful face. Strange to think that not so long ago she'd been in the depths of despair, love and marriage seemingly a far-off dream.

'Of course I'll marry you!' she said.

And he slipped the ring onto her finger. 'To love and to cherish,' he murmured softly.

Then the guests began arriving and they wondered at first why the hostess was laughing and crying at the same time.

* * * * *

A sneaky peek at next month...

MEDICAL ROMANCE™

THE ULTIMATE IN ROMANTIC MEDICAL DRAMA

My wish list for next month's titles...

In stores from 6th June 2014:

❑ 200 Harley Street: The Soldier Prince – Kate Hardy

& 200 Harley Street: The Enigmatic Surgeon
    – Annie Claydon

❑ A Father for Her Baby & The Midwife's Son
    – Sue MacKay

❑ Back in Her Husband's Arms – Susanne Hampton

& Wedding at Sunday Creek – Leah Martyn

Available at WHSmith, Tesco, Asda, Eason, Amazon and Apple

Just can't wait?

0514/03

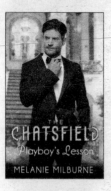

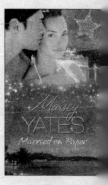

THE
CHATSFIELD®

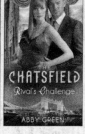

Collect all 8!

Buy now at
www.millsandboon.co.uk/thechatsfield

The World of Mills & Boon

There's a Mills & Boon® series that's perfect for you
There are ten different series to choose from and
new titles every month, so whether you're looking for
glamorous seduction, Regency rakes, homespun
heroes or sizzling erotica, we'll give you plenty of
inspiration for your next read.

By Request

Back by popular demand!
12 stories every month

Cherish™

*Experience the ultimate rush
of falling in love.*
12 new stories every month

INTRIGUE...

*A seductive combination of
danger and desire...*
7 new stories every month

Desire™

*Passionate and dramatic
love stories*
6 new stories every month

nocturne™

*An exhilarating underworld
of dark desires*
3 new stories every month

For exclusive member offers go to
millsandboon.co.uk/subscribe

WORLD_ M&Ba

Discover more romance at

www.millsandboon.co.uk

- ♥ WIN great prizes in our exclusive competitions
- ♥ BUY new titles before they hit the shops
- ♥ BROWSE new books and REVIEW your favourites
- ♥ SAVE on new books with the Mills & Boon® Bookclub™
- ♥ DISCOVER new authors

PLUS, to chat about your favourite reads, get the latest news and find special offers:

- 🇫 Find us on facebook.com/millsandboon
- 🐦 Follow us on twitter.com/millsandboonuk
- ♥ Sign up to our newsletter at millsandboon.co.uk